THE WORLD'S CLASSICS

THE AWKWARD AGE

HENRY JAMES was born in New York in 1843 of ancestry both Irish and Scottish. He received a remarkably cosmopolitan education in New York, London, Paris and Geneva, and entered law school at Harvard in 1862. After 1866, he lived mostly in Europe, at first writing critical articles, reviews, and short stories for American periodicals. He lived in London for more than twenty years, and in 1898 moved to Rye, where his later novels were written. Under the influence of an ardent sympathy for the British cause in the First World War, Henry James was in 1915 naturalized a British subject. He died in 1916.

In his early novels, which include *Roderick Hudson* (1875) and *The Portrait of a Lady* (1881), he was chiefly concerned with the impact of the older civilization of Europe upon American life. He analysed English character with extreme subtlety in such novels as *What Maisie Knew* (1897) and *The Awkward Age* (1899). In his last three great novels, *The Wings of the Dove* (1902), *The Ambassadors* (1903), and *The Golden Bowl* (1904), he returned to the 'international' theme of American and European character.

VIVIEN JONES is Lecturer in English at the University of Leeds.

THE WORLD'S CLASSICS

===

HENRY JAMES
The Awkward Age

===

Edited with
an introduction and notes by
VIVIEN JONES

Oxford   New York
OXFORD UNIVERSITY PRESS
1984

Oxford University Press, Walton Street, Oxford OX2 6DP

London Glasgow New York Toronto
Delhi Bombay Calcutta Madras Karachi
Kuala Lumpur Singapore Hong Kong Tokyo
Nairobi Dar es Salaam Cape Town
Melbourne Auckland

and associated companies
Beirut Berlin Ibadan Mexico City Nicosia

Oxford is a trade mark of Oxford University Press

The Awkward Age first published in book form 1899
First published as a World's Classics paperback 1984
Introduction, Note on the text, Further reading and Notes
© Vivien Jones 1984
Chronology © Leon Edel 1963

British Library Cataloguing in Publication Data

James, Henry, 1843–1916
The awkward age.—(The world's classics)
I. Title   II. Jones, Vivien
813'.4[F]   PS2116
ISBN 0-19-281654-3

Set by New Western Printing Ltd
Printed in Great Britain by
Hazell Watson & Viney Limited
Aylesbury, Bucks

CONTENTS

INTRODUCTION

WHO is at the 'awkward age'? The obvious answer is of
course the novel's adolescent heroine, Nanda Brookenham,
suspended between the schoolroom and marriage, between
innocence and sanctioned knowledge, and inconveniently
exposed to the fast, corrupting talk in her mother's drawing-
room. Certainly this 'coming to the forefront of some vague
slip of a daughter' was how James, in the Preface, remembered the novel's 'scant but quite ponderable germ' and in
his notebook on 4 March 1895, almost four years before
The Awkward Age began serial publication, he jotted down
'The idea of the little London girl who grows up to "sit
with" the free-talking modern young mother'. But, like so
much of the talk in Mrs Brookenham's salon, James's title
is open to interpretation, its referents uncertain, or at least
multiple. It can as easily suggest Mrs Brook herself for
example. 'She had about her the pure light of youth –
would always have it' (p. 27), yet Nanda's presence is both
witness to her age and a threat to her social supremacy: in
the sexual and ideological rivalry which develops between
mother and daughter, Mrs Brook's influence over her close
circle is irrevocably eclipsed. Or the awkwardness could be
that of Mr Longdon, who loved Nanda's grandmother and
whom we see in the first scene through the eyes of one of
Mrs Brook's inner circle: 'though, to Vanderbank, he could
not look young, he came near – strikingly and amusingly –
looking new' (p. 3). Forced, late in life, to come to terms
with an unfamiliar and uncongenial social set, Mr Longdon
is suspended, like Nanda, between innocence and knowledge, between the simplifying social restrictions of his youth
and present freedoms. And as the nostalgic representative
of a lost way of life, Mr Longdon points up the general
awkwardness of *fin-de-siècle* society. Appropriately, *The
Awkward Age* was published in book form in 1899, the last
year of the nineteenth century, and its title reflects and

sustains a self-conscious age of transition when the issue of the education and freedom of women was fiercely debated and the character of Victorian society was altering radically.

As was Victorian fiction. In Hardy's later novels and in the work of James and Conrad we see the awkward age of classic realism. The omniscient narrative voice typical of the novels of, for example, George Eliot or Trollope disappears and with it the reader's guide to interpretation and judgment. The most obvious technical feature of *The Awkward Age* is its 'dramatic' form: most of the novel is conducted through dialogue, authorial commentary is minimized and readers have therefore to interpret the characters' words for themselves and to make their own judgments. Together with other works of James's 'middle' period – *The Turn of the Screw* or *What Maisie Knew*, for example – *The Awkward Age* anticipates the self-conscious, experimental fiction of the great modernists such as Virginia Woolf and James Joyce. To use the French critic, Roland Barthes's, terms, fiction was in a state of transition from being 'readerly' – in which the reader is the passive consumer of a comparatively straightforward form – to being 'writerly' – in which the reader is actively involved in the creation of meaning(s). Not the least important awkwardness in this novel might, indeed, be that of readers trained in and nostalgic for the simpler world of Victorian realism but forced, like Mr Longdon, to assimilate and participate in new conventions.

'Some vague slip of a daughter'

Nanda Brookenham is one of a long line of Jamesian heroines whose careers can be read as moral fables, variations on the theme of the fall from innocence. Daisy Miller, in the story of 1878, is the fresh, brash young American girl whose naïve honesty is tragically misunderstood by the corrupt civilization which finally destroys her; in *The Portrait of a Lady*, Isabel Archer, so sure of her own freedom and ability to judge, is tempted from the paradise of Gardencourt by Gilbert Osmond and has to learn to recognize the facts of her exploitation; Maisie, like Nanda, is exposed at an early age to adult sexual intrigue;

Maggie, in *The Golden Bowl*, experiences through her husband's adultery 'the horror of finding evil seated, all at its ease, where she had only dreamed of good'. In his famous essay of 1884, 'The Art of Fiction', James wrote: 'The essence of moral energy is to survey the whole field'. He was defending the novelist's right to complete freedom of subject matter in the face of the moralistic timidity of English criticism in general and Walter Besant, the influential popular novelist and critic, in particular, but his remark can equally be seen to illuminate the complex attitude to moral knowledge displayed in the novels. Moral maturity and responsibility, he suggests, are the fruits only of experience; innocence like Daisy's, or Pansy's in *The Portrait*, is painfully vulnerable, and can even be in its own way corrupt or dangerous – here in *The Awkward Age* little Aggie runs wild when set free by her marriage; the sheltered governess's over-active imagination might well be responsible for the horrors in *The Turn of the Screw*. Isabel, paradoxically, is morally freer when she acknowledges her imprisonment; Maggie's vision of evil involves her in intrigue and manipulation but it also liberates her into a recognition of her hitherto repressed sexual and emotional needs. In the fallen state, the challenges and difficulties of the moral life, though often tragic in outcome, compensate and qualify a simple regret for lost innocence.

Clearly, Nanda's experience can and frequently has been analysed in such terms. Her tragedy has been described, by Dorothea Krook for example, as that of 'the human condition', since she is in a sense responsible for her misery, fully aware of her responsibility, yet helpless to change it. Nanda values the kind of innocence that life in Buckingham Crescent has denied her – she says at one point of Aggie, '"Ah, say what you will – it *is* the way we ought to be!"' (p. 240). She can therefore only love the man who shares that view and who, exactly because of it, can never love her. Her predicament is fully and painfully understood by Mitchy, who loves her in spite of her knowledge and whom, for that reason, she can of course never love:

'But what's the use,' he persisted as she answered nothing, 'in loving a person with the prejudice — hereditary or other – to which you're precisely obnoxious? Do you positively *like* to love in vain?'

It was a question, the way she turned back to him seemed to say, that deserved a responsible answer. 'Yes.' (p. 241)

Yet, though feeling for Nanda in her suffering, few readers would endorse her admiration for little Aggie's state. The moral maturity, however qualified, which her knowledge and self-knowledge have given her is usually seen as the novel's moral centre. Nanda recognizes her own corruption but aligns herself with Mr Longdon and his Beccles garden, and her choice exposes the unredeemed corruption of Mrs Brook's set. Read thus, the novel has been seen as a restrained endorsement of the 'so morally well-meant and so intellectually helpless compromise', the English solution, as described in James's Preface, to the problem of what to do with the young girl.

Without wanting wholly to deny the interest of this kind of reading, I would like to look at the novel's exploration of innocence and corruption from a rather different perspective. The 'germ' of *The Awkward Age* was a particular social problem in a particular context. James himself stresses this specificity in a letter to Henrietta Reubell of late 1899: 'I had in view a certain special social (highly "modern" and actual) London group and type and tone... and that clever people at least would know who, in general, and what, one meant.' Identifying who James meant other than in very general terms, though possible, can offer us only very limited satisfaction; 'what', on the other hand, is much more interesting. In choosing the subject of girls' education, James was moving, rather late perhaps, into an area of fierce social and literary debate. The 1890s was the era of the New Woman and, in the earlier years of the decade particularly, there was a proliferation of novels, usually by women, which self-consciously spoke on behalf of women and explored problems of female education and sexuality, the double standard and the validity of marriage. Conservative reaction attacked and refuted their premises and methods in periodicals and sometimes in more novels, reasserting the standard of womanliness which they had dared to question. The radicalism of the 'New Fiction' and the often crudely stereotypic plots and characters of novels on both sides of the argument are clearly a long way from James's complexity in *The Awkward Age*, but James was certainly aware of the controversy, his novel inevitably contributes to it in its choice of subject and it even, I shall suggest, shares some organizational features with novels more obviously involved.

Socially, except for a very few, the issue of female emancipation took less daring forms. The sexual candour and visions of feminist utopia in the novels are replaced by questions of whether girls should be allowed to read such novels (or, as in Nanda's case, even more dubious novels of the French Naturalist school), whether they should be allowed to go out unchaperoned during the day, whether they should be given their own latch-key, whether they should ride bicycles or wear divided skirts. In 1894 (again, some years before *The Awkward Age* was published) a series of articles under the title 'The Revolt of the Daughters' appeared in *The Nineteenth Century* and other leading periodicals. Addressed mainly to mothers, they urge sympathy and solidarity with their daughters and deal with just such questions of day-to-day education as occupy Mrs Brook and the Duchess. It has been suggested that these articles were a source for James's novel. Certainly he dined at just this period with their instigator, Mrs Crackanthorpe, and he is very likely to have read them, but, whether or not he actually did so, they are symptomatic of an atmosphere of discussion and change which could be observed throughout the London society in which he moved. Among the most interesting are those by Mrs Crackanthorpe herself. Firmly on the side of the daughters, she deplores the Duchess's policy:

Not a little curious is it that the mothers who so carefully shield their daughters from the faintest breath of adverse criticism before marriage appear to be absolutely indifferent to what is said openly of these same daughters when marriage has set them free. Is this a reality, or is it a monstrous unreality, leading to every kind of social hypocrisy?

(Nineteenth Century, January 1894, p. 30)

And she paints the ideal state which would result from

allowing girls the freedom to make their own mistakes and puts her argument, significantly, in terms of the class struggle:

Salvation comes from within always and everywhere. Since the capitalists have failed them, the operatives must work out their own. Then perhaps we shall have the woman of to-morrow, pure of heart and fearless of speech, who demands of herself and of everyone else, not a flimsy and superficial 'correctness', but that inward sincerity which enables her both to say and to hear, 'I have erred', with equanimity.

(ibid. 30)

A similar endorsement of knowledge as the means to moral responsibility can be discerned in *The Awkward Age*. But Mrs Crackanthorpe's stirring radicalism and her excitement at the prospect of social upheaval find little echo in James – particularly in the James of the *Notebooks*. There, like Mrs Crackanthorpe, he sees a connection between women's emancipation and general social change, but in a much more limited social context and with a very different reaction. In a series of notebook entries, which he interrupts to record the 'germ' of *The Awkward Age*, James cites 'some extremely well-said and suggestive things' in an account in French of contemporary English manners, *Notes sur Londres* by 'Brada' (actually Henriette Consuelo, contessa di Puliga): 'The idea of his [*sic*] little book is the Revolution in English society by the *avènement* of the women, which he sees everywhere and in everything. I saw it long ago – and I saw in it a big subject for the Novelist.' Brada, and James, link this with 'the excellent subject of the *déchéance* of the aristocracy; its ceasing to have style, to take itself seriously.' James quotes a long passage in which Brada regrets the aristocracy's growing failure to believe in its own superiority and to operate on principles of exclusivity – principles which should be upheld by women: '"Aussi longtemps que les femmes entretiennent le feu du sanctuaire on peut avoir bon espoir, mais du moment qu'elles se rient et du sanctuaire et du feu sacré, il est probable qu'il ne tardera pas à s'éteindre" ' ('As long as women maintain the fire in the sanctuary there is hope, but once they start to mock both the sanctuary and the sacred flame, it cannot be long before it goes out'). And they are, of course, beginning to mock this sacred office and to seek to emancipate themselves '"de la tutelle de l'homme – vivre d'une vie personnelle"' ('from the protection of men – to live their own lives'). James, in his comments, describes this movement as the 'masculinization' of women, and he goes on:

I seem to see the great broad, rich theme of a large satirical novel in the picture, gathering a big armful of elements together, of the *train dont va* English society before one's eyes – the great modern collapse of all the forms and 'superstitions' and respects, good and bad, and restraints and mysteries...the general revolution, the failure of fastidiousness.

The 'large satirical novel' was never written, but James's concern for a 'vulgarized' aristocracy, one of whose symptoms was the growing unrest of women no longer satisfied with a role as revered, but largely passive, upholders of a repressive ideal of 'restraints and mysteries', found its way into *The Awkward Age*. The voice of the *Notebooks*, though equivocal, is essentially that of conservative reaction, but the form of the novel makes James's attitude there impossible to define. I am not trying to identify James's intentions in the novel from his notebook entries: his intentions necessarily remain a mystery. I want simply to supply a relevant ideological context for his chosen subject and to register as interesting the gap between the overt conservatism of the *Notebooks* and the inevitable ambiguity of the experimental novel.

In keeping with the novel's later date, society in *The Awkward Age*, at least the impecunious outskirts of society represented by Mrs Brookenham's set, has already suffered some of the dilution feared by Brada. It has been '"trop liberale et de bon accueil"' ('too generous and welcoming') (*Notebooks*, p. 195):[1] minor peers like Lord Petherton not only mix with but live off wealthy businessmen like Mitchy; Mrs Brookenham, the daughter of Lady Julia, married a man with little money for whom she secured, through her connections, a Civil Service position; Mr Longdon finds it

[1] For details of works cited, see 'Further reading'.

difficult to accept

'That your grandmother's daughter should have brought *her* daughter –'

'To stay with a person' – Nanda took it up as, apparently out of delicacy, he fairly failed – 'whose father used to take the measure, down on his knees on a little mat, as mamma says, of my grandfather's remarkably large foot? Yes, we none of us mind. Do you think we should?' (p. 150)

Similarly, though Aggie is still kept in sheltered ignorance, Nanda has already secured the tangible freedoms which, 'The Revolt of the Daughters' suggests, many girls still sought in 1894. She has her own key, walks unchaperoned to Van's rooms for tea, smokes, reads what books she likes. As always, James's concern is not with the facts but with their effect – as he wrote in the Preface to *The Princess Casamassima*: 'the affair of the painter is not the immediate, it is the reflected field of life, the realm not of application, but of *appreciation*' (*The Art of the Novel*, p. 65). And his primary focus, the 'fine consciousness' displaying the consequences of change, is of course Nanda herself.

Nanda is in many ways the victim of unsought emancipation. She accepts the social flexibility and freer mores of her mother's society, but clings emotionally to the ideals and forms they have destroyed, including the ideal of pure womanhood which, had she been able to embody it, would have won for her the happy ending of marriage to Vanderbank. In her dilemma, she shows broad similarities with the heroines of anti-feminist novels – such as *The Yellow Aster* (1894) by 'Iota' – who find themselves deprived by their modern upbringing of essential womanly characteristics. And *The Awkward Age* has another motif in common with these novels: that of contrasted women (often sisters), a motif well established in both fairy-tale and recent fiction (one thinks, for example, of Lucy Snowe and Polly Home in *Villette* or of Maggie and her cousin Lucy in *The Mill on the Floss*) and used in conservative novels to establish images of correct femininity. Nanda is very obviously contrasted with Aggie, but equally importantly with Mrs Brook whose relationship with her daughter has much in common with that of sisters. All three are in constant implicit contrast with the absent ideal of Lady Julia, and typology casts Mrs Brook, who unlike the fair-haired Nanda looks nothing like Lady Julia, as the 'dark sister'. Disliked by Mr Longdon, the custodian of Lady Julia's memory, she represents a kind of emancipation which values past ideals only as potential sources of income. Nanda, on the other hand, strives to emulate the spirit of her grandmother, to re-establish, albeit in modified terms, an older ideal of womanhood.

This conservative position is certainly one of the discourses present in the novel, but as I have already suggested, the form refuses to privilege any one simple reading. Trained in classic realism, we tend instinctively as readers to identify initially with the heroine and thus with Nanda's nostalgia for a former morality (a reflection, after all, of our own desire for certainty), but her view receives no overt authorial sanction and is qualified, as we have seen, by a positive reading of her state of knowledge which allows her to cope, unlike Aggie, with an unstable and often devious society. And some critics have seen Nanda's nostalgia as an empty, sterile idealism which the novel rejects in favour of Mrs Brook's life and brilliance. It is some time since critics of James took sides so crudely, but the fact that they could do so, using the same text to justify diametrically opposed views, suggests the way in which the novel's form problematizes the entrenched positions of the controversy from which it began. The conservative ideal is in constant tension with other possible readings.

One of which, indeed, is perhaps surprisingly radical in its exposure of the position of women. We needn't take sides with Nanda or her mother. Mrs Brook's motives for her apparently mercenary and manipulative strategy, for her behaviour at Tishy's party (Chapter XXX), are never clear but they can anyway be sympathetically seen as the result of her own sad frustration. From one point of view, Mrs Brook is as much a victim as Nanda: brilliant, trapped in an unsatisfactory marriage made when, subject to her own mother's older system of education, she was too young to understand its implications, she has created an edifice of fine talk in defensive compensation for lack of passion or

opportunities for fulfilment – words have had to replace
things. Nanda is a rival not simply because they both love
Van, but because of 'the sight of a freedom on her
daughter's part that suddenly loomed larger than any
freedom of her own' (p. 220). And that freedom is not
simply financial, but moral – the freedom to reject the fabric
of words which is her mother's existence. Nanda's tenderness towards her mother in her last interview with Vanderbank: ' "When I think of her downstairs there so often
nowadays practically alone I feel as if I could scarcely bear
it. She's so fearfully young" ' (p. 339), can be seen as an
acknowledgment of their common plight. Nanda urges
Van to face up to his responsibility towards Mrs Brook
(which he has failed to do in her own case):

'one's feeling that when a person has brought a person out –'
   'A person should take the consequences,' Vanderbank broke
in, 'and see a person through?' (p. 340)

Vanderbank embodies the double standard so fiercely
attacked by the 'New Woman' novelists. Harold, who
claims to know some of the country houses where Van has
'left his tracks' (p. 263), bears witness to his promiscuity –
yet he expects a chaste bride like Aggie. More insidiously,
the double standard operates in Van's use of women like
Nanda and her mother for intellectual satisfaction, only
to reject Nanda for the knowledge he has helped to give
her. He refuses to treat Nanda as a commodity by marrying
her for Mr Longdon's money but does exactly that in
seeing her as soiled. The Duchess, as so often, sees the
situation clearly enough, pointing out to Mr Longdon
Nanda's diminishing chance of securing a husband the
longer she remains in the ' "mal' aria they themselves have
made for her" ' (p. 172). Nanda sees it too, and in her
conversation with Van at Beccles lays bare his hypocrisy in
a way that she must know puts an end to any chance of
him marrying her:

'Girls understand now. It has got to be faced, as Tishy says.'
   'Oh well,' Vanderbank laughed, 'we don't require Tishy to
point that out to us. What are we all doing most of the time but
trying to face it?'

'Doing? Aren't you doing rather something very different? You're just trying to dodge it. You're trying to make believe – not perhaps to yourselves but to *us* – that it isn't so.'

'But surely you don't want us to be any worse!'

She shook her head with brisk gravity. 'We don't care really what you are.' (p. 229)

Nanda here comes closest to the New Woman's polemical rejection of the double standard in favour of an independent existence. But her tragedy is that she lives in a society whose economics offer no possibility of such an existence, other than sad spinsterhood, and her continuing love for Van is an implicit endorsement of its principles. Emancipation remains a matter of educational policy and social detail. Allowing for the important difference between James's equivocation and Hardy's anger, a broad parallel could be drawn with Sue Bridehead in *Jude the Obscure*, whose intellectual emancipation is crushed by a society which offers her no space.

What *The Awkward Age* does offer to Nanda is the unfulfilled possibility of a relationship with Mitchy, the social outsider who loves her as an individual. The roles are still circumscribed – wife, mistress, mentor – but Mitchy's honesty yields a kind of freedom. The last chapter of the novel holds in balance two absences – that of Lady Julia and that of Mitchy: the conservative return towards an irrecoverable ideal of womanhood and the beginning of a way towards an as yet unrealizable independence. The novel refuses closure, refuses us the satisfaction of knowing which, or whether, Nanda chooses. We leave her, awkwardly, between them.

'*Dialogue . . . speaking for itself*'

My reading of *The Awkward Age* as an enactment of tension between various available views of women, symptomatic of social change in a particular period, is based on and validated by its ideological context, but it is just *a* reading. I have tried to take the novel's constant ambiguity into account, but this kind of interpretation must acknowledge that in closing off other possible readings, in subjecting the novel to closure, it necessarily violates its open-endedness, an open-endedness typical of the experimental novels of the period. Growing scepticism and philosophical relativism are paralleled in the novel by a mistrust of authorial omniscience, with its implicit confidence that experience can be conclusively categorized. James's novels break most obviously with the narrative method of classic realism during the 1890s (though the process had begun much earlier, for example in the epistemological pre-occupations of *The Portrait of a Lady*). He spent the first years of the decade writing for the theatre, then after the traumatically unsuccessful first night of his play *Guy Domville* in January 1895, he rededicated himself to the novel: 'I take up my *own* old pen again – the pen of all my old unforgettable efforts and sacred struggles....Large and full and high the future still opens' (*Notebooks*, p. 179). Most often, as in *What Maisie Knew* and *The Turn of the Screw*, omniscience is abandoned in favour of the restricted point of view. Here interpretation is problematized by the 'absolutely scenic lines', as James described it in the Preface, on which the novel is constructed. And, again as he points out in the Preface, his chosen method draws attention to the inseparability of form and subject, 'helps us ever so happily to see the grave distinction between substance and form in a really wrought work of art signally break down': concerned with Nanda's potential effect on the talk in her mother's drawing-room, it is itself made of talk, talk about knowing, reading, interpreting – the processes in which we, as much as the characters, are involved.

We share Mr Longdon's problem as, in the prefatory first book for example, he tries to follow and assess Vanderbank's incessant, elusive conversation. Words are established as slippery and uncertain from the beginning, from the superficial level of unimportant puns ('"What a head you must have!" "Oh yes – our head's Sir Digby Dence"' – p. 4), to the potentially more worrying uncertain identity of Van's sister with her series of names (p. 14), to his indifference to what might be said of London society:

'It's impossible to say too much – it's impossible to say enough. There isn't anything any one can say that I won't agree to.'

'That shows you really don't care,' the old man returned with
acuteness.

'Oh, we're past saving, if that's what you mean!' Vanderbank
laughed.

'You don't care, you don't care!' his visitor repeated, 'and
– if I may be frank with you – I shouldn't wonder if it were
rather a pity.' (p. 13)

Mr Longdon's 'if I may be frank' is characteristic. He still
believes in the possibility of identifying a truth which words
will pellucidly reflect and communicate – hence his concern
at Vanderbank's indifference to what might be said. In
Buckingham Crescent he has glimpsed a kind of talk
which divorces words from certain referents, whose concern
is not communication but the play of talk itself. '"I think I
was rather frightened"' is his parting comment to Vanderbank: frightened, because he speaks a different language
and instead of passively 'reading' the talk according to
pre-established assumptions, he has now to translate, to
interpret it, a subjective process fraught with uncertainty.
Just as our initial instinct as readers trained in classic
realism is, I suggested, to identify with Nanda as heroine,
so here we tend at first to share Mr Longdon's assumption
that we shall be able to reach an accurate conclusion about
Mrs Brookenham and her set. But our sympathy with Nanda
is modified by being in constant play with other possibilities,
and our confidence in Mr Longdon's commonsense morality
is undermined as it is established as just one point of view
among many.

Everyone in *The Awkward Age* is involved in the game of
interpretation – even the narrator. James's scenic method
is not of course completely confined to dialogue, but the
narrative voice really does little more than supply detailed
stage directions, like those of Ibsen or Shaw (or James
himself). We are given physical descriptions of character
and setting, details of gesture – another discourse open to
our interpretation – and, importantly, of silences, but
almost without exception the narrator's interpretative comments are registered as speculative: qualified by 'perhaps',
put in the conditional tense, or attributed to an imaginary
'initiated' or 'ingenious' observer 'disposed to interpret

the scene' (p. 86). A passage during Nanda's crucial conversation with Vanderbank at Beccles is typical. Nanda
has been describing to Van her sense of his fundamental
unease, yet passive acquiescence in London society:

So she *appeared* to put it to him, with something in her lucidity
that *would have been* infinitely touching; a strange, grave, calm
consciousness of their common doom and of what in especial in
it would be worst for herself. He sprang up indeed after an
instant *as if* he had been infinitely touched; he turned away,
taking just near her a few steps to and fro, gazed about the place
again, but this time without the air of particularly seeing it, and
then came back to her as if from a greater distance. *An observer
at all initiated would*, at the juncture, fairly have hung on his
lips, and there was in fact on Vanderbank's part quite the look
of the man – though it lasted but just while we seize it – in
suspense about himself. (p. 231; my italics)

The narrative voice is so consistently tentative that we
respond to it not as authoritative narration but as just
another point of view; when, towards the end of the quoted
passage, we read 'in fact', it has the force of colloquial
emphasis rather than categorical truth. And when we
examine what the 'initiated observer' could tell us (and
initiated into what? Mrs Brook's set? Nanda's particular
problem? the workings of Van's mind? similar situations
in other novels?), it is actually very little. The obvious
assumption is that Van is 'in suspense about himself' because
he is uncertain whether to propose to Nanda, but there are
several other possible explanations: he might be wondering
whether to tell her of Mr Longdon's offer, or considering
the validity of her view of him – or, indeed, thinking about
something quite beyond our speculation. Similarly, Nanda's
'strange, grave, calm consciousness' may or may not exist
for her. Our strategy as readers is to choose the possibility
which we can most readily fit into our sense of consistent
character or of thematic or narrative coherence.

What this suggests is the way in which our reading
habits are based on the notion of character as possessing
a penetrable subjective self, and on belief in meaning and
coherence as recoverable, pre-existent truths. *The Awkward
Age* actually offers no such coherent identities, the staple

of the realist novel. In refusing that '"going behind", to compass explanations and amplifications, to drag out odds and ends from the "mere" storyteller's great property-shop of aids to allusion' (Preface), James's novel, like the conversation in Mrs Brook's salon, offers only a play of surfaces which, in resisting any final interpretation, draw attention to the act of interpretation itself. Character, we realize, is provisional, created by an act of collusion between text and reader. As Mitchy says at one point: '"It's every one's fate to be in one way or another the subject of ideas"' (p. 318). To be, indeed, created by them: when Mrs Brook, for example, talks of Mr Longdon's 'value' or 'worth' we see it as moral or simply financial according to our idea of her. At another point Mrs Brook indignantly asks Van: '"Do you call mamma a 'phrase'?"' (p. 194) – but that is, after all, all Lady Julia is, a phrase which we and the other characters read in different ways according to our particular sense of her significance.

And even if, 'initiated' and sophisticated, we step back and acknowledge this play of meaning, hold possible meanings in tension rather than choosing between them, we are still involved in interpretation – inevitably: to read is to interpret. But in responding thus to James's experimental form we achieve a self-consciousness, painful no doubt, akin to Nanda's growth to knowledge. An astute early reviewer described *The Awkward Age* as 'the wonderful artistic outcome of our national habit of repression.... Let us thank the proprieties, the conventions of this land, the genius of repression, which have created that need for a new realism' (*Critical Heritage*, pp. 286–8). Certainly, as Todorov points out, somewhere behind *The Awkward Age* there is a realist novel about sex, marriage and money and our instinct is to make sense of character and event in its terms. The excitement of reading James's novel is to feel the tension between that nostalgic impulse and the self-consciousness demanded by its form. Like Nanda's, our initiation, though awkward, opens up frightening and exhilarating possibilities.

VIVIEN JONES

NOTE ON THE TEXT

The Awkward Age exists in three editions. It was first published in *Harper's Weekly* in fourteen episodes between October 1898 and January 1899, without the division into ten books. This was followed by publication in book form, by William Heinemann in London on 25 April 1899, and by Harper and Brothers in New York on 12 May, and it was in this form that the ten-book division was added. It was then republished in 1908 as volume IX of the New York Edition. James's revisions for the first book publication are mainly a matter of punctuation – he omits commas, for example, around phrases which the speaking voice would naturally slightly parenthesize – but there are one or two other interesting changes which I have drawn attention to in the Notes. Perhaps because the novel consists largely of dialogue, James's revisions for the New York Edition, unlike many of the works in that edition, are again comparatively minor. More commas are omitted to give the familiar texture of late Jamesian prose to some of the longer narrative passages. Other revisions tend to produce a smoother, more natural, prose: 'accepted, under pressure, his invitation' (2.3), for example, becomes 'accepted his invitation under pressure'; or they improve a speaker's idiom: Mrs Brookenham's 'illustrative anecdote' (275.18) becomes 'racy anecdote' and in her conversation with the Duchess in Book II, she is saved from insulting Aggie when James omits her reference to 'mechanical dolls' (41.3). The Preface is of course taken from the New York Edition but the text of the novel used here is that of the first book publication.

FURTHER READING

JAMES'S WRITINGS

For a complete list of James's work see *A Bibliography of Henry James*, ed. Leon Edel and Dan H. Laurence revised with the assistance of James Rambeau (Oxford: Clarendon Press, 1982, 3rd edn).

The major novels are all easily available, most of them in paperback editions.

James's major critical essays are collected in: *French Poets and Novelists* (London: Macmillan, 1878); *Partial Portraits* (London: Macmillan, 1888); *Essays in London and Elsewhere* (London: Osgood, McIlvaine, 1893); *Notes on Novelists* (London: Dent, 1914). The Prefaces are collected in *The Art of the Novel*, with an introduction by R. P. Blackmur (1934; rpt. New York and London: Charles Scribner's Sons, 1962). Two useful selections of essays are: *The House of Fiction: Essays on the Novel by Henry James*, ed. Leon Edel (London: Rupert Hart-Davies, 1957); *Selected Literary Criticism*, ed. Morris Shapira (1963; rpt. Harmondsworth: Penguin Books, 1968).

James's letters are available in two editions: *The Letters of Henry James*, ed. Percy Lubbock, 2 vols (London: Macmillan, 1920); *Henry James: Letters*, ed. Leon Edel, 3 vols to date (London: Macmillan, 1974–).

James's working notebooks are available as *The Notebooks of Henry James*, ed. F. O. Matthiessen and Kenneth B. Murdock (1947; rpt. Chicago and London: University of Chicago Press, 1981).

BIOGRAPHY AND BACKGROUND

Edel, Leon, *The Life of Henry James*, 2 vols (rev. edn Harmondsworth: Penguin Books, 1977).

Gard, Roger, ed., *Henry James: The Critical Heritage* (London: Routledge and Kegan Paul, 1968).

Adburgham, Alison, *The Punch History of Manners and Modes* (London: Hutchinson, 1961).

For an excellent survey of the 'New Woman' fiction, to which I am much indebted, see:

Boumelha, Penny, *Thomas Hardy and Women: Sexual Ideology and Narrative Form* (Sussex: Harvester Press and New York: Barnes and Noble, 1982).

CRITICISM

Criticism on *The Awkward Age* is not particularly extensive. The following offer traditional critical readings of the novel:

Gregor, Ian, 'The Novel of Moral Consciousness: *The Awkward Age*' in Ian Gregor and Brian Nicholas, *The Moral and the Story* (London: Faber, 1962).

Krook, Dorothea, in *The Ordeal of Consciousness in Henry James* (Cambridge: Cambridge University Press, 1963).

Leavis, F. R. in *The Great Tradition* (1948: rpt. Harmondsworth: Penguin Books, 1972).

More recent critical readings:

Bersani, Leo, 'The Jamesian Lie' in *A Future for Astyanax: Character and Desire in Literature* (Boston and Toronto: Little, Brown, 1977).

Bradbury, Nicola, in *Henry James: The Later Novels* (Oxford: Clarendon Press, 1979).

Culver, Stuart, 'Censorship and Intimacy: Awkwardness in *The Awkward Age*', *English Literary History* 48 (1981), 368–86.

Todorov, Tzvetan, 'The Verbal Age', trans. Patricia Martin Gibby, *Critical Inquiry* 4 (Winter, 1977), 351–71.

Walters, Margaret, 'Keeping the place tidy for the young female mind' in John Goode, ed., *The Air of Reality: New Essays on Henry James* (London: Methuen, 1972).

Other articles on *The Awkward Age*:

Blackall, Jean Frantz, 'Literary Allusion as Imaginative Event in *The Awkward Age*', *Modern Fiction Studies* 26 (Summer, 1980), 179–97.

Girling, H. K., '"Wonder" and "Beauty" in *The Awkward Age*' in Tony Tanner, ed., *Henry James: Modern Judgements* (London: Macmillan, 1968).

Hall, William F., 'James's Conception of Society in *The Awkward Age*', *Nineteenth Century Fiction* 23 (June 1968), 28–48.

Hill, Hamlin L. Jr., '"The Revolt of the Daughters": A Suggested Source for *The Awkward Age*', *Notes and Queries* (Sept. 1961), pp. 347–9.

Owen, Elizabeth, '*The Awkward Age* and the Contemporary English Scene', *Victorian Studies* 11 (Sept. 1967), 63–82.

CHRONOLOGY OF HENRY JAMES

COMPILED BY LEON EDEL

1843	Born 15 April at No. 21 Washington Place, New York City.
1843–4	Taken abroad by parents to Paris and London: period of residence at Windsor.
1845–55	Childhood in Albany and New York.
1855–8	Attends schools in Geneva, London, Paris and Boulogne-sur-mer and is privately tutored.
1858	James family settles in Newport, Rhode Island.
1859	At scientific school in Geneva. Studies German in Bonn.
1860	At school in Newport. Receives back injury on eve of Civil War while serving as volunteer fireman. Studies art briefly. Friendship with John La Farge.
1862–3	Spends term in Harvard Law School.
1864	Family settles in Boston and then in Cambridge. Early anonymous story and unsigned reviews published.
1865	First signed story published in *Atlantic Monthly*.
1869–70	Travels in England, France and Italy. Death of his beloved cousin Minny Temple.
1870	Back in Cambridge, publishes first novel in *Atlantic, Watch and Ward*.
1872–4	Travels with sister Alice and aunt in Europe; writes impressionistic travel sketches for the *Nation*. Spends autumn in Paris and goes to Italy to write first large novel.
1874–5	On completion of *Roderick Hudson* tests New York City as residence; writes much literary journalism for *Nation*. First three books published: *Transatlantic Sketches*, *A Passionate Pilgrim* (tales) and *Roderick Hudson*.
1875–6	Goes to live in Paris. Meets Ivan Turgenev and through him Flaubert, Zola, Daudet, Maupassant and Edmond de Goncourt. Writes *The American*.

1876–7   Moves to London and settles in 3 Bolton Street, Piccadilly. Revisits Paris, Florence, Rome.

1878   'Daisy Miller' published in London establishes fame on both sides of the Atlantic. Publishes first volume of essays, *French Poets and Novelists*.

1879–82   *The Europeans, Washington Square, Confidence, The Portrait of a Lady.*

1882–3   Revisits Boston: first visit to Washington. Death of parents.

1884–6   Returns to London. Sister Alice comes to live near him. Fourteen-volume collection of novels and tales published. Writes *The Bostonians* and *The Princess Casamassima*, published in the following year.

1886   Moves to flat at 34 De Vere Gardens West.

1887   Sojourn in Italy, mainly Florence and Venice. 'The Aspern Papers', *The Reverberator*, 'A London Life'. Friendship with grand-niece of Fenimore Cooper – Constance Fenimore Woolson.

1888   *Partial Portraits* and several collections of tales.

1889–90   *The Tragic Muse.*

1890–1   Dramatizes *The American*, which has a short run. Writes four comedies, rejected by producers.

1892   Alice James dies in London.

1894   Miss Woolson commits suicide in Venice. James journeys to Italy and visits her grave in Rome.

1895   He is booed at first night of his play *Guy Domville*. Deeply depressed, he abandons the theatre.

1896–7   *The Spoils of Poynton, What Maisie Knew.*

1898   Takes long lease of Lamb House, in Rye, Sussex. Writes 'The Turn of the Screw'.

1899–1900   *The Awkward Age, The Sacred Fount.* Friendship with Conrad and Wells.

1902–4   *The Ambassadors, The Wings of the Dove* and *The Golden Bowl.* Friendships with H. C. Andersen and Jocelyn Persse.

1905   Revisits USA after 20-year absence, lectures on Balzac and the speech of Americans.

1906–10   *The American Scene.* Edits selective and revised

'New York Edition' of his works in 24 volumes. Friendship with Hugh Walpole.

1910   Death of brother, William James.

1913   Sargent paints his portrait as 70th birthday gift from some 300 friends and admirers. Writes autobiographies, *A Small Boy and Others*, and *Notes of a Son and Brother*.

1914   *Notes on Novelists*. Visits wounded in hospitals.

1915   Becomes a British subject.

1916   Given Order of Merit. Dies 28 February in Chelsea, aged 72. Funeral in Chelsea Old Church. Ashes buried in Cambridge, Mass., family plot.

1976   Commemorative tablet unveiled in Poets' Corner of Westminster Abbey, 17 June.

PREFACE

I RECALL with perfect ease the idea in which *The Awkward Age* had its origin, but reperusal gives me pause in respect to naming it. This composition, as it stands, makes, to my vision – and will have made perhaps still more to that of its readers – so considerable a mass beside the germ sunk in it and still possibly distinguishable, that I am half-moved to leave my small secret undivulged. I shall encounter, I think, in the course of this copious commentary, no better example, and none on behalf of which I shall venture to invite more interest, of the quite incalculable tendency of a mere grain of subject-matter to expand and develop and cover the ground when conditions happen to favour it. I say all, surely, when I speak of the thing as planned, in perfect good faith, for brevity, for levity, for simplicity, for jocosity, in fine, and for an accommodating irony. I invoked, for my protection, the spirit of the lightest comedy, but *The Awkward Age* was to belong, in the event, to a group of productions, here reintroduced, which have in common, to their author's eyes, the endearing sign that they assisted in each case an unforeseen principle of growth. They were projected as small things, yet had finally to be provided for as comparative monsters. That is my own title for them, though I should perhaps resent it if applied by another critic – above all in the case of the piece before us, the careful measure of which I have just freshly taken. The result of this consideration has been in the first place to render sharp for me again the interest of the whole process thus illustrated, and in the second quite to place me on unexpectedly good terms with the work itself. As I scan my list I encounter none the 'history' of which embodies a greater number of curious truths – or of truths at least by which I find contemplation more enlivened. The thing done and dismissed has ever, at the best, for the ambitious workman, a trick of looking dead if not buried, so that he almost throbs with ecstasy when, on an anxious review, the flush of life re-appears. It is verily on recognizing that flush on a whole side of *The Awkward Age* that I brand it all, but ever so tenderly, as monstrous – which is but my way of noting the *quantity* of finish it stows away. Since I speak so undauntedly, when need is, of the value of composition, I shall not beat about the bush to claim for these pages the maximum of that advantage. If such a feat be possible in this field as really taking a lesson from one's own adventure I feel I have now not failed of it – to so much more demonstration of my profit than I can hope to carry through do I find myself urged. Thus it is that, still with a remnant of self-respect, or at least of sanity, one may turn to complacency, one may linger with pride. Let my pride provoke a frown till I justify it; which – though with more matters to be noted here than I have room for – I shall accordingly proceed to do.

Yet I must first make a brave face, no doubt, and present in its native humility my scant but quite ponderable germ. The seed sprouted in that vast nursery of sharp appeals and concrete images which calls itself, for blest convenience, London; it fell even into the order of the minor 'social phenomena' with which, as fruit for the observer, that mightiest of the trees of suggestion bristles. It was not, no doubt, a fine purple peach, but it might pass for a round ripe plum, the note one had inevitably had to take of the difference made in certain friendly houses and for certain flourishing mothers by the sometimes dreaded, often de-layed, but never fully arrested coming to the forefront of some vague slip of a daughter. For such mild revolutions as these not, to one's imagination, to remain mild one had had, I dare say, to be infinitely addicted to 'noticing'; under the rule of that secret vice or that unfair advantage, at any rate, the 'sitting downstairs', from a given date, of the merciless maiden previously perched aloft could easily be felt as a crisis. This crisis, and the sense for it in those whom it most concerns, has to confess itself courageously the prime propulsive force of *The Awkward Age*. Such a matter might well make a scant show for a 'thick book', and no thick book, but just a quite charmingly thin one, was in fact originally dreamt of. For its proposed scale the little idea seemed happy – happy, that is, above all in having come very straight; but its proposed scale was the limit of a small square canvas. One had been present again and again at the exhibition I refer to – which is what I mean by the 'coming straight' of this particular London impression; yet one was (and through fallibilities that after all had their sweetness, so that one would on the whole rather have kept them than parted with them) still capable of so false a measurement. When I think indeed of those of my many false measurements that have resulted after much anguish, in decent symmetries, I find the whole case, I profess, a theme for the philosopher. The little ideas one wouldn't have treated save for the design of keeping them small, the developed situations that one would never with malice pre-pense have undertaken, the long stories that had thoroughly meant to be short, the short subjects that had underhandedly plotted to be long, the hypocrisy of modest beginnings, the audacity of misplaced middles, the triumph of intentions never entertained – with these patches, as I look about, I see my experience paved: an experience to which nothing is wanting save, I confess, some grasp of its final lesson.

This lesson would, if operative, surely provide some law for the recognition, the determination in advance, of the just limits and the just extent of the situation, *any* situation, that appeals, and that yet, by the presumable, the helpful laws of situations, must have its reserves as well as its promises. The story-teller considers it because it promises, and undertakes it, often, just because also making out, as he believes, where the promise conveniently drops. The promise, for instance, of the case I have just named, the case of the account to be taken, in a circle of free talk, of a new and innocent, a wholly unacclimatized presence, as to which such accommodations have never had to come up, might well have appeared as limited as it was lively; and if these pages were not before us to register my illusion I should never have made a braver claim for it. They them-selves admonish me, however in fifty interesting ways, and they especially emphasize that truth of the vanity of the *a priori* test of what an *idée-mère* may have to give. The truth is that what a happy thought has to give depends immensely on the general turn of the mind capable of it, and on the fact that its loyal entertainer, cultivating fondly its possible relations and extensions, the bright efflorescence latent in it, but having to take other things in their order too, is terribly at the mercy of his mind. That organ has only to exhale, in its degree, a fostering tropic air in order to produce complications almost beyond reckoning. The trap laid for his superficial convenience resides in the fact that, though the relations of a human figure or a social occurrence are what make such objects interesting, they also make them, to the same tune, difficult to isolate, to surround with the sharp black line, to frame in the square, the circle, the charming oval, that helps any arrangement of objects to become a picture. The story-teller has but to have been condemned by nature to a liberally amused and beguiled, a richly sophisticated, view of relations and a fine inquisitive speculative sense for them, to find himself at moments flounder in a deep warm jungle. These are the moments at which he recalls ruefully that the great merit of such and such a small case, the merit for his particular advised use, had been precisely in the smallness.

I may say at once that this had seemed to me, under the first flush of recognition, the good mark for the pretty notion of the 'free circle' put about by having, of a sudden, an ingenuous mind and a pair of limpid searching eyes to count with. Half the attraction was in the current actuality of the thing: repeatedly, right and left, as I have said, one had seen such a drama constituted, and always to the effect of proposing to the interested view one of those questions that are of the essence of drama: what will happen, who suffer, who not suffer, what turn be determined, what crisis created, what issue found? There had of course, to be, as a basis, the free circle, but this was material of that admirable order with which the good London never leaves its true lover and believer long unprovided. One could count them on one's fingers (an abundant allowance), the liberal fire-sides beyond the wide glow of which, in a comparative dimness, female adolescence hovered and waited. The wide

glow was bright, was favourable to 'real' talk, to play of
mind, to an explicit interest in life, a due demonstration of
the interest by persons qualified to feel it: all of which
meant frankness and ease, the perfection, almost, as it were,
of intercourse, and a tone as far as possible removed from
that of the nursery and the schoolroom – as far as possible
removed even, no doubt, in its appealing 'modernity', from
that of supposedly privileged scenes of conversation twenty
years ago. The charm was, with a hundred other things, in
the freedom – the freedom menaced by the inevitable
irruption of the ingenuous mind; whereby, if the freedom
should be sacrificed, what would truly *become* of the
charm? The charm might be figured as dear to members
of the circle consciously contributing to it, but it was none
the less true that some sacrifice in some quarter would have
to be made, and what meditator worth his salt could fail
to hold his breath while waiting on the event? The
ingenuous mind might, it was true, be suppressed altogether,
the general disconcertment averted either by some master-
stroke of diplomacy or some rude simplification; yet these
were ugly matters, and in the examples before one's eyes
nothing ugly, nothing harsh or crude, had flourished. A girl
might be married off the day after her irruption, or better
still the day before it, to remove her from the sphere of the
play of mind; but these were exactly not crudities, and even
then, at the worst, an interval had to be bridged. *The Awkward Age* is precisely a study of one of these curtailed or
extended periods of tension and apprehension, an account of
the manner in which the resented interference with ancient
liberties came to be in a particular instance dealt with.

I note once again that I had not escaped seeing it actually
and traceably dealt with – after (I admit) a good deal of
friendly suspense; also with the nature and degree of the
'sacrifice' left very much to one's appreciation. In circles
highly civilized the great things, the real things, the hard,
the cruel and even the tender things, the true elements of
any tension and true facts of any crisis, have ever, for the
outsider's, for the critic's use, to be translated into terms –
terms in the distinguished name of which, terms for the
right employment of which, more than one situation of the

type I glance at had struck me as all irresistibly appealing.
There appeared in fact at moments no end to the things
they said, the suggestions into which they flowered; one of
these latter in especial arriving at the highest intensity.
Putting vividly before one the perfect system on which the
awkward age is handled in most other European societies,
it threw again into relief the inveterate English trick of the
so morally well-meant and so intellectually helpless
compromise. We live notoriously, as I suppose every age
lives, in an 'epoch of transition'; but it may still be said of
the French for instance, I assume, that their social scheme
absolutely provides against awkwardness. That is it would
be, by this scheme, so infinitely awkward, so awkward
beyond any patching-up, for the hovering female young to
be conceived as present at 'good' talk, that their presence is,
theoretically at least, not permitted till their youth has been
promptly corrected by marriage – in which case they have
ceased to be merely young. The better the talk prevailing in
any circle, accordingly, the more organized, the more complete, the element of precaution and exclusion. Talk – giving
the term a wide application – is one thing, and a proper
inexperience another; and it has never occurred to a logical
people that the interest of the greater, the general, need be
sacrificed to that of the less, the particular. Such sacrifices
strike them as gratuitous and barbarous, as cruel above all to
the social intelligence; also as perfectly preventable by
wise arrangement. Nothing comes home more, on the other
hand, to the observer of English manners than the very
moderate degree in which wise arrangement, in the French
sense of a scientific economy, has ever been invoked; a fact
indeed largely explaining the great interest of their incoherence, their heterogeneity, their wild abundance. The
French, all analytically, have conceived of fifty different
proprieties, meeting fifty different cases, whereas the English
mind, less intensely at work, has never conceived but of one
– the grand propriety, for every case, it should in fairness
be said, of just being English. As practice, however, has
always to be a looser thing than theory, so no application
of that rigour has been possible in the London world without a thousand departures from the grim ideal.

The American theory, if I may 'drag it in', would be, I think, that talk should never become 'better' than the female young, either actually or constructively present, are minded to allow it. *That* system allows as little compromise as the French; it has been absolutely simple, and the beauty of its success shines out in every record of our conditions of intercourse – premising always our 'basic' assumption that the female young read the newspapers. The English theory may be in itself almost as simple, but different and much more complex forces have ruled the application of it; so much does the goodness of talk depend on what there may be to talk about. There are more things in London, I think, than anywhere in the world; hence the charm of the dramatic struggle reflected in my book, the struggle somehow to fit propriety into a smooth general case which is really all the while bristling and crumbling into fierce particular ones. The circle surrounding Mrs Brookenham, in my pages, is of course nothing if not a particular, even a 'peculiar' one – and its rather vain effort (the vanity, the real inexpertness, being precisely part of my tale) is toward the courage of that condition. It has cropped up in a social order where individual appreciations of propriety have not been formally allowed for, in spite of their having very often quite rudely and violently and insolently, rather of course than insidiously, flourished; so that as the matter stands, rightly or wrongly, Nanda's retarded, but eventually none the less real, incorporation means virtually Nanda's exposure. It means this, that is, and many things beside – means them for Nanda herself and, with a various intensity, for the other participants in the action; but what it particularly means, surely, is the failure of successful arrangement and the very moral, sharply pointed, of the fruits of compromise. It is compromise that has suffered her to be in question at all, and that has condemned the freedom of the circle to be self-conscious, compunctious, on the whole much more timid than brave – the consequent muddle, if the term be not too gross, representing meanwhile a great inconvenience for life, but, as I found myself feeling, an immense promise, a much greater one than on the 'foreign' showing, for the painted picture of life. Beyond which let me add that here immediately is a prime specimen of the way in which the obscurer, the lurking relations of a motive apparently simple, always in wait for their spring, may by seizing their chance for it send simplicity flying. Poor Nanda's little case, and her mother's, and Mr Longdon's and Vanderbank's and Mitchy's, to say nothing of that of the others, has only to catch a reflected light from over the Channel in order to double at once its appeal to the imagination. (I am considering all these matters, I need scarce say, only as they are concerned with that faculty. With a relation *not* imaginative to his material the story-teller has nothing whatever to do.)

It exactly happened moreover that my own material here was to profit in a particular way by that extension of view. My idea was to be treated with light irony – it would be light and ironical or it would be nothing; so that I asked myself, naturally, what might be the least solemn form to give it, among recognized and familiar forms. The question thus at once arose: what form so familiar, so recognized among alert readers, as that in which the ingenious and inexhaustible, the charming philosophic 'Gyp' casts most of her social studies? Gyp has long struck me as mistress, in her levity, of one of the happiest of forms – the only objection to my use of which was a certain extraordinary benightedness on the part of the Anglo-Saxon reader. One had noted this reader as perverse and inconsequent in respect to the absorption of 'dialogue' – observed the 'public for fiction' consume it, in certain connexions, on the scale and with the smack of lips that mark the consumption of bread and jam by a children's school-feast, consume it even at the theatre, so far as our theatre ever vouchsafes it, and yet as flagrantly reject it when served, so to speak, *au naturel*. One had seen good solid slices of fiction, well endued, one might surely have thought, with this easiest of lubrications, deplored by editor and publisher as positively not, for the general gullet as known to *them*, made adequately 'slick'. '"Dialogue," always "dialogue"!' I had seemed from far back to hear them mostly cry: 'We can't have too much of it, we can't have enough of it, and no excess of it, in the form of no matter what savourless dilution, or what boneless dispersion, ever began to injure a book so much as even the

very scantest claim put in for form and substance.' This
wisdom had always been in one's ears; but it had at the same
time been equally in one's eyes that really constructive
dialogue, dialogue organic and dramatic, speaking for
itself, representing and embodying substance and form, is
among us an uncanny and abhorrent thing, not to be dealt
with on any terms. A comedy or a tragedy may run for a
thousand nights without prompting twenty persons in
London or in New York to desire that view of its text which
it so desired in Paris, as soon as a play begins to loom at all
large, that the number of copies of the printed piece in
circulation far exceeds at last the number of performances.
But as with the printed piece our own public, infatuated as
it may be with the theatre, refuses all commerce – though
indeed this can't but be, without cynicism, very much
through the infirmity the piece, *if* printed, would reveal –
so the same horror seems to attach to any typographic hint
of the proscribed playbook or any insidious plea for it. The
immense oddity resides in the almost exclusively typographic
order of the offence. An English, an American Gyp would
typographically offend, and that would be the end of her.
There gloomed at me my warning, as well as shone at me
my provocation, in respect to the example of this delightful
writer. I might emulate her, since I presumptuously would,
but dishonour would await me if, proposing to treat the
different faces of my subject in the most completely in-
stituted colloquial form, I should evoke the figure and
affirm the presence of participants by the repeated and pre-
fixed name rather than by the recurrent and *affixed* 'said he'
and 'said she'. All I have space to go into here – much as
the funny fact I refer to might seem to invite us to dance
hand in hand round it – is that I was at any rate duly
admonished, that I took my measures accordingly, and
that the manner in which I took them has lived again for
me ever so arrestingly, so amusingly, on re-examination of
the book.

But that I did, positively and seriously – ah so seriously!
– emulate the levity of Gyp and, by the same token, of that
hardiest of flowers fostered in her school, M. Henri Lavedan,
is a contribution to the history of *The Awkward Age* that

I shall obviously have had to brace myself in order to make.
Vivid enough to me the expression of face of any kindest of
critics, even, moved to declare that he would never in the
least have suspected it. Let me say at once, in extenuation
of the too respectful distance at which I may thus have
appeared to follow my model, that my first care *had* to be
the covering of my tracks – lest I truly should be caught
in the act of arranging, or organizing dialogue to 'speak for
itself'. What I now see to have happened is that I organized
and arranged but too well – too well, I mean, for any
betrayal of the Gyp taint, however faded and feeble. The
trouble appears to have been that while I on the one hand
exorcized the baleful association, I succeeded in rousing on
nobody's part a sense of any other association whatever, or
of my having cast myself into any conceivable or calculable
form. My private inspiration had been in the Gyp plan
(artfully dissimulated, for dear life, and applied with the
very subtlest consistency, but none the less kept in secret
view); yet I was to fail to make out in the event that the
book succeeded in producing the impression of *any* plan on
any person. No hint of that sort of success, or of any critical
perception at all in relation to the business, has ever come
my way; in spite of which when I speak, as just above, of
what was to 'happen' under the law of my ingenious labour,
I fairly lose myself in the vision of a hundred bright
phenomena. Some of these incidents I must treat myself to
naming, for they are among the best I shall have on any
occasion to retail. But I must first give the measure of the
degree in which they were mere matters of the study. This
composition had originally appeared in *Harper's Weekly*
during the autumn of 1898 and the first weeks of the winter,
and the volume containing it was published that spring. I
had meanwhile been absent from England, and it was not
till my return, some time later, that I had from my publisher any news of our venture. But the news then met at a
stroke all my curiosity: 'I'm sorry to say the book has done
nothing to speak of; I've never in all my experience seen
one treated with more general and complete disrespect.'
There was thus to be nothing left me for fond subsequent
reference – of which I doubtless give even now so adequate

an illustration – save the rich reward of the singular interest attaching to the very intimacies of the effort.

It comes back to me, the whole 'job', as wonderfully amusing and delightfully difficult from the first; since amusement deeply abides, I think, in any artistic attempt the basis and ground-work of which are conscious of a particular firmness. On that hard fine floor the element of execution feels it may more or less confidently *dance*; in which case puzzling questions, sharp obstacles, dangers of detail, may come up for it by the dozen without breaking its heart or shaking its nerve. It is the difficulty produced by the loose foundation or the vague scheme that breaks the heart – when a luckless fatuity has over-persuaded an author of the 'saving' virtue of treatment. Being 'treated' is never, in a workable idea, a mere passive condition, and I hold no subject ever susceptible of help that isn't, like the embarrassed man of our proverbial wisdom, first of all able to help itself. I was thus to have here an envious glimpse, in carrying my design through, of that artistic rage and that artistic felicity which I have ever supposed to be intensest and highest, the confidence of the dramatist strong in the sense of his postulate. The dramatist has verily to *build*, is committed to architecture, to construction at any cost; to driving in deep his vertical supports and laying across and firmly fixing his horizontal, his resting pieces – at the risk of no matter what vibration from the tap of his master-hammer. This makes the active value of his basis immense, enabling him, with his flanks protected, to advance undistractedly, even if not at all carelessly, into the comparative fairyland of the mere minor anxiety. In other words his scheme *holds*, and as he feels this in spite of noted strains and under repeated tests, so he keeps his face to the day. I rejoiced, by that same token, to feel *my* scheme hold, and even a little ruefully watched it give me much more than I had ventured to hope. For I promptly found my conceived arrangement of my material open the door wide to ingenuity. I remember that in sketching my project for the conductors of the periodical I have named I drew on a sheet of paper – and possibly with an effect of the cabalistic, it now comes over me, that even anxious amplification may have but vaguely attenuated – the neat figure of a circle consisting of a number of small rounds disposed at equal distance about a central object. The central object was my situation, my subject in itself, to which the thing would owe its title, and the small rounds represented so many distinct lamps, as I liked to call them, the function of each of which would be to light with all due intensity one of its aspects. I had divided it, didn't they see? into aspects – uncanny as the little term might sound (though not for a moment did I suggest we should use it for the public), and by that sign we would conquer.

They 'saw,' all genially and generously – for I must add that I had made, to the best of my recollection, no morbid scruple of not blabbing about Gyp and her strange incitement. I the more boldly held my tongue over this that the more I, by my intelligence, lived in my arrangement and moved about in it, the more I sank into satisfaction. It was clearly to work to a charm and, during this process – by calling at every step for an exquisite management – 'to haunt, to startle and waylay'. Each of my 'lamps' would be the light of a single 'social occasion' in the history and inter-course of the characters concerned, and would bring out to the full the latent colour of the scene in question and cause it to illustrate, to the last drop, its bearing on my theme. I revelled in this notion of the Occasion as a thing by itself, really and completely a scenic thing, and could scarce name it, while crouching amid the thick arcana of my plan, with a large enough O. The beauty of the conception was in this approximation of the respective divisions of my form to the successive Acts of a Play – as to which it was more than ever a case for charmed capitals. The divine distinction of the act of a play – and a greater than any other it easily succeeds in arriving at – was, I reasoned, in its special, its guarded objectivity. This objectivity, in turn, when achieving its ideal, came from the imposed absence of that 'going behind', to compass explanations and amplifications, to drag out odds and ends from the 'mere' story-teller's great property-shop of aids to illusion: a resource under denial of which it was equally perplexing and delightful, for a change, to proceed. Everything, for that matter, becomes

interesting from the moment it has closely to consider, for
full effect positively to bestride, the law of its kind. 'Kinds'
are the very life of literature, and truth and strength come
from the complete recognition of them, from abounding to
the utmost in their respective senses and sinking deep into
their consistency. I myself have scarcely to plead the cause
of 'going behind', which is right and beautiful and fruitful
in its place and order; but as the confusion of kinds is the
inelegance of letters and the stultification of values, so to
renounce that line utterly and do something quite different
instead may become in another connexion the true course
and the vehicle of effect. Something in the very nature, in
the fine rigour, of this special sacrifice (which is capable of
affecting the form-lover, I think, as really more of a projected form than any other) lends it moreover a coercive
charm; a charm that grows in proportion as the appeal to it
tests and stretches and strains it, puts it powerfully to the
touch. To make the presented occasion tell all its story itself,
remain shut up in its own presence and yet on that patch of
staked-out ground become thoroughly interesting and remain thoroughly clear, is a process not remarkable, no
doubt, so long as a very light weight is laid on it, but difficult
enough to challenge and inspire great adroitness so soon as
the elements to be dealt with begin at all to 'size up'.

The disdainers of the contemporary drama deny, obviously, with all promptness, that the matter to be expressed
by its means – richly and successfully expressed that is – *can*
loom with any largeness; since from the moment it does one
of the conditions breaks down. The process simply collapses
under pressure, they contend, proves its weakness as quickly
as the office laid on it ceases to be simple. 'Remember,' they
say to the dramatist, 'that you have to be, supremely, three
things: you have to be true to your form, you have to be
interesting, you have to be clear. You have in other words to
prove yourself adequate to taking a heavy weight. But we
defy you really to conform to your conditions with any but
a light one. Make the thing you have to convey, make the
picture you have to paint, at all rich and complex, and
you cease to be clear. Remain clear – and with the clearness
required by the infantine intelligence of any public consent-

ing to see a play – and what becomes of the "importance" of your subject? If it's important by any other critical measure than the little foot-rule the "produced" piece has to conform to, it is predestined to be a muddle. When it has escaped being a muddle the note it has succeeded in striking at the furthest will be recognized as one of those that are called high but by the courtesy, by the intellectual provinciality, of theatrical criticism, which, as we can see for ourselves any morning, is – well, an abyss even deeper than the theatre itself. Don't attempt to crush us with Dumas and Ibsen, for such values are from any informed and enlightened point of view, that is measured by other high values, literary, critical, philosophic, of the most moderate order. Ibsen and Dumas are precisely cases of men, men in their degree, in their poor theatrical strait-jacket, speculative, who have *had* to renounce the finer thing for the coarser, the thick, in short, for the thin and the curious for the self-evident. What earthly intellectual distinction, what "prestige" of achievement, would have attached to the substance of such things as *Denise*, as *Monsieur Alphonse*, as *Francillon* (and we take the Dumas of the supposedly subtler period) in any other form? What virtues of the same order would have attached to *The Pillars of Society*, to *An Enemy of the People*, to *Ghosts*, to *Rosmersholm* (or taking also Ibsen's "subtler period") to *John Gabriel Borkmann*, to *The Master Builder*? Ibsen is in fact wonderfully a case in point, since from the moment he's clear, from the moment he's "amusing", it's on the footing of a thesis as simple and superficial as that of *A Doll's House* – while from the moment he's by apparent intention comprehensive and searching it's on the footing of an effect as confused and obscure as *The Wild Duck*. From which you easily see *all* the conditions can't be met. The dramatist has to choose but those he's most capable of, and by that choice he's known.'

So the objector concludes, and never surely without great profit from his having been 'drawn'. His apparent triumph – if it be even apparent – still leaves, it will be noted, convenient cover for retort in the riddled face of the opposite stronghold. The last word in these cases is for nobody who can't pretend to an *absolute* test. The terms here used, obviously, are matters of appreciation, and there is no short cut to proof (luckily for us all round) either that *Monsieur Alphonse* develops itself on the highest plane of irony or that *Ghosts* simplifies almost to excruciation. If *John Gabriel Borkmann* is but a pennyworth of effect as to a character we can imagine much more amply presented, and if *Hedda Gabler* makes an appeal enfeebled by remarkable vagueness, there is by the nature of the case no catching the convinced, or call him the deluded, spectator or reader in the act of a mistake. He is to be caught at the worst in the act of attention, of the very greatest attention, and that is all, as a precious preliminary at least, that the playwright asks of him, besides being all the very divinest poet can get. I remember rejoicing as much to remark this, after getting launched in *The Awkward Age*, as if I were in fact constructing a play; just as I may doubtless appear now not less anxious to keep the philosophy of the dramatist's course before me than if I belonged to his order. I felt, certainly, the support he feels, I participated in his technical amusement, I tasted to the full the bitter-sweetness of his draught – the beauty and the difficulty (to harp again on that string) of escaping poverty *even though* the references in one's action can only be, with intensity, to each other, to things exactly on the same plane of exhibition with themselves. Exhibition may mean in a 'story' twenty different ways, fifty excursions, alternatives, excrescences, and the novel, as largely practised in English, is the perfect paradise of the loose end. The play consents to the logic of but one way, mathematically right, and with the loose end as gross an impertinence on its surface, and as grave a dishonour, as the dangle of a snippet of silk or wool on the right side of a tapestry. We are shut up wholly to cross-relations, relations all within the action itself; no part of which is related to anything but some other part – save of course by the relation of the total to life. And, after invoking the protection of Gyp, I saw the point of my game all in the problem of keeping these conditioned relations crystalline at the same time that I should, in emulation of life, consent to their being numerous and fine and characteristic of the London world (as the London world was in this quarter and that to be deciphered). All of which was to make in the event for complications.

I see now of course how far, with my complications, I got away from Gyp; but I see today so much else too that this particular deflection from simplicity makes scarce a figure among the others; after having once served its purpose, I mean, of lighting my original imitative innocence. For I recognize in especial, with a waking vibration of that interest in which, as I say, the plan of the book is embalmed for me, that my subject was probably condemned in advance to appreciable, or more exactly perhaps to almost preposterously appreciative, over-treatment. It places itself for me thus in a group of small productions exhibiting this perversity, representations of conceived cases in which my process has been to pump the case gaspingly dry, dry not only of superfluous moisture, but absolutely (for I have encountered the charge) of breathable air. I may note, in fine, that coming back to the pages before us with a strong impression of their recording, to my shame, that disaster, even to the extent of its disqualifying them for decent reappearance, I have found the adventure taking, to my relief, quite another turn, and have lost myself in the wonder of what 'over-treatment' may, in the detail of its desperate ingenuity, consist of. The revived interest I speak of has been therefore that of following critically, from page to page, even as the red Indian tracks in the forest the paleface, the footsteps of the systematic loyalty I was able to achieve. The amusement of this *constatation* is, as I have hinted, in the detail of the matter, and the detail is so dense, the texture of the figured and smoothed tapestry so close, that the genius of Gyp herself, muse of general looseness, would certainly, once warned, have uttered the first disavowal of my homage. But what has occurred meanwhile is that this high consistency has itself, so to speak, constituted an exhibition, and that an important artistic truth has seemed to me thereby lighted. We brushed against that truth just now in our glance at the denial of expansibility to any idea the mould of the 'stage-play' may hope to express without cracking and bursting; and we bear in mind at the same time that the picture of Nanda Brookenham's situation, though perhaps seeming to a careless eye so to wander and sprawl, yet presents itself on absolutely scenic lines, and that each of these scenes in itself, and each as related to each and to all of its companions, abides without a moment's deflection by the principle of the stage-play.

In doing this then it does more – it helps us ever so happily to see the grave distinction between substance and form in a really wrought work of art signally break down. I hold it impossible to say, before *The Awkward Age*, where one of these elements ends and the other begins: I have been unable at least myself, on re-examination, to mark any such joint or seam, to see the two *discharged* offices as separate. They are separate before the fact, but the sacrament of execution indissolubly marries them, and the marriage, like any other marriage, has only to be a 'true' one for the scandal of a breach not to show. The thing 'done', artistically, is a fusion, or it has not *been* done – in which case of course the artist may be, and all deservedly, pelted with any fragment of his botch the critic shall choose to pick up. But his ground once conquered, in this particular field, he knows nothing of fragments and may say in all security: 'Detach one if you can. You can analyse in *your* way, oh yes – to relate, to report, to explain; but you can't disintegrate my synthesis; you can't resolve the elements of my whole into different responsible agents or find your way at all (for you own fell purpose). My mixture has only to be perfect literally to bewilder you – you are lost in the tangle of the forest. Prove this value, this effect, in the air of the whole result, to be of my subject, and that other value, other effect, to be of my treatment, prove that I haven't so shaken them together as the conjurer I profess to be *must* consummately shake, and I consent but to parade as before a booth at a fair.' The exemplary closeness of *The Awkward Age* even affects me, on reperusal, I confess, as treasure quite instinctively and foreseeingly laid up against my present opportunity for these remarks. I have been positively struck by the quantity of meaning and the number of intentions, the extent of *ground for interest*, as I

may call it, that I have succeeded in working scenically, yet
without loss of sharpness, clearness or 'atmosphere', into
each of my illuminating Occasions – where, at certain
junctures, the due preservation of all these values took, in
the familiar phrase, a good deal of doing.

I should have liked just here to re-examine with the
reader some of the positively most artful passages I have in
mind – such as the hour of Mr Longdon's beautiful and, as
it were, mystic attempt at a compact with Vanderbank, late
at night, in the billiard-room of the country-house at which
they are staying; such as the other nocturnal passage, under
Mr Longdon's roof, between Vanderbank and Mitchy,
where the conduct of so much fine meaning, so many flares
of the exhibitory torch through the labyrinth of mere
immediate appearances, mere familiar allusions, is successfully and safely effected; such as the whole array of the
terms of presentation that are made to serve, all system-
atically, yet without a gap anywhere, for the presentation,
throughout, of a Mitchy 'subtle' no less than concrete and
concrete no less than deprived of that officious explanation
which we know as 'going behind'; such as, briefly, the
general service of co-ordination and vivification rendered, on
lines of ferocious, of really quite heroic compression, by the
picture of the assembled group at Mrs Grendon's, where the
'cross references' of the action are as thick as the green
leaves of a garden, but none the less, as they have scenically
to be, counted and disposed, weighted with responsibility.
Were I minded to use in this connexion a 'loud' word – and
the critic in general hates loud words as a man of taste may
hate loud colours – I should speak of the composition of the
chapters entitled 'Tishy Grendon', with all the pieces of the
game on the table together and each unconfusedly and con-
tributively placed, as triumphantly scientific. I must properly
remind myself, rather, that the better lesson of my retro-
spect would seem to be really a supreme revision of the
question of what it may be for a subject to suffer, to call it
suffering, by over-treatment. Bowed down so long by the
inference that its product had in this case proved such a
betrayal, my artistic conscience meets the relief of having to
recognize truly here no traces of suffering. The thing carries

itself to my maturer and gratified sense as with every symptom of soundness, an insolence of health and joy. And from this precisely I deduce my moral; which is to the effect that, since our only way, in general, of knowing that we have had too much of anything is by *feeling* that too much: so, by the same token, when we don't feel the excess (and I am contending, mind, that in *The Awkward Age* the multiplicity yields to the order) how do we know that the measure not recorded, the notch not reached, does represent adequacy or satiety? The mere feeling helps us for certain degrees of congestion, but for exact science, that is for the criticism of 'fine' art, we want the notation. The notation, however, is what we lack, and the verdict of the mere feeling is liable to fluctuate. In other words an imputed defect is never, at the worst, disengageable, or other than matter for appreciation – to come back to my claim for that felicity of the dramatist's case that his synthetic 'whole' *is* his form, the only one we have to do with. I like to profit in his company by the fact that if our art has certainly, for the impression it produces, to defer to the rise and fall, in the critical temperature, of the tell-tale mercury, it still hasn't to reckon with the engraved thermometer face.

HENRY JAMES

BOOK I

LADY JULIA

I

SAVE when it happened to rain Vanderbank always walked home, but he usually took a hansom when the rain was moderate and adopted the preference of the philosopher when it was heavy. On this occasion he therefore recognized, as the servant opened the door, a congruity between the weather and the 'four-wheeler' that, in the empty street, under the glazed radiance, waited and trickled and blackly glittered. The butler mentioned it as, on such a wild night, the only thing they could get, and Vanderbank, having replied that it was exactly what would do best, prepared, in the doorway, to put up his umbrella and dash down to it. At this moment he heard his name pronounced from behind, and, on turning, found himself joined by the elderly fellow-guest with whom he had talked after dinner and about whom, later on, upstairs, he had sounded his hostess. It was at present a clear question of how this amiable, this apparently unassertive person should get home – of the possibility of the other cab for which even now one of the footmen, with a whistle to his lips, craned out his head and listened through the storm. Mr Longdon wondered, to Vanderbank, if their course might by any chance be the same; which led our young friend immediately to express a readiness to see him safely in any direction that should accommodate him. As the footman's whistle spent itself in vain they got together into the four-wheeler, where, at the end of a few moments more, Vanderbank became conscious of having proposed his own rooms as a wind-up to their drive. Wouldn't that be a better finish of the evening than just separating in the wet? He liked his new acquaintance, who struck him as in a manner clinging to him, who was staying at an hotel presumably at that hour

dismal, and who, confessing with easy humility to a connexion positively timid with a club at which one couldn't
have a visitor, accepted, under pressure, his invitation.
Vanderbank, when they arrived, was amused at the air of
added extravagance with which he said he would keep the
cab: he so clearly enjoyed to that extent the sense of making
a night of it.

'You young men, I believe, keep them for hours, eh? At
least they did in my time,' he laughed – 'the wild ones! But
I think of them as all wild then. I dare say that when one
settles in town one learns how to manage; only I'm afraid,
you know, that I've got completely out of it. I do feel really
quite mouldy. It's a matter of thirty years—'

'Since you've been in London?'

'For more than a few days at a time, upon my honour.
You won't understand that – any more, I dare say, than I
myself quite understand how, at the end of all, I've accepted
this queer view of the doom of coming back. But I don't
doubt I shall ask you, if you'll be so good as to let me, for
the help of a hint or two: as to how to do, don't you know?
and not to – what do you fellows call it? – *be* done. Now
about one of *these* things—!'

One of these things was the lift in which, at no great
pace and with much rumbling and creaking, the porter
conveyed the two gentlemen to the alarming eminence, as
Mr Longdon measured their flight, at which Vanderbank
perched. The impression made on him by this contrivance
showed him as unsophisticated, yet when his companion, at
the top, ushering him in, gave a touch to the quick light and,
in the pleasant, ruddy room, all convenience and character,
had before the fire another look at him, it was not to catch
in him any protrusive angle. Mr Longdon was slight and
neat, delicate of body and both keen and kind of face, with
black brows finely marked and thick, smooth hair in which
the silver had deep shadows. He wore neither whisker nor
moustache and seemed to carry in the flicker of his quick
brown eyes and the positive sun-play of his smile even more
than the equivalent of what might, superficially or stupidly,
elsewhere be missed in him; which was mass, substance,
presence – what is vulgarly called importance. He had

indeed no presence, but he had somehow an effect. He might almost have been a priest, if priests, as it occurred to Vanderbank, were ever such dandies. He had at all events conclusively doubled the Cape of the years – he would never again see fifty-five: to the warning light of that bleak headland he presented a back sufficiently conscious. Yet, though, to Vanderbank, he could not look young, he came near – strikingly and amusingly – looking new: this, after a minute, appeared mainly perhaps indeed in the perfection of his evening dress and the special smartness of the sleeveless overcoat he had evidently had made to wear with it and might even actually be wearing for the first time. He had talked to Vanderbank at Mrs Brookenham's about Beccles and Suffolk; but it was not at Beccles, nor anywhere in the county, that these ornaments had been designed. His action had already been, with however little purpose, to present the region to his interlocutor in a favourable light. Vanderbank, for that matter, had the kind of imagination that liked to place an object, even to the point of losing sight of it in the conditions; he already saw the nice old nook it must have taken to keep a man of intelligence so fresh while suffering him to remain so fine. The product of Beccles accepted at all events a cigarette – still much as a joke and an adventure – and looked about him as if even more pleased than he had expected. Then he broke, through his double eye-glass, into an exclamation that was like a passing pang of envy and regret. 'You young men, you young men—!'

'Well, what about us?' Vanderbank's tone encouraged the courtesy of the reference. 'I'm not so young, moreover, as that comes to.'

'How old are you then, pray?'

'Why, I'm thirty-four.'

'What do you call that? I'm a hundred and three!' Mr Longdon took out his watch. 'It's only a quarter past eleven.' Then with a quick change of interest, 'What did you say is your public office?' he inquired.

'The General Audit. I'm Deputy Chairman.'

'Dear!' Mr Longdon looked at him as if he had had fifty windows. 'What a head you must have!'

'Oh yes – our head's Sir Digby Dence.'

'And what do we do for you?'

'Well, you gild the pill – though not perhaps very thick. But it's a decent berth.'

'A thing a good many fellows would give a pound of their flesh for?'

The old man appeared so to deprecate too faint a picture that his companion dropped all scruples. 'I'm the most envied man I know – so that if I were a shade less amiable I should be one of the most hated.'

Mr Longdon laughed, yet not quite as if they were joking. 'I see. Your pleasant way carries it off.'

Vanderbank was, however, not serious. 'Wouldn't it carry off anything?'

Again his visitor, through the *pince-nez*, appeared to crown him with a Whitehall cornice. 'I think I ought to let you know I'm studying you. It's really fair to tell you,' he continued, with an earnestness not discomposed by the indulgence in Vanderbank's face. 'It's all right – all right!' he reassuringly added, having meanwhile stopped before a photograph suspended on the wall. 'That's your mother!' he exclaimed with something of the elation of a child making a discovery or guessing a riddle. 'I don't make you out in her yet – in my recollection of her, which, as I told you, is perfect; but I dare say I soon shall.'

Vanderbank was more and more aware that the kind of hilarity he excited would never in the least be a bar to affection. 'Please take all your time.'

Mr Longdon looked at his watch again. 'Do you think I *had* better keep it?'

'The cab?' Vanderbank liked him so, found in him such a promise of pleasant things, that he was almost tempted to say: 'Dear and delightful sir, don't weigh that question; I'll pay, myself, for the man's whole night!' His approval at all events was complete. 'Most certainly. That's the only way not to think of it.'

'Oh, you young men, you young men!' his guest again murmured. He had passed on to the photograph – Vanderbank had many, too many photographs – of some other relation, and stood wiping the gold-mounted glasses through which he had been darting admirations and catching side-lights of shocks. 'Don't talk nonsense,' he continued as his friend attempted once more to throw in a protest; 'I belong to a different period of history. There have been things this evening that have made me feel as if I had been disinterred – literally dug up from a long sleep. I assure you there have!' – he really pressed the point.

Vanderbank wondered a moment what things in particular these might be; he found himself wanting to get at everything his visitor represented, to enter into consciousness and be, as it were, on his side. He glanced, with an intention freely sarcastic, at an easy possibility. 'The extraordinary vitality of Brookenham?'

Mr Longdon, with the nippers in place again, fixed on him a gravity that failed to prevent his discovering in the eyes behind them a shy reflection of his irony. 'Oh, Brookenham! You must tell me all about Brookenham.'

'I see that's not what you mean.'

Mr Longdon forbore to deny it. 'I wonder if you'll understand what I mean.' Vanderbank bristled with the wish to be put to the test, but was checked before he could say so. 'And what's *his* place – Brookenham's?'

'Oh, Rivers and Lakes – an awfully good thing. He got it last year.'

Mr Longdon – but not too grossly – wondered. 'How did he get it?'

Vanderbank laughed. 'Well, *she* got it.'

His friend remained grave. 'And about how much now—?'

'Oh, twelve hundred – and lots of allowances and boats and things. To do the work!' Vanderbank, still with a certain levity, exclaimed.

'And what *is* the work?'

The young man hesitated. 'Ask *him*. He'll like to tell you.'

'Yet he seemed to have but little to say.' Mr Longdon exactly measured it again.

'Ah, not about that. Try him.'

He looked more sharply at his host, as if vaguely suspicious of a trap; then, not less vaguely, he sighed. 'Well, it's what I came up for – to try you all. But do they live on that?' he continued.

Vanderbank once more just faltered. 'One doesn't quite know what they live on. But they've means – for it was just that fact, I remember, that showed Brookenham's getting the place wasn't a job. It was given, I mean, not to his mere domestic need, but to his notorious efficiency. He has a property – an ugly little place in Gloucestershire – which they sometimes let. His elder brother has the better one, but they make up an income.'

Mr Longdon, for an instant, lost himself. 'Yes, I remember – one heard of those things at the time. And *she* must have had something.'

'Yes, indeed, she had something – and she always has her intense cleverness. She knows thoroughly how. They do it tremendously well.'

'Tremendously well,' Mr Longdon intelligently echoed. 'But a house in Buckingham Crescent, with the way they seem to have built through to all sorts of other places—'

'Oh, they're all right,' Vanderbank soothingly dropped.

'One likes to feel that of people with whom one has dined. There are four children?' his friend went on.

'The older boy, whom you saw and who, in his way, is a wonder, the older girl, whom you must see, and two youngsters, male and female, whom you mustn't.'

There might by this time, in the growing interest of their talk, have been almost nothing too uncanny for Mr Longdon to fear it. 'You mean the youngsters are – unfortunate?'

'No – they're only, like all the modern young, I think, mysteries, terrible little baffling mysteries.' Vanderbank had broken into mirth again – it flickered so from his friend's face that, really at moments to the point of alarm, his explanations deepened darkness. Then with more interest he harked back. 'I know the thing you just mentioned – the thing that strikes you as odd.' He produced his knowledge quite with elation. 'The talk.' Mr Longdon, on this, only looked at him, in silence, harder, but he went on with assurance: 'Yes, the talk – for we do talk, I think.' Still his guest left him without relief, only fixing him, on his suggestion, with a sort of suspended eloquence. Whatever the old man was on the point of saying, however, he disposed of in a curtailed murmur; he had already turned afresh to the series of portraits, and as he glanced at another Vanderbank spoke afresh. 'It was very interesting to me to hear from you there, when the ladies had left us, how many old threads you were prepared to pick up.'

Mr Longdon had paused. 'I'm an old boy who remembers the mothers,' he at last replied.

'Yes, you told me how well you remember Mrs Brookenham's.'

'Oh, oh!' – and he arrived at a new subject. 'This must be your sister Mary.'

'Yes; it's very bad, but as she's dead—'

'Dead? Dear, dear!'

'Oh long ago' – Vanderbank eased him off. 'It's delightful of you,' he went on, 'to have known also such a lot of *my* people.'

Mr Longdon turned from his contemplation with a visible effort. 'I feel obliged to you for taking it so; it mightn't – one never knows – have amused you. As I told you there, the first thing I did was to ask Fernanda about the company; and when she mentioned your name I immediately said: "Would he like me to speak to him?"'

'And what did Fernanda say?'

Mr Longdon stared. 'Do *you* call her Fernanda?'

Vanderbank felt positively more guilty than he would have expected. 'You think it too much in the manner we just mentioned?'

His friend hesitated; then with a smile a trifle strange: 'Excuse me; *I* didn't mention—'

'No, you didn't; and your scruple was magnificent. In point of fact,' Vanderbank pursued, 'I *don't* call Mrs Brookenham by her Christian name.'

Mr Longdon's clear eyes were searching. 'Unless in speaking of her to others?' He seemed really to wish to know.

Vanderbank was but too ready to satisfy him. 'I dare say we seem to you a vulgar lot of people. That's not the way, I can see, you speak of ladies at Beccles.'

'Oh, if you laugh at me!' And the old man turned off.

'Don't threaten me,' said Vanderbank, 'or I *will* send

away the cab. Of course I know what you mean. It will be tremendously interesting to hear how the sort of thing we've fallen into – oh, we *have* fallen in! – strikes your fresh ear. Do have another cigarette. Sunk as I must appear to you, it sometimes strikes mine. But I'm not sure as regards Mrs Brookenham, whom I've known a long time.'

Mr Longdon again took him up. 'What do you people call a long time?'

Vanderbank considered. 'Ah, there you are! and now we're "we people"! That's right; give it to us. I'm sure that in one way or another it's all earned. Well, I've known her ten years. But awfully well.'

'What do you call awfully well?'

'We people?' Vanderbank's inquirer, with his continued restless observation, moving nearer, the young man had laid on his shoulder the most considerate of hands. 'Don't you perhaps ask too much? But no,' he added, quickly and gaily, 'of course you don't: if I don't look out I shall have, on you, exactly the effect I don't want. I dare say I don't know *how* well I know Mrs Brookenham. Mustn't that sort of thing be put, in a manner, to the proof? What I meant to say just now was that I wouldn't – at least I hope I shouldn't – have named her as I did save to an old friend.'

Mr Longdon looked promptly satisfied and reassured. 'You probably heard me address her myself.'

'I did, but you have your rights, and that wouldn't excuse me. The only thing is that I go to see her every Sunday.'

Mr Longdon pondered; then, a little to Vanderbank's surprise, at any rate to his deeper amusement, candidly asked: 'Only Fernanda? No other lady?'

'Oh yes, several other ladies.'

Mr Longdon appeared to hear this with pleasure. 'You're quite right. We don't make enough of Sunday at Beccles.'

'Oh, we make plenty of it in London!' Vanderbank said. 'And I think it's rather in my interest I should mention that Mrs Brookenham calls *me*—'

His visitor covered him now with an attention that just operated as a check. 'By your Christian name?' Before Vanderbank could in any degree attenuate, 'What *is* your Christian name?' Mr Longdon asked.

Vanderbank felt of a sudden almost guilty – as if his answer could only impute extravagance to the lady. 'My Christian name' – he blushed it out – 'is Gustavus.'

His friend took a droll, conscious leap. 'And she calls you Gussy?'

'No, not even Gussy. But I scarcely think I ought to tell you,' he pursued, 'if she herself gave you no glimpse of the fact. Any implication that she consciously avoided it might make you see deeper depths.'

Vanderbank spoke with pointed levity, but his companion showed him after an instant a face just covered – and a little painfully – with the vision of the possibility brushed away by the joke. 'Oh, I'm not so bad as that!' Mr Longdon modestly ejaculated.

'Well, she doesn't do it always,' Vanderbank laughed, 'and it's nothing, moreover, to what some people are called. Why, there was a fellow there—' He pulled up, however, and, thinking better of it, selected another instance. 'The Duchess – weren't you introduced to the Duchess? – never calls me anything but "Vanderbank" unless she calls me "*caro mio*". It wouldn't have taken much to make her appeal to *you* with an "I say, Longdon!" I can quite hear her.'

Mr Longdon, focussing the effect of the sketch, pointed its moral with an indulgent: 'Oh well, a *foreign* duchess!' He could make his distinctions.

'Yes, she's invidiously, cruelly foreign,' Vanderbank concurred: 'I've never indeed seen a woman avail herself so cleverly, to make up for the obloquy of that state, of the benefits and immunities it brings with it. She has bloomed in the hothouse of her widowhood – she's a Neapolitan hatched by an incubator.'

'A Neapolitan?' – Mr Longdon, civilly, seemed to wish he had only known it.

'Her husband was one; but I believe that dukes at Naples are as thick as princes at Petersburg. He's dead, at any rate, poor man, and she has come back here to live.'

'Gloomily, I should think – after Naples?' Mr Longdon threw out.

'Oh, it would take more than even a Neapolitan past—!'

However,' the young man added, catching himself up, 'she lives not in what is behind her, but in what is before – she lives in her precious little Aggie.'

'Little Aggie?' Mr Longdon took a cautious interest.

'I don't take a liberty there,' Vanderbank smiled. 'I speak only of the young Agnesina, a little girl, the Duchess's niece, or rather, I believe, her husband's, whom she has adopted – in the place of a daughter early lost – and has brought to England to marry.'

'Ah, to some great man, of course.'

Vanderbank thought. 'I don't know.' He gave a vague but expressive sigh. 'She's rather lovely, little Aggie.'

Mr Longdon looked conspicuously subtle. 'Then perhaps *you're* the man—'

'Do I look like a great one?' Vanderbank broke in.

His visitor, turning away from him, again embraced the room. 'Oh dear, yes!'

'Well then, to show how right you are, there's the young lady.' He pointed to an object on one of the tables, a small photograph with a very wide border of something that looked like crimson fur.

Mr Longdon took up the picture; he was serious now. 'She's very beautiful – but she's not a little girl.'

'At Naples they develop early. She's only seventeen or eighteen, I suppose; but I never know how old – or at least how young – girls are, and I'm not sure. An aunt, at any rate, has of course nothing to conceal. She *is* extremely pretty – with extraordinary red hair and a complexion to match; great rarities, I believe, in that race and latitude. She gave me the portrait – frame and all. The frame is Neapolitan enough, and little Aggie is charming.' Then Vanderbank subjoined: 'But not so charming as little Nanda.'

'Little Nanda? – have you got *her*?' The old man was all eagerness.

'She's over there beside the lamp – also a present from the original.'

II

MR LONGDON had gone to the place – little Nanda was in glazed white wood. He took her up and held her out; for a moment he said nothing, but presently, over his glasses, rested on his host a look intenser even than his scrutiny of the faded image. 'Do they give their portraits now?'

'Little girls – innocent lambs? Surely, to old friends. Didn't they in your time?'

Mr Longdon studied the portrait again; after which, with an exhalation of something between superiority and regret, 'They never did to me,' he replied.

'Well, you can have all you want now!' Vanderbank laughed.

His friend gave a slow, droll head-shake. 'I don't want them "now"!'

'You could do with them, my dear sir, still,' Vanderbank continued in the same manner, 'every bit *I* do!'

'I'm sure you do nothing you oughtn't.' Mr Longdon kept the photograph and continued to look at it. 'Her mother told me about her – promised me I should see her next time.'

'You must – she's a great friend of mine.'

Mr Longdon remained absorbed. 'Is she clever?'

Vanderbank turned it over. 'Well, you'll tell me if you think so.'

'Ah, with a child of seventeen—!' Mr Longdon murmured it as if in dread of having to pronounce. 'This one, too, *is* seventeen?'

Vanderbank again considered. 'Eighteen.' He just hung fire once more, then brought out: 'Well, call it nearly nineteen. I've kept her birthdays,' he laughed.

His companion caught at the idea. 'Upon my honour, *I* should like to! When is the next?'

'You've plenty of time – the fifteenth of June.'

'I'm only too sorry to wait.' Laying down the object he had been examining, Mr Longdon took another turn about the room, and his manner was such an appeal to his host to accept his restlessness that, from the corner of a lounge, the latter watched him with encouragement. 'I said to you just now that I knew the mothers, but it would have been more to the point to say the grandmothers.' He stopped before the lounge, then nodded at the image of Nanda. 'I knew *hers*. She put it at something less.'

Vanderbank rather failed to understand. 'The old lady? Put what?'

Mr Longdon's face, for a moment, showed him as feeling his way. 'I'm speaking of Mrs Brookenham. She spoke of her daughter as only sixteen.'

His companion's amusement at the tone of this broke out. 'She usually does! She has done so, I think, for the last year or two.'

Mr Longdon dropped upon the lounge as if with the weight of something sudden and fresh; then, from where he sat, with a sharp little movement, tossed into the fire the end of his cigarette. Vanderbank offered him another, a second, and as he accepted it and took a light he said: 'I don't know what you're doing with me – I never, at home, smoke so much!' But he puffed away, and, seated so near him, laid his hand on Vanderbank's arm as if to help himself to utter something that was too delicate not to be guarded and yet too important not to be risked. 'Now that's the sort of thing I did mean – as one of my impressions.' Vanderbank continued at a loss, and he went on: 'I refer – if you don't mind my saying so – to what you said just now.'

Vanderbank was conscious of a deep desire to draw from him whatever might come; so sensible was it somehow that whatever in him was good was also thoroughly personal. But our young friend had to think a minute. 'I see, I see. Nothing is more probable than that I've said something nasty; but which of my particular horrors?'

'Well, then, your conveying that she makes her daughter out younger—'

'To make herself out the same?' Vanderbank took him straight up. 'It was nasty my doing that? I see, I see. Yes, yes: I rather gave her away, and you're struck by it – as is most delightful you *should* be – because you're, in every way, of a better tradition and, knowing Mrs Brookenham's my friend, can't conceive of one's playing on a friend a trick so vulgar and odious. It strikes you also probably as the kind of thing we must be constantly doing; it strikes you that, right and left, probably, we keep giving each other away. Well, I dare say we do. Yes, "come to think of it," as they say in America, we do. But what shall I tell you? Practically we all know it and allow for it, and it's as broad as it's long. What's London life after all? It's tit for tat!'

'Ah, but what becomes of friendship?' Mr Longdon earnestly and pleadingly asked, while he still held Vanderbank's arm as if under the spell of vivid explanation with which he had been furnished.

The young man met his eyes only the more sociably. 'Friendship?'

'Friendship.' Mr Longdon maintained the full value of the word.

'Well,' his companion risked, 'I dare say it isn't in London by any means what it is at Beccles. I quite literally mean that,' Vanderbank reassuringly added; 'I never really have believed in the existence of friendship in big societies – in great towns and great crowds. It's a plant that takes time and space and air; and London society is a huge "squash", as we elegantly call it – an elbowing, pushing, perspiring, chattering mob.'

'Ah, I don't say *that* of you!' Mr Longdon murmured with a withdrawal of his hand and a visible scruple for the sweeping concession he had evoked.

'Do say it, then – for God's sake; let some one say it, so that something or other, whatever it may be, may come of it! It's impossible to say too much – it's impossible to say enough. There isn't anything any one can say that I won't agree to.'

'That shows you really don't care,' the old man returned with acuteness.

'Oh, we're past saving, if that's what you mean!' Vanderbank laughed.

'You don't care, you don't care!' his visitor repeated, 'and – if I may be frank with you – I shouldn't wonder if it were rather a pity.'

'A pity I don't care?'

'You ought to, you ought to.' Mr Longdon paused. 'May I say all I think?'

'I assure you *I* shall! You're awfully interesting.'

'So are you, if you come to that. It's just what I've had in my head. There's something I seem to make out in you—!' He abruptly dropped this, however, going on in another way. 'I remember the rest of you, but why did I never see *you*?'

'I must have been at school – at college. Perhaps you did know my brothers, elder and younger.'

'There was a boy with your mother at Malvern. I was near her there for three months in – what *was* the year?'

'Yes, I know,' Vanderbank replied while his guest tried to fix the date. 'It was my brother Miles. He was awfully clever, but he had no health, poor chap, and we lost him at seventeen. She used to take houses at such places with him – it was supposed to be for his benefit.'

Mr Longdon listened with a visible recovery. 'He used to talk to me – I remember he asked me questions I couldn't answer and made me dreadfully ashamed. But I lent him books – partly, upon my honour, to make him think that, as I had them, I did know something. He read everything and had a lot to say about it. I used to tell your mother he had a great future.'

Vanderbank shook his head sadly and kindly. 'So he had. And you remember Nancy, who was handsome and who was usually with them?' he went on.

Mr Longdon looked so uncertain that he explained he meant his other sister; on which his companion said: 'Oh, her? Yes, she was charming – she evidently had a future too.'

'Well, she's in the midst of it now. She's married.'

'And whom did she marry?'

'A fellow called Toovey. A man in the City.'

'Oh!' said Mr Longdon a little blankly. Then as if to retrieve his blankness: 'But why do you call her Nancy? Wasn't her name Blanche?'

'Exactly – Blanche Bertha Vanderbank.'

Mr Longdon looked half mystified and half distressed. 'And now she's Nancy Toovey?'

Vanderbank broke into laughter at his dismay. 'That's what everyone calls her.'

'But why?'

'Nobody knows. You see you were right about her future.'

Mr Longdon gave another of his soft, smothered sighs; he had turned back again to the first photograph, which he looked at for a longer time. 'Well, it wasn't *her* way.'

'My mother's? No indeed. Oh, my mother's way!' Vanderbank waited, then added gravely: 'She was taken in time.'

Mr Longdon turned half round and looked as if he were about to reply to this; but instead of so doing he proceeded afresh to an examination of the expressive oval in the red plush frame. He took little Aggie, who appeared to interest him, and abruptly observed: 'Nanda isn't so pretty.'

'No, not nearly. There's a great question whether Nanda is pretty at all.'

Mr Longdon continued to inspect her more favoured friend; which led him after a moment to bring out: 'She ought to be, you know. Her grandmother was.'

'Oh, and her mother,' Vanderbank threw in. 'Don't you think Mrs Brookenham lovely?'

Mr Longdon kept him waiting a little. 'Not so lovely as Lady Julia. Lady Julia had—' He faltered; then, as if there were too much to say, disposed of the question. 'Lady Julia had everything.'

Vanderbank gathered from the sound of the words an impression that determined him more and more to diplomacy. 'But isn't that just what Mrs Brookenham has?'

This time the old man was prompt. 'Yes, she's very brilliant, but it's a totally different thing.' He laid little Aggie down and moved away as if without a purpose; but Vanderbank presently perceived his purpose to be another glance at the other young lady. As if accidentally and absently, he bent again over the portrait of Nanda. 'Lady Julia was exquisite, and this child's exactly like her.'

Vanderbank, more and more conscious of something working in him, was more and more interested. 'If Nanda's so like her, *was* she so exquisite?' he hazarded.

'Oh yes; everyone was agreed about that.' Mr Longdon kept his eyes on the face, trying a little, Vanderbank even thought, to conceal his own. 'She was one of the greatest beauties of her day.'

'Then *is* Nanda so like her?' Vanderbank persisted, amused at his friend's transparency.

'Extraordinarily. Her mother told me all about her.'

'Told you she's as beautiful as her grandmother?'

Mr Longdon turned it over. 'Well, that she has just Lady Julia's expression. She absolutely *ha*s it – I see it here.' He was delightfully positive. 'She's much more like the dead than like the living.'

Vanderbank saw in this too many deep things not to follow them up. One of these was, to begin with, that his friend had not more than half succumbed to Mrs Brookenham's attraction, if indeed, by a fine originality, he had not resisted it altogether. That in itself, for an observer deeply versed in this lady, was delightful and beguiling. Another indication was that he found himself, in spite of such a break in the chain, distinctly predisposed to Nanda. 'If she reproduces then so vividly Lady Julia,' the young man threw out, 'why does she strike you as so much less pretty than her foreign friend there, who is after all by no means a prodigy?'

The subject of this address, with one of the photographs in his hand, glanced, while he reflected, at the other. Then with a subtlety that matched itself for the moment with Vanderbank's: 'You just told me yourself that the little foreign person—'

'Is ever so much the lovelier of the two? So I did. But you've promptly recognized it. It's the first time,' Vanderbank went on, to let him down more gently, 'that I've heard Mrs Brookenham admit the girl's looks.'

'Her own girl's? "Admit" them?'

'I mean grant them to be even as good as they are. I myself, I must tell you, extremely like them. I think Lady Julia's grand-daughter has in her face, in spite of every-thing—'

'What do you mean by everything?' Mr Longdon broke in with such an approach to resentment that his host's amusement overflowed.

'You'll see – when you do see. She has no features. No, not one,' Vanderbank inexorably pursued; 'unless indeed you put it that she has two or three too many. What I was going to say was that she has in her expression all that's charming in her nature. But beauty, in London' – and, feeling that he held his visitor's attention, he gave himself the pleasure of freely unfolding his idea – 'staring, glaring, obvious, knock-down beauty, as plain as a poster on a wall, an advertisement of soap or whisky, something that speaks to the crowd and crosses the foot-lights, fetches such a price in the market that the absence of it, for a woman with a girl to marry, inspires endless terrors and constitutes for the wretched pair – to speak of mother and daughter alone – a sort of social bankruptcy. London doesn't love the latent or the lurking, has neither time, nor taste, nor sense for any-thing less discernible than the red flag in front of the steam-roller. It wants cash over the counter and letters ten feet high. Therefore, you see, it's all as yet rather a dark question for poor Nanda – a question that, in a way, quite occupies the foreground of her mother's earnest little life. How *will* she look, what will be thought of her and what will she be able to do for herself? She's at the age when the whole thing – speaking of her appearance, her possible share of good looks – is still, in a manner, in a fog. But everything depends on it.'

Mr Longdon, by this time, had come back to him. 'Excuse my asking it again – for you take such jumps: what, once more, do you mean by everything?'

'Why, naturally, her marrying. Above all her marrying early.'

Mr Longdon stood before the sofa. 'What do you mean by early?'

'Well, we do doubtless get up later than at Beccles; but that gives us, you see, shorter days. I mean in a couple of seasons. Soon enough.' Vanderbank developed, 'to limit the strain—' He broke down again, in gaiety, at his friend's expression.

'What do you mean by the strain?'

'Well, the complication of her being there.'

'Being where?'

'You do put one through!' Vanderbank laughed. But he showed himself perfectly prepared. 'Out of the school-room, where she is now. In her mother's drawing-room. At her mother's fireside.'

Mr Longdon stared. 'But where else should she be?'

'At her husband's, don't you see?'

Mr Longdon looked as if he quite saw, yet he was nevertheless, as regards his original challenge, not to be put off. 'Ah, certainly,' he replied with a slight stiffness, 'but not as if she had been pushed down the chimney. All in good time.'

Vanderbank turned the tables on him. 'What do you call good time?'

'Why, time to make herself loved.'

Vanderbank wondered. 'By the men who come to the house?'

Mr Longdon slightly attenuated this way of putting it. 'Yes – and in the home circle. Where's the "strain" – of her being suffered to be a member of it?'

III

VANDERBANK, at this, left his corner of the sofa and, with his hands in his pockets, and a manner so amused that it might have passed for excited, took several paces about the room while his interlocutor, watching him, waited for his response. The old man, as this response for a minute hung fire, took his turn at sitting down, and then Vanderbank stopped before him with a face in which something had been still more brightly kindled. 'You ask me more things than I can tell you. You ask me more than I think you suspect. You must come and see me again – you must let me come and see you. You raise the most interesting questions, and we must sooner or later have them all out.'

Mr Longdon looked happy in such a prospect, but he once more took out his watch. 'It wants five minutes to midnight. Which means that I must go now.'

'Not in the least. There are satisfactions you too must give.' Vanderbank, with an irresistible hand, confirmed him in his position and pressed upon him another cigarette. His resistance rang hollow – it was clearly, he judged, such an occasion for sacrifices. His companion's view of it meanwhile was quite as marked. 'You see there's ever so much more you must in common kindness tell me.'

Mr Longdon sat there like a shy singer invited to strike up. 'I told you everything at Mrs Brookenham's. It comes over me now how I dropped on you.'

'What you told me,' Vanderbank returned, 'was excellent so far as it went; but it was only after all that, having caught my name, you had asked of our friend if I belonged to people you had known years before, and then, from what she had said, had, with what you were so good as to call great pleasure, made out that I did. You came round to me, on this, after dinner, and gave me a pleasure still greater. But that only takes us part of the way.' Mr Longdon said nothing, but there was something appreciative in his conscious lapses; they were a tribute to his young friend's frequent felicity. This personage indeed appeared more and more to take them for that; which was not without its effect upon his spirits. At last, with a flight of some freedom, he brought their pause to a close. 'You loved Lady Julia.' Then as the attitude of his guest, who serenely met his eyes, was practically a contribution to the subject, he went on with a feeling that he had positively pleased. 'You lost her, and you're unmarried.'

Mr Longdon's smile was beautiful – it supplied so many meanings that when presently he spoke he seemed already to have told half his story. 'Well, my life took a form. It had to, or I don't know what would have become of me, and several things that all happened at once helped me out. My father died – I came into the little place in Suffolk. My sister, my only one, who had married and was older than I, lost within a year or two both her husband and her little boy. I offered her, in the country, a home, for her trouble was greater than any trouble of mine. She came, she stayed; it went on and on, and we lived there together. We were sorry for each other, and it somehow suited us. But she died two years ago.'

Vanderbank took all this in, only wishing to show – wishing by this time quite tenderly – that he even read into it deeply enough all the unsaid. He filled out another of his friend's gaps. 'And here you are.' Then he invited Mr Longdon himself to make the stride. 'Well, you'll be a great success.'

'What do you mean by that?'

'Why, that we shall be so infatuated with you that it will make your life a burden to you. You'll see soon enough what I mean by it.'

'Possibly,' the old man said; 'to understand you I shall have to. You speak of something that, as yet – with my race practically run – I know nothing about. I was no success as a young man. I mean of the sort that would have made most difference. People wouldn't look at me.'

'Well, *we* shall look at you,' Vanderbank declared. Then he added: 'What people do you mean?' And before his friend could reply: 'Lady Julia?'

Mr Longdon's assent was mute. 'Ah, she was not the worst! I mean that what made it so bad,' he continued, 'was that they all really liked me. Your mother, I think – as to *that*, the dreadful, consolatory "liking" – even more than the others.'

'My mother?' – Vanderbank was surprised. 'You mean there was a question—?'

'Oh, but for half a minute. It didn't take her long. It was five years after your father's death.' This explanation was very delicately made. 'She *could* marry again.'

'And I suppose you know she did,' Vanderbank replied.

'I knew it soon enough!' With this, abruptly, Mr Longdon pulled himself forward. 'Good-night, good-night.'

'Good-night,' said Vanderbank. 'But wasn't that *after* Lady Julia?'

On the edge of the sofa, his hands supporting him, Mr Longdon looked straight. 'There was nothing after Lady Julia.'

'I see.' His companion smiled. 'My mother was earlier.'

'She was extremely good to me. I'm not speaking of that time at Malvern – that came later.'

'Precisely – I understand. You're speaking of the first years of her widowhood.'

Mr Longdon just faltered. 'I should call them rather the last. Six months later came her second marriage.'

Vanderbank's interest visibly improved. 'Ah, it was *then*? That was my seventh year.' He called things back and pieced them together. 'But she must have been older than you.'

'Yes – a little. She was kindness itself to me, at all events, then and afterwards. That was the charm of the weeks at Malvern.'

'I see,' the young man laughed. 'The charm was that you had recovered.'

'Oh dear, no!' Mr Longdon, rather to his mystification, exclaimed. 'I'm afraid I hadn't recovered at all – hadn't, if that's what you mean, got over my misery and my melancholy. She knew I hadn't – and that was what was nice of her. She was a person with whom I could talk about her.'

Vanderbank took a moment to clear up the ambiguity. 'Oh, you mean you could talk about the *other*! You hadn't got over Lady Julia.'

Mr Longdon sadly smiled at him. 'I haven't got over her yet!' Then, however, as if not to look too woeful, he took pains to be lucid. 'The first wound was bad – but from that one always comes round. Your mother, dear woman, had known how to help me. Lady Julia was at that time her intimate friend – it was she who introduced me there. She couldn't help what happened – she did her best. What I meant just now was that, in the after-time, when opportunity occurred, she was the one person with whom I could always talk and who always understood.' Mr Longdon appeared to lose himself an instant in the deep memories to which alone he now survived to testify; then he sighed out as if the taste of it all came back to him with a faint sweetness: 'I think they must both have been good to me. At the period at Malvern – the particular time I just mentioned to you – Lady Julia was already married, and during those first years she was whirled out of my ken. Then her own life took a quieter turn; we met again; I went, for a long time, often to her house. I think she rather liked the state to which she had reduced me, though she didn't, you know, in the least presume upon it. The better a woman is – it has often struck me – the more she enjoys, in a quiet way, some fellow's having been rather bad, rather dark and desperate, about her – for her. I dare say, I mean, that, though Lady Julia insisted I ought to marry, she wouldn't really have liked it much if I had. At any rate it was in those years that

I saw her daughter just cease to be a child – the little girl who was to be transformed by time into the so different person with whom we dined tonight. That comes back to me when I hear you speak of the growing up, in turn, of that person's own daughter.'

'I follow you with a sympathy!' Vanderbank replied. 'The situation's reproduced.'

'Ah, partly – not altogether. The things that are unlike – well, are so *very* unlike.' Mr Longdon for a moment, on this, fixed his companion with eyes that betrayed one of the restless little jumps of his mind. 'I told you just now that there's something I seem to make out in you.'

'Yes, that was meant for better things?' – Vanderbank gaily took him up. 'There *is* something, I really believe – meant for ever so much better ones. Those are just the sort I like to be supposed to have a real affinity with. Help me to them, Mr Longdon; help me to them, and I don't know what I won't do for you!'

'Then, after all' – and the old man made his point with innocent sharpness – 'you're *not* past saving!'

'Well, I individually – how shall I put it to you? If I tell you,' Vanderbank went on, 'that I've that sort of fulcrum for salvation which consists at least in a deep consciousness and the absence of a rag of illusion, I shall appear to say that I'm different from the world I live in and to that extent present myself as superior and fatuous. Try me at any rate. Let me try myself. Don't abandon me. See what can be done with me. Perhaps I'm after all a case. I shall certainly cling to you.'

'You're too clever – you're too clever: that's what's the matter with you all!' Mr Longdon sighed.

'With us *all*?' Vanderbank echoed. 'Dear Mr Longdon, it's the first time I've heard it. If you should say with *me* in particular, why there might be something in it. What you mean, at any rate – I see where you come out – is that we're cold and sarcastic and cynical, without the soft human spot. I think you flatter us even while you attempt to warn; but what's extremely interesting at all events is that, as I gather, we made on you this evening, in a particular way, a collective impression – something in which our trifling varieties are merged.' His visitor's face, at this, appeared to say to him that he was putting the case in perfection, so that he was encouraged to go on. 'There was something particular with which you were not altogether pleasantly struck.'

Mr Longdon, who, decidedly, changed colour easily, showed in his clear cheek the effect at once of feeling a finger on his fault and of admiration for his companion's insight. But he accepted the situation. 'I couldn't help noticing your tone.'

'Do you mean its being so low?'

Mr Longdon, who had smiled at first, looked grave now. 'Do you really want to know?'

'Just how you were affected? I assure you that there's nothing, at this moment, I desire nearly so much.'

'I'm no judge,' the old man went on; 'I'm no critic; I'm no talker myself. I'm old-fashioned and narrow and dull. I've lived for years in a hole. I'm not a man of the world.'

Vanderbank considered him with a benevolence, a geniality of approval, that he literally had to hold in check for fear of seeming to patronize. 'There's not one of us who can touch you. You're delightful, you're wonderful, and I'm intensely curious to hear you,' the young man pursued. 'Were we absolutely odious?' Before his friend's puzzled, finally almost pained face, such an air of appreciating so much candour, yet looking askance at so much freedom, he could only endeavour to smooth the way and light the subject. 'You see we don't in the least know where we are. We're lost – and you find us.' Mr Longdon, as he spoke, had prepared at last really to go, reaching the door with a manner that denoted, however, by no means so much satiety as an attention that felt itself positively too agitated. Vanderbank had helped him on with the Inverness cape and for an instant detained him by it. 'Just tell me as a kindness. *Do* we talk—?'

'Too freely?' Mr Longdon, with his clear eyes so untouched by time, speculatively murmured.

'Too outrageously. I want the truth.'

The truth evidently for Mr Longdon was difficult to tell. 'Well – it was certainly different.'

'From you and Lady Julia, I see. Well, of course with

time *some* change is natural, isn't it? But so different,'
Vanderbank pressed, 'that you were really shocked?'

His visitor, at this, smiled, but the smile somehow made
the face graver. 'I think I was rather frightened. Good-
night.'

BOOK II

LITTLE AGGIE

IV

MRS BROOKENHAM stopped on the threshold with the sharp surprise of the sight of her son, and there was disappointment, though rather of the afflicted than of the irritated sort, in the question that, slowly advancing, she launched at him. 'If you're still lolling about, why did you tell me two hours ago that you were leaving immediately?'

Deep in a large brocaded chair, with his little legs stuck out to the fire, he was so much at his ease that he was almost flat on his back. She had evidently roused him from sleep, and it took him a couple of minutes, during which, without again looking at him, she directly approached a beautiful old French secretary, a fine piece of the period of Louis Seize, to justify his presence. 'I changed my mind – I couldn't get off.'

'Do you mean to say you're not going?'

'Well, I'm thinking it over. What's a fellow to do?' He sat up a little, staring with conscious solemnity at the fire, and if it had been – as it was not – one of the annoyances she in general expected from him, she might have received the impression that his flush was the heat of liquor.

'He's to keep out of the way,' she replied – 'when he has led one so deeply to hope it.' There had been a bunch of keys suspended in the lock of the secretary, of which as she said these words Mrs Brookenham took possession. Her air on observing them had promptly become that of having been in search of them, and a moment after she had passed across the room they were in her pocket. 'If you don't go, what excuse will you give?'

'Do you mean to *you*, mummy?'

She stood before him, and now she dismally looked at

him. 'What's the matter with you? What an extraordinary time to take a nap!'

He had fallen back in the chair, from the depths of which he met her eyes. 'Why, it's *just* the time, mummy, I did it on purpose. I can always go to sleep when I like. I assure you it sees one through things!'

She turned away with impatience and, glancing about the room, perceived on a small table of the same type as the secretary a somewhat massive book with the label of a circulating library, which she proceeded to pick up as for refuge from the impression made on her by the boy. He watched her do this and watched her then slightly pause at the wide window that, in Buckingham Crescent, commanded the prospect they had ramified rearward to enjoy; a medley of smoky brick and spotty stucco, of other undressed backs, of glass invidiously opaque, of roofs and chimney-pots and stables unnaturally near – one of the private pictures that in London, in select situations, run up, as the phrase is, the rent. There was no indication of value now, however, in the character conferred on the scene by a cold spring rain. The place had moreover a confessed out-of-season vacancy. She appeared to have determined on silence for the present mark of her relation with Harold, yet she soon failed to resist a sufficiently poor reason for breaking it. 'Be so good as to get out of my chair.'

'What will you do for me,' he asked, 'if I oblige you?'

He never moved – but as if only the more directly and intimately to meet her – and she stood again before the fire and sounded his strange little face. 'I don't know what it is, but you give me sometimes a kind of terror.'

'A terror, mamma?'

She found another place, sinking sadly down and opening her book, and the next moment he got up and came over to kiss her, on which she drew her cheek wearily aside. 'You bore me quite to death,' she panted, 'and I give you up to your fate.'

'What do you call my fate?'

'Oh, something dreadful – if only by its being publicly ridiculous.' She turned vaguely the pages of her book. 'You're too selfish – too sickening.'

'Oh, dear, dear!' he wonderingly whistled while he wandered back to the hearth-rug on which, with his hands behind him, he lingered awhile. He was small and had a slight stoop, which somehow gave him character – a character somewhat of the insidious sort, carried out in the acuteness, difficult to trace to a source, of his smooth fair face, whose lines were all curves and its expression all needles. He had the voice of a man of forty and was dressed – as if markedly not for London – with an air of experience that seemed to match it. He pulled down his waistcoat, smoothing himself, feeling his neat hair and looking at his shoes; then he said to his mother: 'I took your five pounds. Also two of the sovereigns,' he went on. 'I left you two pound ten.' She jerked up her head at this, facing him in dismay, and, immediately on her feet, passed back to the secretary. 'It's quite as I say,' he insisted; 'you should have locked it *before*, don't you know? It grinned at me there with all its charming brasses, and what was I to do? Darling mummy, I *couldn't* start – that was the truth. I thought I should find something – I had noticed; and I do hope you'll let me keep it, because if you don't it's all up with me. I stopped over on purpose – on purpose, I mean, to tell you what I've done. Don't you call that a sense of honour? And now you only stand and glower at me.'

Mrs Brookenham was, in her forty-first year, still charmingly pretty, and the nearest approach she made at this moment to meeting her son's description of her was by looking beautifully desperate. She had about her the pure light of youth – would always have it; her head, her figure, her flexibility, her flickering colour, her lovely, silly eyes, her natural, quavering tone all played together toward this effect by some trick that had never yet been exposed. It was at the same time remarkable that – at least in the bosom of her family – she rarely wore an appearance of gaiety less qualified than at the present juncture; she suggested, for the most part, the luxury, the novelty, of woe, the excitement of strange sorrows and the cultivation of fine indifferences. This was her special sign – an innocence dimly tragic. It gave immense effect to her other resources. She opened the secretary with the key she had quickly found, then with the aid of another rattled out a small drawer; after which she pushed the drawer back, closing the whole thing. 'You terrify me,' she again said.

'How can you say that when you showed me just now how well you know me? Wasn't it just on account of what you thought I might do that you took out the keys as soon as you came in?' Harold's manner had a way of clearing up whenever he could talk of himself.

'You're too utterly disgusting, and I shall speak to your father,' with which, going to the chair he had given up, his mother sank down again with her heavy book. There was no anger, however, in her voice, and not even a harsh plaint; only a detached, accepted disenchantment. Mrs Brookenham's supreme rebellion against fate was just to show with the last frankness how much she was bored.

'No, darling mummy, you won't speak to my father – you'll do anything in the world rather than that,' Harold replied, quite as if he were kindly explaining her to herself. 'I thank you immensely for the charming way you take what I have done; it was because I had a conviction of that that I waited for you to know it. It was all very well to tell you I would start on my visit – but how the deuce was I to start without a penny in the world? Don't you see that if you want me to go about you must really enter into my needs?'

'I wish to heaven you would leave me – I wish to heaven you would get out of the house,' Mrs Brookenham went on without looking up.

Harold took out his watch. 'Well, mamma, now I *am* ready: I wasn't in the least before. But it will be going forth, you know, quite to seek my fortune. For do you really think – I must have from you what you do think – that it will be all right for me?'

She fixed him at last with her pretty pathos. 'You mean for you to go to Brander?'

'You know,' he answered with his manner as of letting her see her own attitude, 'you know you try to make me do things that you wouldn't at all do yourself. At least I hope you wouldn't. And don't you see that if I so far oblige you I must at least be paid for it?'

His mother leaned back in her chair, gazed for a moment at the ceiling and then closed her eyes. 'You *are* frightful,' she said; 'you're appalling.'

'You're always wanting to get me out of the house,' he continued; 'I think you want to get us *all* out, for you manage to keep Nanda from showing even more than you do me. Don't you think your children are good enough, mummy dear? At any rate it's as plain as possible that if you don't keep us at home you must keep us in other places. One can't live anywhere for nothing – it's all bosh that a fellow saves by staying with people. I don't know how it is for a lady, but a man practically, is let in—'

'Do you know you kill me, Harold?' Mrs Brookenham woefully interposed. But it was with the same remote melancholy that, in the next breath, she asked: 'It wasn't an *invitation* – to Brander?'

'It's as I told you. She said she'd write, fixing a time; but she never did write.'

'But if *you* wrote—'

'It comes to the same thing? *Does* it? – that's the question. If on my note she didn't write – that's what I mean. Should one simply take it that one is wanted? I like to have these things *from* you, mother. I do, I believe, everything you say; but to feel safe and right I must just *have* them. Any one *would* want me, eh?'

Mrs Brookenham had opened her eyes, but she still attached them to the cornice. 'If she hadn't wanted you she would have written. In a great house like that there's always room.'

The young man watched her a moment. 'How you *do* like to tuck us in and then sit up yourself? What do you want to do, anyway? What are you up to, mummy?'

She rose, at this, turning her eyes about the room as if from the extremity of martyrdom or the wistfulness of some deep thought. Yet when she spoke it was with a different expression, an expression that would have served for an observer as a marked illustration of that disconnectedness of her parts which frequently was laughable even to the degree of contributing to her social success. 'You've spent then more than four pounds in five days. It was on Friday I gave them to you. What in the world do you suppose is going to become of me?'

Harold continued to look at her as if the question demanded some answer really helpful. 'Do we live beyond our means?'

She now moved her gaze to the floor. 'Will you *please* get away?'

'Anything to assist you. Only, if I *should* find I'm not wanted—?'

She met, after an instant, his look, and the wan loveliness and silliness of her own had never been greater. '*Be* wanted, and you won't find it. You're odious, but you're not a fool.'

He put his arms about her now for farewell, and she submitted as if it were absolutely indifferent to her to whose bosom she was pressed. 'You do, dearest,' he laughed, 'say such sweet things!' And with that he reached the door, on opening which he pulled up at a sound from below. 'The Duchess! She's coming up.'

Mrs Brookenham looked quickly round the room, but she spoke with utter detachment. 'Well, let her come.'

'As I'd let her go. I take it as a happy sign *she* won't be at Brander.' He stood with his hand on the knob; he had another quick appeal. 'But after Tuesday?'

Mrs Brookenham had passed half round the room with the glide that looked languid but that was really a remarkable form of activity, and had given a transforming touch, on sofa and chairs, to three or four crushed cushions. It was with the sad, inclined head of a broken lily. 'You're to stay till the twelfth.'

'But if I *am* kicked out?'

It was as a broken lily that she considered it. 'Then go to the Mangers.'

'Happy thought! And shall I write?'

His mother raised a little more a window-blind. 'No – I will.'

'Delicious mummy!' And Harold blew her a kiss.

'Yes, rather' – she corrected herself. 'Do write – from Brander. It's the sort of thing for the Mangers. Or even wire.'

'Both?' the young man laughed. 'Oh, you duck!' he cried. 'And from where will *you* let them have it?'

'From Pewbury,' she replied without wincing. 'I'll write on Sunday.'

'Good. How d'ye do, Duchess?' – and Harold, before he disappeared, greeted with a rapid concentration of all the shades of familiarity a large, high lady, the visitor he had announced, who rose in the doorway with the manner of a person used to arriving on thresholds very much as people arrive at stations – with the expectation of being 'met'.

V

'GOOD-BYE. He's off,' Mrs Brookenham, who had remained quite on her own side of the room, explained to her friend.

'Where's he off to?' this friend inquired with a casual advance and a look not so much at her hostess as at the cushions just rearranged.

'Oh, to some places. To Brander today.'

'How he does run about!' And the Duchess, still with a glance hither and yon, sank upon the sofa to which she had made her way unaided. Mrs Brookenham knew perfectly the meaning of this glance: she had but three or four comparatively good pieces, whereas the Duchess, rich with the spoils of Italy, had but three or four comparatively bad. This was the relation, as between intimate friends, that the Duchess visibly preferred, and it was quite groundless, in Buckingham Crescent, ever to enter the drawing-room with an expression suspicious of disloyalty. The Duchess was a woman who so cultivated her passions that she would have regarded it as disloyal to introduce there a new piece of furniture in an underhand way – that is without a full appeal to herself, the highest authority, and the consequent bestowal of opportunity to nip the mistake in the bud. Mrs Brookenham had repeatedly asked herself where in the world she might have found the money to be disloyal. The Duchess's standard was of a height—!' It matched for that matter her other elements, which were as conspicuous as usual as she sat there suggestive of early tea. She always suggested tea before the hour, and her friend always, but with so different a wistfulness, rang for it. 'Who's to be at Brander?' she asked.

'I haven't the least idea – he didn't tell me. But they've always a lot of people.'

'Oh, I know – extraordinary mixtures. Has he been there before?'

Mrs Brookenham thought. 'Oh yes – if I remember – more than once. In fact her note – which he showed me, but which only mentioned "some friends" – was a sort of appeal on the ground of something or other that had happened the last time.'

The Duchess was silent a moment. 'She writes the most extraordinary notes.'

'Well, this was nice, I thought,' Mrs Brookenham said – 'from a woman of her age and her immense position to so young a man.'

Again the Duchess reflected. 'My dear, she's not an American and she's not on the stage. Aren't those what you call positions in this country? And she's also not a hundred.'

'Yes, but Harold's a mere baby.'

'Then he doesn't seem to want for nurses!' the Duchess replied. She smiled at her friend. 'Your children are like their mother – they're eternally young.'

'Well, *I'm* not a hundred!' moaned Mrs Brookenham as if she wished with dim perversity that she were. 'Every one, at any rate, is awfully kind to Harold.' She waited a moment to give her visitor the chance to pronounce it eminently natural, but no pronouncement came – nothing but the footman who had answered her ring and of whom she ordered tea. 'And where did you say *you're* going?' she inquired after this.

'For Easter?' The Duchess achieved a direct encounter with her charming eyes – which was not, in general, an easy feat. 'I didn't say I was going anywhere. I haven't, of a sudden, changed my habits. You know whether I leave my child – except in the sense of having left her an hour ago at Mr Garlick's class in Modern Light Literature. I confess I'm a little nervous about the subjects and am going for her at five.'

'And then where do you take her?'

'Home to her tea – where should you think?'

Mrs Brookenham declined, in connexion with the matter, any responsibility of thought; she did indeed much better by saying after a moment: 'You *are* devoted!'

'Miss Merriman has her afternoon – I can't imagine what they do with their afternoons,' the Duchess went on. 'But she's to be back in the school-room at seven.'

'And you have Aggie till then?'

'Till then,' said the Duchess cheerfully. 'You're off, for Easter, to – where is it?' she continued.

Mrs Brookenham had received with no flush of betrayal the various discriminations thus conveyed by her visitor, and her only revenge for the moment was to look as sweetly resigned as if she really saw what was in them. Where were they going for Easter? She had to think an instant, but she brought it out. 'Oh, to Pewbury – we've been engaged so long that I had forgotten. We go once a year – one does it for Edward.'

'Ah, you spoil him!' smiled the Duchess. 'Who's to be there?'

'Oh, the usual thing, I suppose. A lot of my lord's tiresome supporters.'

'To pay his debt? Then why are you poor things asked?'

Mrs Brookenham looked, on this, quite adorably – that is most wonderingly – grave. 'How do I know, my dear Jane, why in the world we're ever asked anywhere? Fancy people wanting Edward!' she quavered with stupefaction. 'Yet we can never get off Pewbury.'

'You're better for getting on, *cara mia*, than for getting off!' the Duchess blandly returned. She was a person of no small presence, filling her place, however, without ponderosity, with a massiveness indeed rather artfully kept in bounds. Her head, her chin, her shoulders were well aloft, but she had not abandoned the cultivation of a 'figure', or any of the distinctively finer reasons for passing as a handsome woman. She was secretly at war moreover, in this endeavour, with a lurking no less than with a public foe, and thoroughly aware that if she didn't look well she might at times only, and quite dreadfully, look good. There were definite ways of escape, none of which she neglected and from the total of which, as she flattered herself, the air of distinction almost mathematically resulted. This air corresponded superficially with her acquired Calabrian sonorities, from her voluminous title down, but the colourless hair, the passionless forehead, the mild cheek and long lip of the British matron, the type that had set its trap for her earlier than any other, were elements difficult to deal with and were all, at moments, that a sharp observer saw. The battleground then was the haunting danger of the *bourgeois*. She gave Mrs Brookenham no time to resent her last note before inquiring if Nanda were to accompany the couple.

'Mercy, mercy no – she's not asked.' Mrs Brookenham, on Nanda's behalf, fairly radiated obscurity. 'My children don't go where they're not asked.'

'I never said they did, love,' the Duchess returned. 'But what then do you do with her?'

'If you mean socially' – Mrs Brookenham looked as if there might be in some distant sphere, for which she almost yearned, a maternal opportunity very different from that – 'if you mean socially, I don't do anything at all. I've never pretended to do anything. You know as well as I, dear Jane, that I haven't begun yet.' Jane's hostess now spoke as simply as an earnest, anxious child. She gave a vague, patient sigh. 'I suppose I must begin!'

The Duchess remained for a little rather grimly silent. 'How old is she – twenty?'

'Thirty!' said Mrs Brookenham with distilled sweetness. Then with no transition of tone: 'She has gone for a few days to Tishy Grendon's.'

'In the country?'

'She stays with her tonight in Hill Street. They go down together tomorrow. Why hasn't Aggie been?' Mrs Brookenham went on.

The Duchess handsomely stared. 'Been where?'

'Why, here, to see Nanda.'

'Here?' the Duchess echoed, fairly looking again about the room. 'When is Nanda ever here?'

'Ah, you know I've given her a room of her own – the sweetest little room in the world.' Mrs Brookenham never looked so happy as when obliged to explain. 'She has everything there that a girl can want.'

'My dear woman,' asked the Duchess, 'has she sometimes her own mother?'

The men had now come in to place the tea-table, and it was the movements of the red-haired footman that Mrs Brookenham followed. 'You had better ask my child herself.'

The Duchess was frank and jovial. 'I would, I promise you, if I could get at her! But isn't that woman always with her?'

Mrs Brookenham smoothed the little embroidered tea-cloth. 'Do you call Tishy Grendon a woman?'

Again the Duchess had one of her pauses, which were indeed so frequent in her talks with this intimate that an auditor could sometimes wonder what particular form of relief they represented. They might have been a habit proceeding from the fear of undue impatience. If the Duchess had been as impatient with Mrs Brookenham as she would possibly have seemed without them, her frequent visits, in the face of irritation, would have had to be accounted for. 'What do *you* call her?' she demanded.

'Why, Nanda's best friend – if not her only one. That's the place I *should* have liked for Aggie,' Mrs Brookenham ever so graciously smiled.

The Duchess, hereupon, going beyond her, gave way to free mirth. 'My dear thing, you're delightful. Aggie *or* Tishy is a sweet thought. Since you're so good as to ask why Aggie has fallen off, you'll excuse my telling you that you've just named the reason. You've known ever since we came to England what I feel about the proper persons – and the most improper – for her to meet. The Tishy Grendons are far from the proper.'

Mrs Brookenham continued to assist a little in the preparations for tea. 'Why not say at once, Jane' – and her tone, in its appeal, was almost infantine – 'that you've come at last to placing even poor Nanda, for Aggie's wonderful purpose, in the same impossible class?'

The Duchess took her time, but at last she accepted her duty. 'Well, if you will have it. You know my ideas. If it isn't my notion of the way to bring up a girl to give her up, in extreme youth, to an intimacy with a young married woman who is both unhappy and silly, whose conversation has absolutely no limits, who says everything that comes into her head and talks to the poor child about God only knows what – if I should never dream of such an arrangement for my niece I can almost as little face the prospect of throwing her *much*, don't you see? with any young person exposed to such an association. It would be in the natural order certainly' – in spite of which natural order the Duchess made the point with but moderate emphasis – 'that, since dear Edward is my cousin, Aggie should see at least as much of Nanda as of any other girl of their age. But what will you have? I must recognize the predicament I'm placed in by the more and more extraordinary development of English manners. Many things have altered, goodness knows, since I was Aggie's age, but nothing is so different as what you all do with your girls. It's all a muddle, a compromise, a monstrosity, like everything else you produce; there's nothing in it that goes on all-fours. *I* see but one consistent way, which is our fine old foreign way and which makes – in the upper classes, mind you, for it's with them only I'm concerned – *des femmes bien gracieuses*. I allude to the immemorial custom of my husband's race, which was good enough for his mother and his mother's mother, for Aggie's own, for his other sisters, for *toutes ces dames*. It would have been good enough for my child, as I call her – my dear husband called her *his* – if, not losing her parents, she had remained in her own country. She would have been brought up there under an anxious eye – that's the great point; privately, carefully, tenderly, and with what she was *not* to learn – till the proper time – looked after quite as much as the rest. I can only go on with her in that spirit and make of her, under Providence, what I consider any young person of her condition, of her name, of her particular traditions, should be. *Voilà, ma chère.* Should you put it to me if I think you're surrounding Nanda with any such security as that, I shouldn't be able to help it if I offended you by an honest answer. What it comes to, simply stated, is that really she must choose between Aggie and Tishy. I'm afraid I should shock you were I to tell you what I should think of myself for packing *my* child, all alone, off for a week with Mrs Grendon.'

Mrs Brookenham, who had many talents, had none perhaps that she oftener found useful than that of listening with the appearance of being fairly hypnotized. It was the way she listened to her housekeeper at their regular morning conference, and if the rejoinder ensuing upon it frequently appeared to have nothing to do with her manner, that was a puzzle for her interlocutor alone. 'Oh, of course I know your theory, dear Jane, and I dare say it's very charming and old-fashioned and, if you like, aristocratic, in a frowsy, foolish old way – though even upon that, at the same time, there would be something too to be said. But I can only congratulate you on finding it more workable than there can be any question of *my* finding it. If you're all armed for the sacrifices you speak of, I simply am not. I don't think I'm quite a monster, but I don't pretend to be a saint. I'm an English wife and an English mother, and I live in the mixed English world. My daughter, at any rate, is just my daughter – thank Heaven, and one of a good English bunch; she's not the unique niece of my dead Italian husband, nor doubtless either, in spite of her excellent birth, of a lineage, like Aggie's, so very tremendous. I've my life to lead, and she's a part of it. Sugar?' She wound up on a still softer note as she handed the cup of tea.

'Never! Well, with *me*,' said the Duchess with spirit, 'she would be all.'

'"All" is soon said! Life is composed of many things,' Mrs Brookenham gently rang out – 'of such mingled, intertwisted strands!' Then still with the silver bell, 'Don't you really think Tishy nice?' she asked.

'I think little girls should live with little girls, and young *femmes du monde* so immensely initiated should – well,' said the Duchess with a toss of her head, 'let them alone. What do they want of them "at all, at all"?'

'Well, my dear, if Tishy strikes you as "initiated," all one can ask is "Initiated into what?" I should as soon think of applying such a term to a little shivering shorn lamb. Is it your theory,' Mrs Brookenham pursued, 'that our

unfortunate unmarried daughters are to have no intelligent
friends?'

'Unfortunate indeed,' cried the Duchess, 'precisely *because* they're unmarried, and unmarried, if you don't mind
my saying so, a good deal because they're unmarriageable.
Men, after all, the nice ones – by which I mean the possible
ones – are not on the lookout for little brides whose usual
associates are so up to snuff. It's not their idea that the
girls they marry shall already have been pitchforked – by
talk and contacts and visits and newspapers, and the way
the poor creatures rush about and all the extraordinary
things they do – quite into *everything*. A girl's most intelligent friend is her mother – or the relative acting as such.
Perhaps you consider that Tishy takes your place!'

Mrs Brookenham waited so long to say what she considered that before she next spoke the question appeared to
have dropped. Then she only replied as if suddenly remembering her manners: 'Won't you eat something?' She
indicated a particular plate. 'One of the nice little round
ones?' The Duchess appropriated a nice little round one,
and her hostess presently went on: 'There's one thing I
mustn't forget – don't let us eat them *all*. I believe they're
what Lord Petherton really comes for.'

The Duchess finished her mouthful imperturbably before
she took this up. 'Does he come so often?'

Mrs Brookenham hesitated. 'I don't know what he calls
it; but he said yesterday that he'd come today. I've had tea
earlier for you,' she went on with her most melancholy
kindness – 'and he's always late. But we mustn't, between us,
lick the platter clean.'

The Duchess entered very sufficiently into her companion's tone. 'Oh, I don't feel at all obliged to consider
him, for he has not of late particularly put himself out for
me. He has not been to see me since I don't know when, and
the last time he did come he brought Mr Mitchett.'

'Here it was the other way round. It was Mr Mitchett, the
other year, who first brought Lord Petherton.'

'And who,' asked the Duchess, 'had first brought Mr
Mitchett?'

Mrs Brookenham, meeting her friend's eyes, looked for an

instant as if trying to remember. 'I give it up. I muddle beginnings.'

'That doesn't matter, if you only *make* them,' the Duchess smiled.

'No, does it?' To which Mrs Brookenham added: 'Did he bring Mr Mitchett for Aggie?'

'If he did they will have been disappointed. Neither of them has seen, in my house, the tip of her nose.' The Duchess announced this circumstance with a pomp of pride.

'Ah, but with your ideas that doesn't prevent.'

'Prevent what?'

'Why, what you call, I suppose, the *pourparlers*.'

'For Aggie's hand? My dear,' said the Duchess. 'I'm glad you do me the justice of feeling that I'm a person to take time by the forelock. It was not, as you seem to remember, with the sight of Mr Mitchett that the question of Aggie's hand began to occupy me. I should be ashamed of myself if it were not constantly before me and if I had not my feelers out in more quarters than one. But I've not so much as thought of Mr Mitchett – who, rich as he may be, is the son of a shoemaker and superlatively hideous – for a reason I don't at all mind telling you. Don't be outraged if I say that I've for a long time hoped you yourself would find the right use for him.' She paused – at present with a momentary failure of assurance, from which she rallied, however, to proceed with a burst of earnestness that was fairly noble: 'Forgive me if I just tell you once for all how it strikes me. I'm stupefied at your not seeming to recognize either your interest or your duty. Oh, I know you want to, but you appear to me – in your perfect good faith, of course – utterly at sea. They're one and the same thing, don't you make out? your interest and your duty. Why isn't it as plain as a pikestaff that the thing to do with Nanda is simply to marry her – and to marry her soon? That's the great thing – do it while you *can*. If you don't want her downstairs – at which, let me say, I don't in the least wonder – your remedy is to take the right alternative. Don't send her to Tishy—'

'Send her to Mr Mitchett?' Mrs Brookenham unresentfully quavered. Her colour, during her visitor's allocution, had distinctly risen, but there was no irritation in her voice.

'How do you know, Jane, that I don't want her downstairs?'

The Duchess looked at her with an audacity confirmed by the absence from her face of everything but the plaintive. 'There you are, with your eternal English false positions! *J'aime, moi, les situations nettes – je n'en comprends pas d'autres.* It wouldn't be to your honour – to that of your delicacy – that, with your impossible house, you *should* wish to plant your girl in your drawing-room. But such a way of keeping her out of it as throwing her into a worse—'

'Well, Jane, you do say things to me!' Mrs Brookenham blandly broke in. She had sunk back into her chair; her hands, in her lap, pressed themselves together, and her wan smile brought a tear into each of her eyes by the very effort to be brighter. It might have been guessed of her that she hated to seem to care, but that she had other dislikes too. 'If one were to take up, you know, some of the things you say—!' And she positively sighed for the fulness of amusement at them of which her tears were the sign.

Her friend could quite match her indifference. 'Well, my child, *take* them up; if you were to do that with them candidly, one by one, you would do really very much what I should like to bring you to. Do you see?' Mrs Brookenham's failure to repudiate the vision appeared to suffice, and her visitor cheerfully took a further jump. 'As much of Tishy as she wants – *after*. But not before.'

'After what?'

'Well – say after Mr Mitchett. Mr Mitchett won't take her after Mrs Grendon.

'And what are your grounds for assuming that he'll take her at all?' Then as the Duchess hung fire a moment: 'Have you got it by chance from Lord Petherton?'

The eyes of the two women met for a little on this, and there might have been a consequence of it in the manner of the rejoinder. 'I've got it from not being a fool. Men, I repeat, like the girls they marry—'

'Oh, I already know your old song! The way they like the girls they *don't* marry seems to be,' Mrs Brookenham mused, 'what more immediately concerns us. You had better wait till you *have* made Aggie's fortune, perhaps, to be so sure of the working of your system. Excuse me, darling, if I don't take you for an example until you've a little more successfully become one. The sort of men *I* know anything about, at any rate, are not looking for mechanical dolls. They're looking for smart, safe, sensible English girls.'

The Duchess glanced at the clock. 'What is Mr Vanderbank looking for?'

Her hostess appeared to oblige her by anxiously thinking. 'Oh, *he*, I'm afraid, poor dear – for nothing at all!'

The Duchess had taken off a glove to appease her appetite, and now, drawing it on, she smoothed it down. 'I think he has his ideas.'

'The same as yours?'

'Well, more like them than like yours.'

'Ah, perhaps then – for he and I,' said Mrs Brookenham, 'don't agree, I think, on two things in the world. You think poor Mitchy then,' she went on, 'who's the son of a shoemaker and who might be the grandson of a grasshopper, good enough for my child.'

The Duchess appreciated for a moment the superior fit of her glove. 'I look facts in the face. It's exactly what I'm doing for Aggie.' Then she broke into a certain conscious airiness. 'What are you giving her?'

But Mrs Brookenham took without wincing whatever, as between a masterful relative and an exposed frivolity, might have been the sting of it. 'That you must ask Edward. I haven't the least idea.'

'There you are again – the virtuous English mother! I've got Aggie's little fortune in an old stocking, and I count it over every night. If you've no old stocking for Nanda, there are worse fates than shoemakers and grasshoppers. Even *with* one, you know, I don't at all say that I should sniff at poor Mitchy. We must take what we can get, and I shall be the first to take it. You can't have everything for ninepence.' And the Duchess got up, shining, however, with a confessed light of fantasy. 'Speak to him, my dear – speak to him!'

'Do you mean offer him my child?'

The Duchess laughed at the intonation. 'There you are once more – *vous autres*! If you're shocked at the idea, you place *drôlement* your delicacy. I'd offer mine to the son of a chimney-sweep if the principal guarantees were there.

Nanda's charming – you don't do her justice. I don't say Mr
Mitchett is either beautiful or noble, and he hasn't as much
distinction as would cover the point of a pin. He takes,
moreover, his ease in talk – but that,' added the Duchess
with decision, 'is much a matter of whom he talks with. And
after marriage, what does it signify? He has forty thousand
a year, an excellent idea of how to take care of it, and a
good disposition.'

Mrs Brookenham sat still; she only looked up at her
friend. 'Is it by Lord Petherton that you know of his
excellent idea?'

The Duchess showed she was challenged, but also that she
was indulgent. 'I go by my impression. But Lord Petherton
has spoken for him.'

'He ought to do that,' said Mrs Brookenham – 'since he
wholly lives on him.'

'Lord Petherton – on Mr Mitchett?' The Duchess stared,
but rather in amusement than in horror. 'Why, hasn't he
a – property?'

'The loveliest. Mr Mitchett's his property. Didn't you
know?' There was an artless wail in Mrs Brookenham's
surprise.

'How should I know – still a stranger as I'm often rather
happy to feel myself here, and choosing my friends and
picking my steps very much, I can assure you – how should
I know about all your social scandals and things?'

'Oh, we don't call *that* a social scandal!' Mrs Brookenham
inimitably returned.

'Well, if you should wish to, you'd have the way that I
told you of to stop it. Divert the stream of Mr Mitchett's
wealth.'

'Oh, there's plenty for everyone!' – Mrs Brookenham kept
up her tone. 'He's always giving us things – bonbons and
dinners and opera boxes.'

'He has never given *me* any,' the Duchess contentedly
declared.

Mrs Brookenham waited a little. 'Lord Petherton has the
giving of some. He has never in his life before, I imagine,
made so many presents.'

'Ah then it's a shame one has nothing!' On which, before

reaching the door, the Duchess changed the subject. 'You say I never bring Aggie. If you like I'll bring her back.'

Mrs Brookenham wondered. 'Do you mean today?'

'Yes, when I've picked her up. It will be something to do with her till Miss Merriman can take her.'

'Delighted, dearest; do bring her. And I think she should *see* Mr Mitchett.'

'Shall I find him too, then?'

'Oh, take the chance.'

The two women, on this, exchanged, tacitly and across the room – the Duchess at the door, which a servant had arrived to open for her, and Mrs Brookenham still at her tea-table – a further stroke of intercourse, over which the latter was not on this occasion the first to lower her lids. 'I think I've shown high scruples,' the Duchess said, 'but I understand then that I'm free.'

'Free as air, dear Jane.'

'Good.' Then just as she was off, 'Ah, dear old Edward!' the guest exclaimed. Her kinsman, as she was fond of calling him, had reached the top of the staircase, and Mrs Brookenham, by the fire, heard them meet on the landing – heard also the Duchess protest against his turning to see her down. Mrs Brookenham, listening to them, hoped that Edward would accept the protest and think it sufficient to leave her with the footman. Their common consciousness, not devoid of satisfaction, that she was a kind of cousin was quite consistent with a view, early arrived at, of the absurdity of any fuss about her.

VI

WHEN Mr Brookenham appeared his wife was prompt. 'She's coming back for Lord Petherton.'

'Oh!' he simply said.

'There's something between them.'

'Oh!' he merely repeated. But it would have taken many such sounds on his part to represent a spirit of response discernible to any one but his wife.

'There have been things before,' she went on, 'but I

haven't felt sure. Don't you know how one has sometimes a flash?'

It could not be said of Edward Brookenham, who seemed to bend for sitting down more hinges than most men, that he looked as if he knew either this or anything else. He had a pale, cold face, marked and made regular, made even in a manner handsome, by a hardness of line in which, oddly, there was no significance, no accent. Clean shaven, slightly bald, with unlighted grey eyes and a mouth that gave the impression of not working easily, he suggested a stippled drawing by an inferior master. Lean moreover and stiff, and with the air of having here and there in his person a bone or two more than his share, he had once or twice, at fancy-balls, been thought striking in a dress copied from one of Holbein's English portraits. But when once some such meaning as that had been put into him it took a long time to put another, a longer time than even his extreme exposure, or anybody's study of the problem, had yet made possible. If anything particular had finally been expected from him it might have been a summary or an explanation of the things he had always not said, but there was something in him that had long since pacified impatience and drugged curiosity. He had never in his life answered such a question as his wife had just put him and which she would not have put had she feared a reply. So dry and decent and even distinguished did he look, as if he had positively been created to meet a propriety and match some other piece, his wife, with her notorious perceptions, would no more have appealed to him seriously on a general proposition than she would, for such a response, have rung the drawing-room bell. He was none the less held to have a great general adequacy, 'What is it that's between them?' he demanded.

'What's between any woman and the man she's making up to?'

'Why, there may often be nothing, I didn't know she even particularly knew him,' Brookenham added.

'It's exactly what she would like to prevent any one's knowing, and her coming here to be with him when she knows I know *she* knows – don't you see? – that he's to be here, is just one of those calculations that *are* subtle enough to put off the scent a woman who has but half a nose.' Mrs Brookenham, as she spoke, appeared to testify, by the pretty star-gazing way she thrust it into the air, to her own possession of the totality of such a feature. 'I don't know yet quite what I think, but one wakes up to such things soon enough.'

'Do you suppose it's her idea that he'll marry her?' Brookenham asked in his colourless way.

'My dear Edward!' his wife murmured for all answer.

'But if she can see him in other places why should she want to see him here?' Edward persisted in a voice destitute of intonation.

Mrs Brookenham now had plenty of that. 'Do you mean if she can see him in his own house?'

'No cream, please,' her husband said. 'Hasn't she a house too?'

'Yes, but so pervaded all over by Aggie and Miss Merriman.'

'Oh!' Brookenham observed.

'There has always been some man – I've always known there has. And now it's Petherton,' said his companion.

'But where's the attraction?'

'In *him*? Why, lots of women could tell you. Petherton has had a career.'

'But I mean in old Jane.'

'Well, I dare say lots of men could tell you. She's no older than any one else. She has also such great elements.'

'Oh, I dare say she's all right,' Brookenham returned as if his interest in the case had dropped. You might have felt you got a little nearer to him on guessing that in so peopled a circle satiety was never far from him.

'I mean for instance she has such a grand idea of duty. She thinks we're nowhere!'

'Nowhere?'

'With our children – with our home life. She's awfully down on Tishy.'

'Tishy?' – Brookenham appeared for a moment at a loss.

'Tishy Grendon – and her craze for Nanda.'

'Has she a craze for Nanda?'

'Surely I told you Nanda's to be with her for Easter.'

'I believe you did,' Brookenham bethought himself, 'but you didn't say anything about a craze. And where's Harold?' he went on.

'He's at Brander. That is, he will be by dinner. He has just gone.'

'And how does he get there?'

'Why, by the South-Western. They'll send to meet him.'

Brookenham appeared for a moment to view this statement in the dry light of experience. 'They'll only send if there are others too.'

'Of course then there'll be others – lots. The more the better for Harold.'

This young man's father was silent a little. 'Perhaps – if they don't play high.'

'Ah,' said his mother, 'however Harold plays he has a way of winning.'

'He has a way too of being a hopeless ass. What I meant was how he comes there at all,' Brookenham explained.

'Why, as any one comes – by being invited. She wrote to him – weeks ago.'

Brookenham was discoverably affected by this fact, but it would not have been possible to say if his satisfaction exceeded his surprise. 'To Harold? Very good-natured.' He had another short reflection, after which he continued: 'If they don't send he'll be in for five miles in a fly – and the man will see that he gets his money.'

'They *will* send – after her note.'

'Did it say so?'

Mrs Brookenham's melancholy eyes seemed, from afar, to run over the page. 'I don't remember – but it was so cordial.'

Again Brookenham meditated. 'That often doesn't prevent one's being let in for ten shillings.'

There was more gloom in this forecast than his wife had desired to produce. 'Well, my dear Edward, what do you want me to do? Whatever a young man does, it seems to me, he's let in for ten shillings.'

'Ah, but he needn't be – that's my point. *I* wasn't at his age.'

Harold's mother took up her book again. 'Perhaps you weren't the same success! I mean at such places.'

'Well, I didn't borrow money to make me one – as I have a sharp idea our young scamp does.'

Mrs Brookenham hesitated. 'From whom do you mean – the Jews?'

He looked at her as if her vagueness might be assumed. 'No. They, I take it, are not quite so "cordial" to him, as you call it, as the old ladies. He gets it from Mitchy.'

'Oh!' said Mrs Brookenham. 'Are you very sure?' she then demanded.

He had got up and put his empty cup back upon the tea-table, wandering afterwards a little about the room and looking out, as his wife had done half an hour before, at the dreary rain and the now duskier ugliness. He reverted in this attitude, with a complete unconsciousness of making for irritation, to a question they might be supposed to have dropped. 'He'll have a lovely drive for his money!' His companion, however, said nothing, and he presently came round again. 'No, I'm not absolutely sure – of his having had it from Mitchy. If I were I should do something.'

'What would you do?' She put it as if she couldn't possibly imagine.

'I would speak to him.'

'To Harold?'

'No – that might just put it into his head.' Brookenham walked up and down a little with his hands in his pockets; then, with a complete concealment of the steps of the transition, 'Where are we dining tonight?' he brought out.

'Nowhere, thank Heaven. We grace our own board.'

'Oh – with those fellows, as you said, and Jane?'

'That's not for dinner. The Baggers and Mary Pinthorpe and – upon my word, I forget.'

'You'll see when she comes,' suggested Brookenham, who was again at the window.

'It isn't a she – it's two or three he's, I think,' his wife replied with her indifferent anxiety. 'But I don't know what dinner it is,' she bethought herself; 'it may be the one that's after Easter. Then that one's this one,' she added with her eyes once more on her book.

'Well, it's a relief to dine at home' – and Brookenham faced about. 'Would you mind finding out?' he asked with some abruptness.

'Do you mean who's to dine?'

'No, that doesn't matter. But whether Mitchy *has* come down.'

'I can only find out by asking him.'

'Oh, *I* could ask him.' He seemed disappointed at his wife's want of resource.

'And you don't want to?'

He looked coldly, from before the fire, over the prettiness of her brown, bent head, 'It will be such a beastly bore if he admits it.'

'And you think poor I can make him not admit it?' She put the question as if it were really her own thought too, but they were a couple who could, even face to face and unlike the augurs behind the altar, think these things without laughing. 'If he *should* admit it,' Mrs Brookenham threw in, 'will you give me the money?'

'The money?'

'To pay Mitchy back.'

She had now raised her eyes to her husband, but, turning away, he failed to meet them. 'He'll deny it.'

'Well, if they all deny it,' she presently remarked, 'it's a simple enough matter. I'm sure *I* don't want them to come down on us! But that's the advantage,' she almost prattled on, 'of having so many such charming friends – they *don't* come down.'

This again was a remark of a sweep that there appeared to be nothing in Brookenham's mind to match; so that, scarcely pausing in the walk into which he had again fallen, he only said: 'Who do you mean by "all"?'

'Why, if he has had anything from Mitchy I dare say he has had something from Van.'

'Oh!' Brookenham returned, as if with a still greater drop of interest.

'They oughtn't to do it,' she declared; 'they ought to tell us, and when they don't it serves them right.' Even this observation, however, failed to rouse in her husband a response, and, as she had quite formed the habit of doing, she philosophically answered herself. 'But I don't suppose they do it on spec.'

It was less apparent than ever what Edward supposed. 'Oh, Van hasn't money to chuck about.'

'Ah, I only mean a sovereign here and there.'

'Well,' Brookenham threw out after another turn, 'I think Van, you know, is your affair.'

'It *all* seems to be my affair!' she exclaimed with too dolorous a little wail to have other than a comic effect. 'And of course then it will be still more so if he should begin to apply to Mr Longdon.'

'We must stop that in time.'

'Do you mean by warning Mr Longdon and requesting him immediately to tell us? That won't be very pleasant,' Mrs Brookenham sighed.

'Well, then, wait and see.'

She waited only a minute – it might have seemed that she already saw. 'I want him to be kind to Harold, and I can't help thinking he will.'

'Yes, but I fancy that that will be his notion of it – keeping him from making debts. I dare say one needn't trouble about him,' Brookenham added. 'He can take care of himself.'

'He appears to have done so pretty well all these years,' his wife mused. 'As I saw him in my childhood I see him now, and I see now that I saw then even how awfully in love he was with mamma. He's too lovely about mamma,' Mrs Brookenham pursued.

'Oh!' her husband replied.

This delicate past held her a moment. 'I see now I must have known a lot as a child.'

'Oh!' her companion repeated.

'I want him to take an interest in us. Above all in the children. He ought to like us' – she followed it up. 'It will be a sort of "poetic justice". He sees, himself, the reasons, and we mustn't prevent it.' She turned the possibilities over a moment, but they produced another soft wail. 'The thing is that I don't see how he *can* like Harold.'

'Then he won't lend him money,' said Brookenham.

This contingency too she considered. 'You make me feel

as if I wished he would – which is too dreadful. And I don't think he really likes *me*,' she went on.

'Oh!' her husband again ejaculated.

'I mean not utterly *really*. He has to try to. But it won't make any difference,' she next remarked.

'Do you mean his trying?' Brookenham inquired.

'No – I mean his not succeeding. He'll be just the same.' She saw it steadily and saw it whole. 'On account of mamma.'

Her husband, also, with his perfect propriety, put it before himself. 'And will he – on account of your mother – also like *me*?'

Mrs Brookenham weighed it. 'No, Edward.' She covered him with her loveliest expression. 'No, not really either. But it won't make any difference.' This time she had pulled him up.

'Not if he doesn't like Harold, or like you, or like me?' Brookenham, clearly, found himself able to accept only the premise.

'He'll be perfectly loyal. It will be the advantage of mamma!' Mrs Brookenham exclaimed. 'Mamma, Edward,' she brought out with a flash of solemnity – 'mamma *was* wonderful. There have been times when I've felt that she's still with us, but Mr Longdon makes it vivid. Whether she's with me or not, at any rate, she's with *him*; so that when he's with me, don't you see—'

'It comes to the same thing?' her husband intelligently asked. 'I see. And when was he with you last?'

'Not since the day he dined – but that was only last week. He'll come soon – I know from Van.'

'And what does Van know?'

'Oh, all sorts of things. He has taken the greatest fancy to him.'

'The old man – to Van?'

'Van to Mr Longdon. And the other way too. Mr Longdon has been most kind to him.'

Brookenham still moved about. 'Well, if he likes Van and doesn't like *us*, what good will that do us?'

'You would understand soon enough if you felt Van's loyalty.'

'Oh, the things you expect me to feel, my dear!' Edward Brookenham lightly moaned.

'Well, it doesn't matter. But he *is* as loyal to me as Mr Longdon to mamma.'

The statement produced on Brookenham's part an unusual vision of the comedy of things. 'Every Jenny has her Jockey!' Yet perhaps – remarkably enough – there was even more imagination in his next words. 'And what sort of means?'

'Mr Longdon? Oh, very good. Mamma wouldn't have been the loser. Not that she cared. He *must* like Nanda,' Mrs Brookenham wound up.

Her companion appeared to look at the idea and then meet it. 'He'll have to see her first.'

'Oh, he shall see her!' Mrs Brookenham affirmed. 'It's time for her at any rate to sit downstairs.'

'It was time, you know, *I* thought, a year ago.'

'Yes, I know what you thought. But it wasn't.'

She had spoken with decision, but he seemed unwilling to concede the point. 'You admitted yourself that she was ready.'

'*She* was ready – yes. But I wasn't. I am now,' Mrs Brookenham, with a fine emphasis on her adverb, proclaimed as she turned to meet the opening of the door and the appearance of the butler, whose announcement – 'Lord Petherton and Mr Mitchett' – might for an observer have seemed immediately to offer support to her changed state.

VII

LORD PETHERTON, a man of five-and-thirty, whose robust but symmetrical proportions gave to his dark blue double-breasted coat an air of tightness that just failed of compromising his tailor, had for his main facial sign a certain pleasant brutality, the effect partly of a bold, handsome parade of carnivorous teeth, partly of an expression of nose suggesting that this feature had paid a little, in the heat of youth, for some aggression at the time admired and even publicly commemorated. He would have been ugly, he substantively granted, had he not been happy; he would have been dangerous had he not been warranted. Many things doubtless performed for him this last service, but none so much as the delightful sound of his voice, the voice, as it were, of another man, a nature reclaimed, supercivilized, adjusted to the perpetual 'chaff' that kept him smiling in a way that would have been a mistake, and indeed an impossibility, if he had really been witty. His bright familiarity was that of a young prince whose confidence had never had to falter, and the only thing that at all qualified the resemblance was the equal familiarity excited in his subjects.

Mr Mitchett had so little intrinsic appearance that an observer would have felt indebted, as an aid to memory, to the rare prominence of his colourless eyes and the positive attention drawn to his chin by the precipitation of its retreat from detection. Dressed, on the other hand, not as gentlemen dress in London to pay their respects to the fair, he excited, by the exhibition of garments that had nothing in common save the violence and the independence of their pattern, a suspicion that in the desperation of humility he wished to make it public that he had thrown to the winds the effort to please. It was written all over him that he had judged once for all his personal case and that as his character, superficially disposed to gaiety, deprived him of the resource of shyness and shade, the effect of comedy might not escape him if secured by a real plunge. There was comedy therefore in the form of his pot-hat and the colour of his spotted shirt, in the systematic disagreement, above all, of his coat, waistcoat and trousers. It was only on long acquaintance that his so many ingenious ways of showing that he recognized his commonness could present him as secretly rare.

'And where's the child this time?' he asked of his hostess as soon as he was seated near her.

'Why do you say "this time", as if it were different from any other time?' she replied, as she gave him his tea.

'Only because, as the months and the years elapse, it's more and more of a wonder, whenever I don't see her, to think what she does with herself – or what you do with her. What it does show, I suppose,' Mr Mitchett went on, 'is that she takes no trouble to meet me.'

'My dear Mitchy,' said Mrs Brookenham, 'what do *you* know about "trouble" – either poor Nanda's or mine or anybody's else? You've never had to take any in your life, you're the spoiled child of fortune, and you skim over the surface of things in a way that seems often to represent you as supposing that everybody else has wings. Most other people are sticking fast in their native mud.'

'Mud, Mrs Brook – mud, mud!' he protestingly cried as, while he watched his fellow-visitor move to a distance with their host, he glanced about the room, taking in afresh the Louis Seize secretary, which looked better closed than open and for which he always had a knowing eye. 'Remarkably charming mud!'

'Well, that's what a great deal of the element really appears, today, to be thought; and precisely, as a specimen, Mitchy dear, those two French books you were so good as to send me and which – really, this time, you extraordinary man!' She fell back, intimately reproachful, from the effect produced on her, renouncing all expression save that of the rolled eye.

'Why, were they particularly dreadful?' – Mitchy was honestly surprised. 'I rather liked the one in the pink cover – what's the confounded thing called? – I thought it had a sort of a something-or-other.' He had cast his eye about as if for a glimpse of the forgotten title, and she caught the question as he vaguely and good-humouredly dropped it.

'A kind of a morbid modernity? There *is* that,' she dimly conceded.

'Is that what they call it? Awfully good name. You must have got it from old Van!' he gaily declared.

'I dare say I did. I get the good things from him and the bad ones from you. But you're not to suppose,' Mrs Brookenham went on, 'that I've discussed your horrible book with him.'

'Come, I say!' Mr Mitchett protested; 'I've seen you with books from Vanderbank which, if you *have* discussed them with him – well,' he laughed, 'I should like to have been there!'

'You haven't seen me with anything like yours – no, no, never, never!' She was particularly positive. 'He, on the contrary, gives tremendous warnings, makes apologies, in advance, for things that – well, after all, haven't killed one.'

'That have even perhaps a little, after the warnings, let one down?'

Mrs Brookenham took no notice of this pleasantry; she simply adhered to her thesis. 'One has taken one's dose and one isn't such a fool as to be deaf to some fresh, true note, if it happens to turn up. But for abject, horrid, unredeemed vileness from beginning to end—'

'So you read to the end?' Mr Mitchett interposed.

'I read to see what you could possibly have sent such things to me for, and because so long as they were in my hands they were not in the hands of others. Please to remember in future that the children are all over the place, and that Harold and Nanda have their nose in everything.'

'I promise to remember,' Mr Mitchett returned, 'as soon as you make old Van do the same.'

'I do make old Van – I pull old Van up much oftener than I succeed in pulling you. I must say,' Mrs Brookenham went on, 'you're all getting to require among you in general, an amount of what one may call editing!' She gave one of her droll universal sighs. 'I've got your books at any rate locked up, and I wish you'd send for them quickly again; one's too nervous about anything happening and their being perhaps found among one's relics. Charming literary remains!' she laughed.

The friendly Mitchy was also much amused. 'By Jove, the most awful things *are* found! Have you heard about old Randage and what his executors have just come across? The most abominable—'

'I haven't heard,' she broke in, 'and I don't want to; but you give me a shudder, and I beg you'll have your offerings removed, for I can't think of confiding them, for the purpose, to any one in this house. I might burn them up in the dead of night, but even then I should be fearfully nervous.'

'I'll send them my usual messenger,' said Mitchy, 'a person I keep for such jobs, thoroughly seasoned, as you may imagine, and of a discretion – what do you call it? – *à toute épreuve.* Only you must let me say that I like your terror about Harold! Do you suppose he spends his time over Dr Watts's hymns?'

Mrs Brookenham just hesitated, and nothing, in general, was so becoming to her as the act of hesitation. 'Dear Mitchy, do you know I want awfully to talk to you about Harold?'

'About his reading, Mrs Brook?' Mitchy responded with interest. 'The worse things are, let me just mention to you about that, the better they seem positively to be for one's feeling up in the language. They're more difficult, the bad ones – and there's a lot in that. All the young men know it – those who are going up for exams.'

She had her eyes for a little on Lord Petherton and her husband; then, as if she had not heard what her interlocutor had just said, she overcame her last scruple. 'Dear Mitchy, has he had money from you?'

He stared with his good goggle eyes – he laughed out. 'Why on earth—? But do you suppose I'd tell you if he had?'

'He hasn't really borrowed the most dreadful sums?'

Mitchy was highly diverted. 'Why should he? For what, please?'

'That's just it – for what? What does he do with it all? What in the world becomes of it?'

'Well,' Mitchy suggested, 'he's saving up to start a business. Harold's irreproachable – hasn't a vice. Who knows, in these days, what may happen? He sees further than any young man I know. Do let him save.'

She looked far away with her sweet world-weariness. 'If you weren't an angel it would be a horror to be talking to you. But I insist on knowing.' She insisted now with her absurdly pathetic eyes on him. 'What kind of sums?'

'You shall never, never find out,' Mr Mitchett replied with extravagant firmness. 'Harold is one of my great amusements – I really have awfully few; and if you deprive me of him you'll be a fiend. There are only one or two things I want to live for, but one of them is to see how far Harold will go. Please give me some more tea.'

'Do you positively swear?' she asked with intensity as she

helped him. Then without waiting for his answer: 'You have the common charity to *us*, I suppose, to see the position you would put us in. Fancy Edward!' she quite austerely threw off.

Mr Mitchett, at this, had, on his side, a hesitation. 'Does Edward imagine—?'

'My dear man, Edward never "imagined" anything in life.' She still had her eyes on her interlocutor. 'Therefore if he *sees* a thing, don't you know? it must exist.'

Mitchy for a little fixed the person mentioned as he sat with his other guest, but, whatever this person saw, he failed just then to see his wife's companion, whose eyes he never met. His face only offered itself, like a clean domestic vessel, a receptacle with the peculiar property of constantly serving yet never filling, to Lord Petherton's talkative splash. 'Well, only don't let him take it up. Let it be only between you and me,' Mr Mitchett pleaded; 'keep him quiet – don't let him speak to me.' He appeared to convey, with his pleasant extravagance, that Edward looked dangerous, and he went on with a rigour of levity: 'It must be *our* little quarrel.'

There were different ways of meeting such a tone, but Mrs Brookenham's choice was remarkably prompt. 'I don't think I quite understand what dreadful joke you may be making, but I dare say if you *had* let Harold borrow you would have another manner, and I was at any rate determined to have the question out with you.'

'Let us always have everything out – that's quite my own idea. It's you,' said Mr Mitchett, 'who are by no means always so frank with me as I recognize – oh, I do *that*! – what it must have cost you to be over this little question of Harold. There's one thing, Mrs Brook, you do dodge.'

'What do I ever dodge, dear Mitchy?' Mrs Brook quite tenderly asked.

'Why, when I ask you about your other child you're off like a frightened fawn. When have you ever, on my doing so, said "My darling Mitchy, I'll ring for her to be asked to come down, and you can see for yourself" – when have you ever said anything like that?'

'I see,' Mrs Brookenham mused; 'you think I sacrifice her. You're very interesting among you all, and I've certainly a delightful circle. The Duchess has just been letting me have it most remarkably hot, and as she's presently coming back you'll be able to join forces with her.'

Mitchy looked a little of a loss. 'On the subject of your sacrifice—'

'Of my innocent and helpless, yet somehow at the same time, as a consequence of my cynicism, dreadfully damaged and depraved daughter.' She took in for an instant the slight bewilderment against which, as a result of her speech, even so expert an intelligence as Mr Mitchett's had not been proof; then, with a small jerk of her head at the other side of the room, she made the quickest of transitions. 'What *is* there between her and him?'

Mitchy wondered at the other two. 'Between Edward and the girl?'

'Don't talk nonsense. Between Petherton and Jane.'

Mitchy could only stare, and the wide noonday light of his regard was at such moments really the redemption of his ugliness. 'What "is" there? Is there anything?'

'It's too beautiful,' Mrs Brookenham appreciatively sighed, 'your relation with him! You won't compromise him.'

'It would be nicer of me,' Mitchy laughed, 'not to want to compromise *her.*'

'Oh, Jane!' Mrs Brookenham dropped. '*Does* he like her?' she continued. 'You must know.'

'Ah, it's just my knowing that constitutes the beauty of my loyalty – of my delicacy.' He had his quick jumps too. 'Am I never, never to see the child?'

This inquiry appeared only to confirm his companion in the contemplation of what was touching in him. 'You're the most delicate thing I know, and it crops up, in the oddest way, in the intervals of your depravity. Your talk's half the time impossible; you respect neither age nor sex nor condition; one doesn't know what you'll say or do next; and one has to return your books – *c'est tout dire* – under cover of darkness. Yet there's in the midst of all this, and in the depths of you, a little deep-down delicious niceness, a sweet sensibility, that one has actually one's self, shocked as one perpetually is at you, quite to hold one's breath and stay one's hand for fear of ruffling or bruising. There's no one with whom, in talking,' she balmily continued, 'I find myself half so often suddenly moved to pull up short. You've more little toes to tread on – though you pretend you haven't: I mean morally speaking, don't you know? – than even I have myself, and I've so many that I could wish most of them cut off. You never spare me a shock – no, you don't do that: it isn't the form your delicacy takes. But you'll know what I mean, all the same, I think, when I tell you that there are lots I spare *you*!'

Mr Mitchett fairly glowed with the candour of his attention. 'Know what you mean, dearest lady? How can a man handicapped to death, a man of my origin, my appearance, my general weaknesses, drawbacks, immense indebtedness, all round, for the start, as it were, that I feel my friends have been so good as to allow me: how can such a man not be conscious every moment that every one about him goes on tiptoe and winks at every one else? What *can* you all mention in my presence, poor things, that isn't personal?'

Mrs Brookenham's face covered him for an instant as no painted Madonna's had ever covered the little charge at the breast beneath it. 'And the finest thing of all in you is your beautiful, beautiful pride! You're prouder than all of us put together.' She checked a motion that he had apparently meant as a protest – she went on with her muffled wisdom. 'There isn't a man but *you* whom Petherton wouldn't have made vulgar. He isn't vulgar himself – at least not exceptionally; but he's just one of those people, a class one knows well, who are so fearfully, in this country, the cause of it in others. For all I know he's the cause of it in me – the cause of it even in poor Edward. For *I'm* vulgar, Mitchy, dear – very often; and the marvel of you is that you never are.'

'Thank you for everything. Thank you, above all, for "marvel"!' Mitchy grinned.

'Oh, I know what I say!' – she didn't in the least blush. 'I'll tell you something,' she pursued with the same gravity, 'if you'll promise to tell no one on earth. If you're

proud, I'm not. There! It's most extraordinary, and I try
to conceal it, even to myself; but there's no doubt whatever about it – I'm not proud *pour deux sous*. And some
day, on some awful occasion, I shall show it. So – I notify
you. Shall you love me still?'

'To the bitter end,' Mitchy loyally responded. 'For how
can, how need, a woman be "proud" who's so preter-
naturally clever? Pride's only for use when wit breaks
down – it's the train the cyclist takes when his tyre's
deflated. When that happens to *your* tyre, Mrs Brook,
you'll let me know. And you do make me wonder just
now,' he confessed, 'why you're taking such particular
precautions and throwing out such a cloud of skirmishers.
If you want to shoot me dead a single bullet will do.' He
faltered but an instant before completing his sense. 'Where
you really want to come out is at the fact that Nanda
loathes me and that I might as well give up asking for
her.'

'Are you quite serious?' his companion after a moment
asked. 'Do you really and truly like her, Mitchy?'

'I like her as much as I dare to – as much as a man can
like a girl when, from the very first of his seeing her and
judging her, he has also seen, and seen with all the reasons,
that there's no chance for him whatever. Of course, with
all that, he has done his best not to let himself go. But
there are moments,' Mr Mitchett ruefully added, 'when
it would relieve him awfully to feel free for a good spin.'

'I think you exaggerate,' his hostess replied, 'the difficulties in your way. What do you mean by "all the
reasons"?'

'Why, one of them I've already mentioned. I make her
flesh creep.'

'My own Mitchy!' Mrs Brookenham protestingly
moaned.

'The other is that – very naturally – she's in love.'

'With whom, under the sun?'

Mrs Brookenham had, with her startled stare, met his
eyes long enough to have taken something from him before
he next spoke. 'You really have never suspected? With
whom conceivably but old Van?'

'Nanda's in love with old Van?' – the degree to which she had never suspected was scarce to be expressed. 'Why, he's twice her age – he has seen her in a pinafore with a dirty face, and well slapped for it: he has never thought of her in the world.'

'How can a person of your acuteness, my dear woman,' Mitchy asked, 'mention such trifles as having the least to do with the case? How can you possibly have such a fellow about, so beastly good-looking, so infernally well turned out in the way of "culture", and so bringing them down in short on every side, and expect in the bosom of your family the absence of history of the reigns of the good kings? If *you* were a girl, wouldn't *you* turn purple? If I were a girl shouldn't I – unless, as is more likely, I turned green?'

Mrs Brookenham was deeply affected. 'Nanda does turn purple—?'

'The loveliest shade you ever saw. It's too absurd that you haven't noticed.'

It was characteristic of Mrs Brookenham's amiability that, with her sudden sense of the importance of this new light, she should be quite ready to abase herself. 'There are so many thing in one's life; one follows false scents; one doesn't make out everything at once. If you're right you must help me. We must see more of her.'

'But what good will that do me?' Mitchy inquired.

'Don't you care enough for her to want to help *her*?' Then before he could speak, 'Poor little darling dear!' his hostess tenderly ejaculated. 'What does she think or dream? Truly she's laying up treasure!'

'Oh, he likes her,' said Mitchy. 'He likes her in fact extremely.'

'Do you mean he has told you so?'

'Oh no – we never mention it! But he likes her,' Mr Mitchett stubbornly repeated. 'And he's thoroughly straight.'

Mrs Brookenham for a moment turned these things over; after which she came out in a manner that visibly surprised him. 'It isn't as if you wished to be nasty about him, is it? – because I know you like him yourself. You're so wonderful to your friends' – oh, she could let him see that she knew! – 'and in such different and exquisite ways. There are those, like *him*' – she signified her other visitor – 'who get everything out of you and whom you really appear to like, or at least to put up with, just *for* that. Then there are those who ask nothing – and whom you like in spite of it.'

Mitchy leaned back, at this, fist within fist, watching her with a certain disguised emotion. He grinned almost too much for mere amusement. 'That's the class to which *you* belong.'

'It's the best one,' she returned, 'and I'm careful to remain in it. You try to get us, by bribery, into the inferior place, because, proud as you are, it bores you a little that you like us so much. But we won't go – at least *I* won't. You may make Van,' she wonderfully continued. 'There's nothing you wouldn't do for him or give him.' Mitchy admired her from his position, slowly shaking his head with it. 'He's the man – with no fortune and just as he is, to the smallest particular – whom you would have liked to be, whom you intensely envy, and yet to whom you're magnanimous enough to be ready for almost any sacrifice.'

Mitchy's appreciation had fairly deepened to a flush. 'Magnificent – magnificent Mrs Brook! What *are* you, in thunder, up to?'

'Therefore, as I say,' she imperturbably went on, 'it's not to do him an ill turn that you maintain what you've just told me.'

Mr Mitchett for a minute gave no sign but his high colour and his queer glare. 'How could it do him an ill turn?'

'Oh, it *would* be a way, don't you see? to put before me the need of getting rid of him. For he may "like" Nanda as much as you please: he'll never, never,' Mrs Brookenham resolutely quavered – 'he'll never come to the scratch. And to feel that as I do,' she explained, 'can only be, don't you also see? to want to save her.'

It would have appeared at last that poor Mitchy did see. 'By taking it in time? By forbidding him the house?'

She seemed to stand with little nipping scissors in a garden of alternatives. 'Or by shipping *her* off. Will you help me to save her?' she broke out again after a moment. 'It isn't true,' she continued, 'that she has any aversion to you.'

'Have you charged her with it?' Mitchy demanded with a courage that amounted to high gallantry.

It inspired, on the spot, his interlocutress; and her own, of as fine a quality now as her diplomacy, which was saying much, fell but little below. 'Yes, my dear friend – frankly.'

'Good. Then I know what she said.'

'She absolutely denied it.'

'Oh yes – they always do, because they pity me.' Mitchy smiled. 'She said what they always say – that the effect I produce is, though at first upsetting, one that little by little they find it possible to get used to. The world's full of people who are getting used to me,' Mr Mitchett concluded.

'It's what *I* shall never do, for you're quite too delicious!' Mrs Brookenham declared. 'If I haven't threshed you out really *more* with Nanda,' she continued, 'it has been from a scruple of a sort you people never do a woman the justice to impute. You're the object of views that have so much more to set them off.'

Mr Mitchett, on this, jumped up; he was clearly conscious of his nerves; he fidgeted away a few steps, then, with his hands in his pockets, fixed on his hostess a countenance more controlled. 'What does the Duchess mean by your daughter's being – as I understood you to quote her just now – "damaged and depraved"?'

Mrs Brookenham came up – she literally rose – smiling. 'You fit the cap. You know how she would like you for little Aggie!'

'What does she mean, what does she mean?' Mitchy repeated.

The door, as she spoke, was thrown open; Mrs Brookenham glanced round. 'You've the chance to find out from herself!' The Duchess had come back and little Aggie was in her wake.

VIII

THAT young lady, in this relation, was certainly a figure to have offered a foundation for the highest hopes. As slight and white, as delicately lovely, as a gathered garden lily, her admirable training appeared to hold her out to them all as with precautionary finger-tips. She presumed, however, so little on any introduction that, shyly and submissively, waiting for the word of direction, she stopped short in the centre of the general friendliness till Mrs Brookenham fairly became, to meet her, also a shy little girl – put out a timid hand with wonder-struck, innocent eyes that hesitated whether a kiss of greeting might be dared. 'Why, you dear, good, strange "ickle" thing, you haven't been here for ages, but it *is* a joy to see you, and I do hope you've brought your doll!' – such might have been the sense of our friend's fond murmur while, looking at her up and down with pure pleasure, she drew the rare creature to a sofa. Little Aggie presented, up and down, an arrangement of dress exactly in the key of her age, her complexion, her emphasized virginity. She might have been prepared for her visit by a cluster of doting nuns, cloistered daughters of ancient houses and educators of similar products, whose taste, hereditarily good, had grown, out of the world and most delightfully, so queer as to leave on everything they touched a particular shade of distinction. The Duchess had brought in with the child an air of added confidence for which, in a moment, an observer would have seen the grounds, the association of the pair being so markedly favourable to each. Its younger member carried out the style of her aunt's presence quite as one of the accessory figures effectively thrown into old portraits. The Duchess, on the other hand, seemed, with becoming blandness, to draw from her niece the dignity of a kind of office of state – hereditary governess of the children of the blood. Little Aggie had a smile as softly bright as a southern dawn, and the friends of her relative looked at each other, according to a fashion frequent in Mrs Brookenham's drawing-room, in free communication of their happy impression. Mr Mitchett was, none the less, scantly diverted from his recognition of the occasion Mrs Brookenham had just named to him.

'My dear Duchess,' he promptly asked, 'do you mind explaining to me an opinion that I have just heard of your – with marked originality – holding?'

The Duchess, with her head in the air, considered an instant her little ivory princess. 'I'm always ready, Mr Mitchett, to defend my opinions; but if it's a question of going much into the things that are the subjects of some of them, perhaps we had better, if you don't mind, choose our time and our place.'

'No "time", gracious lady, for my impatience,' Mr Mitchett replied, 'could be better than the present – but if you've reasons for wanting a better place, why shouldn't we go, on the spot, into another room?'

Lord Petherton, at this inquiry, broke into instant mirth. 'Well, of all the coolness, Mitchy! – he does go at it, doesn't he, Mrs Brook? What do you want to do in another room?' he demanded of his friend. 'Upon my word, Duchess, under the nose of those—'

The Duchess, on the first blush, lent herself to the humour of the case. 'Well, Petherton, of "those"?' – I defy him to finish his sentence!' she smiled to the others.

'Of those,' said his lordship, 'who flatter themselves that when you do not happen to find them somewhere your first idea is not quite to jump at a pretext for getting off somewhere else. Especially,' he continued to jest, 'with a man of Mitchy's vile reputation.'

'Oh!' Edward Brookenham exclaimed at this, but only as if with quiet relief.

'Mitchy's offer is perfectly safe, I may let him know,' his wife remarked, 'for I happen to be sure that nothing would really induce Jane to leave Aggie five minutes among us here without remaining herself to see that we don't become improper.'

'Well then, if we're already pretty far on the way to it,' Lord Petherton resumed, 'what on earth *might* we arrive at in the absence of your control? I warn you, Duchess,' he joyously pursued, 'that if you go out of the room with Mitchy I shall rapidly become quite awful.'

The Duchess, during this brief passage, never took her eyes from her niece, who rewarded her attention with the sweetness of consenting dependence. The child's foreign origin was so delicately but unmistakably written in all her exquisite lines that her look might have expressed the modest detachment of a person to whom the language of her companions was unknown. The Duchess then glanced round the circle. 'You're very odd people, all of you, and I don't think you quite know how ridiculous you are. Aggie and I are simple stranger-folk; there's a great deal we don't understand; yet we're none the less not easily frightened. In what is it, Mr Mitchett,' she asked, 'that I've wounded your susceptibilities?'

Mr Mitchett hesitated; he had apparently found time to reflect on his precipitation. 'I see what Petherton's up to, and I won't, by drawing you aside just now, expose your niece to anything that might immediately oblige Mrs Brook to catch her up and flee with her. But the first time I find you more isolated – well,' he laughed, though not with the clearest ring, 'all I can say is, Mind your eyes, dear Duchess!'

'It's about your thinking, Jane,' Mrs Brookenham placidly explained, 'that Nanda suffers – in her morals, don't you know? – by my neglect. I wouldn't say anything about you that I can't bravely say *to* you; therefore, since he has plumped out with it, I do confess that I've appealed to him on what, as so good an old friend, *he* thinks of your contention.'

'What in the world *is* Jane's contention?' Edward Brookenham put the question as if they were 'stuck' at cards.

'You really, all of you,' the Duchess replied with excellent coolness, 'choose extraordinary conditions for the discussion of delicate matters. There are decidedly too many things on which we don't feel alike. You're all inconceivable just now. *Je ne peux pourtant pas la mettre à la porte, cette chérie*' – whom she covered again with the gay solicitude that seemed to have in it a vibration of private entreaty: 'Don't understand, my own darling – don't understand!'

Little Aggie looked around with an impartial politeness that, as an expression of the general blind sense of her being, in every particular, in hands at full liberty either to spot or to spare her, was touching enough to bring tears to all eyes. It perhaps had to do with the sudden emotion with which – using now quite a different manner – Mrs Brookenham again embraced her, and even with this lady's equally abrupt and altogether wonderful address to her: 'Between you and me straight, my dear, and as from friend to friend, I know that you'll never doubt that everything must be all right! – What I spoke of to poor Mitchy,' she went on to the Duchess, 'is the dreadful view you take of my letting Nanda go to Tishy – and indeed of the general question of any acquaintance between young unmarried and young married females. Mr Mitchett is sufficiently interested in us, Jane, to make it natural of me to take him into our confidence in one of our difficulties. On the other hand we feel your solicitude, and I needn't tell you at this time of day what weight in every respect we attach to your judgement. Therefore it *will* be a difficulty for us, *cara mia*, don't you see? if we decide suddenly, under the spell of your influence, that our daughter must break off a friendship – it *will* be a difficulty for us to put the thing to Nanda herself in such a way as that she shall have some sort of notion of what suddenly possesses us. Then there'll be the much stiffer job of putting it to poor Tishy. Yet if her house *is* an impossible place, what else is one to do? Carrie Donner's to be there, and Carrie Donner's a nature apart; but how can we ask even a little lamb like Tishy to give up her own sister?'

The question had been launched with an argumentative sharpness that made it for a moment keep possession of the air, and during this moment, before a single member of the circle could rally, Mrs Brookenham's effect was superseded by that of the reappearance of the butler. 'I say, my dear, don't shriek!' – Edward Brookenham had only time to sound this warning before a lady, presenting herself in the open doorway, followed close on the announcement of her name. 'Mrs Beach Donner!' – the impression was naturally marked. Every one betrayed it a little but Mrs Brookenham, who, more than the others, appeared to have the help of seeing that, by a merciful stroke, her visitor had just failed to hear. This visitor, a young woman of striking, of startling appearance, who, in the manner of certain shiny house doors and railings, instantly created a presumption of the lurking label 'Fresh paint', found herself, with an embarrassment oddly opposed to the positive pitch of her complexion, in the presence of a group in which it was yet immediately evident that every one was a friend. Every one, to show no one had been caught, said something extremely easy; so that it was after a moment only poor Mrs Donner who, seated close to her hostess, seemed to be in any degree in the wrong. This moreover was essentially her fault, so extreme was the anomaly of her having, without the means to back it up, committed herself to a 'scheme of colour' that was practically an advertisement of courage. Irregularly pretty and painfully shy, she was retouched, from brow to chin, like a suburban photograph – the moral of which was simply that she should either have left more to nature or taken more from art. The Duchess had quickly reached her kinsman with a smothered hiss, an 'Edward dear, for God's sake take Aggie!' and at the end of a few minutes had formed for herself in one of Mrs Brookenham's admirable 'corners' a society consisting of Lord Petherton and Mr Mitchett, the latter of whom regarded Mrs Donner, across the room, with articulate wonder and compassion.

'It's all right, it's all right – she's frightened only at herself!'

The Duchess watched her as from a box at the play, comfortably shut in, as in the old operatic days at Naples, with a pair of entertainers. 'You're the most interesting nation in the world. One never gets to the end of your hatred of the *nuance*. The sense of the suitable, the harmony of parts – what on earth were you doomed to do that, to be punished sufficiently in advance, you had to be deprived of it in your very cradles? Look at her little black dress – rather good, but not so good as it ought to be, and, mixed up with all the rest, see her type, her beauty, her timidity, her wickedness, her notoriety and her *impudeur*. It's only in this country that a woman is both so shocking and so shaky.' The Duchess's displeasure overflowed. 'If she doesn't know how to be good—'

'Let her at least know how to be bad? Ah,' Mitchy

replied, 'your irritation testifies more than anything else could do to our peculiar genius or our peculiar want of it. Our vice is intolerably clumsy – if it can possibly be a question of vice in regard to that charming child, who looks like one of the new-fashioned bill-posters, only, in the way of "morbid modernity", as Mrs Brook would say, more extravagant and funny than any that have yet been risked. I remember,' he continued, 'Mrs Brook's having spoken of her to me lately as "wild". Wild? – why, she's simply tameness run to seed. Such an expression shows the state of training to which Mrs Brook has reduced the rest of us.'

'It doesn't prevent, at any rate, Mrs Brook's training, some of the rest of you being horrible,' the Duchess declared. 'What did you mean just now, really, by asking me to explain before Aggie this so serious matter of Nanda's exposure?' Then instantly, taking herself up before Mr Mitchett could answer: 'What on earth do you suppose Edward's saying to my darling?'

Brookenham had placed himself, side by side with the child, on a distant little settee, but it was impossible to make out from the countenance of either whether a sound had passed between them. Aggie's little manner was too developed to show, and her host's not developed enough. 'Oh, he's awfully careful,' Lord Petherton reassuringly observed. 'If you or I or Mitchy say anything bad, it's sure to be before we know it and without particularly meaning it. But old Edward means it—!'

'So much that, as a general thing, he doesn't dare to say it?' the Duchess asked. 'That's a pretty picture of him, inasmuch as, for the most part, he never speaks. What therefore must he mean?'

'He's an abyss – he's magnificent!' Mr Mitchett laughed. 'I don't know a man of an understanding more profound, and he's equally incapable of uttering and of wincing. If, by the same token, I'm "horrible", as you call me,' he pursued, 'it's only because, in every way, I'm so beastly superficial. All the same, I do sometimes go into things, and I insist upon knowing,' he again broke out, 'what it exactly was you had in mind in saying to Mrs Brook, about Nanda, what she repeated to me.'

'You "insist", you silly man?' – the Duchess had veered a little to indulgence. 'Pray, on what ground of right, in such a connexion, do you do anything of the sort?'

Poor Mitchy showed but for a moment that he felt pulled up. 'Do you mean that when a girl liked by a fellow likes him so little in return—?'

'I don't mean anything,' said the Duchess, 'that may provoke you to suppose me vulgar and odious enough to try to put you out of conceit of a most interesting and unfortunate creature; and I don't quite, as yet, see – though I dare say I shall soon make it out! – what our friend has in her head in tattling to you on these matters as soon as my back is turned. Petherton will tell you – I wonder he hasn't told you before – why Mrs Grendon, though not perhaps herself quite the rose, is decidedly, in these days, too near it.'

'Oh, Petherton never tells me anything!' Mitchy's answer was brisk and impatient, but evidently quite as sincere as if the person alluded to had not been there.

The person alluded to, meanwhile, fidgeting frankly in his chair, alternately stretching his legs and resting his elbows on his knees, had reckoned as small the profit he might derive from this colloquy. His bored state indeed – if he was bored – prompted in him the honest impulse to clear, as he would have perhaps considered it, the atmosphere. He indicated Mrs Donner with a remarkable absence of precautions. 'Why, what the Duchess alludes to is my poor sister Fanny's stupid grievance – surely you know about that.' He made oddly vivid for a moment the nature of his relative's allegation, his somewhat cynical treatment of which became peculiarly derisive in the light of the attitude and expression, at that minute, of the figure incriminated. 'My brother-in-law's too thick with her. But Cashmore's such a fine old ass. It's excessively unpleasant,' he added, 'for affairs are just in that position in which, from one day to another, there may be something that people will get hold of. Fancy a man,' he robustly reflected while the three took in more completely the subject of Mrs Brookenham's attention – 'fancy a man with that apparition on his hands! The beauty of it is that the two women seem never to have broken off. Blest if they don't still keep seeing each other!'

The Duchess, as on everything else, passed succinctly on this. 'Ah, how can hatreds comfortably flourish without the nourishment of such regular "seeing" as what you call here bosom friendship alone supplies? What are parties given for in London but that enemies may meet? I grant you it's inconceivable that the husband of a superb creature like your sister should find his requirements better met by an object *comme cette petite*, who looks like a pen-wiper – an actress's idea of one – made up for a theatrical bazaar. At the same time, if you'll allow me to say so, it scarcely strikes one that your sister's prudence is such as to have placed all the cards in her hands. She's the most beautiful woman in England, but her *esprit de conduite* isn't quite on a level. One can't have everything!' she philosophically sighed.

Lord Petherton met her comfortably enough on this assumption of his detachments. 'If you mean by that her being the biggest fool alive I'm quite ready to agree with you. It's exactly what makes me afraid. Yet how can I decently say in particular,' he asked, 'of what?'

The Duchess still perched on her critical height. 'Of what but one of your amazing English periodical public washings of dirty linen? There's not the least necessity to "say"!' she laughed. 'If there's anything more remarkable than these purifications, it's the domestic comfort with which, when it has come and gone, you sport the articles purified.'

'It comes back, in all that sphere,' Mr Mitchett instructively suggested, 'to our national, our fatal want of style. We can never, dear Duchess, take too many lessons, and there's probably at the present time no more useful function performed among us than that dissemination of neater methods to which you are so good as to contribute.'

He had had another idea, but before he reached it his companion had gaily broken in. 'Awfully good one for you, Duchess – and I'm bound to say that, for a clever woman, you exposed yourself! I've at any rate a sense of comfort,' Lord Petherton pursued, 'in the good relations now more and more established between poor Fanny and Mrs Brook. Mrs Brook's awfully kind to her and awfully sharp, and Fanny will take things from her that she won't take from me. I keep saying to Mrs Brook – don't you know? – "Do keep hold of her, and let her have it strong." She hasn't, upon my honour, any one in the world but me.'

'And we know the extent of *that* resource!' the Duchess freely exclaimed.

'That's exactly what Fanny says – that *she* knows it,' Petherton good-humouredly assented. 'She says my beastly hypocrisy makes her sick. There are people,' he pleasantly rambled on, 'who are awfully free with their advice, but it's mostly fearful rot. Mrs Brook's isn't, upon my word – I've tried some myself!'

'You talk as if it were something nasty and home-made – gooseberry wine!' the Duchess laughed; 'but one can't know the dear soul, of course, without knowing that she has set up, for the convenience of her friends, a little office for consultations. She listens to the case, she strokes her chin and prescribes—'

'And the beauty of it is,' cried Lord Petherton, 'that she makes no charge whatever!'

'She doesn't take a guinea at the time, but you may still get your account,' the Duchess returned. 'Of course we know that the great business she does is in husbands and wives.'

'This then seems the day of the wives!' Mr Mitchett interposed as he became aware, the first, of the illustration that the Duchess's image was in the act of receiving. 'Lady Fanny Cashmore!' – the butler was already in the field, and the company, with the exception of Mrs Donner, who remained seated, was apparently conscious of a vibration that brought it afresh, but still more nimbly than on Aggie's advent, to its feet.

IX

'Go to her straight – be nice to her: you must have plenty to say. You stay with me – we have our affair.' The latter of these commands the Duchess addressed to Mr Mitchett, while their companion, in obedience to the former and affected, as it seemed, by an unrepressed familiar accent that stirred a fresh flicker of Mitchy's grin, met the new arrival in the middle of the room before Mrs Brookenham had had time to reach her. The Duchess, quickly reseated, watched an instant the inexpressive concussion of the tall brother and sister; then while Mitchy again subsided in his place, 'You're not, as a race, clever, you're not delicate, you're not sane, but you're capable of extraordinary good looks,' she resumed. '*Vous avez parfois la grande beauté.*'

Mitchy was much amused. 'Do you really think Petherton has?'

The Duchess withstood it. 'They've got, both outside and in, the same great general things, only turned, in each, rather different ways, a way safer for him as a man, and more triumphant for her as – whatever you choose to call her! What *can* a woman do,' she richly mused, 'with such beauty as that—'

'Except come desperately to advise with Mrs Brook' – Mitchy undertook to complete her question – 'as to the highest use to make of it? But see,' he immediately added, 'how perfectly competent to instruct her our friend now looks.' Their hostess had advanced to Lady Fanny with an outstretched hand but with an eagerness of greeting merged a little in the sweet predominance of wonder as well as in the habit, at such moments most perceptible, of the languid lily-bend. Nothing in general could have been less poorly conventional than the kind of reception given in Mrs Brookenham's drawing-room to the particular element – the element of physical splendour void of those disparities that make the questions of others tiresome – comprised in Lady Fanny's presence. It was a place in which, at all times, before interesting objects, the unanimous occupants, almost more concerned for each other's vibrations than for anything else, were apt rather more to exchange sharp and silent searchings than to fix their eyes on the object itself. In the case of Lady Fanny, however, the object itself – and quite by the same law that had worked, though less profoundly, on the entrance of little Aggie – superseded the usual rapt communion very much in the manner of some beautiful tame tigress who might really coerce attention. There was in Mrs Brookenham's way of looking up at her a dim, despairing abandonment of the idea of any common personal ground. Lady Fanny, magnificent, simple, stupid,

had almost the stature of her brother, a forehead unsur-
passably low and an air of sombre concentration just
sufficiently corrected by something in her movements that
failed to give it a point. Her blue eyes were heavy in spite of
being perhaps a couple of shades too clear, and the wealth
of her black hair, the disposition of the massive coils of which
was all her own, had possibly a satin sheen depreciated by
the current fashion. But the great thing in her was that she
was, with unconscious heroism, thoroughly herself; and what
were Mrs Brook and Mrs Brook's intimates after all, in their
free surrender to the play of perception, but a happy association for keeping her so? The Duchess was moved to the
liveliest admiration by the grand, simple sweetness of her
encounter with Mrs Donner, a combination indeed in which
it was a question if she or Mrs Brook appeared to the higher
advantage. It was poor Mrs Donner — not, like Mrs Brook,
subtle in sufficiency, nor, like Lady Fanny, almost too simple
— who made the poorest show. The Duchess immediately
marked it to Mitchy as infinitely characteristic that their
hostess, instead of letting one of her visitors go, kept them
together by some sweet ingenuity and while Lord Petherton,
dropping his sister, joined Edward and Aggie in the other
angle, sat there between them as if, in pursuance of some
awfully clever line of her own, she were holding a hand of
each. Mr Mitchett of course did justice all round, or at least,
as would have seemed from an inquiry he presently made,
wished not to fail of it. 'Is it your real impression then that
Lady Fanny has serious grounds——?'

'For jealousy of that preposterous little person? My dear
Mitchett,' the Duchess resumed after a moment's reflection,
'if you're so rash as to ask me in any of these connexions for
my "real" impression you deserve whatever you may get.'
The penalty Mitchy had incurred was apparently grave
enough to make his companion just falter in the infliction of
it; which gave him the opportunity of replying that the little
person was perhaps not more preposterous than any one else,
that there was something in her he rather liked, and that
there were many different ways in which a woman could be
interesting. This further levity it was therefore that laid him
fully open. 'Do you mean to say you've been living with

Petherton so long without becoming aware that he's shockingly worried?'

'My dear Duchess,' Mitchy smiled, 'Petherton carries his worries with a bravery! They're so many that I've long since ceased to count them; and in general I've been disposed to let those pass that I can't help him to meet. *You've* made, I judge,' he went on, 'a better use of opportunities perhaps not so good – such as at any rate enables you to see further than I into the meaning of the impatience he just now expressed.'

The Duchess was admirable, in conversation, for neglecting everything not essential to her present plausibility. 'A woman like Lady Fanny can have no "grounds" for anything – for any indignation, I mean, or for any revenge worth twopence. In this particular case at all events they've been sacrificed with such extravagance that, as an injured wife, she hasn't had the gumption to keep back an inch or two to stand on. She can do absolutely nothing.'

'Then you take the view—?' Mitchy, who had, after all, his delicacies, pulled up as at sight of a name.

'I take the view,' said the Duchess, 'and I know exactly why. *Elle se les passe* – her little fancies! – She's a phenomenon, poor dear. And all with – what shall I call it? – the absence of haunting remorse of a good house-mother who makes the family accounts balance. She looks – and it's what they love her for here when they say "Watch her now!" – like an angry saint; but she's neither a saint, nor, to be perfectly fair to her, really angry at all. She has only just enough reflection to make out that it may some day be a little better for her that her husband shall, on his side too, have committed himself; and she's only, in secret, too pleased to be sure whom it has been with. All the same I must tell you,' the Duchess still more crisply added, 'that our little friend Nanda is of the opinion – which I gather her to be quite ready to defend – that Lady Fanny is wrong.'

Poor Mitchy found himself staring. 'But what has our little friend Nanda to do with it?'

'What indeed, bless her heart? If you *will* ask questions, however, you must take, as I say, your risks. There are days when between you all you stupefy me. One of them was when I happened about a month ago to make some allusion to the charming example of Mr Cashmore's fine taste that we have there before us: what was my surprise at the tone taken by Mrs Brook to deny on this little lady's behalf the soft impeachment? It was quite a mistake that anything had happened – Mrs Donner had pulled through unscathed. She had been but a day or two at the most in danger, for her family and friends – the best influences – had rallied to her support: the flurry was all over. She was now perfectly safe. Do you think she looks so?' the Duchess asked.

This was not a point that Mitchy was conscious of freedom of mind to examine. 'Do I understand you that Nanda was her mother's authority—?'

'For the exact shade of the intimacy of the two friends and the state of Mrs Brook's information? Precisely – it was "the latest before going to press." "Our own correspondent!" Her mother quoted her.'

Mr Mitchett visibly wondered. 'But how should Nanda know—?'

'Anything about the matter? How should she *not* know everything? You've not, I suppose, lost sight of the fact that this lady and Mrs Grendon are sisters. Carrie's situation and Carrie's perils are naturally very present to the extremely unoccupied Tishy, who is unhappily married into the bargain, who has no children, and whose house, as you may imagine, has a good thick air of partisanship. So, as with Nanda, on *her* side, there is no more absorbing interest than her dear friend Tishy, with whom she's at present staying and under whose roof she perpetually meets this victim of unjust aspersions—'

'I see the whole thing from here, you imply?' Mr Mitchett, under the influence of this rapid evocation, had already taken his line. 'Well,' he said bravely, 'Nanda's not a fool.'

A momentary silence on the part of the Duchess might have been her tribute to his courage. 'No. I don't agree with her, as it happens, here; but that there are matters as to which she's not in general at all befogged is exactly the worst I ever said of her. And I hold that in putting it so – on the basis of my little anecdote – you clearly give out that you're answered.'

Mitchy turned it over. 'Answered?'

'In the quarrel that, awhile back, you sought to pick with me. What I touched on to her mother was the peculiar range of aspects and interests she's compelled to cultivate by the special intimacies that Mrs Brook permits her. There they are – and that's all I said. Judge them for yourself.'

The Duchess had risen as she spoke, which was also what Mrs Donner and Mrs Brookenham had done; and Mr Mitchett was on his feet as well, to act on this last admonition. Mrs Donner was taking leave, and there occurred among the three ladies in connexion with the circumstance a somewhat striking exchange of endearments. Mr Mitchett, observing this, expressed himself suddenly as diverted. 'By Jove, they're kissing – she's in Lady Fanny's arms!' But his hilarity was still to deepen. 'And Lady Fanny, by Jove, is in Mrs Brook's!'

'Oh, it's all beyond *me*!' the Duchess cried; and the little wail of her baffled imagination had almost the austerity of a complaint.

'Not a bit – they're all right. Mrs Brook has acted!'

'Oh, it isn't that she doesn't "act"!' his interlocutress ejaculated.

Mrs Donner's face presented, as she now crossed the room, something that resembled the ravage of a death-struggle between its artificial and its natural elegance. 'Well,' Mitchy said with decision as he caught it – 'I back Nanda.' And while a whiff of derision reached him from the Duchess, 'Nothing *has* happened!' he murmured.

As if to reward him for an indulgence that she must much more have divined than overheard, the visitor approached him with her bravery of awkwardness. 'I go on Thursday to my sister's, where I shall find Nanda Brookenham. Can I take her any message from you?'

Mr Mitchett showed a tint that might positively have been reflected. 'Why should you dream of her expecting one?'

'Oh,' said the Duchess with a gaiety that but half carried off her asperity, 'Mrs Brook must have told Mrs Donner to ask you!'

The latter lady, at this, rested strange eyes on the speaker, and they had perhaps something to do with a quick flare of

Mitchy's wit. 'Tell her, please – if, as I suppose you came here to ask the same of her mother – that I adore her still more for keeping in such happy relations with you as enable me thus to meet you.'

Mrs Donner, overwhelmed, took flight with a nervous laugh, leaving Mr Mitchett and the Duchess still confronted. Nothing had passed between the two ladies, yet it was as if there were a trace of something in the eyes of the elder, which, during a moment's silence, moved from the retreating visitor, now formally taken over at the door by Edward Brookenham, to Lady Fanny and her hostess, who, in spite of the embraces just performed, had again subsided together while Mrs Brook gazed up in exalted intelligence. 'It's a funny house,' said the Duchess at last. 'She makes me such a scene over my not bringing Aggie, and still more over my very faint hint of my reasons for it, that I fly off, in compunction, to do what I can, on the spot, to repair my excess of prudence. I reappear, panting, with my niece – and it's to *this* company I introduce her!'

Her companion looked at the charming child, to whom Lord Petherton was talking with evident kindness and gaiety – a conjunction that evidently excited Mitchy's interest. 'May *we* then know her?' he asked with an effect of drollery. 'May I – if *he* may?'

The Duchess's eyes, turned to him, had taken another light. He even gaped a little at their expression, which was, in a manner, carried out by her tone. 'Go and talk to her, you perverse creature, and send him over to me.' Lord Petherton, a minute later, had joined her; Brookenham had left the room with Mrs Donner; his wife and Lady Fanny were still more closely engaged; and the young Agnesina, though visibly a little scared at Mitchy's queer countenance, had begun, after the fashion he had touched on to Mrs Brook, politely to invoke the aid of the idea of habit. 'Look here – you must help me,' the Duchess said to Petherton. 'You can, perfectly – and it's the first thing I've yet asked of you.'

'Oh, oh, oh!' her interlocutor laughed.

'I must have Mitchy,' she went on without noticing his particular shade of humour.

'Mitchy too?' – he appeared to wish to leave her in no doubt of it.

'How low you are!' she simply said. 'There are times when I despair of you. He's in every way your superior, and I like him so that – well, he must like *her*. Make him feel that he does.'

Lord Petherton turned it over as something put to him practically. 'I could wish for him that he would. I see in her possibilities!' he continued to laugh.

'I dare say you do. *I* see them in Mitchett, and I trust you'll understand me when I say that I appeal to you.'

'Appeal to *him* straight. That's much better,' Petherton lucidly observed.

The Duchess wore for a moment her proudest air, which made her, in the connexion, exceptionally gentle. 'He doesn't like me.'

Her interlocutor looked at her with all his bright brutality. 'Oh, my dear, I can speak for you – if *that's* what you want!'

The Duchess met his eyes, and so, for an instant, they sounded each other. 'You're so abysmally coarse that I often wonder—' But as the door reopened she caught herself. It was the effect of a face apparently directed at her. 'Be quiet. Here's Edward.'

BOOK III

MR LONGDON

X

IF MITCHY arrived exactly at the hour it was quite by design and on a calculation – over and above the little pleasure it might give him – of ten minutes clear with his host, whom it rarely befell him to see alone. He had a theory of something special to go into, of a plummet to sink or a feeler to put forth; his state of mind in short was diplomatic and anxious. But his hopes had a drop as he crossed the threshold. His precaution had only assured him the company of a stranger, for the person in the room to whom the servant announced him was not old Van. On the other hand this gentleman would clearly be old – what was it? the fellow Vanderbank had made it a matter of such importance he should 'really know'. But were they then simply to have tea there together? No; the candidate for Mr Mitchett's acquaintance, as if quickly guessing his apprehension, mentioned on the spot that their entertainer would be with them: he had just come home in a hurry, fearing he was late, and then had rushed off to make a change. 'Fortunately,' said the speaker, who offered his explanation as if he had had it on his mind – 'fortunately the ladies haven't yet come.'

'Oh, there *are* to be ladies?' Mr Mitchett genially replied.

His fellow-guest, who was shy and apparently nervous, sidled about a little, swinging an eye-glass, yet glancing in a manner a trifle birdlike from object to object. 'Mrs Edward Brookenham, I think.'

'Oh!' Mitchy himself felt, as soon as this comment had quitted his lips, that it might sound even to a stranger like a sign, such as the votaries of Mrs Edward Brookenham had fallen into the way of constantly throwing off, that he recognized her hand in the matter. There was, however, something in his entertainer's face that somehow encouraged frankness; it had the sociability of surprise – it hadn't the chill. Mitchy saw at the same time that this friend of old Van's would never really understand him; though that was a thing he at times liked people as much for as he liked them little for it at others. It was in fact when he most liked that he was on the whole most tempted to mystify. 'Only Mrs Brook? – no others?'

'"Mrs Brook"?' his friend echoed; staring an instant, as if literally missing the connexion; but quickly after, to show he was not stupid – and indeed it seemed to show he was delightful – smiling with extravagant intelligence. 'Is that the right thing to say?'

Mitchy gave the kindest of laughs. 'Well, I dare say I oughtn't to.'

'Oh, I didn't mean to correct you,' his interlocutor hastened to profess; 'I meant, on the contrary, will it be right for me too?'

Mitchy's great goggle attentively fixed him. 'Try it.'

'To *her*?'

'To every one.'

'To her husband?'

'Oh, to Edward,' Mitchy laughed again, 'perfectly!'

'And must I call him "Edward"?'

'Whatever you do will be right,' Mitchy returned – 'even though it happen to be sometimes what I do.'

His companion, as if to look at him with a due appreciation of this, stopped swinging the nippers and put them on. 'You people here have a pleasant way—'

'Oh, we *have*!' – Mitchy, taking him up, was gaily emphatic. He began, however, already to perceive the mystification which in this case was to be his happy effect.

'Mr Vanderbank,' his victim remarked with perhaps a shade more of reserve, 'has told me a good deal about you.' Then as if, in a finer manner, to keep the talk off themselves: 'He knows a great many ladies.'

'Oh yes, poor chap, he can't help it. He finds a lady wherever he turns.'

The stranger took this in, but seemed a little to challenge it. 'Well, that's reassuring, if one sometimes fancies there are fewer.'

'Fewer than there used to be? – I see what you mean,' said Mitchy. 'But if it has struck you so, that's awfully interesting.' He glared and grinned and mused. 'I wonder.'

'Well, we shall see.' His friend seemed to wish not to dogmatize.

'*Shall* we?' Mitchy considered it again in its high suggestive light. '*You* will – but how shall I?' Then he caught himself up with a blush. 'What a beastly thing to say – as if it were mere years that make you see it!'

His companion this time gave way to the joke. 'What else can it be – if I've thought so?'

'Why, it's the facts themselves, and the fine taste, and above all something *qui ne court pas les rues*, an approach to some experience of what a lady *is*.' The young man's acute reflection appeared suddenly to flower into a vision of opportunity that swept everything else away. 'Excuse my insisting on your time of life – but you *have* seen some?' The question was of such interest that he had already begun to follow it. 'Oh, the charm of talk with some one who can meet one's conception of the really distinguished women of the past! If I could get you,' he continued, 'to be so awfully valuable as to meet mine!'

His fellow-visitor, on this, made, in a pause, a nearer approach to taking visibly his measure. 'Are you sure you've got one?'

Mr Mitchett brightly thought. 'No. That must be just why I appeal to you. And it can't therefore be for confirmation, can it?' he went on. 'It must therefore be for the beautiful primary hint altogether.'

His interlocutor began, with a shake of the eye-glass, to shift and sidle again, as if distinctly excited by the subject. But it was as if his very excitement made him a trifle coy. 'Are there no nice ones now?'

'Oh yes, there must be lots. In fact I know quantities.'

This had the effect of pulling the stranger up. 'Ah, "quantities"! There it is.'

'Yes,' said Mitchy, 'fancy the "lady" in her millions. Have you come up to London, wondering, as you must, about what's happening – for Vanderbank mentioned, I think, that you *have* come up – in pursuit of her?'

'Ah,' laughed the subject of Vanderbank's information, 'I'm afraid "pursuit", with me, is over.'

'Why, you're at the age,' Mitchy returned, 'of the most exquisite form of it. Observation.'

'Yet it's a form, I seem to see, that you've not waited for my age to cultivate.' This was followed by a decisive head-shake. 'I'm not an observer. I'm a hater.'

'That only means,' Mitchy explained, 'that you keep your observation for your likes – which is more admirable than prudent. But between my fear in the one direction and my desire in the other,' he lightly added, 'I scarcely know how to present myself. I must study the ground. Meanwhile *has* old Van told you much about me?'

Old Van's possible confidant, instead of immediately answering, again assumed the *pince-nez*. 'Is that what you call him?'

'In general, I think – for shortness.'

'And also' – the speaker hesitated – 'for esteem?'

Mitchy laughed out. 'For veneration! Our disrespects, I think, are all tender, and we wouldn't for the world do to a person we don't like anything so nice as to call him, or even call her, don't you know—'

His questioner had quickly looked as if he knew. 'Something pleasant and vulgar?'

Mitchy's gaiety deepened. 'That discrimination is our only austerity. You must fall in.'

'Then what will you call me?'

'What can we?' After which, sustainingly, 'I'm "Mitchy",' our friend revealed.

His interlocutor looked slightly queer. 'I don't think I can quite begin. I'm Mr Longdon,' he almost blushed to articulate.

'Absolutely and essentially – that's exactly what I recognize. I defy any one to see you,' Mitchy declared, 'as anything else, and on that footing you'll be, among us, unique.'

Mr Longdon appeared to accept his prospect of isolation with a certain gravity. 'I gather from you – I've gathered indeed from Mr Vanderbank – that you're a little sort of a set that hang very much together.'

'Oh yes; not a formal association nor a secret society – still less a "dangerous gang" or an organization for any definite end. We're simply a collection of natural affinities,' Mitchy explained; 'meeting perhaps principally in Mrs Brook's drawing-room – though sometimes also in old Van's, as you see, sometimes even in mine – and governed at any rate everywhere by Mrs Brook, in our mysterious ebbs and flows, very much as the tides are governed by the moon. As I say,' Mitchy pursued, 'you must join. But if Van has got hold of you,' he added, 'or you've got hold of him, you *have* joined. We're not quite so numerous as I could wish, and we want variety; we want just what I'm sure you'll bring us – a fresh eye, an outside mind.'

Mr Longdon wore for a minute the air of a man knowing but too well what it was to be asked to put down his name. 'My friend Vanderbank swaggers so little that it's rather from you than from himself that I seem to catch the idea—'

'Of his being a great figure among us? I don't know what he may have said to you, or have suppressed; but you may take it from me – as between ourselves, you know – that he's very much the best of us. Old Van, in fact – if you really want a candid opinion,' and Mitchy shone still brighter as he talked, 'is formed for a distinctly higher sphere. I should go so far as to say that on our level he's positively wasted.'

'And are you very sure you're not?' Mr Longdon asked with a smile.

'Dear no – I'm in my element. My element is to grovel before Van. You've only to look at me, as you must already have made out, to see I'm everything dreadful that he isn't. But you've seen him for yourself – I needn't tell you!' Mitchy ejaculated.

Mr Longdon, as if under the coercion of so much confidence, had stood in place longer than for any previous moment, and the spell continued for a minute after Mitchy had paused. Then nervously, abruptly he turned away, and his friend watched him rather aimlessly wander. 'Our host has spoken of you to me in high terms,' he said as he came back. 'You would have no fault to find with them.'

Mitchy took it with his highest light. 'I know from your taking the trouble to remember that, how much what I've said of him pleases and touches you. We're a little sort of a set then, you and I; we're an organization of two, at any rate, and we can't help ourselves. There – that's settled.' He glanced at the clock on the chimney. 'But what's the matter with him?'

'You gentlemen dress so much,' said Mr Longdon.

Mitchy met the explanation quite half-way. '*I* try to look funny – but why should Apollo in person?'

Mr Longdon weighed it. 'Do you think him like Apollo?'

'The very image. Ask any of the women!'

'But do *they* know—'

'How Apollo must look?' Mitchy considered. 'Why, the way it works is that it's just from Van's appearance they get the tip, and that then, don't you see? they've their term of comparison. Isn't it what you call a vicious circle? I borrow a little their vice.'

Mr Longdon, who had once more been arrested, once more sidled away. Then he spoke from the other side of the expanse of a table covered with books for which the shelves had no space – covered with portfolios, with well-worn leather-cased boxes, with documents in neat piles. The place was a miscellany, yet not a litter, the picture of an admirable order. 'If we're an association of two, you and I, let me, accepting your idea, do what, this way, under a gentleman's roof and while enjoying his hospitality, I should in ordinary circumstances think perhaps something of a breach.'

'Oh, strike out!' Mitchy laughed. It possibly chilled his interlocutor, who again hung fire so long that he himself at last adopted his image. 'Why doesn't he marry, you mean?'

Mr Longdon fairly flushed with recognition. 'You're very deep, but with what we perceive – why doesn't he?'

Mitchy continued visibly to have his amusement, which might have been, this time and in spite of the amalgamation he had pictured, for what 'they' perceived. But he threw off after an instant an answer clearly intended to meet the case. 'He thinks he hasn't the means. He has great ideas of what a fellow must offer a woman.'

Mr Longdon's eyes travelled awhile over the amenities about him. 'He hasn't such a view of himself alone—'

'As to make him think he's enough as he stands? No,' said Mitchy, 'I don't fancy he had a very awful view of himself alone. And since we *are* burning this incense under his nose,' he added, 'it's also my impression that he has no private means. Women in London cost so much.'

Mr Longdon was silent a little. 'They come very high, I dare say.'

'Oh, tremendously. They want so much. I mean the sort of women he lives with. A modest man – who's also poor – isn't in it. I give you that, at any rate, as his view. There are lots of them that would – and only too glad – "love him for himself"; but things are much mixed, and these not necessarily the right ones, and at all events he doesn't see it. The result of which is that he's waiting.'

'Waiting to feel himself in love?'

Mitchy just hesitated. 'Well, we're talking of marriage. Of course you'll say there are women with money. There *are* – he seemed for a moment to meditate – 'dreadful ones!'

The two men, on this, exchanged a long regard. 'He mustn't do that.'

Mitchy again hesitated. 'He won't.'

Mr Longdon had also a silence, which he presently terminated by one of his jerks into motion. 'He sha'n't!'

Once more Mitchy watched him revolve a little, but now, familiarly yet with a sharp emphasis, he himself resumed their colloquy. 'See here, Mr Longdon. Are you seriously taking him up?'

Yet again, at the tone of this appeal, the old man perceptibly coloured. It was as if his friend had brought to the surface an inward excitement, and he laughed for embarrassment. 'You see things with a freedom—'

'Yes, and it's so I express them. I see them, I know, with a *raccourci*; but time after all rather presses, and at any rate we understand each other. What I want now is just to say' – and Mitchy spoke with a simplicity and a gravity he had not yet used – 'that if your interest in him should at any time reach the point of your wishing to do something or other (no matter what, don't you see?) *for* him—'

Mr Longdon, as he faltered, appeared to wonder, but emitted a sound of gentleness. 'Yes?'

'Why,' said the stimulated Mitchy, 'do, for God's sake, just let me have a finger in it.'

Mr Longdon's momentary mystification was perhaps partly but the natural effect of constitutional prudence. 'A finger?'

'I mean – let me help.'

'Oh!' breathed the old man thoughtfully and without meeting his eyes.

Mitchy, as if with more to say, watched him an instant; then before speaking caught himself up. 'Look out – here he comes.'

Hearing the stir of the door by which he had entered, he looked round; but it opened at first only to admit Vanderbank's servant. 'Miss Brookenham!' the man announced; on which the two gentlemen in the room were – audibly, almost violently – precipitated into a union of surprise.

XI

HOWEVER she might have been discussed, Nanda was not one to shrink, for, though she drew up an instant on failing to find in the room the person whose invitation she had obeyed, she advanced the next moment as if either of the gentlemen before her would answer as well. 'How do you do, Mr Mitchy? How do you do, Mr Longdon?' She made no difference for them, speaking to the elder, whom she had not yet seen, as if they were already acquainted. There was moreover in the air of that personage at this juncture little to invite such a confidence: he appeared to have been startled, in the oddest manner, into stillness, and, holding out no hand to meet her, only stared rather stiffly and without a smile. An observer disposed to interpret the scene might have fancied him a trifle put off by the girl's familiarity, or even, as by a singular effect of her self-possession, stricken into deeper diffidence. This self-possession, however, took on her own part no account of any awkwardness; it seemed the greater from the fact that she was almost unnaturally grave; and it overflowed in the immediate challenge: 'Do you mean to say Van isn't here? – I've come without mother – she said I could, to see *him*,' she went on, addressing herself more particularly to Mitchy. 'But she didn't say I might do anything of that sort to see *you*.'

If there was something serious in Nanda and something blank in their companion, there was, superficially at least, nothing in Mr Mitchett but his usual flush of gaiety. 'Did she really send you off this way alone?' Then while the girl's face met his own with the clear confession of it, 'Isn't she too splendid for anything?' he asked with immense enjoyment. 'What do you suppose is her idea?' Nanda's eyes had now turned to Mr Longdon, whom she fixed with her mild straightness; which led to Mitchy's carrying on and repeating the appeal. 'Isn't Mrs Brook charming? What do you suppose is her idea?'

It was a bound into the mystery, a bound of which his fellow-visitor stood quite unconscious, only looking at Nanda still with the same coldness of wonder. All expression had for the minute been arrested in Mr Longdon, but he at last began to show that it had merely been retarded. Yet it was almost with solemnity that he put forth his hand. 'How do you do? How do you do? I'm so glad!'

Nanda shook hands with him as if she had done so already, though it might have been just her look of curiosity that detracted from her air of amusing herself. 'Mother has wanted me awfully to see you. She told me to give you her love,' she said. Then she added with odd irrelevance: 'I didn't come in the carriage, nor in a cab or an omnibus.'

'You came on a bicycle?' Mitchy inquired.

'No, I walked.' She still spoke without a gleam. 'Mother wants me to do everything.'

'Even to walk!' Mitchy laughed. 'Oh yes, we must, in these times, keep up our walking!' The ingenious observer just now suggested might even have detected in the still higher rise of this visitor's spirits a want of mere inward ease.

She had taken no notice of the effect upon him of her mention of her mother, and she took none, visibly, of Mr Longdon's manner or of his words. What she did, while the two men, without offering her, either, a seat, practically lost themselves in their deepening vision, was to give her attention to all the place, looking at the books, pictures and other significant objects, and especially at the small table set out for tea, to which the servant who had admitted her now returned with a steaming kettle. 'Isn't it charming here? Will there be any one else? Where *is* Mr Van? Shall I make tea?' There was just a faint quaver, showing a command of the situation more desired perhaps than achieved, in the very rapid sequence of these ejaculations. The servant meanwhile had placed the hot water above the little silver lamp and left the room.

'Do you suppose there's anything the matter? Oughtn't the man – or do you know our host's room?' Mr Longdon, addressing Mitchy with solicitude, yet began to show, in a countenance less blank, a return of his sense of relations. It was as if something had happened to him and he were in haste to convert the signs of it into an appearance of care for the proprieties.

'Oh,' said Mitchy, 'Van's only making himself beautiful' – which account of their absent entertainer drew some point from his appearance at the moment in the doorway furthest removed from the place where the three were gathered.

Vanderbank came in with friendly haste and with something of the look indeed – refreshed, almost rosy, brightly brushed and quickly buttoned – of emerging, out of breath, from pleasant ablutions and renewals. 'What a brute to have kept you waiting! I come back from work quite begrimed. How d'ye do, how d'ye do, how d'ye do? What's the matter with you, huddled there as if you were on a street-crossing? I want you to think this a refuge – but not of that kind!' he laughed. 'Sit down, for heaven's sake; lie down – be happy! Of course you've made acquaintance all – except that Mitchy's so modest! Tea, tea!' – and he bustled to the table, where, the next minute, he appeared rather helpless. 'Nanda, you blessed child, do *you* mind making it? How jolly of you! – are you all right?' He seemed, with this, for the first time, to be aware of somebody's absence. 'Your mother isn't coming? She let you come alone? How jolly of her!' Pulling off her gloves, Nanda had come immediately to his assistance; on which, quitting the table and laying hands on Mr Longdon's shoulders to push him toward a sofa, he continued to talk, to sound a note of which the humour was the exaggeration of his flurry. 'How jolly of you to be willing to come – most awfully kind! I hope she isn't ill? Do, Mitchy, lie down. Down, Mitchy, down! – that's the only way to keep you.' He had waited for no account of Mrs Brookenham's health, and it might have been apparent – still to our sharp spectator – that he found nothing wonderful in her daughter's unsupported arrival.

' I can make tea beautifully,' she said from behind her table. 'Mother showed me how this morning.'

'This morning?' – and Mitchy, who, before the fire and still erect, had declined to be laid low, greeted the simple remark with uproarious mirth. 'Dear young lady, you're the most delicious family!'

'She showed me at breakfast about the little things to do. She thought I might have to make it here and told me to offer,' the girl went on. 'I haven't yet done it this way at home – I usually have my tea upstairs. They bring it up in a cup, all made and very weak, with a piece of bread-and-butter in the saucer. That's because I'm so young. Tishy never lets me touch hers either; so we had to make up for lost time. That's what mother said' – she followed up her story, and her young distinctness had clearly something to do with a certain pale concentration in Mr Longdon's face. 'Mother isn't ill, but she told me already yesterday she wouldn't come. She said it's really all for *me*. I'm sure I hope it is!' – with which there flickered in her eyes, dimly but perhaps all the more prettily, the first intimation they had given of the light of laughter. 'She told me you would understand, Mr Van – from something you've said to her. It's for my seeing Mr Longdon without – she thinks – her spoiling it.'

'Oh, my dear child, "spoiling it"!' Vanderbank protested as he took a cup of tea from her to carry to their friend. 'When did your mother ever spoil anything? I told her Mr Longdon wanted to see you, but I didn't say anything of his not yearning also for the rest of the family.'

A sound of protest rather formless escaped from the gentleman named, but Nanda continued to carry out her duty. 'She told me to ask why he hadn't been again to see her. Mr Mitchy, sugar? isn't that the way to say it? Three lumps? You're like me, only that I more often take five.'

Mitchy had dashed forward for his tea; she gave it to him; then she added with her eyes on Mr Longdon's, which she had had no difficulty in catching: 'She told me to ask you all sorts of things.'

The old man had got up to take his cup from Vanderbank, whose hand, however, dealt with him on the question of sitting down again. Mr Longdon, resisting, kept erect with a low gasp that his host only was near enough to catch. This suddenly appeared to confirm an impression gathered by Vanderbank in their contact, a strange sense that his visitor was so agitated as to be trembling in every limb. It brought to his lips a kind of ejaculation – 'I *say*!' But even as he spoke Mr Longdon's face, still white, but with a smile that was not all pain, seemed to supplicate him not to notice; and he was not a man to require more than this to achieve a divination as deep as it was rapid. 'Why, we've all been scattered for Easter, haven't we?' he asked of Nanda. 'Mr Longdon has been at home, your mother and father have been paying visits, I myself have been out of London, Mitchy has been to Paris, and you – oh yes, I know where you've been.'

'Ah, we all know that – there has been such a row made about it!' Mitchy said.

'Yes, I've heard of the feeling there is,' Nanda replied. 'It's supposed to be awful, my knowing Tishy – quite too awful.'

Mr Longdon, with Vanderbank's covert aid, had begun to appear to have pulled himself together, dropping back upon his sofa and giving some attention to his tea. It might have been with the notion of showing himself at ease that he turned, on this, a benevolent smile to the girl. 'But what, my dear, is the objection—?'

She looked gravely from him to Vanderbank and to Mitchy, and then back again from one of these to the other. 'Do you think I ought to say?'

They both laughed, and they both just appeared uncertain, but Vanderbank spoke first. 'I don't imagine, Nanda, that you really know.'

'No – as a family, you're perfection!' Mitchy broke out. Before the fire again, with his cup, he addressed his hilarity to Mr Longdon. 'I told you a tremendous lot, didn't I? But I didn't tell you about that.'

The old man maintained, yet with a certain vagueness, the attitude of amiable inquiry. 'About the – a – family?'

'Well,' Mitchy smiled, 'about its ramifications. This young lady has a tremendous friendship – and in short it's all very complicated.'

'My dear Nanda,' said Vanderbank, 'it's all very simple. Don't believe a word of anything of the sort.'

He had spoken as with the intention of a large, light optimism; but there was clearly something in the girl that would always make for lucidity. 'Do you mean about Carrie Donner? I *don't* believe it, and at any rate I don't think it's any one's business. I shouldn't have a very high opinion of a person who would give up a friend.' She stopped short, with the sense apparently that she was saying more than she meant, though, strangely, as if it had been an effect of her type and of her voice, there was neither pertness nor passion in the profession she had just made. Curiously wanting as she seemed both in timidity and in levity, she was to a certainty not self-conscious – she was extraordinarily simple. Mr Longdon looked at her now with an evident surrender to his extreme interest, and it might well have perplexed him to see her at once so downright and yet of so fresh and sweet a tenderness of youth.

'That's right, that's right, my dear young lady: never, never give up a friend for anything any one says!' It was Mitchy who rang out with this lively wisdom, the action of which on Mr Longdon – unless indeed it was the action of something else – was to make that personage, in a manner that held the others watching him in slight suspense, suddenly spring to his feet again, put down his teacup carefully on a table near him and then, without a word, as if no one had been present, quietly wander away and disappear through the door left open on Vanderbank's entrance. It opened into a second, a smaller sitting-room, into which the eyes of his companions followed him.

'What's the matter?' Nanda asked. 'Has he been taken ill?'

'He *is* "rum", my dear Van,' Mitchy said; 'but you're

right – of a charm, a distinction! In short just the sort of thing we want.'

'The sort of thing we "want" – I dare say!' Vanderbank laughed. 'But it's not the sort of thing that's to be had for the asking – it's a sort we shall be mighty lucky if we can get!'

Mitchy turned with amusement to Nanda. 'Van has invented him and, with the natural greed of the inventor, won't let us have him cheap. Well,' he went on, 'I'll pay my share of the expense.'

'The difficulty is that he's so much too good for us,' Vanderbank explained.

'Ungrateful wretch,' his friend cried, 'that's just what I've been telling him that *you* are! Let the return you make not be to deprive me—!'

'Mr Van's not at all too good for *me*, if you mean that,' Nanda broke in. She had finished her tea-making and leaned back in her chair with her hands folded on the edge of the tray.

Vanderbank only smiled at her in silence, but Mitchy took it up. 'There's nobody too good for you, of course; only you're not quite, don't you know? *in* our set. You're in Mrs Grendon's. I know what you're going to say – that she hasn't got any set, that she's just a loose little white flower dropped on the indifferent bosom of the world. But you're the small sprig of tender green that, added to her, makes her immediately "compose".'

Nanda looked at him with her cold kindness. 'What nonsense you do talk!'

'Your tone's sweet to me,' he returned, 'as showing that you don't think *me*, either, too good for you. No one, remember, will take that for your excuse when the world some day sees me annihilated by your having put an end to our so harmless relations.'

The girl appeared to lose herself a moment in the abysmal humanity over which his fairly fascinating ugliness played like the whirl of an eddy. 'Martyr!' she gently exclaimed. But there was no smile with it. She turned to Vanderbank, who, during the previous minute, had moved toward the neighbouring room, then, hesitating, taking counsel of discretion, had come back a little nervous. 'What *is* the matter?'

'What do you want to get out of him, you wretch?' Mitchy went on as their host for an instant produced no answer.

Vanderbank, whose handsome face had a fine thought in it, looked a trifle absently from one of them to the other; but it was to Nanda he spoke. 'Do you like him, Nanda?'

She showed surprise at the question. 'How can I know so soon?'

'*He* knows already.'

Mitchy, with his eyes on her, became radiant to interpret. 'He knows that he's pierced to the heart!'

'The matter with him, as you call it,' Vanderbank brought out, 'is one of the most beautiful things I've even seen.' He looked at her as with a hope that she would understand it. 'Beautiful, beautiful, beautiful!'

'Precisely,' Mitchy continued, 'the victim done for by one glance of the goddess!'

Nanda, motionless in her chair, fixed her other friend with clear curiosity. '"Beautiful"? Why beautiful?'

Vanderbank, about to speak, checked himself. 'I won't spoil it. Have it from *him*!' – and, returning to the old man, he this time went out.

Mitchy and Nanda looked at each other. 'But isn't it rather awful?' Mitchy demanded.

She got up without answering; she slowly came away from the table. 'I think I do know if I like him.'

'Well you may,' Mitchy exclaimed, 'after his putting before you probably, on the whole, the greatest of your triumphs.'

'And I also know, I think, Mr Mitchy, that I like *you*.' She spoke without attention to this hyperbole.

'In spite of my ineffectual attempts to be brilliant? That's a joy,' he went on, 'if it's not drawn out by the mere clumsiness of my flattery.' She had turned away from him, kindly enough, as if time for his talk in the air were always to be allowed him; she took in vaguely Vanderbank's books and prints. 'Why didn't your mother come?' Mitchy then inquired.

At this she again looked at him. 'Do you mention her as a way of alluding to something you guess she must have told me?'

'That I've always supposed I make your flesh creep? Yes,' Mitchy admitted; 'I see that she must have said to you: "Be nice to him, to show him it isn't quite so bad as that!" So you *are* nice – so you always *will* be nice. But I adore you, all the same, without illusions.'

She had opened at one of the tables, unperceivingly, a big volume of which she turned the leaves. 'Don't "adore" a girl, Mr Mitchy – just help her. That's more to the purpose.'

'Help you?' he cried. 'You bring tears to my eyes!'

'Can't a girl have friends?' she went on. 'I never heard of anything so idiotic.' Giving him, however, no chance to take her up on this, she made a quick transition. 'Mother didn't come because she wants me now, as she says, more to share her own life.'

Mitchy looked at it. 'But is this the way for her to share yours?'

'Ah, that's another matter – about which you must talk to *her*. She wants me not, any more, to see only with her eyes. She's throwing me into the world.'

Mitchy had listened with the liveliest interest, but he presently broke into a laugh. 'What a good thing, then, that I'm there to catch you!'

Without – it might have been seen – having gathered the smallest impression of what they enclosed, she carefully drew together again the covers of her folio. There was deliberation in her movements. 'I shall always be glad when you're there. But where do you suppose they've gone?' Her eyes were on what was visible of the other room, from which there arrived no sound of voices.

'They are there,' said Mitchy, 'but simply looking unutterable things about you. The impression's too deep. Let them look, and tell me meanwhile if Mrs Donner gave you my message.'

'Oh yes, she told me some humbug.'

'The humbug then was in the tone my perfectly sincere speech took from herself. She gives things, I recognize, rather that sound. It's her weakness,' he continued, 'and perhaps

even one may say her danger. All the more reason you
should help her, as I believe you're supposed to be doing,
aren't you? I hope you feel that you are,' he earnestly added.

He had spoken this time gravely enough, and with magnificent gravity Nanda replied. 'I *have* helped her. Tishy is
sure I have. That's what Tishy wants me for. She says that
to be with some nice girl is really the best thing for her.'

Poor Mitchy's face hereupon would have been interesting,
would have been distinctly touching to other eyes; but
Nanda's were not heedful of it. 'Oh,' he returned after an
instant and without profane mirth, 'that seems to me the
best thing for any one.'

Vanderbank, however, might have caught his expression,
for Vanderbank now reappeared, smiling on the pair as if
struck by their intimacy. 'How you *are* keeping it up!' Then
to Nanda, persuasively: 'Do you mind going to him in
there? I want him so really to see you. It's quite, you know,
what he came for.'

Nanda seemed to wonder. 'What will he do to me? Anything dreadful?'

'He'll tell you what I meant just now.'

'Oh,' said Nanda, 'if he's a person who can tell me sometimes what you mean—!' With which she went quickly off.

'And can't *I* hear?' Mitchy asked of his host while they
looked after her.

'Yes, but only from me.' Vanderbank had pushed him to
a seat again and was casting about for cigarettes. 'Be quiet
and smoke, and I'll tell you.'

Mitchy, on the sofa, received with meditation a light.
'Will she understand? She has everything in the world but
one,' he added. 'But that's half.'

Vanderbank, before him, lighted for himself. 'What is it?'

'A sense of humour.'

'Oh yes, she's serious.'

Mitchy smoked a little. 'She's tragic.'

His friend, at the fire, watched a moment the empty
portion of the other room, then walked across to give the
door a light push that all but closed it. 'It's rather odd,' he
remarked as he came back – 'that's quite what I just said to
him. But he won't treat her to comedy.'

XII

'Is it the shock of her resemblance to her grandmother?'
Vanderbank had asked of Mr Longdon on rejoining him in
his retreat. The old man, with his back turned, was gazing
out of the window, and when in answer he showed his face
there were tears in his eyes. His answer in fact was just these
tears, the significance of which Vanderbank immediately
recognized. 'It's still greater then than you gathered from
her photograph.'

'It's the most extraordinary thing in the world. I'm too
absurd to be so upset' – Mr Longdon smiled through his
tears – 'but if you had known Lady Julia you would understand. It's *she* again, as I first knew her, to the life; and not
only in feature, in stature, in colour, in movement, but in
every bodily mark and sign, in every look of the eyes, above
all – oh, to a degree! – in the sound, in the charm of the
voice.' He spoke low and confidentially, but with an intensity
that now relieved him – he was restless in his emotion. He
moved about, in his excitement, gently, as if with a sacred
awe – as if, but a few steps away, he had been in the very
presence. 'She's *all* Lady Julia. There isn't a touch of her
mother. It's unique – an absolute revival. I see nothing of
her father, either – I see nothing of any one else. Isn't it
thought wonderful by every one?' he went on. 'Why didn't
you tell me?'

'To have prepared you a little?' – Vanderbank felt almost
guilty. 'I see – I should have liked to make more of it;
though,' he added, smiling, 'I might so, by putting you on
your guard, have caused myself to lose what, if you'll allow
me to say so, strikes me as one of the most touching tributes
I've ever seen rendered to a woman. In fact, however, how
could I know? I never saw Lady Julia, and you had in
advance all the evidence that I could have: the portrait –
pretty bad, in the taste of the time, I admit – and the three
or four photographs that, with it, you must have noticed at
Mrs Brook's. These things must have compared themselves,
for you, with my photograph in there of the grand-daughter.
The similarity of course we had all observed, but it has

taken your wonderful memory and your admirable vision to put into it all the detail.'

Mr Longdon thought a moment, giving a dab with his pocket-handkerchief. 'Very true – you're quite right. It's far beyond any identity in the pictures. But why did you tell me,' he added more sharply, 'that she isn't beautiful?'

'You've deprived me,' Vanderbank laughed, 'of the power of expressing civilly any surprise at your finding her so. But I said to you, please remember, nothing that qualified a jot my sense of the curious character of her face. I have always positively found in it a recall of the type of the period you must be thinking of. It isn't a bit modern. It's a face of Sir Thomas Lawrence—'

'It's a face of Gainsborough!' Mr Longdon returned with spirit. 'Lady Julia herself harked back.'

Vanderbank, clearly, was equally touched and amused. 'Let us say at once that it's a face of Raphael.'

His old friend's hand was instantly on his arm. 'That's exactly what I often said to myself of Lady Julia's.'

'The forehead's a little too high,' said Vanderbank.

'But it's just that excess that, with the exquisite eyes and the particular disposition round it of the fair hair, makes the individual grace, makes the beauty of the reminder.'

Released by Lady Julia's lover, the young man in turn grasped him as an encouragement to confidence. 'It's a face that should have the long side-ringlets of 1830. It should have the rest of the personal arrangement, the pelisse, the shape of bonnet, the sprigged muslin dress and the cross-laced sandals. It should have arrived in a pea-green "tilbury" and it should be a reader of Mrs Radcliffe. And all this to complete the Raphael!'

Mr Longdon, who, relieved by expression, had begun to recover himself, looked hard a moment at his companion. 'How you've observed her!'

Vanderbank met it without confusion. 'Whom haven't I observed? Do you like her?' he then rather oddly and abruptly asked.

The old man broke away again. 'How can I tell – with such disparities?'

'The manner must be different,' Vanderbank suggested. 'And the things she says.'

His visitor was before him again. 'I don't know what to make of them. They don't go with the rest of her. Lady Julia,' said Mr Longdon, 'was rather shy.'

On this too his host could meet him. 'She must have been. And Nanda – yes, certainly – doesn't give that impression.'

'On the contrary. But Lady Julia was gay!' he added, with an eagerness that made Vanderbank smile.

'I can also see that. Nanda doesn't joke. And yet,' Vanderbank continued with his exemplary candour, 'we mustn't speak of her, must we? as if she were bold and grim.'

Mr Longdon fixed him. 'Do you think she's sad?'

They had preserved their dropped tone and might, with their heads together, have been conferring as the party 'out' in some game with the couple in the other room. 'Yes. Sad.' But Vanderbank broke off. 'I'll send her to you.' Thus it was he had come back to her.

Nanda, on joining Mr Longdon, went straight to the point. 'He says it's so beautiful – what you feel on seeing me: if that *is* what he meant.' The old man said nothing again at first; he only smiled at her, but less strangely now, and then appeared to look about him for some place where she could sit near him. There was a sofa in this room too, on which, observing, she quickly sank down, so that they were presently together, placed a little sideways and face to face. She had shown perhaps that she supposed him to have wished to take her hand, but he forbore to touch her, only letting her feel all the kindness of his eyes and their long, backward vision. These things she evidently felt soon enough; she went on before he had spoken. 'I know how well you knew my grandmother. Mother has told me – and I'm so glad. She told me to say to you that she wants *you* to tell me.' Just a shade, at this, might, over the old man's face, have appeared to drop; but who was there to detect whether the girl observed it? It didn't prevent at any rate her completing her statement. 'That's why, today, she wished me to come alone. She wished you to have me, she said, all to yourself.'

No, decidedly, she was not shy: that mute reflection was

in the air an instant. 'That, no doubt, is the best way. I thank her very much. I called, after having had the honour of dining – I called, I think, three times,' he went on, with a sudden displacement of the question; 'but I had the misfortune each time to miss her.'

She kept looking at him with her crude young clearness. 'I didn't know about that. Mother thinks she's more at home than almost any one. She does it on purpose: she knows what it is,' Nanda pursued, with her perfect gravity, 'for people to be disappointed of finding her.'

'Oh, I shall find her yet,' said Mr Longdon. 'And then I hope I shall also find *you*.'

She appeared simply to consider the possibility and after an instant to think well of it. 'I dare say you will now, for now I shall be down.'

Her companion just blinked. 'In the drawing-room, you mean – always?'

It was quite what she meant. 'Always. I shall see all the people who come. It will be a great thing for me. I want to hear all the talk. Mr Mitchett says I ought to – that it helps to form the young mind. I hoped, for that reason,' she went on with the directness that made her honesty almost violent – 'I hoped there would be more people here today.'

'I'm very glad there are not!' – the old man rang equally clear. 'Mr Vanderbank kindly arranged the matter for me just this way. I met him at dinner, at your mother's, three weeks ago, and he brought me home here that night, when, as knowing you so differently, we took the liberty of talking you all over. It had the effect, naturally, of making me want to begin with you afresh – only that seemed difficult too without further help. This he good-naturedly offered me; he said' – and Mr Longdon recovered his spirits to repeat it – '"Hang it, I'll have them here for you!"'

'I see – he knew we would come.' Then she caught herself up. 'But we haven't come, have we?'

'Oh, it's all right – it's all right. To me the occasion's brilliant and the affluence great. I've had such talk with those young men—'

'I see' – she was again prompt, but beyond any young person he had ever met she might have struck him as literal.

'You're not used to such talk. Neither am I. It's rather wonderful, isn't it? They're thought awfully clever, Mr Van and Mr Mitchy. Do you like them?' she pushed on.

Mr Longdon, who, as compared with her, might have struck a spectator as infernally subtle, took an instant to think. 'I've not met Mr Mitchett before.'

'Well, he always thinks one doesn't like him,' Nanda explained. 'But one does. One ought to,' she added.

Her companion had another pause. 'He likes *you*.'

Oh, Mr Longdon needn't have hesitated! 'I know he does. He has told mother. He has told lots of people.'

'He has told even you,' Mr Longdon smiled.

'Yes — but that isn't the same. I don't think he's a bit dreadful,' she pursued. Still, there was a greater interest. 'Do you like Mr Van?'

This time her interlocutor indeed hung fire. 'How can I tell? He dazzles me.'

'But don't you like that?' Then before he could really say: 'You're afraid he may be false?'

At this he fairly laughed. 'You go to the point!' She just coloured to have amused him so, but he quickly went on: 'I think one has a little natural nervousness at being carried off one's feet. I'm afraid I've always liked too much to see where I'm going.'

'And you don't with him?' She spoke with her curious hard interest. 'I understand. But I think I like to be dazzled.'

'Oh, you've got time — you can come round again; you've a margin for accidents, for disappointments and recoveries; you can take one thing with another. But I've only my last little scrap.'

'And you want to make no mistakes — I see.'

'Well, I'm too easily upset.'

'Ah, so am I,' said Nanda. 'I assure you that in spite of what you say I want to make no mistakes either. I've seen a great many — though you mightn't think it,' she persisted; 'I really know what they may be. Do you like *me*?' she brought forth. But even on this she spared him too; a look appeared to have been enough for her. 'How can you say, of course, already? — if you can't say for Mr Van. I mean as you've seen him so much. When he asked me just now if I liked *you* I told him it was too soon. But it isn't now; you see it goes fast. I *do* like you.' She gave him no time to acknowledge this tribute, but, as if it were a matter of course, tried him quickly with something else. 'Can you say if you like mother?'

He could meet it pretty well now. 'There are immense reasons why I should.'

'Yes – I know about them, as I mentioned: mother has told me.' But what she had to put to him kept up his surprise. 'Have reasons anything to do with it? I don't believe you like her!' she exclaimed. '*She* doesn't think so,' she added.

The old man's face at last, partly bewildered, partly reassured, showed even more something finer still in the effect she produced. 'Into what mysteries you plunge!'

'Oh, we do; that's what every one says of us. We discuss everything and every one – we're always discussing each other. I think we must be rather celebrated for it, and it's a kind of trick – isn't it? – that's catching. But don't you think it's the most interesting sort of talk? Mother says we haven't any prejudices. *You* have, probably, quantities – and beautiful ones: so perhaps I oughtn't to tell you. But you'll find out for yourself.'

'Yes – I'm rather slow; but I generally end by finding out. And I've got, thank heaven,' said Mr Longdon, 'quite prejudices enough.'

'Then I hope you'll tell me some of them,' Nanda replied in a tone evidently marking how much he pleased her.

'Ah, you must do as *I* do – you must find out for yourself. Your resemblance to your grandmother is quite prodigious,' he immediately added.

'That's what I wish you'd tell me about – your recollection of her and your wonderful feeling about her. Mother has told me things, but that I should have something straight from you is exactly what she also wants. My grandmother must have been awfully nice,' the girl rambled on, 'and I somehow don't see myself at all as the same sort of person.'

'Oh, I don't say you're in the least the same sort: all I allude to,' Mr Longdon returned, 'is the miracle of the physical heredity. Nothing could be less like her than your manner and your talk.'

Nanda looked at him with all her honesty. 'They're not so good, you must think.'

He hung fire an instant, but was as honest as she. 'You're separated from her by a gulf – and not only of time. Personally, you see, you breathe a different air.'

She thought – she quite took it in. 'Of course. And you breathe the same – the same old one, I mean, as my grandmother.'

'The same old one,' Mr Longdon smiled, 'as much as possible. Some day I'll tell you more of what you desire. I can't go into it now.'

'Because I've upset you so?' Nanda frankly asked.

'That's one of the reasons.'

'I think I can see another too,' she observed after a moment. 'You're not sure how much I shall understand. But I shall understand,' she went on, 'more, perhaps, than you think. In fact,' she said earnestly. 'I *promise* to understand. I've some imagination. Had my grandmother?' she asked. Her actual sequences were not rapid, but she had already anticipated him. 'I've thought of that before, because I put the same question to mother.'

'And what did your mother say?'

'"Imagination – dear mamma? Not a grain!"'

The old man showed a faint flush. 'Your mother then has a supply that makes up for it.'

The girl fixed him, on this, with a deeper attention. 'You don't like her having said that.'

His colour came stronger, though a slightly strained smile did what it could to diffuse coolness. 'I don't care a single scrap, my dear, in respect to the friend I'm speaking of, for any judgement but my own.'

'Not even for her daughter's?'

'Not even for her daughter's.' Mr Longdon had not spoken loud, but he rang as clear as a bell.

Nanda, for admiration of it, broke almost for the first time into the semblance of a smile. 'You feel as if my grandmother were quite *your* property!'

'Oh, quite.'

'I say – that's splendid!'

'I'm glad you like it,' he answered kindly.

The very kindness pulled her up. 'Excuse my speaking so, but I'm sure you know what I mean. You mustn't think,' she eagerly continued, 'that mother won't also want to hear you.'

'On the subject of Lady Julia?' He gently, but very effectively, shook his head. 'Your mother shall never hear me.'

Nanda appeared to wonder at it an instant, and it made her completely grave again. 'It will be all for *me*?'

'Whatever there may be of it, my dear.'

'Oh, I shall get it all out of you,' she returned without hesitation. Her mixture of free familiarity and of the vividness of evocation of something, whatever it was, sharply opposed – the little worry of this contradiction, not altogether unpleasant, continued to fill his consciousness more discernibly than anything else. It was really reflected in his quick brown eyes that she alternately drew him on and warned him off, but also that what they were beginning more and more to make out was an emotion of her own trembling there beneath her tension. His glimpse of it widened – his glimpse of it fairly triumphed when suddenly, after this last declaration, she threw off with quite the same accent but quite another effect: 'I'm glad to be like any one the thought of whom makes you feel so good! You *are* good,' she continued: 'I see already how I shall feel it.' She stared at him with tears, the sight of which brought his own straight back, so that thus for a moment they sat there together.

'My dear child!' he at last simply murmured. But he laid his hand on her now, and her own immediately met it.

'You'll get use to me,' she said with the same gentleness that the response of her touch had tried to express; 'and I shall be so careful with you that – well, you'll see!' She broke short off with a quaver and the next instant she turned – there was some one at the door. Vanderbank, still not quite at his ease, had come back to smile upon them. Detaching herself from Mr Longdon, she got straight up to meet him. 'You were right, Mr Van. It's beautiful, beautiful, beautiful!'

BOOK IV

MR CASHMORE

XIII

HAROLD BROOKENHAM, whom Mr Cashmore, ushered in and announced, had found in the act of helping himself to a cup of tea at the table apparently just prepared – Harold Brookenham arrived at the point with a dash so direct as to leave the visitor an option between but two suppositions: that of a desperate plunge, to have his shame soon over, or that of the acquired habit of such appeals, which had taught him the easiest way. There was no great sharpness in the face of Mr Cashmore, who was somehow massive without majesty; yet he might not have been proof against the suspicion that his young friend's embarrassment was an easy precaution, a conscious corrective to the danger of audacity. It would not have been impossible to divine that if Harold shut his eyes and jumped it was mainly for the appearance of doing so. Experience was to be taken as showing that one might get a five-pound note as one got a light for a cigarette; but one had to check the friendly impulse to ask for it in the same way. Mr Cashmore had in fact looked surprised, yet not on the whole so surprised as the young man seemed to have expected of him. There was almost a quiet grace in the combination of promptitude and diffidence with which Harold took over the responsibility of all proprietorship of the crisp morsel of paper that he slipped with slow firmness into the pocket of his waistcoat, rubbing it gently in its passage against the delicately buff-coloured duck of which that garment was composed. 'So quite too awfully kind of you that I really don't know what to say' – there was a marked recall, in the manner of this speech, of the sweetness of his mother's droop and the tenderness of her wail. It was as if he had been moved for the moment to moralize, but the eyes he raised to his benefactor had the oddest effect of marking that personage himself as the source of the lesson.

Mr Cashmore, who would have been very red-haired if he had not been very bald, showed a single eye-glass and a long upper lip; he was large and jaunty, with little petulant movements and intense ejaculations that were not in the line of his type. 'You may say anything you like if you don't say you'll repay it. That's always nonsense – I hate it.'

Harold remained sad, but showed himself really superior. 'Then I won't say it.' Pensively, a minute, he appeared to figure the words, in their absurdity, on the lips of some young man not, like himself, tactful. 'I know just what you mean.'

'But I think, you know, that you ought to tell your father,' Mr Cashmore said.

'Tell him I've borrowed of you?'

Mr Cashmore good-humouredly demurred. 'It would serve me right – it's so shocking my having listened to you. Tell him, certainly,' he went on after an instant. 'But what I mean is that if you're in such straits you should speak to him like a man.'

Harold smiled at the innocence of a friend who could suppose him not to have exhausted that resource. 'I'm *always* speaking to him like a man, and that's just what puts him so awfully out. He denies to my face that I *am* one. One would suppose, to hear him, not only that I'm a small objectionable child, but that I'm scarcely even human. He doesn't conceive me as with any wants.'

'Oh,' Mr Cashmore laughed, 'you've all – you youngsters – as many wants, I know, as an advertisement page of *The Times*.'

Harold showed an admiration. 'That's awfully good. If you think you ought to speak of it,' he continued, 'do it rather to mamma.' He noted the hour. 'I'll go, if you'll excuse me, to give you the chance.'

The visitor referred to his own watch. 'It's your mother herself who gives the chances – the chances *you* take.'

Harold looked kind and simple. 'She *has* come in, I know. She'll be with you in a moment.'

He was half-way to the door, but Mr Cashmore, though so easy, had not done with him. 'I suppose you mean that if it's only your mother who's told, you may depend on her to shield you.'

Harold turned this over as if it were a questionable sovereign, but on second thoughts he wonderfully smiled. 'Do you think that after you've let me have it you can tell? You could, of course, if you hadn't.' He appeared to work it out for Mr Cashmore's benefit. 'But I don't mind,' he added, 'your telling mamma.'

'Don't mind, you mean really, its annoying her so awfully?'

The invitation to repent thrown off in this could only strike the young man as absurd – it was so previous to any enjoyment. Harold liked things in their proper order; but at the same time his evolutions were quick. 'I dare say I *am* selfish, but what I was thinking was that the terrific wigging, don't you know? – well, I'd take it from *her*. She knows about one's life – about our having to go on, by no fault of our own, as our parents start us. She knows all about wants – no one has more than mamma.'

Mr Cashmore stared, but there was amusement in it too. 'So she'll say it's all right?'

'Oh no; she'll let me have it hot. But she'll recognize that at such a pass more must be done for a fellow, and that may lead to something – indirectly, don't you see? for she won't *tell* my father, she'll only, in her own way, work on him – that will put me on a better footing, and for which therefore at bottom I shall have to thank *you*.'

The eye assisted by Mr Cashmore's glass had fixed, during this address, with a discernible growth of something like alarm, the subject of his beneficence. The thread of their relations somehow lost itself in this subtler twist, and he fell back on mere stature, position and property, things always convenient in the presence of crookedness. 'I shall say nothing to your mother, but I think I shall be rather glad that you're not a son of mine.'

Harold wondered at this new element in their talk. 'Do your sons never—'

'Borrow money of their mother's visitors?' Mr Cashmore had taken him up, eager, evidently, quite to satisfy him; but the question was caught on the wing by Mrs

Brookenham herself, who had opened the door as her friend spoke and who quickly advanced with an echo of it.

'Lady Fanny's visitors?' — and, though her eyes rather avoided than met his own, she seemed to cover her ladyship's husband with a vague but practised sympathy. 'What on earth are you saying to Harold about them?' Thus it was that at the end of a few minutes Mr Cashmore, on the sofa face to face with her, found his consciousness quite purged of its actual sense of his weakness and a new turn given to the idea of what, in one's very drawing-room, might go on behind one's back. Harold had quickly vanished — had been tacitly disposed of, and Mrs Brook's caller had moved even in the short space of time so far in quite another direction as to have drawn from her the little cold question: '"Presents"? You don't mean money?'

He clearly felt the importance of expressing at least by his silence and his eye-glass what he meant. 'Her extravagance is beyond everything, and though there are bills enough, God knows, that do come in to me, I don't see how she pulls through unless there are others that go elsewhere.'

Mrs Brookenham had given him his tea — her own she had placed on a small table near her, and she could now respond freely to the impulse felt, on this, of settling herself to something of real interest. Except to Harold she was incapable of reproach, though there were shades, of course, in her resignation, and her daughter's report of her to Mr Longdon as conscious of an absence of prejudice would have been justified for a spectator by the particular feeling that Mr Cashmore's speech caused her to disclose. What did this feeling wonderfully appear unless strangely irrelevant? 'I've no patience when I hear you talk as if you weren't horribly rich.'

He looked at her an instant as if with the fancy that she might have derived that impression from Harold. 'What has that to do with it? Does a rich man enjoy any more than a poor his wife's making a fool of him?'

Her eyes opened wider: it was one of her very few ways of betraying amusement. There was little indeed to be amused at here except his choice of the particular invidious name. 'You know I don't believe a word you say.'

Mr Cashmore drank his tea, then rose to carry the cup somewhere and put it down, declining with a motion any assistance. When he was on the sofa again he resumed their intimate talk. 'I like tremendously to be with you, but you mustn't think I've come here to let you say to me such deadful things as that.' He was an odd compound, Mr Cashmore, and the air of personal good health, the untarnished bloom which sometimes lent a monstrous serenity to his mention of the barely mentionable, was an occasion balanced or matched by his playful application of extravagant terms to matters of much less moment. 'You know what I come to you for, Mrs Brook: I won't come any more if you're going to be horrid and impossible.'

'You come to me, I suppose, because – for my deep misfortune, I assure you – I've a kind of vision of things, of the wretched miseries in which you all knot yourselves up, which you yourselves are as little blessed with as if, tumbling about together in your heap, you were a litter of blind kittens.'

'Awfully good, that – you do lift the burden of my trouble!' He had laughed out in the manner of the man who made notes for platform use of things that might serve; but the next moment he was grave again, as if his observation had reminded him of Harold's praise of his wit. It was in this spirit that he abruptly brought out: 'Where, by the way, is your daughter?'

'I haven't the least idea. I do all I can to enter into her life, but you can't get into a railway train while it's on the rush.'

Mr Cashmore swung back to hilarity. 'You give me lots of things. Do you mean she's so "fast"?' He could keep the ball going.

Mrs Brookenham hesitated. 'No; she's a tremendous dear, and we're great friends. But she has her free young life, which, by that law of our time that I'm sure I only want, like all other laws, once I know what they *are*, to accept – she has her precious freshness of feeling which I say to myself that, so far as control is concerned, I ought to respect. I try to get her to sit with me, and she does so often, because she's kind. But before I know it she leaves me again: she feels that her presence makes a difference in one's liberty of talk.'

Mr Cashmore was struck by this picture. 'That's awfully charming of her.'

'Isn't it too dear?' The thought of it, for Mrs Brook, seemed fairly to open out vistas. 'The modern daughter!'

'But not the ancient mother!' Mr Cashmore smiled.

She shook her head with a world of accepted woe. '"Give me back, give me back one hour of my youth"! Oh, I haven't a single thrill left to answer a compliment. I sit here now face to face with things as they are. They come in their turn, I assure you – and they find me,' Mrs Brook sighed, 'ready. Nanda has stepped on the stage, and I give her up the house. Besides,' she went on musingly, 'it's awfully interesting. It *is* the modern daughter – we're really "doing" her, the child and I; and as the modern has always been my own note – I've gone in, I mean, frankly for my very own Time – who is one, after all, that one should pretend to decline to go where it may lead?' Mr Cashmore was unprepared with an answer to this question, and his hostess continued in a different tone: 'It's sweet her sparing one!'

This, for the visitor, was firmer ground. 'Do you mean about talking before her?'

Mrs Brook's assent was positively tender. 'She won't have a difference in my freedom. It's as if the dear thing *knew*, don't you see? what we must keep back. She wants us not to have to think. It's quite maternal!' she mused again. Then as if with the pleasure of presenting it to him afresh: 'That's the modern daughter!'

'Well,' said Mr Cashmore, 'I can't help wishing she were a trifle less considerate. In that case I might find her with you, and I may tell you frankly that I get more from her than I do from you. She has the great merit for me, in the first place, of not being such an admirer of my wife.'

Mrs Brookenham took this up with interest. 'No – you're right; she doesn't, as I do, *see* Lady Fanny, and that's a kind of mercy.'

'There you are, then, you inconsistent creature,' he cried with a laugh; 'after all you *do* believe me. You recognize how benighted it would be for your daughter not to feel that Fanny's bad.'

'You're too tiresome, my dear man,' Mrs Brook returned,

'with your ridiculous simplifications. Fanny's *not* "bad";
she's magnificently good – in the sense of being generous
and simple and true, too adorably unaffected and without
the least *mesquinerie*. She's a great calm silver statue.'

Mr Cashmore showed, on this, something of the strength
that comes from the practice of public debate. 'Then why
are you glad that your daughter doesn't like her?'

Mrs Brook smiled as with the sadness of having too much
to triumph. 'Because I'm not, like Fanny, without *mesquinerie*. I'm not generous and simple. I'm exaggeratedly
anxious about Nanda. I care, in spite of myself, for what
people may say. Your wife doesn't – she towers above them.
I can be a shade less brave through the chance of my girl's
not happening to feel as the rest of us do.'

Mr Cashmore too heavily followed. 'To "feel" her?'

Mrs Brook floated over. 'There would be, in that case
perhaps, something to hint to her not to shriek on the
house-tops. When you say,' she continued, 'that one admits,
as regards Fanny, anything wrong, you pervert dreadfully
what one does freely grant – that she's a great glorious
pagan. It's a real relief to know such a type – it's like a
flash of insight into history. None the less, if you ask me
why then it isn't all right for young things to "shriek" as I
say, I have my answer perfectly ready.' After which, as her
visitor seemed not only too reduced to doubt it, but too
baffled to distinguish audibly, for his credit, between resignation and admiration, she produced: 'Because she's purely
instinctive. Her instincts are splendid – but it's terrific.'

'That's all I ever maintained it to be!' Mr Cashmore
cried. 'It *is* terrific.'

'Well,' his friend answered. 'I'm watching her. We're all
watching her. It's like some great natural poetic thing – an
Alpine sunrise or a big high tide.'

'You're amazing!' Mr Cashmore laughed. 'I'm watching
her too.'

'And I'm also watching *you*,' Mrs Brook lucidly continued. 'What I don't for a moment believe is that her bills
are paid by anyone. It's *much* more probable,' she sagaci-
ously observed, 'that they're not paid at all.'

'Oh, well, if she can get on that way—!'

'There can't be a place in London,' Mrs Brook pursued, 'where they're not delighted to dress such a woman. She shows things, don't you see? as some fine tourist region shows the placards in the fields and the posters on the rocks. And what proof can you adduce?' she asked.

Mr Cashmore had grown restless; he picked a stray thread off the knee of his trousers. 'Ah, when you talk about "adducing"—!' He appeared to intimate, as if with the hint that if she didn't take care she might bore him, that it was the kind of word he used only in the House of Commons.

'When I talk about it you can't meet me,' she placidly returned. But she fixed him with her weary penetration. 'You try to believe what you *can't* believe, in order to give yourself excuses. And *she* does the same – only less, for she recognizes less, in general, the need of them. She's so grand and simple.'

Poor Mr Cashmore stared. 'Grander and simpler than I, you mean?'

Mrs Brookenham thought. 'Not simpler – no; but very much grander. She wouldn't, in the case you conceive, recognize really the need of *what* you conceive.'

Mr Cashmore wondered – it was almost mystic. 'I don't understand you.'

Mrs Brook, seeing it all from dim depths, tracked it further and further. 'We've talked her over so!'

Mr Cashmore groaned as if too conscious of it. 'Indeed we have!'

'I mean *we*' – and it was wonderful how her accent discriminated. 'We've talked you too – but of course we talk every one.' She had a pause through which there glimmered a ray from luminous hours, the inner intimacy which, privileged as he was, he couldn't pretend to share; then she broke out almost impatiently: 'We're looking after her – leave her to *us*!'

He looked suddenly so curious as to seem really envious, but he tried to throw it off. 'I doubt if after all you're good for her.'

But Mrs Brookenham knew. 'She's just the sort of person we *are* good for, and the thing for her is to be with us as much as possible – just live with us naturally and easily, listen to our talk, feel our confidence in her, be kept up, don't you know? by the sense of what we expect of her splendid type, and so, little by little, let our influence act. What I meant to say just now is that I do perfectly see her taking what you call presents.'

'Well, then,' Mr Cashmore inquired, 'what do you want more?'

Mrs Brook hung fire an instant – she seemed on the point of telling him. 'I don't see her, as I said, recognizing the obligation.'

'The obligation—?'

'To give anything back. Anything at all.' Mrs Brook was positive. 'The comprehension of petty calculations? Never!'

'I don't say the calculations are petty,' Mr Cashmore objected.

'Well, she's a great creature. If she does fall—!' His hostess lost herself in the view, which was at last all before her. 'Be sure we shall all know it.'

'That's exactly what I'm afraid of!'

'Then don't be afraid till we do. She would fall, as it were, on *us*, don't you see? and,' said Mrs Brook, with decision this time in her head-shake, 'that couldn't be. We *must* keep her up – that's your guarantee. It's rather too much,' she added with the same increase of briskness, 'to have to keep *you* up too. Be very sure that if Carrie really wavers—'

'Carrie?'

His interruption was clearly too vague to be sincere, and it was as such that, going straight on, she treated it. 'I shall never again give her three minutes' attention. To answer to you for Fanny without being able—'

'To answer to Fanny for me, do you mean?' He had flushed quickly as if he awaited her there. 'It wouldn't suit you, you contend? Well then, I hope it will ease you off,' he went on with spirit, 'to know that I wholly *loathe* Mrs Donner.'

Mrs Brook, staring, met the announcement with an absolute change of colour. 'And since when, pray?' It was as if a fabric had crumbled. 'She was here but the other day, and as full of you, poor thing, as an egg of meat.'

Mr Cashmore could only blush for her. 'I don't say she wasn't. My life's a burden from her.'

Nothing, for a spectator, could have been so odd as Mrs Brook's disappointment unless it had been her determination. 'Have you done with her already?'

'One has never done with a buzzing insect——!'

'Until one has literally killed it?' Mrs Brookenham wailed. 'I can't take that from you, my dear man: it was yourself who originally distilled the poison that courses through her veins.' He jumped up at this as if he couldn't bear it, presenting as he walked across the room, however, a large, foolish, fugitive back, on which her eyes rested as on a proof of her penetration. 'If you spoil everything by trying to deceive me, how can I help you?'

He had looked, in his restlessness, at a picture or two, but he finally turned round. 'With whom is it you talk us over? With Petherton and his friend Mitchy? With your adored Vanderbank? With your awful Duchess?'

'You know my little circle, and you've not always despised it.' She met him on his return with a figure that had visibly flashed out for her. 'Don't foul your own nest! Remember that after all we've more or less produced you.' She had a smile that attenuated a little her image, for there were things that on a second thought he appeared ready to take from her. She patted the sofa as if to invite him again to be seated, and though he still stood before her it was with a face that seemed to show how her touch went home. 'You know I've never quite thought you do us full honour, but it was because *she* took you for one of us that Carrie first——'

At this, to stop her, he dropped straight into the seat. 'I assure you there has really been nothing.' With a continuation of his fidget he pulled out his watch. 'Won't she come in at all?'

'Do you mean Nanda?'

'Talk me over with *her*,' he smiled, 'if you like. If you don't believe Mrs Donner is dust and ashes to me,' he continued, 'you do little justice to your daughter.'

'Do you wish to break it to me that you're in love with Nanda?'

He hesitated, but only as if to give weight to his reply. 'Awfully. I can't tell you how I like her.'

She wondered. 'And pray how will *that* help me? Help me, I mean, to help you. Is it what I'm to tell your wife?'

He sat looking away, but he evidently had his idea, which he at last produced. 'Why wouldn't it be just the thing? It would exactly prove my purity.'

There might have been in her momentary silence a hint of acceptance of it as a practical contribution to their problem, and there were indeed several lights in which it could be considered. Mrs Brook, on a quick survey, selected the ironic. 'I see, I see. I might by the same law arrange somehow that Lady Fanny should find herself in love with Edward. That would "prove" *her* purity. And you could be quite at ease,' she laughed – 'he wouldn't make any presents!'

Mr Cashmore regarded her with a candour that was almost a reproach to her mirth. 'I like your daughter better than I like you.'

But it only amused her more. 'Is that perhaps because *I* don't prove your purity?'

What he might have replied remained in the air, for the door opened so exactly at the moment she spoke that he rose again with a start, and the butler, coming in, received her inquiry full in the face. This functionary's answer to it, however, had no more than the usual austerity. 'Mr Vanderbank and Mr Longdon.'

These visitors took a minute to appear, and Mrs Brook, not stirring – still only looking from the sofa calmly up at Mr Cashmore – used the time, it might have seemed, for correcting any impression of undue levity made by her recent question. 'Where did you last meet Nanda?'

He glanced at the door to see if he were heard. 'At the Grendons'.'

'So you do go there?'

'I went over from Hicks the other day for an hour.'

'And Carrie was there?'

'Yes. It was a dreadful horrid bore. But I talked only to your daughter.'

She got up – the others were at hand – and offered Mr Cashmore a face that might have struck him as strange. 'It's serious.'

'Serious?' – he had no eyes for the others.

'She didn't tell me.'

He gave a sound, controlled by discretion, which sufficed none the less to make Mr Longdon – beholding him for the first time – receive it with a little of the stiffness of a person greeted with a guffaw. Mr Cashmore visibly liked this silence of Nanda's about their meeting.

XIV

MRS BROOKENHAM, who had introduced him to the elder of her visitors, had also found, in serving these gentlemen with tea, a chance to edge at him with an intensity not to be resisted: 'Talk to Mr Longdon – take him off *there*.' She had indicated the sofa at the opposite end of the room and had set him an example by possessing herself, in the place she already occupied, of her 'adored' Vanderbank. This arrangement, however, when she had made it constituted for her, in her own corner, the ground of an instant appeal. 'Will he hate me any worse for doing that?'

Vanderbank glanced at the others. 'Will Cashmore, do you mean?'

'Dear no – I don't care whom *he* hates. But with Mr Longdon I want to avoid mistakes.'

'Then don't try quite so hard!' Vanderbank laughed. 'Is that your reason for throwing him into Cashmore's arms?'

'Yes, precisely – so that I shall have these few moments to ask you for directions: you must know him, by this time, so well. I only want, heaven help me, to be as nice to him as I possibly can.'

'That's quite the best thing for you and altogether why, this afternoon, I brought him: he might have better luck in finding you – it was he who suggested it – than he has had by himself. I'm in a general way,' Vanderbank added, 'watching over him.'

'I see – and he's watching over you.' Mrs Brook's lovely

vacancy had already taken in so much. 'He wants to judge of what I may be doing to you – he wants to save you from me. He quite detests me.'

Vanderbank, with the interest as well as the amusement, fairly threw himself back. 'There's nobody like you – you're too magnificent!'

'I *am*; and that I can look the truth in the face and not be angry or silly about it is, as you know, the one thing in the world for which I think a bit well of myself.'

'Oh yes, I know – I know; you're too wonderful!'

Mrs Brookenham, in a brief pause, completed her consciousness. 'They're doing beautifully – he's taking Cashmore with a seriousness!'

'And with what is Cashmore taking him?'

'With the hope that, from one moment to another, Nanda may come in.'

'But how on earth does that concern him?'

'Through an extraordinary fancy he has suddenly taken to her.' Mrs Brook had been swift to master the facts. 'He has been meeting her at Tishy's, and she has talked to him so effectually about his behaviour that she has quite made him cease to think about Carrie. He prefers *her* now – and of course she's much nicer.'

Vanderbank's attention, it was clear, had now been fully seized. 'She's much nicer. Rather! What you mean is,' he asked the next moment, 'that Nanda, this afternoon, has been the object of his call?'

'Yes – really; though he tried to keep it from me. She makes him feel,' she went on, 'so innocent and good.'

Her companion for a moment said nothing; but then at last: 'And *will* she come in?'

'I haven't the least idea.'

'Don't you know where she is?'

'I suppose she's with Tishy, who has returned to town.'

Vanderbank turned this over. 'Is that your system now – to ask no questions?'

'Why *should* I ask any – when I want her life to be as much as possible like my own? It's simply that the hour has struck, as you know. From the moment she *is* down, the only thing for us is to live as friends. I think it's so vulgar,' Mrs

Brook sighed, 'not to have the same good manners with one's children as one has with other people. She asks *me* nothing.'

'Nothing?' Vanderbank echoed.

'Nothing.'

He paused again; after which, 'It's very disgusting!' he exclaimed. Then as she took it up as he had taken her word of a moment before, 'It's very preposterous,' he continued.

Mrs Brook appeared at a loss. 'Do you mean her helping him?'

'It's not of Nanda I'm speaking – it's of him.' Vanderbank spoke with a certain impatience. 'His being with her in any sort of direct relation at all. His mixing her up with his other beastly affairs.'

Mrs Brook looked intelligent and wan about it, but also perfectly good-humoured. 'My dear man, he and his affairs *are* such twaddle!'

Vanderbank laughed in spite of himself. 'And does that make it any better?'

Mrs Brook thought, but presently had a light – she almost smiled with it. 'For *us*.' Then more woefully, 'Don't you want Carrie to be saved?' she asked.

'Why should I? Not a jot. Carrie be hanged!'

'But it's for Fanny,' Mrs Brook protested. 'If Carrie *is* rescued, it's a pretext the less for *her*.' As the young man looked for an instant rather gloomily vague she softly quavered: 'I suppose you don't positively *want* her to bolt?'

'To bolt?'

'Surely I've not to remind you at this time of day how Captain Dent-Douglas is always round the corner with the post-chaise, and how tight, on our side, we're all clutching her.'

'But why not let her go?'

Mrs Brook, at this, showed a sentiment more sharp. '"Go"? Then what would become of us?' She recalled his wandering fancy. 'She's the delight of our life.'

'Oh!' Vanderbank sceptically murmured.

'She's the ornament of our circle,' his companion insisted. 'She will, she won't – she won't, she will! It's the excitement, every day, of plucking the daisy over.' Vanderbank's attention, as she spoke, had attached itself, across the room, to Mr Longdon; it gave her thus an image of the way his imagination had just seemed to her to stray, and she saw a reason in it moreover for her coming up in another place. 'Isn't he rather rich?' She allowed the question all its effect of abruptness.

Vanderbank looked round at her. 'Mr Longdon? I haven't the least idea.'

'Not after becoming so intimate? It's usually, with people, the very first thing I get my impression of.' There came into her face, for another glance at their friend, no crudity of curiosity, but an expression more tenderly wistful. 'He must have some mysterious box under his bed.'

'Down in Suffolk? – a miser's hoard? Who knows? I dare say,' Vanderbank went on. 'He isn't a miser, but he strikes me as careful.'

Mrs Brook meanwhile had thought it out. 'Then he has something to be careful of; it would take something really handsome to inspire in a man like him that sort of interest. With his small expenses all these years his savings must be immense. And how could he have proposed to mamma unless he had originally had money?'

If Vanderbank hesitated he also laughed. 'You must remember your mother refused him.'

'Ah, but not because there was not enough.'

'No – I imagine the force of the blow, for him, was just in the other reason.'

'Well, it would have been in that one just as much if that one had been the other.' Mrs Brook was sagacious, though a trifle obscure, and she pursued the next moment: 'Mamma was so sincere. The fortune was nothing to her. That shows it was immense.'

'It couldn't have been as great as your logic,' Vanderbank smiled; 'but of course if it has been growing ever since—!'

'I can see it grow while he sits there,' Mrs Brook declared. But her logic had in fact its own law, and her next transition was an equal jump. 'It was too lovely, the frankness of your admission a minute ago that I affect him uncannily. Ah, don't spoil it by explanations!' she beautifully pleaded: 'he's

not the first and he won't be the last with whom I shall not
have been what they call a combination. The only thing that
matters is that I shouldn't if possible make the case worse.
So you must guide me. What *is* one to do?'

Vanderbank, now amused again, looked at her kindly.
'Be yourself, my dear woman. Obey your fine instincts.'

'How can you be,' she sweetly asked, 'so hideously hypocritical? You know as well as you sit there that my fine
instincts are the thing in the world you're most in terror of.
"Be myself"?' she echoed. 'What you would *like* to say is:
"Be somebody else – that's your only chance." Well, I'll
try – I'll try.'

He laughed again, shaking his head. 'Don't – don't.'

'You mean it's too hopeless? There's no way of effacing
the bad impression or of starting a good one?' On this, with
a drop of his mirth, he met her eyes, and for an instant
through the superficial levity of their talk they might have
appeared to sound each other. It lasted till Mrs Brook went
on: 'I should really like not to lose him.'

Vanderbank seemed to understand at last and said: 'I
think you won't lose him.'

'Do you mean you'll help me, Van – you *will*?' Her voice
had at moments the most touching tones of any in England,
and, humble, helpless, affectionate, she spoke with a familiarity of friendship. 'It's for the sense of the link with
mamma,' she explained. 'He's simply full of her.'

'Oh, I know. He's prodigious.'

'He has told you more – he comes back to it?' Mrs
Brook eagerly asked.

'Well,' the young man replied a trifle evasively, 'we've
had a great deal of talk, and he's the jolliest old boy
possible, and in short I like him.'

'I see,' said Mrs Brook blandly, 'and he likes you, in
return, as much as he despises *me*. That makes it all right
– makes me somehow so happy for you. There's something
in him – what is it? – that suggests the *oncle d'Amérique*, the
eccentric benefactor, the fairy godmother. He's a little of an
old woman – but all the better for it.' She hung fire but an
instant before she pursued: 'What can we make him do for
you?'

Vanderbank at this was very blank. 'Do for me?'

'How can any one love you,' she asked, 'without wanting
to show it in some way? You know all the ways, dear Van,'
she breathed, 'in which *I* want to show it.'

He might have known them, something suddenly fixed
in his face appeared to say, but they were not what was,
on this speech of hers, most immediately present to him.
'That, for instance, is the tone not to take with him.'

'There you are!' she sighed with discouragement. 'Well,
only *tell* me.' Then as he said nothing: 'I must be more like
mamma?'

His expression confessed to his feeling an awkwardness.
'You're perhaps not quite enough like her.'

'Oh, I know that if he deplores me as I am now she
would have done so quite as much; in fact probably, as
seeing it nearer, a good deal more. She would have despised
me even more than he. But if it's a question,' Mrs Brook
went on, 'of not saying what mamma wouldn't, how can I
know, don't you see, what she *would* have said?' Mrs Brook
became as wonderful as if she saw in her friend's face some
admiring reflection of the fine freedom of mind that – in
such a connexion quite as much as in any other – she could
always show. 'Of course I revere mamma just as much as he
does, and there was everything in her to revere. But she was
none the less in every way a charming woman too, and I
don't know, after all, do I? what even she – in their peculiar
relation – may not have said to him.'

Vanderbank's laugh came back. 'Very good – very good.
I return to my first idea. Try with him whatever comes into
your head. You're a woman of genius after all, and genius
mostly justifies itself. To make you right,' he went on
pleasantly and inexorably, 'might perhaps be to make you
wrong. Since you *have* so great a charm, trust it not at all or
all in all. That, I dare say, is all you can do. Therefore – yes
– be yourself.'

These remarks were followed on either side by the
repetition of a somewhat intenser mutual gaze, though
indeed the speaker's eyes had more the air of meeting his
friend's than of seeking them. 'I can't be *you*, certainly,
Van,' Mrs Brook sadly brought forth.

'I know what you mean by that,' he rejoined in a moment. 'You mean I'm hypocritical.'

'Hypocritical?'

'I'm diplomatic and calculating – I don't show him how bad I am; whereas with you he knows the worst.'

Of this observation Mrs Brook, whose eyes attached themselves again to Mr Longdon, took at first no further notice than might have been indicated by the way it set her musing. '"Calculating"?' – she at last took him up. 'On what is there to calculate?'

'Why,' said Vanderbank, 'if, as you just hinted, he's a blessing in disguise—! I perfectly admit,' he resumed, 'that I'm capable of sacrifices to keep on good terms with him.'

'You're not afraid he'll bore you?'

'Oh yes – distinctly.'

'But it will be worth it? Then,' Mrs Brook said as he appeared to assent, 'it will be worth a great deal.' She continued to watch Mr Longdon, who, without his glasses, stared straight at the floor while Mr Cashmore talked to him. She pursued, however, dispassionately enough: 'He must be of a narrowness—!'

'Oh, beautiful!'

She was silent again. 'I shall broaden him. *You* won't.'

'Heaven forbid!' Vanderbank heartily concurred. 'But none the less, as I've said, I'll help you.'

Her attention was still fixed. 'It will be him you'll help. If you're to make sacrifices to keep on good terms with him, the first sacrifice will be of me.' Then on his leaving this remark so long unanswered that she had finally looked at him again: 'I'm perfectly prepared for it.'

It was as if, jocosely enough, he had had time to make up his mind how to meet her. 'What will you have – when he loved my mother?'

Nothing could have been droller than the gloom of her surprise. 'Yours too?'

'I didn't tell you the other day – out of delicacy.'

Mrs Brookenham darkly thought. '*He* didn't tell me either.'

'The same consideration deterred him. But if I didn't speak of it,' Vanderbank continued, 'when I arranged with you, after meeting him here at dinner, that you should come to tea with him at my rooms – if I didn't mention it then it wasn't because I hadn't learnt it early.'

Mrs Brook more deeply sounded this affair, but she spoke with the exaggerated mildness which was the form mostly taken by her gaiety. 'It was because of course it makes him out such a wretch! What becomes in that case of his loyalty?'

'To *your* mother's memory? Oh, it's all right – he has it quite straight. She came later. Mine, after my father's death, had refused him. But you see he might have been my step-father.'

Mrs Brookenham took it in, but she had suddenly a brighter light. 'He might have been my *own* father! Besides,' she went on, 'if his line is to love the mothers why on earth doesn't he love *me*? I'm in all conscience enough of one.'

'Ah, but isn't there in your case the fact of a daughter?' Vanderbank asked with a slight embarrassment.

Mrs Brookenham stared. 'What good does that do me?'

'Why, didn't she tell you?'

'Nanda? She told me he doesn't like her any better than he likes me.'

Vanderbank in his turn showed surprise. 'That's really what she said?'

'She had on her return from your rooms a most unusual fit of frankness, for she generally tells me nothing.'

'Well,' said Vanderbank, 'how did she put it?'

Mrs Brook reflected – recovered it. '"I like him awfully, but I'm not in the least *his* idea."'

'His idea of what?'

'That's just what I asked her. Of the proper grandchild for mamma.'

Vanderbank hesitated. 'Well, she isn't.' Then after another pause: 'But she'll do.'

His companion gave him a deep look. 'You'll make her?'

He got up, and on seeing him move Mr Longdon also rose, so that, facing each other across the room, they exchanged a friendly signal or two. 'I'll make her.'

XV

THEIR hostess's account of Mr Cashmore's motive for not
staying on was so far justified as that Vanderbank, while
Mr Longdon came over to Mrs Brook, appeared without
difficulty further to engage him. The lady in question
meanwhile had drawn her old friend down, and her present
method of approach would have interested an observer
aware of the unhappy conviction that she had just privately
expressed. Some trace indeed of the glimpse of it enjoyed by
Mr Cashmore's present interlocutor might have been detected in the restlessness that Vanderbank's desire to keep
the other pair uninterrupted was still not able to banish from
his attitude. Not, however, that Mrs Brook took the smallest
account of it as she quickly broke out: 'How can we thank
you enough, my dear man, for your extraordinary kindness?'
The reference was vivid, yet Mr Longdon looked so blank
about it that she had immediately to explain. 'I mean to
dear Van, who has told us of your giving him the great
happiness – unless he's too dreadfully mistaken – of letting
him really know you. He's such a tremendous friend of ours
that nothing so delightful can befall him without its affecting
us in the same way.' She had proceeded with confidence,
but suddenly she pulled up. 'Don't tell me he *is* mistaken –
I shouldn't be able to bear it.' She challenged the pale old
man with a loveliness that was for the moment absolutely
juvenile. 'Aren't you letting him – really?'

Mr Longdon's smile was queer. 'I can't prevent him. I'm
not a great house – to give orders to go over me. The kindness is Mr Vanderbank's own, and I've taken up, I'm afraid,
a great deal of his time.'

'You have indeed.' Mrs Brook was undiscouraged. 'He
has been talking with me just now of nothing else. You may
say,' she went on, 'that it's I who have kept him at it. So I
have, for his pleasure's a joy to us. If you can't prevent what
he feels, you know, you can't prevent either what *we* feel.'

Mr Longdon's face reflected for a minute something he
could scarcely have supposed her acute enough to make out,
the struggle between his real mistrust of her, founded on the

unconscious violence offered by her nature to his every memory of her mother, and his sense, on the other hand, of the high propriety of his liking her; to which latter force his interest in Vanderbank was a contribution, inasmuch as he was obliged to recognize on the part of the pair an alliance it would have been difficult to explain at Beccles. 'Perhaps I don't quite see the value of what your husband and you and I are in a position to do for him.'

'Do you mean because he's himself so clever?'

'Well,' said Mr Longdon, 'I dare say that's at the bottom of my feeling so proud to be taken up by him. I think of the young men of *my* time, and I see that he takes in more. But that's what you all do,' he rather helplessly sighed. 'You're very, very wonderful!'

She met him with an almost extravagant eagerness that the meeting should be just where he wished. 'I don't take in everything, but I take in all I can. That's a great affair in London today, and I often feel as if I were a circus-woman, in pink tights and no particular skirts, riding half a dozen horses at once. We're all in the troupe now, I suppose,' she smiled, 'and we must travel with the show. But when you say we're different,' she added, 'think, after all, of mamma.'

Mr Longdon stared. 'It's from her you *are* different.'

'Ah, but she had an awfully fine mind. We're not cleverer than she.'

His conscious, honest eyes looked away an instant. 'It's perhaps enough for the present that you're cleverer than I! I was very glad the other day,' he continued, 'to make the acquaintance of your daughter. I hoped I should find her with you.'

If Mrs Brook cast about it was but for a few seconds. 'If she had known you were coming, she would certainly have been here. She wanted so to please you.' Then as her visitor took no further notice of this speech than to ask if Nanda were out of the house, she had to admit it as an aggravation of failure; but she pursued in the next breath: 'Of course you won't care, but she raves about you.'

He appeared indeed at first not to care. 'Isn't she eighteen?' – it was oddly abrupt.

'I have to think. Wouldn't it be nearer twenty?' Mrs Brook audaciously returned. She tried again. 'She told me all about your interview. I stayed away on purpose – I had my idea.'

'And what *was* your idea?'

'I thought she would remind you more of mamma if I wasn't there. But she's a little person who sees. Perhaps you didn't think it, but she knew.'

'And what did she know?' asked Mr Longdon, who was unable, however, to keep from his tone a certain coldness which really deprived the question of its proper curiosity.

Mrs Brook just showed the chill of it, but she had always her courage. 'Why, that you don't like her.' She had the courage of carrying off as well as of backing out. 'She too has her little place with the circus – it's the way we earn our living.'

Mr Longdon said nothing for a moment and when he at last spoke it was almost with an air of contradiction. 'She's your mother to the life.'

His hostess, for three seconds, looked at him hard. 'Ah, but with such differences! You'll lose it,' she added with a head-shake of pity.

He had his eyes only on Vanderbank. 'Well, my losses are my own affair.' Then his eyes came back. 'Did she tell you I didn't like her?'

The indulgence in Mrs Brook's view of his simplicity was marked. 'You thought you succeeded so in hiding it? No matter – she bears up. I think she really feels a great deal as I do – that it's no matter how many of us you hate if you'll only go on feeling as you do about mamma. To show us *that* – that's what we want.'

Nothing could have expressed more the balm of re-assurance, but the mild drops had fallen short of the spot to which they were directed. '"Show" you?'

Oh, how he had sounded the word! 'I see – you *don't* show. That's just what Nanda saw you thought! But you can't keep us from knowing it – can't keep it in fact, I think, from affecting your own behaviour. You'd be much worse to us if it wasn't for the still warm ashes of your old passion.' It was an immense pity that Vanderbank was at

this moment too far off to fit, for his amusement, to the
expression of his old friend's face so much of the cause of it
as had sprung from the deeply informed tone of Mrs
Brook's allusion. To what degree the speaker herself made
the connexion will never be known to history, nor whether
as she went on she thought she bettered her case or simply
lost her head. 'The great thing for us is that we can never
be for you quite like other ordinary people.'

'And what's the great thing for *me*?'

'Oh, for you, there is nothing, I'm afraid, but small
things – so small that they can scarcely be worth the trouble
of your making them out. Our being so happy that you've
come back to us – if only just for a glimpse and to leave us
again, in no matter what horror, for ever; our positive
delight in your being exactly so different; the pleasure we
have in talking about you, and shall still have – or indeed all
the more – even if we've seen you only to lose you: whatever all this represents for ourselves, it's for none of us to
pretend to say how much or how little *you* may pick out of
it. And yet,' Mrs Brook wandered on, 'however much we
may disappoint you, some little spark of the past can't help
being in us – for the past is the one thing beyond all spoiling;
there it is, don't you think? – to speak for itself and, if need
be, only *of* itself.' She stopped a moment, but she appeared
to have destroyed all power of speech in him, so that while
she waited she had time for a fresh inspiration. It might
perhaps frankly have been mentioned as on the whole her
finest. 'Don't you think it possible that if you once get the
point of view of realizing that I *know*?'

She held the note so long that he at last supplied a
sound. 'That you know what?'

'Why, that, compared with her, I'm a poor creeping
thing. I mean' – she hastened to forestall any protest of mere
decency that would spoil her idea – 'that of course I ache in
every limb with the certainty of my dreadful difference. It
isn't as if I *didn't* know it, don't you see? There it is, as a
matter of course: I've helplessly, but finally and completely,
accepted it. Won't *that* help you?' she so ingeniously pleaded.
'It isn't as if I tormented you with any recall of her whatever. I can quite see how awful it would be for you if, with

the effect I produce on you, I did have her lovely eyes or her distinguished nose or the shape of her forehead or the colour of her hair. Strange as it is in a daughter, I'm disconnected altogether, and don't you think I *may* be a little saved for you by becoming thus simply out of the question? Of course,' she continued, 'your real trial is poor Nanda – she's likewise so fearfully out of it and yet she's so fearfully in it. And she,' said Mrs Brook wonderfully – '*she* doesn't know!'

A strange faint flush, while she talked, had come into Mr Longdon's face, and, whatever effect, as she put it, she produced on him, it was clearly not that of causing his attention to wander. She held him at least, for weal or woe; his bright eyes grew brighter and opened into a stare that finally seemed to offer him as submerged in mere wonder. At last, however, he rose to the surface, and he appeared to have lighted, at the bottom of the sea, on the pearl of the particular wisdom he needed. 'I dare say there may be something in what you so extraordinarily suggest.'

She jumped at it as if in pleasant pain. 'In just letting me go—'

But at this he dropped. 'I shall never let you go.'

It renewed her fear. 'Not just for what I *am*?'

He rose from his place beside her, but looking away from her and with his colour marked. 'I shall never let you go,' he repeated.

'Oh, you angel!' She sprang up more quickly, and the others were by this time on their feet. 'I've done it, I've done it!' she joyously cried to Vanderbank; 'he likes me, or at least he can bear me – I've found him the way; and now I don't care even if he *says* I haven't.' Then she turned again to her old friend. 'We can manage about Nanda – you needn't ever see her. She's "down" now, but she can go up again. We can arrange it at any rate – *c'est la moindre des choses*.'

'Upon my honour I protest,' Mr Cashmore exclaimed, 'against anything of the sort! I defy you to "arrange" that young lady in any such manner without also arranging *me*. I'm one of her great admirers,' he gaily announced to Mr Longdon.

Vanderbank said nothing, and Mr Longdon seemed to show that he would have preferred to do the same: the old man's eyes might have presented an appeal to him somehow to intervene, to show the due acquaintance, springing from practice and wanting in himself, with the art of conversation developed to the point at which it could thus sustain a lady in the upper air. Vanderbank's silence might, without his mere kind, amused look, have seemed almost inhuman. Poor Mr Longdon had finally to do his own simple best. 'Will you bring your daughter to see me?' he asked of Mrs Brookenham.

'Oh, oh – that's an idea: will you bring her to see *me*?' Mr Cashmore again broke out.

Mrs Brook had only fixed Mr Longdon with the air of unutterable things. 'You angel, you angel!' – they found expression but in that.

'*I* don't need to ask you to bring her, do I?' Vanderbank now said to his hostess. 'I hope you don't mind my bragging all over the place of the great honour she did me the other day in appearing quite by herself.'

'Quite by herself? I say, Mrs Brook!' Mr Cashmore flourished on.

It was only now that she noticed him; which she did indeed but by answering Vanderbank. 'She didn't go for *you*, I'm afraid – though of course she might: she went because you had promised her Mr Longdon. But I should have no more feeling about her going to you – and should expect her to have no more – than about her taking a pound of tea, as she sometimes does, to her old nurse, or her going to read to the old women at the workhouse. May you never have less to brag of!'

'I wish she'd bring *me* a pound of tea!' Mr Cashmore resumed. 'Or ain't I enough of an old woman for her to come and read to me at home?'

'Does she habitually visit the workhouse?' Mr Longdon inquired of Mrs Brook.

This lady kept him in a moment's suspense, which another pair of eyes might moreover have detected that Vanderbank in some degree shared. 'Every Friday at three.'

Vanderbank, with a sudden turn, moved slowly to one

of the windows, and Mr Cashmore had a happy remembrance. 'Why, this is Friday – she must have gone today. But does she stay so late?'

'She was to go afterwards to little Aggie: I'm trying so, in spite of difficulties,' Mrs Brook explained, 'to keep them on together.' She addressed herself with a new thought to Mr Longdon. 'You must know little Aggie – the niece of the Duchess: I forget if you've met the Duchess, but you must know *her* too – there are so many things on which, I'm sure, she'll feel with you. Little Aggie's the one,' she continued; 'you'll delight in her; *she* ought to have been mamma's grandchild.'

'Dearest lady, how can you pretend, or for a moment compare her—?' Mr Cashmore broke in. 'She says nothing to me at all.'

'She says nothing to any one,' Mrs Brook serenely replied; 'that's just her type and her charm – just, above all, her education.' Then she appealed to Vanderbank. 'Won't Mr Longdon be struck with little Aggie, and won't he find it interesting to talk about all that sort of thing with the Duchess?'

Vanderbank came back laughing, but Mr Longdon anticipated his reply. 'What sort of thing do you mean?'

'Oh,' said Mrs Brook, 'the whole question, don't you know? of bringing girls forward or not. The question of – well, what do you call it? – their exposure. It's *the* question, it appears – the question of the future; it's awfully interesting, and the Duchess at any rate is great on it. Nanda of course is exposed,' Mrs Brook pursued – 'fearfully.'

'And what on earth is she exposed to?' Mr Cashmore gaily demanded.

'She's exposed to *you*, it would seem, my dear fellow!' Vanderbank spoke with a certain discernible impatience not so much of the fact he mentioned as of the turn of their talk.

It might have been in almost compassionate deprecation of this weak note that Mrs Brookenham looked at him. Her reply to Mr Cashmore's question, however, was uttered at Mr Longdon. 'She's exposed – it's much worse – to *me*. But Aggie isn't exposed to anything – never has been and never is to be; and we're watching to see if the Duchess can carry it through.'

'Why not,' asked Mr Cashmore, 'if there's nothing she *can* be exposed to but the Duchess herself?'

He had appealed to his companions impartially, but Mr Longdon, whose attention was now all for his hostess, appeared unconscious. 'If you're all watching, is it your idea that I should watch *with* you?'

The inquiry, on his lips, was a waft of cold air, the sense of which clearly led Mrs Brook to put her invitation on the right ground. 'Not of course on the chance of anything's happening to the dear child – to whom nothing obviously *can* happen but that her aunt will marry her off in the shortest possible time and in the best possible conditions. No, the interest is, much more, in the way the Duchess herself steers.'

'Ah, she's in a boat,' Mr Cashmore fully concurred, 'that will take a good bit of that.'

It is not for Mr Longdon's historian to overlook that if he was not unnaturally mystified, he was yet also visibly interested. 'What boat is she in?'

He had addressed his curiosity, with politeness, to Mr Cashmore, but they were all arrested by the wonderful way in which Mrs Brook managed to smile at once very dimly, very darkly, and yet make it take them all in. 'I think *you* must tell him, Van.'

'Heaven forbid!' – and Vanderbank again retreated.

'*I'll* tell him like a shot – if you really give me leave,' said Mr Cashmore, for whom any scruple referred itself manifestly not to the subject of the information, but to the presence of a lady.

'I *don't* give you leave, and I beg you'll hold your tongue,' Mrs Brookenham replied. 'You handle such matters with a minuteness—!' In short,' she broke off to Mr Longdon, 'he would tell you a good deal more than you'll care to know. She *is* in a boat – but she's an experienced mariner. *Basta*, as she would say. Do you know Mitchy?' Mrs Brook suddenly asked.

'Oh yes, he knows Mitchy' – Vanderbank had approached again.

'Then make *him* tell him' – she put it before the young man as a charming turn for them all. 'Mitchy *can* be refined when he tries.'

'Oh dear – when Mitchy "tries"!' Vanderbank laughed. 'I think I should rather, for the job, offer him to Mr Longdon as abandoned to his native wild impulse.'

'I *like* Mr Mitchett,' the old man said, endeavouring to look his hostess straight in the eye and speaking as if somewhat to defy her to convict him, even from the point of view of Beccles, of a mistake.

Mrs Brookenham took it with a wonderful bright emotion. 'My dear friend, *vous me rendez la vie*! If you can stand Mitchy you can stand any of us!'

'Upon my honour, I should think so!' Mr Cashmore was eager to remark. 'What on earth do you mean,' he demanded of Mrs Brook, 'by saying that I'm more "minute" than he?'

She turned her beauty an instant on this visitor. 'I don't say you're more minute – I say he's more brilliant. Besides, as I've told you before, you're not one of us.' With which, as a check to further discussion, she went straight on to Mr Longdon: 'The point about Aggie's conservative education is the wonderful sincerity with which the Duchess feels that one's girl may so perfectly and consistently be hedged in without one's really ever (for it comes to that) depriving one's own self—'

'Well, of what?' Mr Longdon boldly demanded while his hostess appeared thoughtfully to falter.

She addressed herself mutely to Vanderbank, in whom the movement produced a laugh. 'I defy you,' he exclaimed, 'to say!'

'Well, you don't defy *me*!' Mr Cashmore cried as Mrs Brook failed to take up the challenge. 'If you know Mitchy,' he went on to Mr Longdon, 'you must know Petherton.'

The old man remained vague and not imperceptibly cold. 'Petherton?'

'My brother-in-law – whom, God knows why, Mitchy runs.'

'Runs?' Mr Longdon again echoed.

Mrs Brook appealed afresh to Vanderbank. 'I think we

ought to spare him. I may not remind you of mamma,' she continued to their companion, 'but I hope you don't mind my saying how much you remind me. Explanations, after all, spoil things, and if you *can* make anything of us and will sometimes come back you'll find everything in its native freshness. You'll see, you'll feel for yourself.'

Mr Longdon stood before her and raised to Vanderbank, when she had ceased, the eyes he had attached to the carpet while she talked. 'And must I go now?' Explanations, she had said, spoiled things, but he might have been a stranger at an Eastern court, comically helpless without his interpreter.

'If Mrs Brook desires to "spare" you,' Vanderbank kindly replied, 'the best way to make sure of it would perhaps indeed be to remove you. But hadn't we a hope of Nanda?'

'It might be of use for us to wait for her?' – it was still to his young friend that Mr Longdon put it.

'Ah, when she's once on the loose—!' Mrs Brookenham sighed: 'Unless *la voilà*,' she said as a hand was heard at the door-latch. It was only, however, a footman who entered with a little tray that, on his approaching his mistress, offered to sight the brown envelope of a telegram. She immediately took leave to open this missive, after the quick perusal of which she had another vision of them all. 'It *is* she – the modern daughter. "Tishy keeps me dinner and opera; clothes all right; return uncertain, but if before morning have latch-key." She won't come home till morning!' said Mrs Brook.

'But think of the comfort of the latch-key!' Vanderbank laughed. 'You might go to the opera,' he said to Mr Longdon.

'Hanged if *I* don't!' Mr Cashmore exclaimed.

Mr Longdon appeared to have caught from Nanda's message an obscure agitation; he met his young friend's suggestion at all events with a visible intensity. 'Will you go with me?'

Vanderbank just hesitated, recalling engagements; which gave Mrs Brook time to intervene. 'Can't you live without him?' she asked of her elder friend.

Vanderbank had looked at her an instant. 'I think I can get there late,' he then replied to Mr Longdon.

'I think *I* can get there early,' Mr Cashmore declared. 'Mrs Grendon must have a box; in fact I know which, and *they* don't,' he jocosely continued to his hostess.

Mrs Brook meanwhile had given Mr Longdon her hand. 'Well, at any rate, the child *shall* soon come to you. And oh, alone,' she insisted: 'you needn't make phrases – I know too well what I'm about.'

'One hopes really you do,' pursued the unquenched Mr Cashmore. 'If that's what one gets by having known your mother—!'

'It wouldn't have helped *you*,' Mrs Brook retorted. 'And won't you have to say it's *all* you were to get?' she pityingly murmured to her other visitor.

He turned to Vanderbank with a strange gasp, and Vanderbank said 'Come!'

BOOK V

THE DUCHESS

XVI

THE lower windows of the great white house, which stood high and square, opened to a wide flagged terrace, the parapet of which, an old balustrade of stone, was broken in the middle of its course by a flight of stone steps that descended to a wonderful garden. The terrace had the afternoon shade and fairly hung over the prospect that dropped away and circled it – the prospect, beyond the series of gardens, of scattered, splendid trees and green glades, an horizon mainly of woods. Nanda Brookenham, one day at the end of July, coming out to find the place unoccupied as yet by other visitors, stood there awhile with an air of happy possession. She moved from end to end of the terrace, pausing, gazing about her, taking in with a face that showed the pleasure of a brief independence the combination of delightful things – of old rooms with old decorations that gleamed and gloomed through the high windows, of old gardens that squared themselves in the wide angles of old walls, of wood-walks rustling in the afternoon breeze and stretching away to further reaches of solitude and summer. The scene had an expectant stillness that she was too charmed to desire to break; she watched it, listened to it, followed with her eyes the white butterflies among the flowers below her, then gave a start as the cry of a peacock came to her from an unseen alley. It set her after a minute into less difficult motion; she passed slowly down the steps, wandering further, looking back at the big bright house but pleased again to see no one else appear. If the sun was still high enough she had a pink parasol. She went through the gardens one by one, skirting the high walls that were so like 'collections' and thinking how, later on, the nectarines and plums would flush there. She exchanged a friendly greeting with a man at work, passed through an open door and, turning this way and that, finally found herself in the park, at some distance from the house. It was a point she had had to take another rise to reach, a place marked by an old green bench for a larger sweep of the view, which, in the distance, where the woods stopped, showed, in the most English way in the world, the colour-spot of an old red village and the tower of an old grey church. She had sunk down upon the bench almost with a sense of adventure, yet not too fluttered to wonder if it wouldn't have been happy to bring a book; the charm of which precisely would have been in feeling everything about her too beautiful to let her read.

The sense of adventure grew in her, presently becoming aware of a stir in the thicket below, followed by the coming into sight, on a path that, mounting, passed near her seat, of a wanderer whom, had his particular, his exceptional identity not quickly appeared, it might have disappointed her a trifle to have to recognize as a friend. He saw her immediately, stopped, laughed, waved his hat, then bounded up the slope and, brushing his forehead with his handkerchief, confessing to being hot, was rejoicingly there before her. Her own ejaculation on first seeing him – 'Why, Mr Van!' – had had an ambiguous sharpness that was rather for herself than for her visitor. She made room for him on the bench, and in a moment he was cooling off and they were both explaining. The great thing was that he had walked from the station to stretch his legs, coming far round, for the lovely hour and the pleasure of it, by a way he had learnt on some previous occasion of being at Mertle.

'You've already stayed here then?' Nanda, who had arrived but half an hour before, spoke as if she had lost the chance to give him a new impression.

'I've stayed here – yes, but not with Mitchy; with some people or other – who the deuce can they have been? – who had the place for a few months a year or two ago.'

'Don't you even remember?'

Vanderbank wondered and laughed. 'It will come to me. But it's a charming sign of London relations, isn't it? – that one *can* come down to people in this way and be awfully well "done for" and all that, and then go away and lose the whole thing, quite forget to whom one has been beholden. It's a queer life.'

Nanda seemed for an instant to wish to say that one might deny the queerness, but she said something else instead. 'I suppose a man like you doesn't quite feel that he *is* beholden: it's awfully good of him – it's doing a great deal for anybody – that he should come down at all; so that it would add immensely to his burden if anybody had to be remembered for it.'

'I don't know what you mean by a man "like me",' Vanderbank returned. 'I'm not any particular kind of a man.' She had been looking at him, but she looked away on this, and he continued good-humoured and explanatory. 'If you mean that I go about such a lot, how do you know it but by the fact that you're everywhere now yourself? – so that, whatever I am, in short, you're just as bad.'

'You admit then that you *are* everywhere. I may be just as bad,' the girl went on, 'but the point is that I'm not nearly so good. Girls are such hacks – they can't be anything else.'

'And, pray, what are fellows who are in the beastly grind of fearfully busy offices? There isn't an old cabhorse in London that's kept at it, I assure you, as I am. Besides,' the young man added, 'if I'm out every night and off somewhere like this for Sunday, can't you understand, my dear child, the fundamental reason of it?'

Nanda, with her eyes on him again, studied an instant this mystery. 'Am I to infer with delight that it's the sweet hope of meeting *me*? It isn't,' she continued in a moment, 'as if there were any necessity for your saying that. What's the use—?' But, impatiently, she stopped short.

He was eminently gay even if his companion was not. 'Because we're such jolly old friends that we really needn't so much as speak at all? Yes, thank goodness – thank goodness.' He had been looking around him, taking in the scene; he had dropped his hat on the ground and, completely at his ease, though still more wishing to show it, had crossed his legs and closely folded his arms. 'What a tremendously jolly place! If I can't for the life of me recall who they were

– the other people – I've the comfort of being sure their minds are an equal blank. Do they even remember the place they had? "We had some fellows down at – where was it, the big white house last November? – and there was one of them, out of the What-do-you-call-it? – *you* know – who might have been a decent enough chap if he had not presumed so on his gifts."' Vanderbank paused a minute, but his companion said nothing, and he pursued: 'It does show, doesn't it? – the fact that we do meet this way – the tremendous change that has taken place in your life in the last three months. I mean, if I'm everywhere as you said just now, your being just the same.'

'Yes – you see what you've done.'

'How, what *I've* done?'

'You plunge into the woods for a change, for solitude,' the girl said, 'and the first thing you do is to find me waylaying you in the depths of the forest. But I really couldn't – if you'll reflect upon it – know you were coming this way.'

Vanderbank sat there with his position unchanged, but with a constant little shake in the foot that hung down, as if everything – and what she now put before him not least – was much too pleasant to be reflected on. 'May I smoke a cigarette?'

Nanda waited a little; her friend had taken out his silver case, which was of ample form, and as he extracted a cigarette she put forth her hand. 'May *I*?' She turned the case over with admiration.

Vanderbank demurred. 'Do you smoke with Mr Longdon?'

'Immensely. But what has that to do with it?'

'Everything, everything.' He spoke with a faint ring of impatience. 'I want you to do with me exactly as you do with him.'

'Ah, that's soon said!' the girl replied in a peculiar tone. 'How do you mean, to "do"?'

'Well then, to *be*. What shall I say?' Vanderbank pleasantly wondered while his foot kept up its motion. 'To feel.'

She continued to handle the cigarette-case, without, however, having profited by its contents. 'I don't think that, as regards Mr Longdon and me, you know quite so much as you suppose.'

Vanderbank laughed and smoked. 'I take for granted he tells me everything.'

'Ah, but you scarcely take for granted *I* do!' She rubbed her cheek an instant with the polished silver, again, the next moment, turning over the case. 'This is the kind of one I should like.'

Her companion glanced down at it. 'Why, it holds twenty.'

'Well, I want one that holds twenty.'

Vanderbank only threw out his smoke. 'I want so to give you something,' he said at last, 'that in my relief at lighting on an object that will do, I will, if you don't look out, give you either that or a pipe.'

'Do you mean this particular one?'

'I've had it for years – but even that one if you like it.'

She kept it – continued to finger it. 'And by whom was it given you?'

At this he turned to her smiling. 'You think I've forgotten that too?'

'Certainly you must have forgotten, to be willing to give it away again.'

'But how do you know it was a present?'

'Such things always are – people don't buy them for themselves.'

She had now relinquished the object, laying it upon the bench, and Vanderbank took it up. 'Its origin is lost in the night of time – it has no history except that I've used it. But I assure you that I do want to give you something. I've never given you anything.'

She was silent a little. 'The exhibition you're making,' she seriously sighed at last, 'of your inconstancy and super-ficiality! All the relics of you that I've treasured and that I supposed at the time to have meant something!'

'The "relics"? Have you a lock of my hair?' Then as her meaning came to him: 'Oh, little Christmas things? Have you really kept them?'

'Laid away in a drawer of their own – done up in pink paper.'

'I know what you're coming to,' Vanderbank said. 'You've given *me* things, and you're trying to convict me of having lost the sweet sense of them. But you can't do it. Where my heart's concerned I'm a walking reliquary. Pink paper? *I* use gold paper – and the finest of all, the gold paper of the mind.' He gave a flip with a finger-nail to his cigarette, and looked at its quickened fire; after which he pursued very familiarly, but with a kindness that of itself qualified the mere humour of the thing: 'Don't talk, my dear child, as if you didn't really know me for the best friend you have in the world.' As soon as he had spoken he pulled out his watch, so that if his words had led to something of a pause this movement offered a pretext for breaking it. Nanda asked the hour and, on his replying 'Five-fifteen,' remarked that there would now be tea on the terrace with every one gathered at it. 'Then shall we go and join them?' her companion demanded.

He had made, however, no other motion, and when, after hesitating, she said, 'Yes, with pleasure,' it was also without a change of position. 'I like this,' she inconsequently added.

'So do I, awfully. Tea on the terrace,' Vanderbank went on, 'isn't "in" it. But who's here?'

'Oh, every one. All your set.'

'Mine? Have I still a set – with the universal vagabondism you accuse me of?'

'Well then Mitchy's – whoever they are.'

'And nobody of yours?'

'Oh yes,' Nanda said, 'all mine. He must at least have arrived by this time. My set's Mr Longdon,' she explained. 'He's all of it now.'

'Then where in the world am I?'

'Oh, you're an extra. There are always extras.'

'A complete set and one over?' Vanderbank laughed. 'Where then is Tishy?'

Charming and grave, the girl thought a moment. 'She's in Paris with her mother – on their way to Aix-les-Bains.' Then with impatience she continued: 'Do you know that's a great deal to say – what you said just now? I mean about your being the best friend I have.'

'Of course I do, and that's exactly why I said it. You see

I'm not in the least delicate or graceful or shy about it – I just come out with it and defy you to contradict me. Who, if I'm not the best, is a better one?'

'Well,' Nanda replied, 'I feel since I've known Mr Longdon that I've almost the sort of friend who makes nobody else count.'

'Then at the end of three months he has arrived at a value for you that I haven't reached in all these years?'

'Yes,' she returned – 'the value of my not being afraid of him.'

Vanderbank, on the bench, shifted his position, turning more to her with an arm over the back. 'And you're afraid of *me*?'

'Horribly – hideously.'

'Then our long, happy relations——?'

'They're just what make my terror,' she broke in, 'particularly abject. Happy relations don't matter. I always think of you with fear.'

His elbow was on the back of the seat and his hand supported his head. 'How awfully curious – if it be true!'

She had been looking away to the sweet English distance, but at this she made a movement. 'Oh Mr Van, I'm "true"!'

As Mr Van himself could not have expressed at any subsequent time, to any interested friend the particular effect upon him of the tone of these words his chronicler takes advantage of the fact not to pretend to a greater intelligence – to limit himself on the contrary to the simple statement that they produced in Mr Van's cheek a flush just discernible. 'Fear of what?'

'I don't know. Fear is fear.'

'Yes, yes – I see.' He took out another cigarette and occupied a moment in lighting it. 'Well, kindness is kindness too – that's all one can say.'

He had smoked again awhile before she turned to him. 'Have I wounded you by saying that?'

A certain effect of his flush was still in his smile. 'It seems to me I should like you to wound me. I did what I wanted a moment ago,' he continued with some precipitation: 'I brought you out handsomely on the subject of Mr Longdon. That was my idea – just to draw you.'

'Well,' said Nanda, looking away again, 'he has come into my life.'

'He couldn't have come into a place where it gives me more pleasure to see him.'

'But he didn't like, the other day, when I used it to him, that expression,' the girl returned. 'He called it "mannered modern slang" and came back again to the extraordinary difference between my speech and my grandmother's.'

'Of course,' the young man understandingly assented. 'But I rather like your speech. Hasn't he by this time, with you,' he pursued, 'crossed the gulf? He has with me.'

'Ah, with you there was no gulf. He liked you from the first.'

Vanderbank wondered. 'You mean I managed him so well?'

'I don't know how you managed him, but liking me has been for him a painful, gradual process. I think he does now,' Nanda declared. 'He accepts me at last as different – he's trying with me on that basis. He has ended by understanding that when he talks to me of Granny I can't even imagine her.'

Vanderbank puffed away. '*I* can.'

'That's what Mitchy says too. But you've both probably got her wrong.'

'I don't know,' said Vanderbank – 'I've gone into it a good deal. But it's too late. We can't be Greeks if we would.'

Even for this Nanda had no laugh, though she had a quick attention. 'Do you call Granny a Greek?'

Her companion rose slowly. 'Yes – to finish her off handsomely and have done with her.' He looked again at his watch. 'Shall we go? – I want to see if my man and my things have turned up.'

She kept her seat; there was something to revert to. 'My fear of you isn't superficial. I mean it isn't immediate – not of you just as you stand,' she explained. 'It's of some dreadfully possible future you.'

'Well,' said the young man, smiling down at her, 'don't forget that if there's to be such a monster, there'll also be a future you, proportionately developed, to deal with him.'

Nanda in the shade had closed her parasol, and her eyes attached themselves to the small hole she had dug in the ground with its point. 'We shall both have moved, you mean?'

'It's charming to think that we shall probably have moved together.'

'Ah, if moving is changing,' she returned, 'there won't be much for me in that. I shall never change – I shall be always just the same. The same old-mannered, modern, slangy hack,' she continued quite gravely. 'Mr Longdon has made me feel that.'

Vanderbank laughed aloud, and it was especially at her seriousness. 'Well, upon my soul!'

'Yes,' she pursued, 'what I am I must remain. I haven't what's called a principle of growth.' Making marks in the earth with her umbrella, she appeared to cipher it out. 'I'm about as good as I can be – and about as bad. If Mr Longdon can't make me different, nobody can.'

Vanderbank could only speak in the tone of high amusement. 'And he has given up the hope?'

'Yes – though not *me* quite, altogether. But the hope he originally had.'

'He gives up quickly – in three months!'

'Oh, these three months,' she answered, 'have been a long time: the fullest, the most important, for what has happened in them, of my life.' She still poked at the ground; then she added: 'And all thanks to *you*.'

'To me?' – Vanderbank couldn't fancy.

'Why, for what we were speaking of just now – my being now so in everything and squeezing up and down no matter whose staircase. Isn't it one crowded hour of glorious life?' she asked. 'What preceded it was an age, no doubt – but an age without a name.'

Vanderbank watched her a little in silence, then spoke quite beside the question. 'It's astonishing how at moments you remind me of your mother!'

At this she got up. 'Ah, there it is! It's what I shall never shake off. That, I imagine, is what Mr Longdon feels.'

Both on their feet now, as if ready for the others, they yet – and even a trifle awkwardly – lingered. It might in fact have appeared to a spectator that some climax had come, on the young man's part, to some state of irresolution as to the utterance of something. What were the words repeatedly on his lips, yet repeatedly not sounded? It would have struck our observer that they were probably not those his lips even now actually formed. 'Doesn't he perhaps talk to you too much about yourself?'

Nanda gave him a dim smile, and he might indeed then have exclaimed on a certain resemblance, a resemblance of expression that had nothing to do with form. It would not have been diminished for him moreover by her successful suppression of every sign that she felt his inquiry a little of a snub. The recall he had previously mentioned could, however, as she answered him, only have been brushed away by a supervening sense of his roughness. 'It isn't so much that probably as my own way of going on.' She spoke with a mildness that could scarce have been so full without being an effort. 'Between his patience and my egotism anything is possible. It isn't his talking – it's his listening.' She gave up the point at any rate as if from softness to her actual companion. 'Wasn't it you who spoke to mamma about my sitting with her? That's what I mean by my debt to you. It's through you that I'm always there – through you and perhaps a little through Mitchy.'

'Oh, through Mitchy – it *must* have been – more than through me.' Vanderbank spoke with the manner of humouring her about a trifle. 'Mitchy, delightful man, felt on the subject, I think, still more strongly.'

They quitted their place together and at the end of a few steps became aware of the approach of one of the others, a figure but a few yards off, arriving from the quarter from which Nanda had come. 'Ah, Mr Longdon!' – she spoke with eagerness now.

Vanderbank instantly waved a hat. 'Dear old boy!'

'Between you all, at any rate,' she said more gaily, 'you've brought me down.'

Vanderbank made no answer till they met their friend, when, by way of greeting, he simply echoed her words. 'Between us all, you'll be glad to know, we've brought her down.'

Mr Longdon looked from one of them to the other. 'Where have you been together?'

Nanda was the first to respond. 'Only talking – on a bench.'

'Well, *I* want to talk on a bench!' The old man showed a spirit.

'With me, of course?' – Vanderbank met it with eagerness.

The girl said nothing, but Mr Longdon sought her eyes. 'No – with Nanda. You must mingle in the crowd.'

'Ah,' their companion laughed, 'you two are the crowd!'

'Well – have your tea first.'

Vanderbank, on this, giving it up with his laugh, offered to Mr Longdon, before withdrawing, the handshake of greeting he had omitted – a demonstration really the warmer for the tone of the joke that went with it. '*Intrigant!*'

XVII

NANDA praised to Mr Longdon the charming spot she had quitted, with the effect that they presently took a fresh possession of it, finding the beauty of the view deepened as the afternoon grew old and the shadows long. They were of a comfortable agreement on these matters, by which more-over they were not long delayed, one of the pair at least being too conscious, for the hour, of still other phenomena than the natural and peaceful process that filled the air. 'Well, you must tell me about these things,' Mr Longdon sociably said: he had joined his young friend with a budget of impressions rapidly gathered at the house; as to which his appeal to her for a light or two may be taken as the measure of the confidence now ruling their relations. He had come to feel at last, he mentioned, that he could allow for most differences; yet in such a situation as the present bewilder-ment could only come back. There were no differences in the world – so it had all ended for him – but those that marked at every turn the manners he had for three months been observing in good society. The general wide deviation of this body occupied his mind to the exclusion of almost everything else, and he had finally been brought to believe that even in his slow-placed prime he must have hung behind his contemporaries. He had not supposed at the moment – in the fifties and the sixties – that he passed for old-fashioned, but life couldn't have left him so far in the rear had the start between them originally been fair. This was the way that, more than once, he had put the matter to the girl: which gives a sufficient hint, it is hoped, of the range of some of their talk. It had always wound up indeed, their talk, with the assumption of the growth of his actual understanding; but it was just these pauses in the fray that seemed to lead from time to time to a sharper clash. It was when he felt, in a word, as if he had exhausted surprises that he received his greatest shocks. There were no such strange tastes as some of those drawn from the bucket that had repeatedly, as he imagined, touched the bottom of the well. 'Now this sudden invasion of somebody's – Heaven knows whose – house, and our dropping down on it like a swarm of locusts: I dare say it isn't civil to criticize it when one's going too, so almost culpably, with the stream; but what are people made of that they consent, just for money, to the violation of their homes?'

Nanda wondered; she cultivated the sense that he made her intensely reflect. 'But haven't people in England always let their places?'

'If we're a nation of shopkeepers, you mean, it can't date, on the scale on which we show it, only from last week? No doubt, no doubt, and the more one thinks of it the more one seems to see that society – for we're *in* society, aren't we, and that's our horizon? – can never have been anything but increasingly vulgar. The point is that in the twilight of time – and I belong, you see, to the twilight – it had made out much less how vulgar it *could* be. It did its best, very probably, but there were too many superstitions it had to get rid of. It has been throwing them overboard one by one, so that now the ship sails uncommonly light. That's the way' – and the old man, with his eyes on the golden distance, ingeniously followed it out – 'I come to feel so the lurching and pitching. If I weren't a pretty fair sailor – well, as it is, my dear,' he interrupted himself with a laugh, 'I show you often enough what grabs I make for support.' He gave a faint gasp, half amusement, half anguish, then abruptly relieved himself by a question. 'To whom in point of fact does the place belong?'

'I'm awfully ashamed, but I'm afraid I don't know. That just came up here,' the girl went on, 'for Mr Van.'

Mr Longdon seemed to think an instant. 'Oh, it came up, did it? And Mr Van couldn't tell?'

'He has quite forgotten – though he has been here before. Of course it may have been with other people,' she added in extenuation. 'I mean it mayn't have been theirs then any more than it's Mitchy's.'

'I see. They too had just bundled in.'

Nanda completed the simple history. 'Today it's Mitchy who bundles, and I believe that really he bundled only yesterday. He turned in his people, and here we are.'

'Here we are, here we are!' her friend more gravely echoed. 'Well, it's splendid!'

As if at a note in his voice her eyes, while his own still strayed away, just fixed him. 'Don't you think it's really rather exciting? Everything's ready, the feast all spread, and with nothing to blunt our curiosity but the general knowledge that there will be people and things, we comfortably take our places.' He answered nothing, though her picture apparently reached him. 'There *are* people, there *are* things, and all in a plenty. Had every one, when you came away, turned up?' she asked as he was still silent.

'I dare say. There were some ladies and gentlemen on the terrace that I didn't know. But I looked only for you and came this way on an indication of your mother's.'

'And did she ask that if you should find me with Mr Van you would make him come to her?'

Mr Longdon replied to this with some delay but without movement. 'How could she have supposed he was here?'

'Since he had not yet been to the house? Oh, it has always been a wonder to me, the things that mamma supposes! I see she asked you,' Nanda observed.

At this her old friend turned to her. 'But it wasn't because of that I got rid of him.'

Nanda hesitated. 'No – you don't mind everything mamma says.'

'I don't mind "everything" anybody says: not even, my dear, when the person's you.'

Again she waited an instant. 'Not even when it's Mr Van?'

Mr Longdon candidly considered. 'Oh, I take him up on all sorts of things.'

'That shows then the importance they have for you. Is *he* like his grandmother?' the girl pursued. Then as her companion looked vague: 'Wasn't it his grandmother too you knew?'

He had an extraordinary smile. 'His mother.' She exclaimed, colouring, on her mistake, and he added: 'I'm not so bad as that. But you're none of you like them.'

'Wasn't she pretty?' Nanda inquired.

'Very handsome. But it makes no difference. She herself, today, wouldn't know him.'

She gave a small gasp. 'His own mother wouldn't—?'

His head-shake just failed of sharpness. 'No, nor he her. There's a link missing.' Then as if after all she might take him too seriously. 'Of course it's I,' he more gently moralized, 'who have lost the link in my sleep. I've slept half the century – I'm Rip Van Winkle.' He went back after a moment to her question. 'He's not, at any rate, like his mother.'

Nanda turned it over. 'Perhaps you wouldn't think so much of her now.'

'Perhaps not. At all events my parting you from Mr Vanderbank was my own idea.'

'I wasn't thinking,' Nanda said, 'of your parting me. I was thinking of your parting yourself.'

'I might have sent *you* to the house? Well,' Mr Longdon replied, 'I find I take more and more the economical view of my pleasures. I run them less and less together – I get all I can out of each.'

'So now you're getting all you can out of *me*?'

'All I can, my dear – all I can.' He watched a little the flushed distance, then mildly broke out: 'It *is*, as you said just now, exciting! But it makes me' – and he became abrupt again – 'want you, as I've already told you, to come to *my* place. Not, however, that we may be still more mad together.'

The girl from the bench shared his contemplation. 'Do you call *this* madness?'

He hesitated. 'You spoke of it yourself as excitement. You'll make of course one of your fine distinctions, but I take it, in my rough way, as a whirl. We're going round and round.' In a minute he had folded his arms with the same closeness Vanderbank had used – in a minute he too was nervously shaking his foot. 'Steady, steady; if we sit close we shall see it through. But come down to Suffolk for sanity.'

'You do mean then that I may come alone?'

'I won't receive you, I assure you, on any other terms. I want to show you,' he continued, 'what life *can* give. Not of course,' he subjoined, 'of this sort of thing.'

'No – you've told me. Of peace.'

'Of peace,' said Mr Longdon. 'Oh, you don't know – you haven't the least idea. That's just why I want to show you.'

Nanda looked as if already she saw it in the distance. 'But will it be peace if I'm there? I mean for *you*,' she added.

'It isn't a question of "me". Everybody's omelette is made of somebody's eggs. Besides, I think that when we're alone together—'

He had dropped for so long that she wondered. 'Well, when we are—?'

'Why, it will be all right,' he simply concluded. 'Temples of peace, the ancients used to call them. We'll set up one, and I shall be at least doorkeeper. You'll come down whenever you like.'

She gave herself to him in her silence more than she could have done in words. 'Have you arranged it with mamma?' she said, however, at last.

'I've arranged everything.'

'*She* won't want to come?'

Her friend's laugh turned him to her. 'Don't be nervous. There are things as to which your mother trusts me.'

'But others as to which not.'

Their eyes met for some time on this, and it ended in his saying: 'Well, you must help me.' Nanda, but without shrinking, looked away again, and Mr Longdon, as if to consecrate their understanding by the air of ease, passed to another subject. 'Mr Mitchett's the most princely host.'

'Isn't he too kind for anything? Do you know what he pretends?' Nanda went on. 'He says, in the most extraordinary way, that he does it all for *me*.'

'Takes this great place and fills it with servants and company—?'

'Yes, just so that I may come down for a Sunday or two. Of course he has only taken it for three or four weeks, but even for that time it's a handsome compliment. He doesn't care what he does. It's his way of amusing himself. He amuses himself at our expense,' the girl continued.

'Well, I hope that makes up, my dear, for the rate at which we're doing so at his!'

'His amusement,' said Nanda, 'is to see us believe what he says.'

Mr Longdon thought a moment. 'Really, my child, you're most acute.'

'Oh, I haven't watched life for nothing! Mitchy doesn't care,' she repeated.

Her companion seemed divided between a desire to draw and a certain fear to encourage her. 'Doesn't care for what?'

She reflected an instant, in her seriousness, and it might have added to Mr Longdon's impression of her depth. 'Well, for himself. I mean for his money. For anything any one may think. For Lord Petherton, for instance, really at all. Lord Petherton thinks he has helped him – thinks, that is, that Mitchy thinks he has. But Mitchy's more amused at *him* than at anybody else. He takes every one in.'

'Every one but you?'

'Oh, I like him.'

'My poor child, you're of a profundity!' Mr Longdon murmured.

He spoke almost uneasily, but she was not too much alarmed to continue lucid. 'And he likes me, and I know just how much – and just how little. He's the most generous man in the world. It pleases him to feel that he's indifferent and splendid – there are so many things it makes up to him for.' The old man listened with attention, and his young friend, conscious of it, proceeded as on ground of which she knew every inch. 'He's the son, as you know, of a great bootmaker – "to all the Courts of Europe" – who left him a large fortune, which had been made, I believe, in the most extraordinary way, in building-speculations as well.'

'Oh yes, I know. It's astonishing!' her companion sighed.

'That he should be of such extraction?'

'Well, everything. That you should be talking as you are – that you should have "watched life", as you say, to such purpose. That we should any of us be here – most of all that Mr Mitchett himself should. That your grandmother's daughter should have brought *her* daughter—'

'To stay with a person' – Nanda took it up as, apparently out of delicacy, he fairly failed – 'whose father used to take the measure, down on his knees on a little mat, as mamma says, of my grandfather's remarkably large foot? Yes, we none of us mind. Do you think we should?' Nanda asked.

Mr Longdon turned it over. 'I'll answer you by a question. Would you marry him?'

'Never.' Then as if to show there was no weakness in her mildness, 'Never, never, never,' she repeated.

'And yet I dare say you know—?' But Mr Longdon once more faltered; his scruple came uppermost. 'You don't mind my speaking of it?'

'Of his thinking he wants to marry me? Not a bit. I positively enjoy telling you there's nothing in it.'

'Not even for *him*?'

Nanda considered. 'Not more than is made up to him by his having found out, through talk and things – which mightn't otherwise have occurred – that I do like him. I wouldn't have come down here if I hadn't.'

'Not for any other reason?' Mr Longdon gravely inquired.

'Not for *your* being here, do you mean?'

He hesitated. 'Me and other persons.'

She showed somehow that she wouldn't flinch. 'You weren't asked till after he had made sure I'd come. We've become, you and I,' she smiled, 'one of the couples who are invited together.'

These were couples, his speculative eye seemed to show, he didn't even yet know about, and if he mentally took them up a moment it was only promptly to drop them. 'I don't think you put it quite strong enough, you know.'

'That Mitchy *is* hard hit? He puts it so strong himself that it will surely do for both of us. I'm a part of what I just spoke of – his indifference and magnificence. It's as if he could only afford to do what's not vulgar. He might perfectly marry a duke's daughter, but that *would* be vulgar – would be the absolute necessity and ideal of nine out of ten of the sons of shoemakers made ambitious by riches. Mitchy says "No; I take my own line; I go in for a beggar-maid." And it's only because I'm a beggar-maid that he wants me.'

'But there are plenty of others,' Mr Longdon objected.

'Oh, I admit I'm the one he least dislikes. But if I had any money,' Nanda went on, 'or if I were really good-looking – for that today, the real thing, will do as well as being a duke's daughter – he wouldn't come near me. And I think that ought to settle it. Besides, he must marry Aggie. She's a beggar-maid too – as well as an angel; so there's nothing against it.'

Mr Longdon stared, but even in his surprise seemed to take from the swiftness with which she made him move over the ground a certain agreeable glow. 'Does "Aggie" like him?'

'She likes every one. As I say, she's an angel – but a real, real, real one. The kindest man in the world is therefore the proper husband for her. If Mitchy wants to do something thoroughly nice,' she declared with the same high competence, 'he'll take her out of her situation, which is awful.'

Mr Longdon looked graver. 'In what way awful?'

'Why, don't you know?' His eye was now cold enough to give her, in her chill, a flurried sense that she might displease him least by a graceful lightness. 'The Duchess and Lord Petherton are like you and me.'

'Is it a conundrum?' He was serious indeed.

'They're one of the couples who are invited together.' But his face reflected so little success for her levity that it was in another tone she presently added: 'Mitchy really oughtn't.' Her friend, in silence, fixed his eyes on the ground;

an attitude in which there was something to make her strike rather wild. 'But of course, kind as he is, he can scarcely be called particular. He has his ideas – he thinks nothing matters. He says we've all come to a pass that's the end of everything.'

Mr Longdon remained mute awhile, and when he at last raised his eyes it was without meeting Nanda's and with some dryness of manner. 'The end of everything? One might easily receive that impression.'

He again became mute, and there was a pause between them of some length, accepted by Nanda with an anxious stillness that it might have touched a spectator to observe. She sat there as if waiting for some further sign, only wanting not to displease her friend, yet unable to pretend to play any part and with something in her really that she couldn't take back now, something involved in her original assumption that there was to be a kind of intelligence in their relation. 'I dare say,' she said at last, 'that I make allusions you don't like. But I keep forgetting.'

He waited a moment longer, then turned to her with a look rendered a little strange by the way it happened to reach over his glasses. It was even austerer than before. 'Keep forgetting what?'

She gave after an instant a faint, feeble smile which seemed to speak of helplessness and which, when at rare moments it played in her face, was expressive from her positive lack of personal, superficial diffidence. 'Well – I don't know.' It was as if appearances became at times so complicated that – so far as helping others to understand was concerned – she could only give up.

'I hope you don't think I want you to be with me as you wouldn't be – as it were – with yourself. I hope you don't think I don't want you to be frank. If you were to try to *appear* to me anything—!' He ended in simple sadness; that, for instance, would be so little what he should like.

'Anything different, you mean, from what I am? That's just what I've thought from the first. One's just what one *is* – isn't one? I don't mean so much,' she went on, 'in one's character or temper – for they have, haven't they? to be what's called "properly controlled" – as in one's mind and

what one sees and feels and the sort of thing one notices.'
Nanda paused an instant; then 'There you are!' she simply
but rather desperately brought out.

Mr Longdon considered this with visible intensity. 'What
you suggest is that the things you speak of depend upon
other people?'

'Well, every one isn't so beautiful as you.' Nanda had
met him with promptitude, yet no sooner had she spoken
than she appeared again to encounter a difficulty. 'But there
it is – my just saying even that. Oh, how I always know –
as I've told you before – whenever I'm different! I can't
ask you to tell me the things Granny *would* have said,
because that's simply arranging to keep myself back from
you, and so being nasty and underhand, which you naturally
don't want, nor I either. Nevertheless when I say the things
she wouldn't, then I put before you too much – too much
for your liking it – what I know and see and feel. If we're
both partly the result of other people, *her* other people were
so different.' The girl's sensitive boldness kept it up, but
there was something in her that pleaded for patience. 'And
yet if she had *you*, so I've got you too. It's the flattery of
that, or the sound of it, I know, that must be so unlike her.
Of course it's awfully like mother; yet it isn't as if you
hadn't already let me see – is it? – that you don't really
think me the same.' Again she stopped a minute, as if to
find her way with him; and again, for the time, he gave no
sign. She struck out again with her strange, cool limpidity:
'Granny wasn't the kind of girl she *couldn't* be – and so
neither am I.'

Mr Longdon had fallen while she talked into something
that might have been taken for a conscious temporary submission to her; he had uncrossed his fidgety legs and,
thrusting them out with his feet together, sat looking very
hard before him, his chin sunk on his breast and his hands,
clasped as they met, rapidly twirling their thumbs. So he
remained for a time that might have given his young
friend the sense of having made herself right with him so
far as she had been wrong. He still had all her attention,
just as previously she had had his, but while he now simply
gazed and thought she watched him with a discreet solici-

tude that would almost have represented him as a near relative whom she supposed unwell. At the end he looked round, and then, obeying some impulse that had gathered in her while they sat mute, she put out to him the tender hand she might have offered to a sick child. They had been talking about frankness, but she showed a frankness in this instance that made him perceptibly colour. For that in turn, however, he responded only the more completely, taking her hand and holding it, keeping it a long minute during which their eyes met and something seemed to clear up that had been too obscure to be dispelled by words. Finally he brought out as if, though it was what he had been thinking of, her gesture had most determined him: 'I wish immensely you'd get married!'

His tone betrayed so special a meaning that the words had a sound of suddenness; yet there was always in Nanda's face that odd preparedness of the young person who has unlearned surprise through the habit, in company, of studiously not compromising her innocence by blinking at things said. 'How *can* I?' she asked, but appearing rather to take up the proposal than to put it by.

'Can't you, *can't* you?' He spoke pressingly and kept her hand. She shook her head slowly, markedly; on which he continued: 'You don't do justice to Mr Mitchy.' She said nothing, but her look was there, and it made him resume: 'Impossible?'

'Impossible.' At this, letting her go, Mr Longdon got up; he pulled out his watch. 'We must go back.' She had risen with him, and they stood face to face in the faded light while he slipped the watch away. 'Well, that doesn't make me wish it any less.'

'It's lovely of you to wish it, but I shall be one of the people who don't. I shall be at the end,' said Nanda, 'one of those who haven't.'

'No, my child,' he returned gravely – 'you shall never be anything so sad.'

'Why not – if *you've* been?'

He looked at her a little, quietly; then, putting out his hand, passed her own into his arm. 'Exactly because I have.'

XVIII

'WOULD you,' the Duchess said to him the next day, 'be for five minutes awfully kind to my poor little niece?' The words were spoken in charming entreaty as he issued from the house late on the Sunday afternoon – the second evening of his stay, which the next morning was to bring to an end – and on his meeting the speaker at one of the extremities of the wide cool terrace. There was at this point a subsidiary flight of steps by which she had just mounted from the grounds, one of her purposes being apparently to testify afresh to that anxious supervision of little Aggie from which she had momentarily suffered herself to be diverted. This young lady, established in the pleasant shade on a sofa of light construction designed for the open air, offered the image of a patience of which it was a questionable kindness to break the spell. It was that beautiful hour when, towards the close-of the happiest days of summer, such places as the great terrace at Mertle present to the fancy a recall of the banquet-hall deserted – deserted by the company lately gathered at tea and now dispersed, according to affinities and combinations promptly felt and perhaps quite as promptly criticized, either in quieter chambers where intimacy might deepen or in gardens and under trees where the stillness knew the click of balls and the good humour of games. There had been chairs, on the terrace, pushed about; there were ungathered teacups on the level top of the parapet; the servants in fact, in the manner of 'hands' mustered by a whistle on the deck of a ship, had just arrived to restore things to an order soon again to be broken. There were scattered couples in sight below and an idle group on the lawn, out of the midst of which, in spite of its detachment, somebody was sharp enough sometimes to cry 'Out!' The high daylight was still in the sky, but with just the foreknowledge already of the long golden glow in which the many-voiced caw of the rooks would sound at once sociable and sad. There was a great deal all about to be aware of and to look at, but little Aggie had her eyes on a book over which her pretty head was bent with a docility visible even from afar. 'I've a friend – down there by the lake – to go back to,' the Duchess went on, 'and I'm on my way to my room to get a letter that I've promised to show him. I shall immediately bring it down and then in a few minutes be able to relieve you. I don't leave her alone too much – one doesn't, you know, in a house full of people, a child of that age. Besides' – and Mr Longdon's interlocutress was even more confiding – 'I do want you so very intensely to know her. You, *par exemple*, you're what I *should* like to give her.' Mr Longdon looked the Duchess, in acknowledgement of her appeal, straight in the face, and who can tell whether or no she acutely guessed from his expression that he recognized this particular juncture as written on the page of his doom? – whether she heard him inaudibly say 'Ah, here it is: I knew it would have to come!' She would at any rate have been astute enough, had this miracle occurred, quite to complete his sense for her own understanding and suffer it to make no difference in the tone in which she still confronted him. 'Oh, I take the bull by the horns – I know you haven't wanted to know me. If you had you would have called on me – I've given you plenty of hints and little coughs. Now, you see, I don't cough any more – I just rush at you and grab you. You don't call on me – so I call on *you*. There isn't any indecency moreover that I won't commit for my child.'

Mr Longdon's impenetrability crashed like glass at the elbow-touch of this large, handsome, practised woman who walked for him, like some brazen pagan goddess, in a cloud of queer legend. He looked off at her child, who, at a distance and not hearing them, had not moved. 'I know she's a great friend of Nanda's.'

'Has Nanda told you that?'

'Often – taking such an interest in her.'

'I'm glad she thinks so then – though really her interests are so various. But come to my baby. I don't make *her* come,' she explained as she swept him along, 'because I want you just to sit down by her there and keep the place, as one may say—!'

'Well, for whom?' he demanded as she stopped.

It was her step that had checked itself as well as her

tongue, and again, suddenly, they stood quite consciously and vividly opposed. 'Can I trust you?' the Duchess brought out. Again then she took herself up. 'But as if I weren't already doing it! It's because I do trust you so utterly that I haven't been able any longer to keep my hands off you. The person I want the place for is none other than Mitchy himself, and half my occupation now is to get it properly kept for him. Lord Petherton's immensely kind, but Lord Petherton can't do everything. I know you really like our host—'

Mr Longdon, at this, interrupted her with a certain coldness. 'How, may I ask, do you know it?'

But with a brazen goddess to deal with—! This personage had to fix him but an instant. 'Because, you dear honest man, you're here. You wouldn't be if you hated him, for you don't practically condone—!'

This time he broke in with his eyes on the child. 'I feel on the contrary, I assure you, that I condone a great deal.'

'Well, don't boast of your cynicism,' she laughed, 'till you're sure of all it covers. Let the right thing for you be,' she went on, 'that Nanda herself wants it.'

'Nanda herself?' He continued to watch little Aggie, who had never yet turned her head. 'I'm afraid I don't understand you.'

She swept him on again. 'I'll come to you presently and explain. I *must* get my letter for Petherton; after which I'll give up Mitchy, whom I was going to find, and, since I've broken the ice – if it isn't too much to say to such a polar bear! – I'll show you *le fond de ma pensée*. Baby darling,' she said to her niece, 'keep Mr Longdon. Show him,' she benevolently suggested, 'what you've been reading.' Then again to her fellow-visitor, as arrested by this very question: 'Caro signore, have *you* a possible book?'

Little Aggie had got straight up and was holding out her volume, which Mr Longdon, all courtesy for her, glanced at. '*Stories from English History*. Oh!'

His ejaculation, though vague, was not such as to prevent the girl from venturing gently: 'Have you read it?'

Mr Longdon, receiving her pure little smile, showed he felt that he had never so taken her in as at this moment and also that she was a person with whom he should surely get on. 'I think I must have.'

Little Aggie was still more encouraged, but not to the point of keeping anything back. 'It hasn't any author. It's anonymous.'

The Duchess borrowed, for another question to Mr Longdon, not a little of her gravity. 'Is it all right?'

'I don't know' – his answer was to Aggie. 'There have been some horrid things in English history.'

'Oh, horrid – *haven*'*t* there?' Aggie, whose speech had the prettiest, faintest foreignness, sweetly and eagerly quavered.

'Well, darling, Mr Longdon will recommend to you some nice historical work – for we love history, don't we? – that leaves the horrors out. We like to know,' the Duchess explained to the authority she invoked, 'the cheerful, happy, *right* things. There are so many, after all, and this is the place to remember them. *A tantôt.*'

As she passed into the house by the nearest of the long windows that stood open Mr Longdon placed himself beside her little charge, whom he treated, for the next ten minutes, with an exquisite courtesy. A person who knew him well would, if present at the scene, have found occasion in it to be freshly aware that he was in his quiet way master of two distinct kinds of urbanity, the kind that added to distance and the kind that diminished it. Such an analyst would furthermore have noted, in respect to the aunt and the niece, of which kind each had the benefit, and might even have gone so far as to detect in him some absolute betrayal of the impression produced on him by his actual companion, some irradiation of his certitude that, from the point of view under which she had been formed, she was a remarkable, a rare success. Since to create a particular little rounded and tinted innocence had been aimed at, the fruit had been grown to the perfection of a peach on a sheltered wall, and this quality of the object resulting from a process might well make him feel himself in contact with something wholly new. Little Aggie differed from any young person he had ever met in that she had been deliberately prepared for consumption and in that furthermore the gentleness of her spirit had immensely helped the preparation. Nanda, beside her, was a northern savage, and the reason was partly that the elements of that young lady's nature were already, were publicly, were almost indecorously active. They were practically there for good or for ill; experience was still to come and what they might work out to still a mystery; but the sum would get itself done with the figures now on the slate. On little Aggie's slate the figures were yet to be written; which sufficiently accounted for the difference of the two surfaces. Both the girls struck him as lambs with the great shambles of life in their future; but while one, with its neck in pink ribbon, had no consciousness but that of being fed from the hand with the small sweet biscuit of unobjectionable knowledge, the other struggled with instincts and forebodings, with the suspicion of its doom and the far-borne scent, in the flowery fields, of blood.

'Oh, Nanda, she's my best friend after three or four others.'

'After so many?' Mr Longdon laughed. 'Don't you think that's rather a back seat, as they say, for one's best?'

'A back seat?' – she wondered with a purity!

'If you don't understand,' said her companion, 'it serves me right, as your aunt didn't leave me with you to teach you the slang of the day.'

'The "slang"?' – she again spotlessly speculated.

'You've never even heard the expression? I should think that a great compliment to our time if it weren't that I fear it may have been only the name that has been kept from you.'

The light of ignorance in the child's smile was positively golden. 'The name?' she again echoed.

She understood too little – he gave it up. 'And who are all the other best friends whom poor Nanda comes after?'

'Well, there's my aunt, and Miss Merriman, and Gelsomina, and Dr Beltram.'

'And who, please, is Miss Merriman?'

'She's my governess, don't you know? – but such a deliciously easy governess.'

'That, I suppose, is because she has such a deliciously easy pupil. And who is Gelsomina?' Mr Longdon inquired.

'She's my old nurse – my old maid.'

'I see. Well, one must always be kind to old maids. But who is Dr Beltram?'

'Oh, the most intimate friend of all. We tell him everything.'

There was for Mr Longdon in this, with a slight uncertainty, an effect of drollery. 'Your little troubles?'

'Ah, they're not always so little! And he takes them all away.'

'Always? – on the spot?'

'Sooner or later,' said little Aggie with serenity. 'But why not?'

'Why not indeed?' he laughed. 'It must be very plain sailing.' Decidedly, she was, as Nanda had said, an angel, and there was a wonder in her possession on this footing of one of the most expressive little faces that even her expressive race had ever shown him. Formed to express everything, it scarce expressed as yet even a consciousness. All the elements of play were in it, but they had nothing to play with. It was a rest moreover, after so much that he had lately been through, to be with a person for whom questions were so simple. 'But he sounds all the same like the kind of doctor whom, as soon as one hears of him, one wants to send for.'

The young girl had at this a small light of confusion. 'Oh, I don't mean he's a doctor for medicine. He's a clergyman – and my aunt says he's a saint. I don't think you've many in England,' little Aggie continued to explain.

'Many saints? I'm afraid not. Your aunt's happy to know one. We should call Dr Beltram in England a priest.'

'Oh, but he's English. And he knows everything we do – and everything we think.'

'"We" – your aunt, your governess and your nurse? What a varied wealth of knowledge!'

'Ah, Miss Merriman and Gelsomina tell him only what they like.'

'And do you and the Duchess tell him what you *don't* like?'

'Oh, often – but we always like *him* – no matter what we tell him. And we know that just the same he always likes us.'

'I see then of course,' said Mr Longdon, very gravely now, 'what a friend he must be. So it's after all this,' he continued in a moment, 'that Nanda comes in?'

His companion had to consider, but suddenly she caught assistance. 'This one, I think, comes before.' Lord Petherton, arriving apparently from the garden, had drawn near unobserved by Mr Longdon, and the next moment was within hail. 'I see him very often,' she continued – 'oftener than Nanda. Oh, but *then* Nanda. And then,' little Aggie wound up, 'Mr Mitchy.'

'Oh, I'm glad *he* comes in,' Mr Longdon returned, 'though rather far down in the list.' Lord Petherton was now before them, there being no one else on the terrace to speak to, and, with the odd look of an excess of physical power that almost blocked the way, he seemed to give them in the flare of his big teeth the benefit of a kind of brutal geniality. It was always to be remembered for him that he could scarce show without surprising you an adjustment to the smaller conveniences; so that when he took up a trifle it was not perforce in every case the sign of an uncanny calculation. When the elephant in the show plays the fiddle it must be mainly with the presumption of consequent apples; which was why, doubtless, this personage had half the time the air of assuring you that, really civilized as his type had now become, no apples were required. Mr Longdon viewed him with a vague apprehension and as if quite unable to meet the question of what he would have called for such a personage the social responsibility. Did this specimen of his class pull the tradition down or did he just take it where he found it – in the very different place from that in which, on ceasing so long ago to 'go out', Mr Longdon had left it? Our friend doubtless averted himself from the possibility of a mental dilemma; if the man didn't lower the position was it the position then that let down the man? Somehow he wasn't positively up. More evidence would be needed to decide; yet it was just of more evidence that one remained rather in dread. Lord Petherton was kind to little Aggie, kind to her companion, kind to every one, after Mr Longdon had explained that she was so good as to be giving him the list of her dear friends. 'I'm only a little dismayed,' the elder man said, 'to find Mr Mitchett at the bottom.'

'Oh, but it's an awfully short list, isn't it? If it consists only of me and Mitchy he's not so very low down. We don't allow her very *many* friends; we look out too well for ourselves.' He addressed the child as on an easy jocose understanding. 'Is the question, Aggie, whether we shall allow you Mr Longdon? Won't that rather "do" for us – for Mitchy and me? I say, Duchess,' he went on as this lady reappeared, '*are* we going to allow her Mr Longdon and do we quite realize what we're about? We mount guard awfully, you know' – he carried the joke back to the person he had named. 'We sift and we sort, we pick the candidates over, and I should like to hear any one say that in this case at least I don't keep a watch on my taste. Oh, we close in!'

The Duchess, with the object of her quest in her hand, had come back. 'Well then Mr Longdon will close *with* us – you'll consider henceforth that he's as safe as yourself. Here's the letter that I wanted you to read – with which you'll please take a turn, in strict charge of the child, and then restore her to us. If you don't come I shall know you have found Mitchy and shall be at peace. Go, little heart,' she continued to the child, 'but leave me your book to look over again. I don't know that I'm quite sure!' She sent them off together, but had a grave protest as her friend put out his hand for the volume. 'No, Petherton – not for books; for her reading I can't say I do trust you. But for everything else – quite!' she declared to Mr Longdon with a look of conscientious courage as their companion withdrew. 'I do believe,' she pursued in the same spirit, 'in a certain amount of intelligent confidence. Really nice men are steadied by the sense of your having had it. But I wouldn't,' she added gaily, 'trust *him* all round!'

XIX

MANY things at Mertle were strange for her interlocutor, but nothing perhaps as yet had been so strange as the sight of this arrangement for little Aggie's protection – an arrangement made in the interest of her remaining as a young person of her age and her *monde*, as her aunt would have said, should remain. The strangest part of this impression too was that the provision might really have its happy side and his lordship really understand better than any one else his noble friend's whole theory of perils and precautions. The child herself, the spectator of the incident was sure enough, understood nothing, but the understandings that surrounded her, filling all the air, made it a heavier compound to breathe than any Mr Longdon had yet tasted. This heaviness had grown for him through the long, sweet summer day, and there was something in his at last finding himself ensconced with the Duchess that made it supremely oppressive. The contact was one that, none the less, he would not have availed himself of a decent pretext to avoid. With so many fine mysteries playing about him there was relief, at the point he had reached, rather than alarm, in the thought of knowing the worst; which it pressed upon him somehow that the Duchess must not only supremely know but must in any relation most naturally communicate. It fluttered him rather that a person who had an understanding with Lord Petherton should so single him out as to wish for one also with himself: such a person must either have a great variety of mind or have a wonderful idea of *his* variety. It was true indeed that Mr Mitchett must have the most extraordinary understanding, and yet with Mr Mitchett he now found himself quite pleasantly at his ease. Their host, however, was a person *sui generis*, whom he had accepted, once for all, the inconsequence of liking in pursuance of the need he occasionally felt to put it on record that he was not narrow-minded. Perhaps at bottom he most liked Mitchy because Mitchy most liked Nanda; there hung about him still moreover the faded fragrance of the superstition that hospitality not declined is one of the things that 'oblige'. It obliged the thoughts for Mr Longdon as well as the manners and in the especial form in which he was now committed to it would have made him, had he really thought any ill, ask himself what the deuce then he was doing in the man's house. All of which didn't prevent some of Mitchy's queer condonations – if condonations in fact they were – from not wholly, by themselves, soothing his vague unrest, an unrest which never had been so great as at the moment he heard the Duchess abruptly say to him: 'Do you know my idea about Nanda? It's my particular desire that you should – the reason, really, why I've thus laid violent hands on you. Nanda, my dear man, should marry the very first moment.'

This was more interesting than he had expected, and the effect produced by his interlocutress, and doubtless not lost on her, was shown in his suppressed start. 'There has been no reason why I should attribute to you any judgement of the matter; but I've had one myself, and I don't see why I shouldn't say frankly that it's very much the one you express. It should be a very good thing.'

'A very good thing, but none of my business?' – the Duchess's briskness was not unamiable.

It was on this circumstance that her companion for an instant perhaps meditated. 'It's probably not in my interest to say that – I should give you too easy a retort. It would strike any one as quite as much your business as mine.'

'Well, it ought to be somebody's, you know. One would suppose it to be her mother's – her father's; but in this country the parents are even more emancipated than the children. Suppose, really, since it appears to be nobody's affair, that you and I *do* make it ours. We needn't either of us,' she continued, 'be concerned for the other's reasons, though I'm perfectly ready, I assure you, to put my cards on the table. You've your feelings – we know they're beautiful. I, on my side, have mine – for which I don't pretend anything but that they're strong. They can dispense with being beautiful, when they're so perfectly settled. Besides, I may mention, they're rather nice than otherwise. Edward and I have a *cousinage*, though for all he does to keep it up—! If he leaves his children to play in the street I take it seriously enough to make an occasional dash for them before they're run over. And I want for Nanda simply the man she herself wants – it isn't as if I wanted for her a dwarf or a hunchback or a *coureur* or a drunkard. Vanderbank's a man whom any woman, don't you think? might be – whom more than one woman *is* – glad of for herself: *beau comme le jour*, awfully conceited and awfully patronizing, but clever and successful and yet liked, and without, so far as I know, any of the terrific appendages which in this country so often diminish the value of even the pleasantest people. He hasn't five horrible unmarried sisters for his wife to have always on a visit. The way your women don't marry is the ruin here of society, and I've been assured in good quarters – though I don't know so much about that – the ruin also of conversation and of literature. Isn't it precisely just a little to keep Nanda herself from becoming that kind of appendage – say to poor Harold, say, one of these days, to her younger brother and sister – that friends like you and me feel the importance of bestirring ourselves in time? Of course she's supposedly young, but she's really any age you like: your London world so fearfully batters and bruises them.'

She had gone fast and far, but it had given Mr Longdon time to feel himself well afloat. There were so many things in it all to take up that he laid his hand – of which, he was not unconscious, the feebleness exposed him – on the nearest. 'Why, I'm sure her mother – after twenty years of it – is fresh enough.'

'Fresh? You find Mrs Brook fresh?'

The Duchess had a manner that, in its all-knowingness, rather humiliated than encouraged; but he was all the more resolute for being conscious of his own reserves. 'It seems to me it's fresh to look about thirty.'

'That indeed would be perfect. But she doesn't – she looks about three. She simply looks a baby.'

'Oh Duchess, you're really too particular!' he returned, feeling that, as the trodden worm will turn, anxiety itself may sometimes tend to wit.

She met him in her own way. 'I know what I mean. My niece is a person *I* call fresh. It's warranted, as they say in the shops. Besides,' she went on, 'if a married woman has been knocked about, that's only a part of her condition. *Elle l'a bien voulu*, and if you're married you're married; it's the smoke – or call it the soot! – of the fire. You know, yourself,' she roundly pursued, 'that Nanda's situation appals you.'

'Oh, "appals"!' he restrictively murmured.

It even tried a little his companion's patience. 'There you are, you English – you'll never face your own music. It's amazing what you'd rather do with a thing – anything not to shoot at or to make money with – than look at its meaning. If I wished to save the girl as *you* wish it I should know exactly from what. But why differ about reasons,' she asked, 'when we're at one about the fact? I don't mention the greatest of Vanderbank's merits,' she added – 'his having so delicious a friend. By whom, let me hasten to assure you,' she laughed, 'I don't in the least mean Mrs Brook! She *is* delicious, if you like, but believe me when I tell you, *caro mio* – if you need to be told – that for effective action on him you're worth twenty of her.'

What was most visible in Mr Longdon was that, however it came to him, he had rarely before, all at once, had so much given him to think about. Again the only way to manage was to take what came uppermost. 'By effective action you mean on the matter of his proposing for Nanda?'

The Duchess's assent was noble. 'You can make him propose – you can make, I mean, a sure thing of it. You can *doter* the bride.' Then as with the impulse to meet benevolently and more than half-way her companion's imperfect apprehension: 'You can settle on her something that will make her a *parti*.' His apprehension was perhaps imperfect, but it could still lead somehow to his flushing all over, and this demonstration the Duchess as quickly took into account. 'Poor Edward, you know, won't give her a penny.'

Decidedly she went fast, but Mr Longdon in a moment had caught up. 'Mr Vanderbank – your idea is – would require on the part of his wife something of that sort?'

'Pray, who wouldn't – in the world we all move in – require it quite as much? Mr Vanderbank, I'm assured, has no means of his own at all, and if he doesn't believe in impecunious marriages it's not I who shall be shocked at him. For myself I simply despise them. He has nothing but a poor official salary. If it's enough for one it would be little enough for two, and would be still less for half a dozen. They're just the people to have, that blessed pair, a fine old English family.'

Mr Longdon was now fairly abreast of it. 'What it comes to then, the idea you're so good as to put before me, is to bribe him to take her.'

The Duchess remained bland, but she fixed him. 'You say that as if you were scandalized, but if you try Mr Van with it I don't think he'll be. And you won't persuade me,' she went on finely, 'that you haven't, yourself, thought of it.' She kept her eyes on him, and the effect of them, soon enough visible in his face, was such as presently to make her exult at her felicity. 'You're of a limpidity, dear man! – you've only to be said "bo!" to and you confess. Consciously or unconsciously – the former, really, I'm inclined to think – you've wanted him for her.' She paused an instant to enjoy her triumph; after which she continued: 'And you've wanted her for him. I make you out, you'll say – for I see you coming – one of those horrible benevolent busybodies who are the worst of the class, but you've only to think a little – if I may go so far – to see that no "making" at all is required. You've only one link with the Brooks, but that link is golden. How can we, all of us, by this time, not have grasped and admired the beauty of your feeling for Lady Julia? There it is – I make you wince: to speak of it is to profane it. Let us by all means not speak of it then, but let us act on it.' He had at least turned his face from her, and it now took in, from the vantage of his high position, only the loveliness of the place and the hour, which included a glimpse of Lord Petherton and little Aggie, who, down in the garden, slowly strolled in familiar union. Each had a hand in the other's, swinging easily as they went; their talk was evidently of flowers and fruits and birds; it was quite like father and daughter. And one could see half a mile off in short that *they* weren't flirting. Our friend's bewilderment came in odd, cold gusts: these were unreasoned and capricious; one of them, at all events, during his companion's pause, must have roared in his ears. Was it not therefore through some continuance of the sound that he heard her go on speaking? 'Of course you know the poor child's own condition.'

It took him a good while to answer. 'Do *you* know it?' he asked with his eyes still away.

'If your question's ironical,' she laughed, 'your irony's perfectly wasted. I should be ashamed of myself if, with my relationship and my interest, I hadn't made sure. Nanda's fairly sick – as sick as a little cat – with her passion.' It was with an intensity of silence that Mr Longdon appeared to accept this; he was even so dumb for a minute that the oddity of the image could draw from him no natural sound. The Duchess once more, accordingly, recognized an opportunity. 'It has doubtless already occurred to you that, since your sentiment for the living is the charming fruit of your sentiment for the dead, there would be a sacrifice to Lady Julia's memory more exquisite than any other.'

At this finally Mr Longdon turned. 'The effort – on the lines you speak of – for Nanda's happiness?'

She fairly glowed with hope. 'And, by the same token such a piece of poetic justice! Quite the loveliest it would be, I think, one had ever heard of.'

So, for some time more, they sat confronted. 'I don't quite see your difficulty,' he said at last. 'I do happen to know, I confess, that Nanda herself extremely desires the execution of your project.'

His friend's smile betrayed no surprise at this effect of her eloquence. 'You're bad at dodging. Nanda's desire is inevitably to stop off for herself every question of any one but Vanderbank. If she wants me to succeed in arranging with Mr Mitchett can you ask for a plainer sign of her private predicament? But you've signs enough, I see' – she caught herself up: 'we may take them all for granted. I've seen perfectly from the first that the only difficulty would come from her mother – but also that that would be stiff.'

The movement with which Mr Longdon removed his glasses might have denoted a certain fear to participate in too much of what the Duchess could see. 'I've not been ignorant that Mrs Brookenham favours Mr Mitchett.'

But he was not to be let off with that. 'Then you've not been blind, I suppose, to her reason for doing so.' He might not have been blind, but his vision, at this, scarce showed sharpness, and it determined in his interlocutress the shortest of short-cuts. 'She favours Mr Mitchett because she wants "old Van" herself.'

He was evidently conscious of looking at her hard. 'In what sense – herself?'

'Ah, you must supply the sense; I can give you only the fact – and it's the fact that concerns us. *Voyons*,' she almost impatiently broke out; 'don't try to create unnecessary obscurities by being unnecessarily modest. Besides, I'm not touching your modesty. Supply any sense whatever that may miraculously satisfy your fond English imagination: I don't insist in the least on a bad one. She does want him herself – that's all I say. "*Pourquoi faire?*" you ask – or rather, being too shy, don't ask, but would like to if you dared or didn't fear I'd be shocked. I *can't* be shocked, but, frankly, I can't tell you either. The situation belongs, I think, to an order I don't understand. I understand either one thing or the other – I understand taking a man up or letting him alone. But I don't really get at Mrs Brook. You must judge at any rate for yourself. Vanderbank could of course tell you if he would – but it wouldn't be right that he should. So the one thing we have to do with is that she's in fact against us. I can only work Mitchy through Petherton, but Mrs Brook can work him straight. On the other hand that's the way you, my dear man, can work Vanderbank.'

One thing evidently beyond the rest, as a result of this vivid demonstration, disengaged itself to Mr Longdon's undismayed sense, but his consternation needed a minute or two to produce it. 'I can absolutely assure you that Mr Vanderbank entertains no sentiment for Mrs Brookenham—'

'That he may not keep under by just setting his teeth and holding on? I never dreamed that he does, and have nothing so alarming in store for you – *rassurez-vous bien!* – as to propose that he shall be invited to sink a feeling for the mother in order to take one up for the child. Don't, please, flutter out of the whole question by a premature scare. I never supposed it's he who wants to keep *her*. He's not in love with her – be comforted! But she's amusing – highly amusing. I do her perfect justice. As your women go, she's rare. If she were French she'd be a *femme d'esprit*.

She has invented a *nuance* of her own and she has done it
all by herself, for Edward figures in her drawing-room only
as one of those queer extinguishers of fire in the corridors of
hotels. He's just a bucket on a peg. The men, the young and
the clever ones, find it a house – and heaven knows they're
right – with intellectual elbow-room, with freedom of talk.
Most English talk is like a quadrille in a sentry box. You'll
tell me we go further in Italy, and I won't deny it, but in
Italy we have the common-sense not to have little girls in
the room. The young men hang about Mrs Brook and the
clever ones ply her with the uproarious appreciation that
keeps her up to the mark. She's in a prodigious fix – she must
sacrifice either her daughter or what she once called to me
her intellectual habits. Mr Vanderbank, you've seen for
yourself, is of these one of the most cherished, the most confirmed. Three months ago – it couldn't be any longer kept
off – Nanda began definitely to "sit" – to be there and look,
by the tea-table, modestly and conveniently abstracted.'

'I beg your pardon – I don't think she looks *that*, Duchess,'
Mr Longdon lucidly broke in. How much she had carried
him with her in spite of himself was betrayed by the very
terms of his dissent. 'I don't think it would strike any one
that she looks "convenient."'

His companion, laughing, gave a shrug. 'Try her and
perhaps you'll find her so!' But his objection had none the
less pulled her up a little. 'I don't say she's a hypocrite, for
it would certainly be less decent for her to giggle and wink.
It's Mrs Brook's theory moreover, isn't it? that she has, from
five to seven at least, lowered the pitch. Doesn't she pretend
that she bears in mind every moment the tiresome difference
made by the presence of sweet virginal eighteen?'

'I haven't, I'm afraid, a notion of what she pretends!'

Mr Longdon had spoken with a curtness to which his
friend's particular manner of overlooking it only added
significance. 'They've become,' she pursued, 'superficial or
insincere or frivolous, but at least they've become, with the
way the drag's put on, quite as dull as other people.'

He showed no sign of taking this up; instead of it he
said abruptly: 'But if it isn't Mr Mitchett's own idea?'

His fellow-visitor barely hesitated. 'It would be his own

if he were free – and it would be Lord Petherton's *for* him. I mean by his being free Nanda's becoming definitely lost to him. Then it would be impossible for Mrs Brook to continue to persuade him, as she does now, that by a waiting game he'll come to his chance. His chance will cease to exist, and he wants so, poor darling, to marry. You've really now seen my niece,' she went on. 'That's another reason why I hold you can help me.'

'Yes – I've seen her.'

'Well, there she is.' It was as if in the pause that followed this they sat looking at little absent Aggie with a wonder that was almost equal. 'The good God has given her to me,' the Duchess said at last.

'It seems to me then that she herself is, in her remarkable loveliness, really your help.'

'She will be doubly so if you give me proofs that you believe in her.' And the Duchess, appearing to consider that with this she had made herself clear and her interlocutor plastic, rose in confident majesty. 'I leave it to you.'

Mr Longdon did the same, but with more consideration now. 'Is it your expectation that I will speak to Mr Mitchett?'

'Don't flatter yourself he won't speak to *you*!'

Mr Longdon made it out. 'As supposing me, you mean, an interested party?'

She clapped her gloved hands with joy. 'It's a delight to hear you practically admit that you *are* one! Mr Mitchett will take anything from you – above all perfect candour. It isn't every day one meets *your* kind, and he's a connoisseur. I leave it to you – I leave it to you.'

She spoke as if it were something she had thrust bodily into his hands and wished to hurry away from. He put his hands behind him – straightening himself a little, half kindled, still half confused. 'You're all extraordinary people!'

She gave a toss of her head that showed a limited enthusiasm. 'You're the best of us, *caro mio* – you and Aggie: for Aggie's as good as you. Mitchy's good too, however – Mitchy's beautiful. You see it's not only his money. He's a gentleman. So are you. There aren't so many. But we move fast,' she added more sharply.

'What do you mean by fast?'

'What should I mean but what I say? If Nanda doesn't get a husband early in the business—'

'Well?' said Mr Longdon, as she appeared to pause with the weight of her idea.

'Why, she won't get one late – she won't get one at all. One, I mean, of the kind she'll take. She'll have been in it too long for *their* taste.'

She had moved, looking off and about her – little Aggie always on her mind – to the flight of steps, where she again hung fire; and had really succeeded in producing in him the manner of keeping up with her to challenge her. 'Been in what?'

She went down a few steps while he stood with his face full of perceptions strained and scattered. 'Why, in the *mal' aria* they themselves have made for her!'

XX

LATE that night in the smoking-room at Mertle, as the smokers – talkers and listeners alike – were about to disperse, Mr Longdon asked Vanderbank to stay, and then it was that the young man, to whom all the evening he had not addressed a word, could make out why, a little unnaturally, he had prolonged his vigil. 'I've something particular to say to you, and I've been waiting. I hope you don't mind. It's rather important.' Vanderbank expressed on the spot the liveliest desire to oblige him and, quickly lighting another cigarette, mounted again to the deep divan with which a part of the place was furnished. The smoking-room at Mertle was not unworthy of the general nobleness, and the fastidious spectator had clearly been reckoned on in the great leather-covered lounge that, raised by a step or two above the floor, applied its back to two quarters of the wall and enjoyed, most immediately, a view of the billiard-table. Mr Longdon continued for a minute to roam with the air of dissimulated absence that, during the previous hour and among the other men, his companion's eye had not lost; he pushed a ball or two about, examined the form of an ash-stand, swung his glasses almost with violence and declined either to smoke or to sit down. Vanderbank, perched aloft on the bench and awaiting developments, had a little the look of some prepossessing criminal who, in court, should have changed places with the judge. He was unlike many a man of marked good looks in that the effect of evening dress was not, with a perversity often observed in such cases, to overemphasize his fineness. His type was rather chastened than heightened, and he sat there moreover with a primary discretion quite in the note of the deference that, from the first with this friend of the elder fashion, he had taken as imposed. He had a strong sense for shades of respect and was now careful to loll scarcely more than with an official superior. 'If you ask me,' Mr Longdon presently continued, 'why at this hour of the night – after a day at best too heterogeneous – I don't keep over till tomorrow whatever I may have to say, I can only tell you that I appeal to you now because I've something on my mind that I shall sleep the better for being rid of.'

There was space to circulate in front of the dais, where he had still paced and still swung his glasses; but with these words he had paused, leaning against the billiard-table, to meet the interested urbanity of the reply they produced. 'Are you very sure that, having got rid of it, you *will* sleep? Is it a pure confidence,' Vanderbank said, 'that you do me the honour to make to me? Is it something terrific that requires a reply, so that I shall have to take account, on my side, of the rest I may deprive you of?'

'Don't take account of anything – I'm myself a man who always takes too much. It isn't a matter about which I press you for an immediate answer. You can give me no answer probably without a good deal of thought. *I've* thought a good deal – otherwise I wouldn't speak. I only want to put something before you and leave it there.'

'I never see you,' said Vanderbank, 'that you don't put something before me.'

'That sounds,' his friend returned, 'as if I rather over-loaded – what's the sort of thing you fellows nowadays say?

– your intellectual board. If there's a congestion of dishes sweep everything without scruple away. I've never put before you anything like this.'

He spoke with a weight that in the great space, where it resounded a little, made an impression – an impression marked by the momentary pause that fell between them. He partly broke the silence first by beginning to walk again, and then Vanderbank broke it as though the apprehension of their becoming perhaps too solemn. 'Well, you immensely interest me and you really couldn't have chosen a better time. A secret – for we shall make it that of course, shan't we? – at this witching hour, in this great old house, is all that my visit here will have required to make the whole thing a rare remembrance. So, I assure you, the more you put before me the better.'

Mr Longdon took up another ash-tray, but with the air of doing so as a direct consequence of Vanderbank's tone. After he had laid it down he put on his glasses; then fixing his companion he brought out: 'Have you no idea at all—?'

'Of what you have in your head? Dear Mr Longdon, how *should* I have?'

'Well, I'm wondering if I shouldn't perhaps have a little in your place. There's nothing that in the circumstances occurs to you as likely for me to want to say?'

Vanderbank gave a laugh that might have struck an auditor as slightly uneasy. 'When you speak of "the circumstances" you do a thing that – unless you mean the simple thrilling ones of this particular moment – always of course opens the door of the lurid for a man of any imagination. To such a man you've only to give a nudge for his conscience to jump. That's at any rate the case with mine. It's never quite on its feet – so it's now already on its back.' He stopped a little – his smile was a trifle strained. 'Is what you want to put before me something awful I've done?'

'Excuse me if I press this point.' Mr Longdon spoke kindly, but if his friend's want of ease grew his own thereby diminished. 'Can you think of nothing at all?'

'Do you mean that I've done?'

'No, but that – whether you've done it or not – I may have become aware of.'

There could have been no better proof than Vanderbank's expression, on this, of his having mastered the secret of humouring without appearing to patronize. 'I think you ought to give me a little more of a clue.'

Mr Longdon took off his glasses. 'Well – the clue's Nanda Brookenham.'

'Oh, I see.' Vanderbank had responded quickly, but for a minute he said nothing more, and the great marble clock that gave the place the air of a club ticked louder in the stillness. Mr Longdon waited with a benevolent want of mercy, yet with a look in his face that spoke of what depended for him – though indeed very far within – on the upshot of his patience. The hush, for that matter, between them, became a conscious public measure of the young man's honesty. He evidently at last felt it as such, and there would have been for an observer of his handsome, controlled face a study of some sharp things. 'I judge that you ask me for an utterance,' he finally said, 'that very few persons at any time have the right to expect of a man. Think of the people – and very decent ones – to whom on many a question one can only reply at best that it's none of their business.'

'I see you know what I mean,' said Mr Longdon.

'Then you know also the distinguished exception I make of you. There isn't another man with whom I'd talk of it.'

'And even to me you don't! But I'm none the less obliged to you,' Mr Longdon added.

'It isn't only the gravity,' his friend went on; 'it's the ridicule that inevitably attaches—'

The manner in which Mr Longdon indicated the empty room was in itself an interruption. 'Don't I sufficiently spare you?'

'Thank you, thank you,' said Vanderbank.

'Besides, it's not for nothing.'

'Of course not!' the young man returned, but with a look of noting the next moment a certain awkwardness in his concurrence. 'But don't spare me now.'

'I don't mean to.' Mr Longdon had his back to the table again, on which he rested with each hand on the rim. 'I don't mean to,' he repeated.

His companion gave a laugh that betrayed at least the drop of a tension. 'Yet I don't quite see what you can do to me.'

'It's just what, for some time past, I've been trying to think.'

'And at last you've discovered?'

'Well – it has finally glimmered out a little in this extraordinary place.'

Vanderbank frankly wondered. 'In consequence of anything particular that has happened?'

Mr Longdon had a pause. 'For an old idiot who notices as much as I, something particular is always happening. If you're a man of imagination—'

'Oh,' Vanderbank broke in. 'I know how much more in that case you're one! It only makes me regret,' he continued, 'that I've not attended more since yesterday to what you've been about.'

'I've been about nothing but what among you people I'm always about. I've been seeing, feeling, thinking. That makes no show, of course I'm aware, for any one but myself, and it's wholly my own affair. Except indeed,' he added, 'so far as I've taken into my head to make, on it all, this special appeal. There are things that have come home to me.'

'Oh, I see, I see' – Vanderbank showed the friendliest alertness. 'I'm to take it from you then, with all the avidity of my vanity, that I strike you as the person best able to understand what they are.'

Mr Longdon appeared to wonder an instant if his intelligence now had not almost too much of a glitter; he kept the same position, his back against the table, and while Vanderbank, on the settee, pressed upright against the wall, they recognized in silence that they were trying each other. 'You're much the best of them. I've my ideas about you. You've great gifts.'

'Well then, we're worthy of each other. When Greek meets Greek—!' and the young man laughed as, a little with the air of bracing himself, he folded his arms. 'Here we are.'

His companion looked at him a moment longer, then, turning away, went slowly round the table. On the further side of it he stopped again and, after a minute, with a nervous movement, set a ball or two in motion. 'It's beautiful – but it's terrible!' he finally murmured. He had not his eyes on Vanderbank, who for a minute said nothing, and he presently went on: 'To see it and not to want to try to help – well, I can't do that.' Vanderbank still neither spoke nor moved, remained as if he might interrupt something of high importance to him, and his friend, passing along the opposite edge of the table, continued to produce in the stillness, without the cue, the small click of the ivory. 'How long – if you don't mind my asking – have you known it?'

Even for this at first Vanderbank had no answer – none but to rise from his place, come down to the floor and, standing there, look at Mr Longdon across the table. He was serious now, but without being solemn. 'How can one tell? One can never be sure. A man may fancy, may wonder, but with a girl, a person so much younger than himself and so much more helpless, he feels a – what shall I call it?'

'A delicacy?' Mr Longdon suggested.

'It may be that; the name doesn't matter; at all events he's embarrassed. He wants not to be an ass on the one side and yet not some other kind of brute on the other.'

Mr Longdon listened with consideration – with a beautiful little air indeed of being, in his all but finally contracted state, earnestly open to information on such points from a magnificent young man. 'He doesn't want, you mean, to be a coxcomb? – and he doesn't want to be cruel?'

Vanderbank, visibly preoccupied, produced a faint, kind smile. 'Oh, *you* know!'

'I? I should know less than any one.'

Mr Longdon had turned away from the table on this, and the eyes of his companion, who after an instant had caught his meaning, watched him move along the room and approach another part of the divan. The consequence of the passage was that Vanderbank's only rejoinder was presently to say: 'I can't tell you how long I've imagined – have asked myself. She's so charming – so interesting, and I feel as if I had known her always. I've thought of one thing and another to do – and then, on purpose, I haven't thought at all. That has mostly seemed to me best.'

'Then I gather,' said Mr Longdon, 'that your interest in her—'

'Hasn't the same character as her interest in *me*?' Vanderbank had taken him up responsively, but after speaking looked about for a match and lighted a new cigarette. 'I'm sure you understand,' he broke out, 'what an extreme effort it is to me to talk of such things!'

'Yes, yes. But it's just effort only? It gives you no pleasure? I mean the fact of her condition,' Mr Longdon explained.

Vanderbank had really to think a little. 'However much it might give me I should probably not be a fellow to gush. I'm a self-conscious stick of a Briton.'

'But even a stick of a Briton—!' Mr Longdon hesitated. 'I've gushed in short to *you*.'

'About Lady Julia?' the young man frankly asked. 'Is that what you call it?'

'Say then we're sticks of Britons. You're not in any degree at all in love?'

There fell between them, before Vanderbank replied, another pause, of which he took advantage to move once more round the table. Mr Longdon meanwhile had mounted to the high bench and sat there as if the judge were now in his proper place. At last his companion spoke. 'What you're coming to is of course that you've conceived a desire.'

'That's it – strange as it may seem. But, believe me, it has not been precipitate. I've watched you both.'

'Oh, I knew you were watching *her*,' said Vanderbank.

'To such a tune that I've made up my mind. I want her so to marry—' But on the odd little quaver of longing with which he brought it out the old man fairly hung.

'Well?' said Vanderbank.

'Well, so that on the day she does she'll come into the

interest of a considerable sum of money – already very decently invested – that I've determined to settle upon her.'

Vanderbank's instant admiration flushed across the room. 'How awfully jolly of you – how beautiful!'

'Oh, there's a way to show practically your appreciation of it.'

But Vanderbank, for enthusiasm, scarcely heard him. 'I can't tell you how admirable I think you.' Then eagerly, 'Does Nanda know it?' he demanded.

Mr Longdon, after an hesitation, spoke with comparative dryness. 'My idea has been that for the present you alone shall.'

Vanderbank also hesitated. 'No other man?'

His companion looked still graver. 'I need scarcely say that I depend on you to keep the fact to yourself.'

'Absolutely then and utterly. But that won't prevent what I think of it. Nothing for a long time has given me such joy.'

Shining and sincere, he had held for a minute Mr Longdon's eyes. 'Why, you do care for her.'

'Immensely. Never, I think, so much as now. That sounds of a grossness, doesn't it?' he laughed. 'But your announcement really lights up the mind.'

His friend for a moment almost glowed with his pleasure. 'The sum I've settled upon would be, I may mention, substantial, and I should of course be prepared with a clear statement – a very definite pledge – of my intentions.'

'So much the better! Only' – Vanderbank suddenly pulled himself up – 'to get it she *must* marry?'

'It's not in my interest to allow you to suppose she needn't, and it's only because of my intense wish for her marriage that I've spoken to you.'

'And on the ground also, with it' – Vanderbank so far concurred – 'of your quite taking for granted my only having to put myself forward?'

If his friend seemed to cast about, it proved but to be for the fullest expression. Nothing in fact could have been more charged than the quiet way in which he presently said: 'My dear boy, I back you.'

Vanderbank clearly was touched by it. 'How extra-

ordinarily kind you are to me!' Mr Longdon's silence
appeared to reply that he was willing to let it go for that,
and the young man next went on: 'What it comes to then –
as you put it – is that it's a way for me to add something
handsome to my income.'

Mr Longdon sat for a little with his eyes attached to the
green field of the billiard-table, vivid in the spreading
suspended lamp-light. 'I think I ought to tell you the
figure I have in mind.'

Another person present might have felt rather taxed
either to determine the degree of provocation represented
by Vanderbank's considerate smile, or to say if there was
an appreciable interval before he rang out: 'I think, you
know, you oughtn't to do anything of the sort. Let that
alone, please. The great thing is the interest – the great
thing is the wish you express. It represents a view of me, an
attitude toward me—!' He pulled up, dropping his arms
and turning away before the complete image.

'There's nothing in those things that need overwhelm
you. It would be odd if you hadn't yourself, about your
value and your future, a feeling quite as lively as any feeling
of mine. There *is* mine at all events. I can't help it. Accept
it. Then of the other feeling – how *she* moves me – I won't
speak.'

'You sufficiently show it!'

Mr Longdon continued to watch the bright circle on the
table, lost in which a moment he let his friend's answer pass.
'I won't begin to you on Nanda.'

'Don't,' said Vanderbank. But in the pause that ensued
each, in one way or another, might have been thinking of
her for himself.

It was broken by Mr Longdon's presently going on: 'Of
course what it superficially has the air of is my offering to
pay you for taking a certain step. It's open to you to be
grand and proud – to wrap yourself in your majesty and
ask if I suppose you bribeable. I haven't spoken without
having thought of that.'

'Yes,' said Vanderbank sympathetically, 'but it isn't as if
you proposed to me, is it, anything dreadful? If one cares
for a girl one's deucedly glad she has money. The more of

anything good she has the better. I may assure you,' he added with the brightness of his friendly intelligence and quite as if to show his companion the way to be least concerned – 'I may assure you that once I were disposed to act on your suggestion I would make short work of any vulgar interpretation of my motive. I should simply try to be as magnificent as yourself.' He smoked, he moved about; then he came up in another place. 'I dare say you know that dear old Mitchy, under whose blessed roof we're plotting this midnight treason, would marry her like a shot and without a penny.'

'I think I know everything – I think I've thought of everything. Mr Mitchett,' Mr Longdon added, 'is impossible.'

Vanderbank appeared for an instant to wonder. 'Wholly then through *her* attitude?'

'Altogether.'

Again he hesitated. 'You've asked her?'

'I've asked her.'

Once more Vanderbank faltered. 'And that's how you know?'

'About *your* chance? That's how I know.'

The young man, consuming his cigarette with concentration, took again several turns. 'And your idea *is* to give one time?'

Mr Longdon had for a minute to turn his idea over. 'How much time do you want?'

Vanderbank gave a head-shake that was both restrictive and indulgent. 'I must live into it a little. Your offer has been before me only these few minutes, and it's too soon for me to commit myself to anything whatever. Except,' he added gallantly, 'my gratitude.'

Mr Longdon, at this, on the divan, got up, as Vanderbank had previously done, under the spring of emotion; only, unlike Vanderbank, he still stood there, his hands in his pockets and his face, a little paler, directed straight. There was disappointment in him even before he spoke. 'You've no strong enough impulse—?'

His friend met him with admirable candour. 'Wouldn't it seem that if I had I would by this time have taken the jump?'

'Without waiting, you mean, for anybody's money?' Mr Longdon cultivated for a little a doubt. 'Of course she has seemed – till now – tremendously young.'

Vanderbank looked about once more for matches and occupied a time with relighting. 'Till now – yes. But it's not,' he pursued, 'only because she's so young that – for each of us, and for dear old Mitchy too – she's so interesting.' Mr Longdon had now stepped down, and Vanderbank's eyes followed him till he stopped again. 'I make out that, in spite of what you said to begin with, you're conscious of a certain pressure.'

'In the matter of time? Oh yes, I do want it *done*. That,' the old man simply explained, 'is why I myself put on the screw.' He spoke with a ring of impatience. 'I want her got out.'

' "Out"?'

'Out of her mother's house.'

Vanderbank laughed, though, more immediately, he had coloured. 'Why her mother's house is just where I see her!'

'Precisely; and if it only were not we might get on faster.'

Vanderbank, for all his kindness, looked still more amused. 'But if it only were not, as you say, I seem to see that you wouldn't have your particular vision of urgency.'

Mr Longdon, through adjusted glasses, took him in with a look that was sad as well as sharp, then jerked the glasses off. 'Oh, you understand me.'

'Ah,' said Vanderbank, 'I'm a mass of corruption!'

'You may perfectly be, but you shall not,' Mr Longdon returned with decision, 'get off on any such plea. If you're good enough for me you're good enough, as you thoroughly know, on whatever head, for any one.'

'Thank you.' But Vanderbank, for all his happy appreciation, thought again. 'We ought, at any rate to remember, oughtn't we? that we should have Mrs Brook against us.'

His companion faltered but an instant. 'Ah, that's another thing I know. But it's also exactly why. Why I want Nanda away.'

'I see, I see.'

The response had been prompt, yet Mr Longdon seemed

suddenly to show that he suspected the superficial. 'Unless it's with Mrs Brook you're in love.' Then on his friend's taking the idea with a mere head-shake of negation, a repudiation that might even have astonished by its own lack of surprise, 'Or unless Mrs Brook's in love with you,' he amended.

Vanderbank had for this any decent gaiety. 'Ah, that of course may perfectly be!'

'But *is* it? That's the question.'

He continued light. 'If she had declared her passion shouldn't I rather compromise her—?'

'By letting me know?' Mr Longdon reflected. 'I'm sure I can't say – it's a sort of thing for which I haven't a measure or a precedent. In my time women didn't declare their passion. I'm thinking of what the meaning is of Mrs Brookenham's wanting you – as I've heard it called – herself.'

Vanderbank, still with his smile, smoked a minute. 'That's what you've heard it called?'

'Yes, but you must excuse me from telling you by whom.'

He was amused at his friend's discretion. 'It's unimaginable. But it doesn't matter. We all call everything – anything. The meaning of it, if you and I put it so, is – well, a modern shade.'

'You must deal then yourself,' said Mr Longdon, 'with your modern shades.' He spoke now as if the case simply awaited such dealing.

But at this his young friend was more grave. '*You* could do nothing? – to bring, I mean, Mrs Brook round?'

Mr Longdon fairly started. 'Propose, on your behalf, for her daughter? With your authority – tomorrow. Authorize me, and I instantly act.'

Vanderbank's colour again rose – his flush was complete. 'How awfully you want it!'

Mr Longdon, after a look at him, turned away. 'How awfully *you* don't!'

The young man continued to blush. 'No – you must do me justice. You've not made a mistake about me – I see in your proposal all, I think, that you can desire I should. Only *you* see it much more simply – and yet I can't just now explain. If it *were* so simple I should say to you in a moment "Do speak to them for me" – I should leave the matter with delight in your hands. But I require time, let me remind you, and you haven't yet told me how much I may take.'

This appeal had brought them again face to face, and Mr Longdon's first reply to it was a look at his watch. 'It's one o'clock.'

'Oh, I require' – Vanderbank had recovered his pleasant humour – 'more than tonight!'

Mr Longdon went off to the smaller table that still offered to view two bedroom candles. 'You must take of course the time you need. I won't trouble you – I won't hurry you. I'm going to bed.'

Vanderbank, overtaking him, lighted his candle for him; after which, handing it and smiling: 'Shall we have conduced to your rest?'

Mr Longdon looked at the other candle. 'You're not coming to bed?'

'To *my* rest we shall not have conduced. I stay up a while longer.'

'Good.' Mr Longdon was pleased. 'You won't forget then, as we promised, to put out the lights?'

'If you trust me for the greater you can trust me for the less. Good-night.'

Vanderbank had put out his hand. 'Good-night.' But Mr Longdon kept him a moment. 'You *don't* care for my figure?'

'Not yet – not yet. *Please.*' Vanderbank seemed really to fear it, but on Mr Longdon's releasing him with a little drop of disappointment they went together to the door of the room, where they had another pause.

'She's to come down to me – alone – in September.'

Vanderbank hesitated. 'Then may *I* come?'

His friend, on this footing, had to consider. 'Shall you know by that time?'

'I'm afraid I can't promise – if you must regard my coming as a pledge.'

Mr Longdon thought on; then raising his eyes: 'I don't quite see why you won't suffer me to tell you—'

'The detail of your intention? *I* do then. You've said quite enough. If my visit positively must commit me,' Vanderbank pursued, 'I'm afraid I can't come.'

Mr Longdon, who had passed into the corridor, gave a dry sad little laugh. 'Come then – as the ladies say – "as you are"!'

On which, rather softly closing the door, Vanderbank remained alone in the great empty, lighted billiard-room.

BOOK VI

MRS BROOK

XXI

PRESENTING himself in Buckingham Crescent three days after the Sunday spent at Mertle, Vanderbank found Lady Fanny Cashmore in the act of taking leave of Mrs Brook, and found Mrs Brook herself in the state of muffled exaltation that was the mark of all her intercourse – and most of all perhaps of her farewells – with Lady Fanny. This splendid creature gave out, as it were, so little that Vanderbank was freshly struck with all Mrs Brook could take in, though nothing, for that matter, in Buckingham Crescent, had been more fully formulated than the imperturbable grandeur of the almost total absence, on the part of the famous beauty, of articulation. Every aspect of the phenomenon had been freely discussed there and endless ingenuity lavished on the question of how exactly it was that so much of what the world would in another case have called complete stupidity could be kept by a mere wonderful face from boring one to death. It was Mrs Brook who, in this relation as in many others, had arrived at the supreme expression of the law, had thrown off, happily enough, to whomever it might have concerned: 'My dear thing, it all comes back, as everything always does, simply to personal pluck. It's only a question, no matter when or where, of having enough. Lady Fanny has the courage of all her silence – so much therefore that it sees her completely through and is what really makes her interesting. Not to be afraid of what may happen to you when you've no more to say for yourself than a steamer without a light – that truly is the highest heroism, and Lady Fanny's greatness is that she's never afraid. She takes the risk every time she goes out – takes, as you may say, her life in her hand. She just turns that glorious mask upon you and practically

says: "No, I won't open my lips – to call it really open –
for the forty minutes I shall stay; but I calmly defy you, all
the same, to kill me for it." And we don't kill her – we
delight in her; though when either of us watches her in a
circle of others it's like seeing a very large blind person in
the middle of Oxford Street. One fairly looks about for the
police.' Vanderbank, before his fellow-visitor withdrew it,
had the benefit of the glorious mask and could scarce have
failed to be amused at the manner in which Mrs Brook
alone showed the stress of thought. Lady Fanny, in the
other scale, sat aloft and Olympian, so that though visibly
much had happened between the two ladies it had all
happened only to the hostess. The sense in the air in short
was just of Lady Fanny herself, who came to an end like a
banquet or a procession. Mrs Brook left the room with
her and, on coming back, was full of it. 'She'll go, she'll
go!'

'Go where?' Vanderbank appeared to have for the
question less attention than usual.

'Well, to the place her companion will propose;
probably – like Anna Karénine – to one of the smaller
Italian towns.'

'Anna Karénine? She isn't a bit like Anna.'

'Of course she isn't so clever,' said Mrs Brook. 'But that
would spoil her. So it's all right.'

'I'm glad it's all right,' Vanderbank laughed. 'But I dare
say we shall still have her with us awhile.'

'We shall do that, I trust, whatever happens. She'll come
up again – she'll remain, I feel, one of those enormous
things that fate seems somehow to have given me as the
occupation of my odd moments. I don't see,' Mrs Brook
added, 'what still keeps her on the edge, which isn't an inch
wide.'

Vanderbank looked this time as if he only tried to
wonder. 'Isn't it *you*?'

Mrs Brook mused more deeply. 'Sometimes I think so.
But I don't know.'

'Yes, how can you of course know, since she can't tell
you?'

'Oh, if I depended on her telling—!' Mrs Brook shook

out, with this, a sofa cushion or two and sank into the
corner she had arranged. The August afternoon was hot
and the London air heavy; the room moreover, though
agreeably bedimmed, gave out the staleness of the season's
end. 'If you hadn't come today,' she went on, 'you would
have missed me till I don't know when, for we've let the
Hovel again – wretchedly, but still we've let it – and I go
down on Friday to see that it isn't too filthy. Edward, who's
furious at what I've taken for it, had his idea that we
should go there this year ourselves.'

'And now' – Vanderbank took her up – 'that fond fancy
has become simply the ghost of a dead thought, a ghost
that, in company with a thousand predecessors, haunts the
house in the twilight and pops at you out of odd corners.'

'Oh, Edward's dead thoughts are indeed a cheerful company and worthy of the perpetual mental mourning we
seem to go about in. They're worse than the relations we're
always losing without seeming to have any fewer, and I
expect every day to hear that the *Morning Post* regrets to
have to announce in that line too some new bereavement.
The apparitions following the deaths of so many thoughts
are particularly awful in the twilight, so that at this season,
while the day drags and drags, I'm glad to have any one
with me who may keep them at a distance.'

Vanderbank had not sat down; slowly, familiarly he
turned about. 'And where's Nanda?'

'Oh, *she* doesn't help – she attracts rather the worst of
the bogies. Edward and Nanda and Harold and I seated
together are fairly a case for that – what do you call it? –
investigating Society. Deprived of the sweet resource of the
Hovel,' Mrs Brook continued, 'we shall each, from about
the tenth on, forage somehow or other for ourselves. Mitchy
perhaps,' she added, 'will insist on taking us to Baireuth.'

'That will be the form, you mean, of his own forage?'

Mrs Brook just hesitated. 'Unless you should prefer to
take it as the form of yours.'

Vanderbank appeared for a moment obligingly enough
to turn this over, but with the effect of perceiving an
objection. 'Oh, I'm afraid I shall have to grind straight
through the month and that by the time I'm free every

Ring at Baireuth will certainly have been rung. Is it your idea to take Nanda?' he asked.

She reached out for another cushion. 'If it's impossible for you to manage what I suggest why should that question interest you?'

'My dear woman' – and her visitor dropped into a chair – 'do you suppose my interest depends on such poverties as what *I* can manage? You know well enough,' he went on in another tone, 'why I care for Nanda and inquire about her.'

She was perfectly ready. 'I know it, but only as a bad reason. Don't be too sure!'

For a moment they looked at each other. 'Don't be so sure, you mean, that the elation of it may go to my head? Are you really warning me against vanity?'

'Your "reallys," my dear Van, are a little formidable, but it strikes me that, before I tell you, there's something I've a right to ask. Are you "really" what they call thinking of my daughter?'

'Your asking,' Vanderbank returned, 'exactly shows the state of your knowledge of the matter. I don't quite see moreover why you speak as if I were paying an abrupt and unnatural attention. What have I done the last three months but talk to you about her? What have you done but talk to *me* about her? From the moment you first spoke to me – "monstrously", I remember you called it – of the difference made in your social life by her finally established, her perpetual, her inexorable participation: from that moment what have we both done but put our heads together over the question of keeping the place tidy, as you called it – or as *I* called it, was it? – for the young female mind?'

Mrs Brook faced serenely enough the directness of this challenge. 'Well, what are you coming to? I spoke of the change in my life of course; I happen to be so constituted that my life has something to do with my mind and my mind something to do with my talk. Good talk: you know – no one, dear Van, should know better – what part for me that plays. Therefore when one has deliberately to make one's talk bad—!'

' "Bad"?' Vanderbank, in his amusement, fell back in his chair. 'Dear Mrs Brook, you're too delightful!'

'You know what I mean – stupid, flat, fourth-rate. When one has to take in sail to that degree – and for a perfectly outside reason – there's nothing strange in one's taking a friend sometimes into the confidence of one's irritation.'

'Ah,' Vanderbank protested, 'you do yourself injustice. Irritation hasn't been for you the only consequence of the affair.'

Mrs Brook gloomily thought. 'No, no – I've had my calmness: the calmness of deep despair. I've seemed to see everything go.'

'Oh, how can you say that,' her visitor demanded, 'when just what we've most been agreed upon so often is the practical impossibility of making any change? Hasn't it seemed as if we really can't overcome conversational habits so thoroughly formed?'

Again Mrs Brook reflected. 'As if our way of looking at things were too serious to be trifled with. I don't know – I think it's only you who have denied our sacrifices, our compromises and concessions. I myself have constantly felt smothered in them. But there it is,' she impatiently went on. 'What I don't admit is that you've given me ground to take for a proof of your "intentions" – to use the odious term – your association with me on behalf of the preposterous fiction, as it after all is, of Nanda's blankness of mind.'

Vanderbank's head, in his chair, was thrown back; his eyes ranged over the top of the room. 'There never has been any mystery about my thinking her – all in her own way – the nicest girl in London. She *is*.'

His companion was silent a little. 'She is, by all means. Well,' she then added, 'so far as I may have been alive to the fact of any one's thinking her so, it's not out of place I should mention to you the difference made in my appreciation of it by our delightful little stay at Mertle. My views of Nanda,' said Mrs Brook, 'have somehow gone up.'

Vanderbank was prompt to show how he could understand it. 'So that you wouldn't consider even Mitchy now?'

But his friend took no notice of the question. 'The way Mr Longdon distinguishes her is quite the sort of thing that gives a girl, as Harold says, a "leg up". It's awfully curious and has made me think: he isn't anything whatever, as London estimates go, in himself – so that what is it, pray, that makes him, when "added on" to her, so double Nanda's value? I somehow or other see, through his being known to back her and through the pretty story of his loyalty to mamma and all the rest of it (oh, if one chose to *work* that!) ever so much more of a chance for her.'

Vanderbank's eyes were on the ceiling. 'It *is* curious, isn't it? – though I think he's rather more "in himself", even for the London estimate, than you quite understand.' He appeared to give her time to take this up, but as she said nothing he pursued: 'I dare say that if even I now *were* to enter myself it would strike you as too late.'

Her attention to this was but indirect. 'It's awfully vulgar to be talking about it, but I can't help feeling that something possibly rather big will come of Mr Longdon.'

'Ah, we've talked of that before,' said Vanderbank, 'and you know you did think something might come even for me.'

She continued however, as if she scarce heard him, to work out her own vision. 'It's very true that up to now—'

'Well, up to now?' he asked as she faltered.

She faltered still a little. 'I do say the most hideous things. But we *have* said worse, haven't we? Up to now, I mean, he hasn't given her anything. Unless indeed,' she mused, 'she may have had something without telling me.'

Vanderbank went much straighter. 'What sort of thing have you in mind? Are you thinking of money?'

'Yes. Isn't it awful?'

'That you should think of it?'

'That I should talk this way.' Her friend was apparently not prepared with an assent, and she quickly enough pursued: 'If he *had* given her any it would come out somehow in her expenditure. She has tremendous liberty and is very secretive, but still it would come out.'

'He wouldn't give her any without letting you know.

Nor would she, without doing so,' Vanderbank added, 'take it.'

'Ah,' Mrs Brook quietly said, 'she hates me enough for anything.'

'That's only your romantic theory.'

Once more she appeared not to hear him; she came up suddenly in another place. 'Has he given *you* anything?'

Her visitor smiled. 'Not so much as a cigarette. I've always my pockets full of them, and *he* never; so he only takes mine. Oh, Mrs Brook,' he continued, 'with me too – though I've also tremendous liberty! – it would come out.'

'I think you'd let me know,' she returned.

'Yes, I'd let you know.'

Silence, upon this, fell between them a little; which Mrs Brook was the first to break. 'She has gone with him this afternoon – by solemn appointment – to the South Kensington Museum.'

There was something in Mrs Brook's dolorous drop that yet presented the news as a portent so great that he was moved again to mirth. 'Ah, that's where she is? Then I confess she has scored. He has never taken *me* to the South Kensington Museum.'

'You were asking what we're going to do,' she went on. 'What I meant was – about Baireuth – that the question for Nanda is simplified. He has pressed her so to pay him a visit.'

Vanderbank's assent was marked. 'I see: so that if you do go abroad she'll be provided for by that engagement.'

'And by lots of other invitations.'

These were such things as, for the most part, the young man could turn over. 'Do you mean you'd let her go alone—?'

'To wherever she's asked?' said Mrs Brook. 'Why not? Don't talk like the Duchess.'

Vanderbank seemed for a moment to try not to. 'Couldn't Mr Longdon take her? Why not?'

His friend looked really struck with it. 'That *would* be working him. But to a beautiful end!' she meditated. 'The only thing would be to get him also asked.'

'Ah, but there you are, don't you see? Fancy "getting"

Mr Longdon anything or anywhere whatever! Don't you feel,' Vanderbank threw out, 'how the impossibility of exerting that sort of patronage for him immediately places him?'

Mrs Brook gave her companion one of those fitful glances of almost grateful appreciation with which their intercourse was even at its darkest hours frequently illumined. 'As if he were the Primate or the French Ambassador? Yes, you're right – one couldn't do it; though it's very odd and one doesn't quite see why. It does place him. But he becomes thereby exactly the very sort of person with whom it would be most of an advantage for her to go about. What a pity,' Mrs Brook sighed, 'he doesn't know more people!'

'Ah well, we *are*, in our way, bringing that to pass. Only we mustn't rush it. Leave it to Nanda herself,' Vanderbank presently added; on which his companion so manifestly left it that she touched after a moment's silence on quite a different matter.

'I dare say he'd tell *you* – wouldn't he? – if he were to give her any considerable sum.'

She had only obeyed his injunction, but he stared at the length of her jump. 'He might attempt to do so, but I shouldn't at all like it.' He was moved immediately to drop this branch of the subject and, apparently to help himself, take up another. 'Do you mean she understands he has asked her down for a regular long stay?'

Mrs Brook barely hesitated. 'She understands, I think, that what I expect of her is to make it as long as possible.'

Vanderbank laughed out – as it was even after ten years still possible to laugh – at the childlike innocence with which her voice could invest the hardest teachings of life; then with something a trifle nervous in the whole sound and manner he sprang up from his chair. 'What a blessing he is to us all!'

'Yes, but think what we must be to *him*.'

'An immense interest, no doubt.' He took a few aimless steps and, stooping over a basket of flowers, inhaled it with violence, almost buried his face. 'I dare say we *are* interesting.'

He had spoken rather vaguely, but Mrs Brook knew

exactly why. 'We render him no end of a service. We keep him in touch with old memories.'

Vanderbank had reached one of the windows, shaded from without by a great striped sun-blind beneath which and between the flowerpots of the balcony he could see a stretch of hot, relaxed street. He looked a minute at these things. 'I do so like your phrases!'

She had a pause that challenged his tone. 'Do you call mamma a "phrase"?'

He went off again, quite with extravagance, but quickly, leaving the window, pulled himself up. 'I dare say we *must* put things for him – he does it, cares or is able to do it, so little himself.'

'Precisely. He just quietly acts. That's his nature, dear thing. We must *let* him act.'

Vanderbank seemed to stifle again too vivid a sense of her particular emphasis. 'Yes, yes – we must let him.'

'Though it won't prevent Nanda, I imagine,' his hostess pursued, 'from finding the fun of a whole month at Beccles – or whatever she puts in – not exactly fast and furious.'

Vanderbank had the look of measuring what the girl might 'put in'. 'The place will be quiet, of course, but when a person's so fond of a person—!'

'As she is of him, you mean?'

He hesitated. 'Yes. Then it's all right.'

'She *is* fond of him, thank God!' said Mrs Brook.

He was before her now with the air of a man who had suddenly determined on a great blind leap. 'Do you know what he has done? He wants me so to marry her that he has proposed a definite basis.'

Mrs Brook got straight up. '"Proposed"? To *her*?'

'No, I don't think he has said a word to Nanda – in fact I'm sure that, very properly, he doesn't mean to. But he spoke to me on Sunday night at Mertle – I had a big talk with him there alone, very late, in the smoking-room.' Mrs Brook's stare was serious, and Vanderbank now went on as if the sound of his voice helped him to meet it. 'We had things out very much and his kindness was extraordinary – he's the most beautiful old boy that ever lived.

I don't know, now that I come to think of it, if I'm within my rights in telling you – and of course I shall immediately let him know that I *have* told you; but I feel I can't arrive at any respectable sort of attitude in the matter without taking you into my confidence – which is really what I came here today to do, though till this moment I've funked it.'

It was either, as her friends chose to think it, an advantage or a drawback of intercourse with Mrs Brook that, her face being at any moment charged with the woe of the world, it was unavoidable to remain rather in the dark as to the effect of particular strokes. There was therefore something in Vanderbank's present study of the signs that showed he had had to learn to feel his way and had more or less mastered the trick. That she had turned a little pale was really the one fresh mark. ' "Funked" it? Why in the world—?' His own colour deepened at her accent, which was a sufficient light on his having been stupid. 'Do you mean you've declined the arrangement?'

He only, with a smile somewhat strained, continued for a moment to look at her; clearly, however, at last feeling, and not much caring, that he got in still deeper. 'You're magnificent. You're magnificent.'

Her lovely gaze widened out. '*Comment donc?* Where – why? You *have* declined her?' she went on. After which, as he replied only with a slow head-shake that seemed to say it was not for the moment all so simple as that, she had one of the inspirations to which she was constitutionally subject. 'Do you imagine I want you to myself?'

'Dear Mrs Brook, you're so admirable,' he answered, laughing, 'that if by any chance you did, upon my honour I don't see how I should be able not to say "All right." ' Then he spoke more gravely. 'I was shy of really bringing out to you what has happened to me, for a reason that I have of course to look in the face. Whatever you want yourself, for Nanda you want Mitchy.'

'I see, I see.' She did full justice to his explanation. 'And what did you say about a "basis"? The blessed man offers to settle—?'

'You're a wonderful woman,' her visitor returned, 'and

your imagination takes its fences in a way that, when I'm out with you, quite puts mine to shame. When he mentioned it to me I was quite surprised.'

'And I,' Mrs Brook asked, 'am not surprised a bit? Isn't it only,' she modestly suggested, 'because I've taken him in more than you? Didn't you know he *would*?' she quavered.

Vanderbank thought or at least pretended to. 'Make *me* the condition? How could I be sure of it?'

But the point of his question was lost for her in the growing light. 'Oh then the condition's you only—?'

'That, at any rate, is all I have to do with. He's ready to settle if I'm ready to do the rest.'

'To propose to her straight, you mean?' She waited, but as he said nothing she went on: 'And you're not ready. Is that it?'

'I'm taking my time.'

'Of course you know,' said Mrs Brook, 'that she'd jump at you.'

He turned away from her now, but after some steps came back. 'Then you do admit it.'

She hesitated. 'To *you*.'

He had a strange faint smile. 'Well, as I don't speak of it—!'

'No – only to me. What is it he settles?' Mrs Brook demanded.

'I can't tell you.'

'You didn't ask?'

'On the contrary I stopped him off.'

'Oh then,' Mrs Brook exclaimed, 'that's what I call declining.'

The words appeared for an instant to strike her companion. 'Is it? Is it?' he almost musingly repeated. But he shook himself the next moment free of his wonder, was more what would have been called in Buckingham Crescent on the spot. 'Isn't there rather something in my having thus thought it my duty to warn you that I'm definitely his candidate?'

Mrs Brook turned impatiently away. 'You've certainly – with your talk about "warning" – the happiest expressions!' She put her face into the flowers as he had done just before;

then as she raised it: 'What kind of a monster are you trying to make me out?'

'My dear lady' – Vanderbank was prompt – 'I really don't think I say anything but what's fair. Isn't it just my loyalty to you in fact that has in this case positively strained my discretion?'

She shook her head in mere mild despair. '"Loyalty" again is exquisite. The tact of men has a charm quite its own. And you're rather good,' she continued, 'as men go.'

His laugh was now a little awkward, as if she had already succeeded in making him uncomfortable. 'I always become aware with you sooner or later that they don't go at all – in your sense; but how am I, after all, so far out if you *have* put your money on another man?'

'You keep coming back to that?' she wearily sighed.

He thought a little. 'No, then. You've only to tell me not to, and I'll never speak of it again.'

'You'll be in an odd position for speaking of it if you do really go in. You deny that you've declined,' said Mrs Brook; 'which means then that you've allowed our friend to hope.'

Vanderbank met it bravely. 'Yes, I think he hopes.'

'And imparts this hope to my child?'

This arrested the young man, but only for a moment. 'I've the most perfect faith in his wisdom with her. I trust his particular delicacy. He cares more for her,' he presently added, 'even than we do.'

Mrs Brook gazed away at the infinite of space. '"We", my dear Van,' she at last returned, 'is one of your own real, wonderful touches. But there's something in what you say: I *have*, as between ourselves – between me and him – been backing Mitchy. That is I've been saying to him "Wait, wait: don't at any rate do anything else." Only it's just from the depth of my thought for my daughter's happiness that I've clung to this resource. He would so absolutely, so unreservedly do anything for her.' She had reached now, with her extraordinary self-control, the pitch of quiet, bland demonstration. 'I want the poor thing, *que diable*, to have another string to her bow and another loaf, for her desolate old age, on the shelf. When everything else is gone, Mitchy

will still be there. Then it will be at least her own fault—!'
Mrs Brook continued. 'What can relieve me of the primary
duty of taking precautions,' she wound up, 'when I know
as well as that I stand here and look at you—'

'Yes, what?' he asked as she just paused.

'Why, that so far they count on you, they count, my dear
Van, on a blank.' Holding him a minute as with the soft,
low voice of his fate, she sadly but firmly shook her head.
'You won't do it.'

'Oh!' he almost too loudly protested.

'You won't do it,' she went on.

'I *say*!' – he made a joke of it.

'You won't do it,' she repeated.

It was as if he could not at last but show himself really
struck; yet what he exclaimed on was what might in truth
most have impressed him. 'You *are* magnificent, really!'

'Mr Mitchett!' the butler, appearing at the door, almost
familiarly dropped; on which Vanderbank turned straight
to the person announced.

Mr Mitchett was there, and, anticipating Mrs Brook in
receiving him, her companion passed it straight on. 'She's
magnificent!'

Mitchy was already all interest. 'Rather! But what's her
last?'

It had been, though so great, so subtle, as they said in
Buckingham Crescent, that Vanderbank scarce knew how
to put it. 'Well, she's so thoroughly superior.'

'Oh, to whom do you say it?' Mitchy cried as he greeted
her.

XXII

THE subject of this eulogy had meanwhile returned to her
sofa, where she received the homage of her new visitor. 'It's
not I who am magnificent, a bit – it's dear Mr Longdon.
I've just had from Van the most wonderful piece of news
about him – his announcement of his wish to make it worth
somebody's while to marry my child.'

' "Make it"?' – Mitchy stared. 'But *isn't* it?'

'My dear friend, you must ask Van. Of course you've

always thought so. But I must tell you, all the same,' Mrs Brook went on, 'that I'm delighted.'

Mitchy had seated himself, but Vanderbank remained erect and became perhaps even slightly stiff. He was not angry – none of the inner circle at Buckingham Crescent was ever angry – but he looked grave and rather troubled. 'Even if it *is* decidedly fine' – he addressed his hostess straight – 'I can't make out quite why you're doing *this*. I mean immediately making it known.'

'Ah, but what do we keep from Mitchy?' Mrs Brook asked.

'What *can* you keep? It comes to the same thing,' Mitchy said. 'Besides, here we are together, share and share alike – one beautiful intelligence. Mr Longdon's "somebody" is of course Van. Don't try to treat me as an outsider.'

Vanderbank looked a little foolishly, though it was but the shade of a shade, from one of them to the other. 'I think I've been rather an ass!'

'What then by the terms of our friendship – just as Mitchy says – can he and I have a better right to know and to feel with you about? You will want, Mitchy, won't you?' Mrs Brook went on, 'to hear all about *that*?'

'Oh, I only mean,' Vanderbank explained, 'in having just now blurted my tale out to you. However, I of course do know,' he pursued to Mitchy, 'that whatever is really between us will remain between us. Let me then tell you myself exactly what's the matter.' The length of his pause after these words showed at last that he had stopped short; on which his companions, as they waited, exchanged a sympathetic look. They waited another minute, and then he dropped into a chair where, leaning forward, his elbows on the arms and his gaze attached to the carpet, he drew out the silence. Finally he looked at Mrs Brook. '*You* make it clear.'

The appeal called up for some reason her most infantine manner. 'I don't think I *can*, dear Van – really *clear*. You know however yourself,' she continued to Mitchy, 'enough by this time about Mr Longdon and mamma.'

'Oh, rather!' Mitchy laughed.

'And about mamma and Nanda.'

'Oh, perfectly: the way Nanda reminds him, and the "beautiful loyalty" that has made him take such a fancy to her. But I've already embraced the facts – you needn't dot any i's.' With another glance at his fellow-visitor Mitchy jumped up and stood there florid. 'He has offered you money to marry her.' He said this to Vanderbank as if it were the most natural thing in the world.

'Oh *no*,' Mrs Brook interposed with promptitude: 'he has simply let him know before any one else that the money is there *for* Nanda, and that therefore—'

'First come, first served?' Mitchy had already taken her up. 'I see, I see. Then, to make sure of the money,' he inquired of Vanderbank, 'you *must* marry her?'

'If it depends upon that she'll never get it,' Mrs Brook returned. 'Dear Van will think conscientiously a lot about it, but he won't do it.'

'Won't you, Van, really?' Mitchy asked from the hearth-rug.

'Never, never. We shall be very kind to him, we shall help him, hope and pray for him, but we shall be at the end,' said Mrs Brook, 'just where we are now. Dear Van will have done his best, and we shall have done ours. Mr Longdon will have done his – poor Nanda even will have done hers. But it will all have been in vain. However,' Mrs Brook continued to expound, 'she'll probably have the money. Mr Longdon will surely consider that she'll want it if she doesn't marry still more than if she does. So we shall be *so* much at least,' she wound up – 'I mean Edward and I and the child will be – to the good.'

Mitchy, for an equal certainty, required but an instant's thought. 'Oh, there can be no doubt about *that*. The things about which your mind may now be at ease—!' he cheerfully explained.

'It does make a great difference!' Mrs Brook comfortably sighed. Then in a different tone: 'What dear Van will find at the end that he can't face will be, don't you see? just this fact of appearing to have accepted a bribe. He won't want, on the one hand – out of kindness for Nanda – to have the money suppressed; and yet he won't want to have the pecuniary question mixed up with the matter – to look in short as if he had had to be paid. He's like you, you know – he's proud; and it will be there we shall break down.'

Mitchy had been watching his friend, who, a few minutes before perceptibly embarrassed, had now recovered himself and, at his ease, though still perhaps with a smile a trifle strained, leaned back and let his eyes play everywhere but over the faces of the others. Vanderbank evidently wished now to show a good-humoured detachment.

'See here,' Mitchy said to him: 'I remember your once submitting to me a case of some delicacy.'

'Oh, he'll submit it to you – he'll submit it even to *me*,' Mrs Brook broke in. 'He'll be charming, touching, confiding – above all he'll be awfully *interesting* about it. But he'll make up his mind in his own way, and his own way won't be to accommodate Mr Longdon.'

Mitchy continued to study their companion in the light of these remarks, then turned upon his hostess his sociable glare. 'Splendid, isn't it, the old boy's infatuation with him?'

Mrs Brook just hesitated. 'From the point of view of the immense interest it – just now, for instance – makes for you and me? Oh yes, it's one of our best things yet. It places him a little with Lady Fanny – "He will, he won't; he won't, he will!" Only, to be perfect, it lacks, as I say, the element of real suspense.'

Mitchy frankly wondered. 'It does, you think? Not for me – not wholly.' He turned again quite pleadingly to their friend. 'I hope it doesn't for yourself totally either?'

Vanderbank, cultivating his detachment, made at first no more reply than if he had not heard, and the others meanwhile showed faces that testified perhaps less than their respective speeches had done to the absence of anxiety. The only token he immediately gave was to get up and approach Mitchy, before whom he stood a minute laughing kindly enough but not altogether gaily. As if then for a better proof of gaiety he presently seized him by the shoulders and, still without speaking, pushed him backward into the chair he himself had just quitted. Mrs Brook's eyes, from the sofa, while this went on attached themselves to her visitors. It took Vanderbank, as he moved about and his companions waited, a minute longer to produce what he had in mind. 'What *is* splendid, as we call it, is this extraordinary freedom and good humour of our intercourse and the fact that we do care – so independently of our personal interests, with so little selfishness or other vulgarity – to get at the idea of things. The beautiful specimen Mrs Brook had just given me of that,' he continued to Mitchy, 'was what made me break out to you about her when you came in.' He spoke to one friend, but he looked at the other. 'What's really "superior" in her is that, though I suddenly show her an interference with a favourite plan, her personal resentment is nothing – all she wants is to see what may really happen, to take in the truth of the case and make the best of that. She offers me the truth, as she sees it, about myself, and with no nasty elation if it does chance to be the truth that suits her best. It was a charming, charming stroke.'

Mitchy's appreciation was no bar to his amusement. 'You're wonderfully right about us. But still it was a stroke.'

If Mrs Brook was less diverted she followed perhaps more closely. 'If you do me so much justice then, why did you put me such a cold, cruel question? – I mean when you so oddly challenged me on my handing on your news to Mitchy. If the principal beauty of our effort to live together is – and quite according to your own eloquence – in our sincerity, I simply obeyed the impulse to do the sincere thing. If we're not sincere, we're nothing.'

'Nothing!' – it was Mitchy who first responded. 'But we *are* sincere.'

'Yes, we *are* sincere,' Vanderbank presently said. 'It's a great chance for us not to fall below ourselves; no doubt therefore we shall continue to soar and sing. We pay for it, people who don't like us say, in our self-consciousness—'

'But people who don't like us,' Mitchy broke in, 'don't matter. Besides, how can we be properly conscious of each other—?'

'That's it!' – Vanderbank completed his idea: 'without my finding myself, for instance, in you and Mrs Brook? We see ourselves reflected – we're conscious of the charming whole. I thank you,' he pursued after an instant to Mrs Brook – 'I thank you for your sincerity.'

It was a business sometimes really to hold her eyes,

but they had, it must be said for her, their steady moments. She exchanged with Vanderbank a somewhat remarkable look, then, with an art of her own, broke short off without appearing to drop him. 'The thing is, don't you think?' – she appealed to Mitchy – 'for us not to be so awfully clever as to make it believed that we can never be simple. We mustn't see *too* tremendous things – even in each other.' She quite lost patience with the danger she glanced at. 'We *can* be simple!'

'We *can*, by God!' Mitchy laughed.

'Well, we are now – and it's a great comfort to have it settled,' said Vanderbank.

'Then you see,' Mrs Brook returned, 'what a mistake you would make to see abysses of subtlety in my having been merely natural.'

'We *can* be natural,' Mitchy declared.

'We can, by God!' Vanderbank laughed.

Mrs Brook had turned to Mitchy. 'I just wanted you to know. So I spoke. It's not more complicated than that. As for *why* I wanted you to know—'

'What better reason could there be,' Mitchy interrupted, 'than your being filled to the finger-tips with the sense of how I would want it myself, and of the misery, the absolute pathos, of my being left out? Fancy, my dear chap' – he had only to put it to Van – 'my *not* knowing!'

Vanderbank evidently couldn't fancy it, but he said quietly enough: 'I should probably have told you myself.'

'Well, what's the difference?'

'Oh, there *is* a difference,' Mrs Brook loyally said. Then she opened an inch or two, for Vanderbank, the door of her dim radiance. 'Only I should have thought it a difference for the better. Of course,' she added, 'it remains absolutely with us three alone, and don't you already feel from it the fresh charm – with it here between us – of our being together?'

It was as if each of the men had waited for the other to assent better than he himself could and Mitchy then, as Vanderbank failed, had gracefully, to cover him, changed the subject. 'But isn't Nanda, the person most interested, to know?'

Vanderbank gave on this a strange sound of hilarity. 'Ah, that would finish it off!'

It produced for a few seconds something like a chill, a chill that had for consequence a momentary pause which in its turn added weight to the words next uttered. 'It's not I who shall tell her,' Mrs Brook said gently and gravely. 'There! – you may be sure. If you want a promise, it's a promise. So that if Mr Longdon's silent,' she went on, 'and you are, Mitchy, and I am, how in the world shall she have a suspicion?'

'You mean of course except by Van's deciding to mention it himself.'

Van might have been, from the way they looked at him, some beautiful unconscious object, but Mrs Brook was quite ready to answer. 'Oh, poor man, *he'll* never breathe.'

'I see. So there we are.'

To this discussion the subject of it had for the time nothing to contribute, even when Mitchy, rising with the words he had last uttered from the chair in which he had been placed, took sociably as well, on the hearth-rug, a position before their hostess. This move ministered apparently only to Vanderbank's mere silence, for it was still without speaking that, after a little, he turned away from his friend and dropped once more into the same seat. 'I've shown you already, you of course remember,' Vanderbank presently said to him, 'that I'm perfectly aware of how much better Mrs Brook would like *you* for the position.'

'He thinks I want him myself,' Mrs Brook blandly explained.

She was indeed, as they always thought her, 'wonderful', but she was perhaps not even now so much so as Mitchy found himself able to be. 'But how would you lose old Van – even at the worst?' he earnestly asked of her.

She just hesitated. 'What do you mean by the worst?'

'Then even at the best,' Mitchy smiled. 'In the event of his falsifying your prediction; which, by the way, has the danger, hasn't it? – I mean for your intellectual credit – of making him, as we all used to be called by our nurse-maids, "contrary".'

'Oh, I've thought of that,' Mrs Brook returned. 'But he

won't do, on the whole, even for the sweetness of spiting me, what he won't want to do. *I* haven't said I should lose him,' she went on; 'that's only the view he himself takes – or, to do him perfect justice, the idea he candidly imputes to me; though without, I imagine – for I don't go so far as that – attributing to me anything so unutterably *bête* as a feeling of jealousy.'

'You wouldn't dream of my supposing anything inept of you,' Vanderbank said on this, 'if you understood to the full how I keep on admiring you. Only what stupefies me a little,' he continued, 'is the extraordinary critical freedom – or we may call it if we like the high intellectual detachment – with which we discuss a question touching you, dear Mrs Brook, so nearly and engaging so your most private and most sacred sentiments. What are we playing with, after all, but the idea of Nanda's happiness?'

'Oh, I'm not playing!' Mrs Brook declared with a little rattle of emotion.

'She's not playing' – Mr Mitchett gravely confirmed it. 'Don't you feel in the very air the vibration of the passion that she's simply too charming to shake at the window as the house-maid shakes the table-cloth or the jingo the flag?' Then he took up what Vanderbank had previously said. 'Of course, my dear man, I'm "aware", as you just now put it, of everything, and I'm not indiscreet, am I, Mrs Brook? in admitting for you as well as for myself that there *was* an impossibility that you and I used sometimes to turn over together. Only – Lord bless us all! – it isn't as if I hadn't long ago seen that there's nothing at all *for* me.'

'Ah, wait, wait!' Mrs Brook put in.

'She has a theory' – Vanderbank, from his chair, lighted it up for Mitchy, who hovered before them – 'that your chance *will* come, later on, after I've given my measure.'

'Oh, but that's exactly,' Mitchy was quick to respond, 'what you'll never do! You'll walk in magnificent mystery "later on" not a bit less than you do today; you'll continue to have the benefit of everything that our imagination, perpetually engaged, often baffled and never fatigued, will continue to bedeck you with. Nanda, in the same way, to the end of all her time, will simply remain exquisite, or genuine, or generous – whatever we choose to call it. It may make a difference to us, who are comparatively vulgar, but what difference will it make to *her* whether you do or you don't decide for her? You can't belong to her more, for herself, than you do already – and that's precisely so much that there's no room for any one else. Where, therefore, without that room, do I come in?'

'Nowhere, I see' – Vanderbank seemed obligingly to muse.

Mrs Brook had followed Mitchy with marked admiration, but she gave on this at Van, a glance that was like the toss of a blossom from the same branch. 'Oh then, shall I just go on with you *both*? That *will* be joy!' she had, however, the next thing, a sudden drop which shaded the picture. 'You're so divine, Mitchy, that how can you not, in the long run, break *any* woman down?'

It was not as if Mitchy was struck – it was only that he was courteous. 'What do you call the long run? Taking about till I'm eighty?'

'Ah, your genius is of a kind to which middle life will be particularly favourable. You'll reap then somehow, one feels, everything you've sown.'

Mitchy still accepted the prophecy only to control it. 'Do you call eighty middle life? Why, my moral beauty, my dear woman – if that's what you mean by my genius – is precisely my curse. What on earth is left for a man just rotten with goodness? It renders necessary the kind of liking that renders *un*necessary anything else.'

'Now that *is* cheap paradox!' Vanderbank patiently sighed. 'You're down for a fine.'

It was with less of the patience perhaps that Mrs Brook took this up. 'Yes, on that we *are* stiff. Five pounds, please.'

Mitchy drew out his pocket-book even though he explained. 'What I mean is that I don't give out the great thing.' With which he produced a crisp bank-note.

'*Don't* you? asked Vanderbank, who, having taken it from him to hand to Mrs Brook, held it a moment, delicately, to accentuate the doubt.

'The great thing's the sacred terror. It's you who give *that* out.'

'Oh!' – and Vanderbank laid the money on the small stand at Mrs Brook's elbow.

'Ain't I right, Mrs Brook? – doesn't he, tremendously, and isn't that more than anything else what does it?'

The two again, as if they understood each other, gazed in a unity of interest at their companion, who sustained it with an air clearly intended as the happy mean between embarrassment and triumph. Then Mrs Brook showed she liked the phrase. 'The sacred terror! Yes, one feels it. It *is* that.'

'The finest case of it,' Mitchy pursued, 'that I've ever met. So my moral's sufficiently pointed.'

'Oh, I don't think it can be said to be that,' Vanderbank returned, 'till you've put the whole thing into a box by doing for Nanda what she does most want you to do.'

Mitchy caught on without a shade of wonder. 'Oh, by proposing to the Duchess for little Aggie?' He took but an instant to turn it over. 'Well, I *would* propose, to please Nanda. Only I've never yet quite made out the reason of her wish.'

'The reason is largely,' his friend answered, 'that, being very fond of Aggie, and in fact extremely admiring her, she wants to do something good for her and to keep her from anything bad. Don't you know – it's too charming – she regularly believes in her?'

Mitchy, with all his recognition, vibrated to the touch. 'Isn't it too charming?'

'Well then,' Vanderbank went on, 'she secures for her friend a phoenix like you, and secures for you a phoenix like her friend. It's hard to say for which of you she desires most to do the handsome thing. She loves you both in short' – he followed it up – 'though perhaps, when one thinks of it, the price she puts on you, Mitchy, in the arrangement, is a little the higher. Awfully fine at any rate – and yet awfully odd too – her feeling for Aggie's type, which is divided by such abysses from her own.'

'Ah,' laughed Mitchy, 'but think then of her feeling for mine!'

Vanderbank, still more at his ease now and with his head back, had his eye aloft and afar. 'Oh, there are things in Nanda—!' The others exchanged a glance at this, while their companion added: 'Little Aggie's really the sort of creature she would have liked to be able to be.'

'Well,' Mitchy said, 'I should have adored her even if she *had* been able.'

Mrs Brook, for some minutes, had played no audible part, but the acute observer we are constantly taking for granted would perhaps have detected in her, as one of the effects of the special complexion today of Vanderbank's presence, a certain smothered irritation. 'She couldn't possibly have been able,' she now interposed, 'with so loose – or rather, to express it more properly, with so perverse – a mother.'

'And yet, my dear lady,' Mitchy promptly reflected 'how if, in little Aggie's case, the Duchess hasn't prevented—?'

Mrs Brook was full of wisdom. 'Well, it's a different thing. I'm not, as a mother – am I, Van? – bad *enough*. That's what's the matter with me. Aggie, don't you see? is the Duchess's morality, her virtue; which, by having it, that way, outside of you, as one may say, you can make a much better thing of. The child has been for Jane, I admit, a capital little subject, but Jane has kept her on hand and finished her like some wonderful piece of stitching. Oh, as work, it's of a *soigné*! There it is – to show. A woman like me has to be *herself*, poor thing, her virtue and her morality. What will you have? It's our lumbering English plan.'

'So that her daughter,' Mitchy sympathized, 'can only, by the arrangement, hope to become at the best her immorality and her vice?'

But Mrs Brook, without an answer for the question, appeared suddenly to have plunged into a sea of thought. 'The only way for Nanda to have been *really* nice—'

'Would have been for you to be like Jane?'

Mitchy and his hostess seemed for a minute, on this, to gaze together at the tragic truth. Then she shook her head. 'We see our mistakes too late.' She repeated the movement, but as if to let it all go, and Vanderbank meanwhile, pulling out his watch, had got up with a laugh that showed some inattention and made to Mitchy a remark about their walking away together. Mitchy, engaged for the instant with Mrs Brook, had assented only with a nod, but the attitude of the two men had become that of departure. Their friend looked at them as if she would like to keep one of them, and for a purpose connected somehow with the other, but was oddly, almost ludicrously embarrassed to choose. What was in her face indeed during this short passage might prove to have been, should we penetrate, the flicker of a sense that, in spite of all intimacy and amiability, they could, at bottom and as things commonly turned out, only be united against her. Yet she made at the end a sort of choice in going on to Mitchy: 'He hasn't at all told you the real reason of Nanda's idea that you should go in for Aggie.'

'Oh, I draw the line there,' said Vanderbank. 'Besides, he understands that too.'

Mitchy did, on the spot, himself and every one justice. 'Why, it just disposes of me, doesn't it?'

Vanderbank, restless now and turning about the room, stopped, on this, with a smile for Mrs Brook. 'We understand too well!'

'Not if he doesn't understand,' she replied after a moment while she turned to Mitchy, 'that his real "combination" can in the nature of the case only be—'

'Oh yes' – Mitchy took her straight up – 'with the young thing who is, as you say, positively and helplessly modern and the pious fraud of whose classic identity with a sheet of white paper has been – oh tacitly of course, but none the less practically – dropped. You've so often reminded me. I do understand. If I were to go in for Aggie it would only be to oblige. The modern girl, the product of our hard London facts and of her inevitable consciousness of them just as they are – she, wonderful being, *is*, I fully recognize, my real affair, and I'm not ashamed to say that when I like the individual I'm not afraid of the type. She knows too much – I don't say; but she doesn't know after all a millionth part of what *I* do.'

'I'm not sure!' Mrs Brook earnestly exclaimed.

He had rung out and he kept it up with a limpidity unusual. 'And product for product, when you come to that, I'm a queerer one myself than any other. The traditions *I* smash!' Mitchy laughed.

Mrs Brook had got up and Vanderbank had gone again

to the window. 'That's exactly why,' she returned: 'you're a pair of monsters and your monstrosity fits. She does know too much,' she added.

'Well,' said Mitchy, with resolution, 'it's all my fault.'

'Not *all* – unless,' Mrs Brook returned, 'that's only a sweet way of saying that it's mostly mine.'

'Oh, yours too – immensely; in fact every one's. Even Edward's. I dare say; and certainly, unmistakably, Harold's. Ah, and Van's own – rather!' Mitchy continued; 'for all he turns his back and will have nothing to say to it.'

It was on the back Vanderbank turned that Mrs Brook's eyes now rested. 'That's precisely why he shouldn't be afraid of her.'

He faced straight about. 'Oh, I don't deny my part.'

He shone at them brightly enough, and Mrs Brook, thoughtful, wistful, candid, took in for a moment the radiance. 'And yet to think that after all it has been mere *talk*!'

Something in her tone again made her hearers laugh out; so it was still with the air of good humour that Vanderbank rejoined: 'Mere, mere, mere. But perhaps it's exactly the "mere" that has made us range so wide.'

Mrs Brook's intelligence abounded. 'You mean that we haven't had the excuse of passion?'

Her companions once more gave way to merriment, but 'There you are!' Vanderbank said after an instant less sociably. With it too he held out his hand.

'You *are* afraid,' she answered as she gave him her own; on which, as he made no rejoinder, she held him before her. 'Do you mean you *really* don't know if she gets it?'

'The money, if he *doesn't* go in?' – Mitchy broke almost with an air of responsibility into Vanderbank's silence. 'Ah but, as we said, surely—!'

It was Mitchy's eyes that Vanderbank met. 'Yes, I should suppose she gets it.'

'Perhaps then, as a compensation, she'll even get *more*—!'

'If I don't go in? Oh!' said Vanderbank. And he changed colour.

He was by this time off, but Mrs Brook kept Mitchy a moment. 'Now – by that suggestion – he has something to show. He won't go in.'

XXIII

HER visitors had been gone half an hour, but she was still in the drawing-room when Nanda came back. The girl found her, on the sofa, in a posture that might have represented restful oblivion but that, after a glance, our young lady appeared to interpret as mere intensity of thought. It was a condition from which at all events Mrs Brook was quickly roused by her daughter's presence; she opened her eyes and put down her feet, so that the two were confronted as closely as persons may be when it is only one of them who looks at the other. Nanda, gazing vaguely about and not seeking a seat, slowly drew off her gloves while her mother's sad eyes considered her from top to toe. 'Tea's gone,' Mrs Brook then said as if there were something in the loss peculiarly irretrievable. 'But I suppose,' she added, 'he gave you all you want.'

'Oh dear yes, thank you – I've had lots.'

Nanda hovered there slim and charming, feathered and ribboned, dressed in thin, fresh fabrics and faint colours, with something in the effect of it all to which the sweeter, deeper melancholy in her mother's eyes seemed happily to testify. 'Just turn round, dear.' The girl immediately obeyed, and Mrs Brook once more took everything in. 'The back's best – only she didn't do what she said she would. How they do lie!' she gently quavered.

'Yes, but we lie so to *them*.' Nanda had swung round again, producing evidently on her mother's part, by the admirable 'hang' of her light skirts, a still deeper peace. 'Do you mean the middle fold? – I knew she wouldn't. I don't want my back to be best – I don't walk backward.'

'Yes,' Mrs Brook resignedly mused; 'you dress for yourself.'

'Oh, how can you say that,' the girl asked, 'when I never stick in a pin but what I think of *you*?'

'Well,' Mrs Brook moralized, 'one must always, I consider, think, as a sort of *point de repère*, of some one good person. Only it's best if it's a person one's afraid of. You do very well, but I'm not enough. What one really requires is a kind of salutary terror. *I* never stick in a pin without thinking of your cousin Jane. What is it that some one quotes somewhere about some one's having said that "Our antagonist is our helper – he prevents our being superficial"? The extent to which, with my poor clothes, the Duchess prevents *me*—!' It was a measure Mrs Brook could give only by the general soft wail of her submission to fate.

'Yes, the Duchess isn't a woman, is she? She's a standard.' The speech had for Nanda's companion, however, no effect of pleasantry or irony, and it was a mark of the special intercourse of these good friends that though they had for each other, in manner and tone, such a fund of consideration as might almost have given it the stamp of diplomacy, there was yet in it also something of that economy of expression which is the result of a common experience. The recurrence of opportunity to observe them together would have taught a spectator that – on Mrs Brook's side, doubtless, more particularly – their relation was governed by two or three remarkably established and, as might have been said, refined laws, the spirit of which was to guard against the vulgarity so often coming to the surface between parent and child. That they *were* as good friends as if Nanda had not been her daughter was a truth that no passage between them might fail in one way or another to illustrate. Nanda had gathered up, for that matter, early in life, a flower of maternal wisdom: 'People talk about the conscience, but it seems to me one must just bring it up to a certain point and leave it there. You can let your conscience alone if you're nice to the second housemaid.' Mrs Brook was as 'nice' to Nanda as she was to Sarah Curd – which involved, as may easily be imagined, the happiest conditions for Sarah. 'Well,' she resumed, reverting to the Duchess on a final appraisement of the girl's air, 'I really think I do well by you and that Jane wouldn't have anything to say today. You look awfully like mamma,' she then threw off as if for the first time of mentioning it.

'Oh, Cousin Jane doesn't care for that,' Nanda returned. 'What I don't look like is Aggie, for all I try.'

'Ah, you shouldn't try – you can do nothing with it. One must be what one is.'

Mrs Brook was almost sententious, but Nanda, with civility, let it pass. 'No one in London touches her. She's quite by herself. When one sees her one feels her to be the real thing.'

Mrs Brook, without harshness, wondered. 'What do you mean by the real thing?'

Even Nanda, however, had to think a moment. 'Well, the real young one. That's what Lord Petherton calls her,' she mildly joked—' "the young 'un".'

Her mother's echo was not for the joke, but for something else. 'I know what you mean. What's the use of being good?'

'Oh, I didn't mean that,' said Nanda. 'Besides, isn't Aggie of a goodness—?'

'I wasn't talking of her. I was asking myself what's the use of *my* being.'

'Well, you can't help it any more than the Duchess can help—'

'Ah, but she could if she would!' Mrs Brook broke in with a sharper ring than she had yet given. 'We can't help being good perhaps, if that burden is laid on us – but there are lengths in other directions we're not absolutely obliged to go. And what I think of when I stick in the pins,' she went on, 'is that Jane seems to me really never to have had to pay.' She appeared for a minute to brood on this till she could no longer bear it; after which she jerked out: 'Why, she has never had to pay for *any*thing!'

Nanda had by this time seated herself, taking her place, under the interest of their talk, on her mother's sofa, where, except for the removal of her long, soft gloves, which one of her hands again and again drew caressingly through the other, she remained very much as if she were some friendly yet circumspect young visitor to whom Mrs Brook had on some occasion dropped '*Do* come.' But there was something perhaps more expressly conciliatory in the way she had kept everything on: as if, in particular serenity and to confirm kindly Mrs Brook's sense of what had been done for her, she had neither taken off her great feathered hat nor laid down her parasol of pale green silk, the 'match' of hat and ribbons and which had an expensive, precious knob. Our spectator would possibly have found too much earnestness in her face to be sure if there was also candour. 'And do you mean that *you* have had to pay—?'

'Oh yes – all the while.' With this Mrs Brook was a little short, and also as she added as if to banish a slight awkwardness: 'But don't let it discourage you.'

Nanda seemed an instant to weigh the advice, and the whole thing would have been striking as another touch in the picture of the odd want, on the part of each, of any sense of levity in the other. Whatever escape when together mother or daughter might ever seek would never be the humorous one – a circumstance, notwithstanding, that would not in every case have failed to make their interviews droll for a third person. It would always indeed for such a person have produced an impression of tension beneath the surface. 'I could have done much better at the start and have lost less time,' the girl at last said, 'if I hadn't had the drawback of not really remembering Granny.'

'Oh well, *I* remember her!' Mrs Brook moaned with an accent that evidently struck her the next moment as so much out of place that she slightly deflected. She took Nanda's parasol and held it as if – a more delicate thing much than any one of hers – she simply liked to have it. 'Her clothes – at your age at least – must have been hideous. Was it at the place he took you to that he gave you tea?' she then went on.

'Yes, at the Museum. We had an orgy in the refreshment-room. But he took me afterwards to Tishy's, where we had another.'

'He went *in* with you?' Mrs Brook had suddenly flashed into eagerness.

'Oh yes – I made him.'

'He didn't want to?'

'On the contrary – very much. But he doesn't do everything he wants,' said Nanda.

Mrs Brook seemed to wonder. 'You mean you've also to want it?'

'Oh no – *that* isn't enough. What I suppose I mean,'

Nanda continued, 'is that he doesn't do anything he doesn't want to. But he does quite enough,' she added.

'And who then was at Tishy's?'

'Oh, poor Tish herself, naturally, and Carrie Donner.'

'And no one else?'

The girl just waited. 'Yes, Mr Cashmore came in.'

Her mother gave a groan of impatience. 'Ah, *again?*'

Nanda thought an instant. 'How do you mean, "again"? He just lives there as much as he ever did, and Tishy can't prevent him.'

'I was thinking of Mr Longdon – of *their* meeting. When he met him here that time he liked it so little. Did he like it any more today?' Mrs Brook quavered.

'Oh no, he hated it.'

'But hadn't he – if he should go in – known he *would?*'

'Yes, perfectly – but he wanted to see.'

'To see—?' Mrs Brook just threw out.

'Well, where I go so much. And he knew I wished it.'

'I don't quite see why,' Mrs Brook mildly observed. And then as her daughter said nothing to help her: 'At any rate he did loathe it?'

Nanda, for a reply, simply after an instant put a question. 'Well, how can he understand?'

'You mean, like me, why you do go there so much? How can he indeed?'

'I don't mean that,' the girl returned – 'it's just that he understands perfectly, because he saw them all, in such an extraordinary way – well, what can I ever call it? – clutch me and cling to me.'

Mrs Brook with full gravity considered this picture. 'And was Mr Cashmore, today, so ridiculous?'

'Ah, he's not ridiculous, mamma – he's very unhappy. He thinks now Lady Fanny probably won't go, but he feels that may be, after all, only the worse for him.'

'She *will* go,' Mrs Brook answered with one of her round-about approaches to decision. 'He *is* too great an idiot. She was here an hour ago, and if ever a woman was packed—!'

'Well,' Nanda objected, 'but doesn't she spend her time in packing and unpacking?'

This inquiry, however, scarce pulled up her mother. 'No – though she *has*, no doubt, hitherto wasted plenty of labour. She has now a dozen boxes – I could see them there in her wonderful eyes – just waiting to be called for. So if you're counting on her not going, my dear—!' Mrs Brook gave a head-shake that was the warning of wisdom.

'Oh, I don't care what she does!' Nanda replied. 'What I meant just now was that Mr Longdon couldn't understand why, with so much to make them so, they couldn't be decently happy.'

'And did he wish you to explain?'

'I tried to, but I didn't make it any better. He doesn't like them. He doesn't even care for Tish.'

'He told you so – right out?'

'Oh,' Nanda said, 'of course I asked him. I didn't press him, because I never do—!'

'You never do?' Mrs Brook broke in as with the glimpse of a new light.

The girl showed an indulgence for this interest that was for a moment almost elderly. 'I enjoy awfully, with him, seeing just how to take him.'

Her tone and her face evidently put forth for her companion at this juncture something freshly, even quite supremely suggestive; and yet the effect of them on Mrs Brook's part was only a question so off-hand that it might already often have been asked. The mother's eyes, to ask it, we may none the less add, attached themselves closely to the daughter's, and her own face just glowed. 'You like him so very awfully?'

It was as if the next instant Nanda felt herself on her guard. Yet she spoke with a certain surrender. 'Well, it's rather intoxicating to be one's self—!' She had only a drop over the choice of her term.

'So tremendously made up to, you mean – even by a little fussy, ancient man? But *doesn't* he, my dear,' Mrs Brook continued with encouragement, 'make up to you?'

A supposititious spectator would certainly on this have imagined in the girl's face the delicate dawn of a sense that her mother had suddenly become vulgar, together with a general consciousness that the way to meet vulgarity was always to be frank and simple. 'He makes one enjoy being liked so much – liked better, I do think, than I've ever been liked by any one.'

If Mrs Brook hesitated it was, however, clearly not because she had noticed. 'Not better surely than by dear Mitchy? Or even if you come to that by Tishy herself.'

Nanda's simplicity maintained itself. 'Oh, Mr Longdon's different from Tishy.'

Her mother again hesitated. 'You mean of course he knows more?'

The girl considered it. 'He doesn't know *more*. But he knows other things – and he's pleasanter than Mitchy.'

'You mean because he doesn't want to marry you?'

It was as if she had not heard that Nanda continued: 'Well, he's more beautiful.'

'O-oh!' cried Mrs Brook, with a drawn-out extravagance of comment that amounted to an impugnment even by herself of her taste.

It contributed to Nanda's quietness. 'He's one of the most beautiful people in the world.'

Her companion at this, with a quick wonder, fixed her. '*Does* he, my dear, want to marry you?'

'Yes – to all sorts of ridiculous people.'

'But I mean – would you take *him*?'

Nanda, rising, met the question with a short ironic 'Yes!' that showed her first impatience. 'It's so charming being liked,' she went on, 'without being approved.'

But Mrs Brook only wanted to know. 'He doesn't approve——?'

'No, but it makes no difference. It's all exactly right, all the same.'

Mrs Brook seemed to wonder, however, exactly how it could be. 'He doesn't want you to give up anything?' She looked as if she were rapidly thinking what Nanda *might* give up.

'Oh yes, everything.'

It was as if for an instant she found her daughter inscrutable; then she had a strange smile. 'Me?'

The girl was perfectly prompt. 'Everything. But he wouldn't like me nearly so much if I really did.'

Her mother had a further pause. 'Does he want to *adopt* you?' Then more quickly and sadly, though also a little as if lacking courage to push the inquiry: 'We couldn't give you up, Nanda.'

'Thank you so much, mamma. But we shan't be very much tried,' Nanda said, 'because what it comes to seems to be that I'm really what you may call adopting *him*. I mean I'm little by little changing him – gradually showing him that, as I couldn't possibly have been different, and as also of course one can't keep giving up, the only way is for him not to mind and to take me just as I am. That, don't you see? is what he would never have expected to do.'

Mrs Brook recognized, in a manner the explanation, but still had her wistfulness. 'But – a – to take you, "as you are", *where*?'

'Well, to the South Kensington Museum.'

'Oh!' said Mrs Brook. Then, however, in a more exemplary tone: 'Do you enjoy so very much your long hours with him?'

Nanda appeared for an instant to think how to express it. 'Well, we're great friends.'

'And always talking about Granny?'

'Oh no – really almost never now.'

'He doesn't think so awfully much of her?' There was an oddity of eagerness in the question – a hope, a kind of dash, for something that might have been in Nanda's interest.

The girl met these things only with obliging gravity. 'I think he's losing any sense of my likeness. He's too used to it, or too many things that are too different now cover it up.'

'Well,' said Mrs Brook as she took this in, 'I think it's awfully clever of you to get only the good of him and have none of the worry.'

Nanda wondered. 'The worry?'

'You leave that all to *me*,' her mother went on, but quite forgivingly. 'I hope at any rate that the good, for you, will be real.'

'Real?' the girl, remaining vague, again echoed.

Mrs Brook at this showed, though not an irritation, a flicker of austerity. 'You must remember that we've a great many things to think about. There are things we must take for granted in each other – we must all help, in our way, to pull the coach. That's what I mean by worry, and if you don't have any, so much the better for you. For me it's in the day's work. Your father and I have most to think about always at this time, as you perfectly know – when we have to turn things round and manage somehow or other to get out of town, have to provide and pinch, to meet all the necessities, with money, money, money, at every turn running away like water. The children this year seem to fit into nothing, into nowhere, and Harold's more dreadful than he has ever been, doing nothing at all for himself and requiring everything to be done for him. He talks about his American girl, with millions, who's so awfully taken with him, but I can't find out anything about her; the only one, just now, that people seem to have heard of is the one Booby Manger's engaged to. The Mangers literally snap up everything,' Mrs Brook quite wailingly now continued: 'the Jew man, so gigantically rich – who is he? Baron Schack or Schmack – who has just taken Cumberland House and who has the awful stammer – or what is it? no roof to his mouth – is to give that horrid little Algie, to do his conversation for him, four hundred a year, which Harold pretended to me that, of all the rush of young men – dozens! – *he* was most in the running for. Your father's settled gloom is terrible, and I bear all the brunt of it; we get literally nothing this year for the Hovel, yet have to spend on it heaven knows what; and everybody, for the next three months, in Scotland and everywhere, has asked us for the wrong time and nobody for the right: so that I assure you I don't know where to turn – which doesn't, however, in the least prevent every one coming to me with their own selfish troubles.' It was as if Mrs Brook had found the cup of her secret sorrows suddenly jostled by some touch of which the perversity, though not completely noted at the moment, proved, as she a little let herself go, sufficient to make it flow over; but she drew, the next thing, from her daughter's stillness a reflection of the vanity of such heat and speedily recovered herself as if in order with more dignity to point the moral. 'I can carry my burden and shall do so to the end; but we must each remember that we shall fall to pieces if we don't manage to keep hold of some little idea of responsibility. I positively can't arrange without knowing when it is you go to him.'

'To Mr Longdon? Oh, whenever I like,' Nanda replied very gently and simply.

'And when shall you be so good as to like?'

'Well, he goes himself on Saturday, and if I want I can go a few days later.'

'And what day can you go if *I* want?' Mrs Brook spoke as with a small sharpness — just softened indeed in time — produced by the sight of a freedom on her daughter's part that suddenly loomed larger than any freedom of her own. It was still a part of the unsteadiness of the vessel of her anxieties; but she never after all remained publicly long subject to the influence that she often comprehensively designated to others as well as to herself as 'nastiness'. 'What I mean is that you might go the same day, mightn't you?'

'With him — in the train? I should think so if you wish it.'

'But would *he* wish it? I mean would he hate it?'

'I don't think so at all, but I can easily ask him.'

Mrs Brook's head inclined to the chimney and her eyes to the window. 'Easily?'

Nanda looked for a moment mystified by her mother's insistence. 'I can at any rate perfectly try it.'

'Remembering even that mamma would never have pushed so?'

Nanda's face seemed to concede even that condition. 'Well,' she at all events serenely replied, 'I really think we're good friends enough for anything.'

It might have been, for the light it quickly produced, exactly what her mother had been working to make her say. 'What do you call that then, I should like to know, but his adopting you?'

'Ah, I don't know that it matters much what it's called.'

'So long as it brings with it, you mean,' Mrs Brook asked, 'all the advantages?'

'Well yes,' said Nanda, who had now begun dimly to smile — 'call them advantages.'

Mrs Brook had a pause. 'One would be quite ready to do that if one only knew a little more exactly what they're to consist of.'

'Oh, the great advantage, I feel, is doing something for *him*.'

Nanda's companion, at this, hesitated afresh. 'But doesn't that, my dear, put the extravagance of your surrender to him on rather an odd footing? Charity, love, begins at home, and if it's a question of merely *giving*, you've objects enough for your bounty without going so far.'

The girl, as her stare showed, was held a moment by her surprise, which presently broke out. 'Why, I thought you wanted me so to be nice to him!'

'Well, I hope you won't think me very vulgar,' said Mrs Brook, 'if I tell you that I want you still more to have some idea of what you'll get by it. I've no wish,' she added, 'to keep on boring you with Mitchy—'

'Don't, don't!' Nanda pleaded.

Her mother stopped short, as if there were something in her tone that set the limit all the more utterly for being unstudied. Yet poor Mrs Brook couldn't leave it there. 'Then what do you get instead?'

'Instead of Mitchy? Oh,' said Nanda, 'I shall never marry.'

Mrs Brook at this turned away, moving over to the window with quickened weariness. Nanda, on her side, as if their talk had ended, went across to the sofa to take up her parasol before leaving the room, an impulse rather favoured than arrested by the arrival of her brother Harold, who came in at the moment both his relatives had turned a back to the door and who gave his sister, as she faced him, a greeting that made their mother look round. 'Hallo, Nan – you *are* lovely! Ain't she lovely, mother?'

'No! Mrs Brook answered, not, however, otherwise noticing him. Her domestic despair centred at this instant all in her daughter. 'Well then, we shall consider – your father and I – that he must take the consequence.'

Nanda had now her hand on the door, while Harold had dropped on the sofa. ' "He"?' she just sounded.

'I mean Mr Longdon.'

'And what do you mean by the consequence?'

'Well, it will do for the beginning of it that you'll please go down *with* him.'

'On Saturday then? Thanks, mamma,' the girl returned.

She was instantly gone, on which Mrs Brook had more attention for her son. This, after an instant, as she approached the sofa and raised her eyes from the little table beside it, came straight out. 'Where in the world is that five-pound note?'

Harold looked vacantly about him. 'What five-pound note?'

BOOK VII

MITCHY

XXIV

MR LONGDON'S garden took in three acres and, full of charming features, had for its greatest wonder the extent and colour of its old brick wall, of which the pink and purple surface was the fruit of the mild ages and the protective function, for a visitor strolling, sitting, talking, reading, that of a sort of nurse of reverie. The air of the place, in the August time, thrilled all the while with the bliss of birds, the hum of little lives unseen and the flicker of white butterflies. It was on the large flat enclosed lawn that Nanda spoke to Vanderbank of the three weeks that she would have completed there on the morrow and that had been – she made no secret of it – the happiest she had yet spent anywhere. The greyish day was soft and still and the sky faintly marbled, while the more newly arrived of the visitors from London, who had come late on the Friday afternoon, lounged away the morning in an attitude of which every relaxed line referred to the holiday he had, as it were – at first merely looking about and victualling – sat down in front of as a captain before a city. There were sitting-places, just there, out of the full light, cushioned benches in the thick wide spread of old mulberry boughs. A large book of facts lay in the young man's lap, and Nanda had come out to him, half an hour before luncheon, somewhat as Beatrice came out to Benedick: not to call him immediately indeed to the meal, but mentioning promptly that she had come at a bidding. Mr Longdon had rebuked her, it appeared, for her want of attention to their guest, showing her in this way, to her pleasure, how far he had gone toward taking her, as he called it, into the house.

'You've been thinking of yourself,' Vanderbank asked,

'as a mere clerk at a salary, and you now find that you're a partner and have a share in the concern?'

'It seems to be something like that. But doesn't a partner put in something? What have I put in?'

'Well — *me*, for one thing. Isn't it your being here that has brought me down?'

'Do you mean you wouldn't have come for him alone? Then don't you make anything of his attraction? You ought to,' said Nanda, 'when he likes you so.'

Vanderbank, longing for a river, was in white flannels, and he took her question with a happy laugh, a handsome face of good humour, that completed the effect of his long, cool fairness. 'Do you mind my just sitting still, and letting me smoke and staying with me awhile? Perhaps after a little we'll walk about — shan't we? But face to face with this dear old house, in this jolly old nook, one is too contented to move, lest raising a finger even should break the spell. What *will* be perfect will be your just sitting down — *do* sit down — and scolding me a little. That, my dear Nanda, will deepen the peace.' Some minutes later, while, near him but in another chair, she fingered the impossible book, as she pronounced it, that she had taken from him, he came back to what she had last said. 'Has he talked to you much about his "liking" me?'

Nanda waited a minute, turning over the book. 'No.'

'Then how are you just now so struck with it?'

'I'm not struck only with what I'm talked to about. I don't only know,' she went on, 'what people tell me.'

'Ah no — you're too much your mother's daughter for that!' Vanderbank leaned back and smoked, and though all his air seemed to say that when one was so at ease for gossip almost any subject would do, he kept jogging his foot with the same small nervous motion as during the half-hour at Mertle that this record has commemorated. 'You're too much one of us all,' he continued. 'We've tremendous perceptions,' he laughed. 'Of course I *should* have come for him. But after all,' he added as if all sorts of nonsense would equally serve, 'he mightn't, except for you, you know, have asked me.'

Nanda so far accepted this view as to reply: 'That's

awfully weak. He's so modest that he might have been afraid of your boring yourself.'

'That's just what I mean.'

'Well, if you do,' Nanda returned, 'the explanation's a little conceited.'

'Oh, I only made it,' Vanderbank said, 'in reference to his modesty.' Beyond the lawn the house was before him, old, square, red-roofed, well assured of its right to the place it took up in the world. This was a considerable space – in the little world at least of Beccles – and the look of possession had everywhere mixed with it, in the form of old windows and doors, the tone of old red surfaces, the style of old white facings, the age of old high creepers, the long confirmation of time. Suggestive of panelled rooms, of precious mahogany, of portraits of women dead, of coloured china glimmering through glass doors and delicate silver reflected on bared tables, the thing was one of those impressions of a particular period that it takes two centuries to produce. 'Fancy,' the young man incoherently exclaimed, 'his caring to leave anything so lovable as all this to come up and live with *us*!'

The girl, for a little, also lost herself. 'Oh, you don't know what it is – the charm comes out so as one stays. Little by little it grows and grows. There are old things everywhere that are too delightful. He lets me explore so – he lets me rummage and rifle; and every day I make discoveries.'

Vanderbank wondered as he smoked. 'You mean he lets you take things—?'

'Oh yes – up to my room, to study or to copy. There are old patterns that are too dear for anything. It's when you live with them, you see, that you know. Everything in the place is such good company.'

'Your mother ought to be here,' Vanderbank presently suggested. 'She's so fond of good company.' Then as Nanda answered nothing he went on: 'Was your grandmother ever?'

'Never,' the girl promptly said. 'Never,' she repeated in a tone quite different. After which she added: 'I'm the only one.'

'Oh, and I. "Me and you", as they say,' her companion amended.

'Yes, and Mr Mitchy, who's to come down – please don't forget – this afternoon.'

Vanderbank had another of his contemplative pauses. 'Thank you for reminding me. I shall spread myself as much as possible before he comes – try to produce so much of my effect that I shall be safe. But what did Mr Longdon ask him for?'

'Ah,' said Nanda gaily, 'what did he ask *you* for?'

'Why, for the reason you just now mentioned – that his interest in me is so uncontrollable.'

'Then isn't his interest in Mitchy—'

'Of the same general order?' Vanderbank broke in. 'Not in the least.' He seemed to look for a way to express the distinction, which suddenly occurred to him. 'He wasn't in love with Mitchy's mother.'

'No' – Nanda turned it over. 'Mitchy's mother, it appears, was awful. Mr Cashmore knew her.'

Vanderbank's smoke-puffs were profuse and his pauses frequent. 'Awful to Mr Cashmore? I'm glad to hear it – he must have deserved it. But I believe in her all the same. Mitchy's often awful himself,' the young man rambled on. 'Just so I believe in *him*.'

'So do I,' said Nanda – 'and that's why I asked him.'

'*You* asked him, my dear child? Have you the inviting?'

'Oh yes.'

The eyes he turned on her seemed really to ask if she jested or were serious. 'So you arranged for me too?'

She turned over again a few leaves of his book and, closing it with something of a clap, transferred it to the bench beside him – a movement in which, as if through a drop into thought, he rendered her no assistance. 'What I mean is that I proposed it to Mr Longdon, I suggested he should be asked. I've a reason for seeing him – I want to talk to him. And do you know,' the girl went on, 'what Mr Longdon said?'

'Something splendid of course.'

'He asked if you wouldn't perhaps dislike his being here with you.'

Vanderbank, throwing back his head, laughed, smoked, jogged his foot more than ever. 'Awfully nice. Dear old Mitch! How little afraid of him you are!'

Nanda wondered. 'Of Mitch?'

'Yes, of the tremendous pull he really has. It's all very well to talk – he *has* it. But of course I don't mean I don't know' – and as with the effect of his nervous sociability he shifted his position. 'I perfectly see that you're *not* afraid. I perfectly know what you have in your head. I should never in the least dream of accusing you – as far as *he* is concerned – of the least disposition to flirt; any more indeed,' Vanderbank pleasantly pursued, 'than even of any general tendency of that sort. No, my dear Nanda' – he kindly kept it up – 'I *will* say for you that, though a girl, thank heaven, and awfully *much* a girl, you're really not on the whole more of a flirt than a respectable social ideal prescribes.'

'Thank you most tremendously,' his companion quietly replied.

Something in the tone of it made him laugh out, and the particular sound went well with all the rest, with the August day and the charming spot and the young man's lounging figure and Nanda's own little hovering hospitality. 'Of course I strike you as patronizing you with unconscious sublimity. Well, that's all right, for what's the most natural thing to do in these conditions but the most luxurious? Won't Mitchy be wonderful for feeling and enjoying them? I assure you I'm delighted he's coming.' Then in a different tone a moment later, 'Do you expect to be here long?' he asked.

It took Nanda some time to say, 'As long as Mr Longdon will keep me, I suppose – if that doesn't sound very horrible.'

'Oh, he'll keep you! Only won't he himself,' Vanderbank went on, 'be coming up to town in the course of the autumn?'

'Well, in that case I would perfectly stay here without him.'

'And leave him in London without *you*? Ah, that's not what we want: he wouldn't be at all the same thing without you. Least of all for himself!' Vanderbank declared.

Nanda again thought. 'Yes, that's what makes him funny, I suppose – his curious infatuation. I set him off – what do you call it? – show him off: by his going round and round me as the acrobat on the horse in the circus goes round the clown. He has said a great deal to me of your mother,' she irrelevantly added.

'Oh, everything that's kind, of course, or you wouldn't mention it.'

'That's what I mean,' said Nanda.

'I see, I see – most charming of him.' Vanderbank kept his high head thrown back as if for the view, with a bright, equal, general interest, of everything that was before them, whether talked of or seen. 'Who do you think I yesterday had a letter from? An extraordinary funny one from Harold. He gave me all the family news.'

'And what *is* the family news?' the girl after a minute inquired.

'Well, the first great item is that he himself—'

'Wanted,' Nanda broke in, 'to borrow five pounds of you? I say that,' she added, 'because if he wrote to you—'

'It couldn't have been in such a case for the simple pleasure of the intercourse?' Vanderbank hesitated, but continued not to look at her. 'What do you know, pray, of poor Harold's borrowings?'

'Oh, I know as I know other things. Don't I know everything?'

'*Do* you? I should rather ask,' the young man gaily enough replied.

'Why should I not? How should I not? You know what I know.' Then, as if to explain herself and attenuate a little the sudden emphasis with which she had spoken: 'I remember you once telling me that I must take in things at my pores.'

Her companion stared, but with his laugh again changed his posture. 'That you "*must*"—?'

'That I do – and you were quite right.'

'And when did I make this extraordinary charge?'

'Ah then,' said Nanda, 'you admit it *is* a charge. It was

a long time ago – when I was a little girl. Which made it worse!' she dropped.

It made it at all events now for Vanderbank more amusing. 'Ah, not worse – better!'

She thought a moment. 'Because in that case I mightn't have understood? But that I do understand is just what you've always meant.'

' "Always", my dear Nanda? I feel somehow,' he rejoined very kindly, 'as if you overwhelmed me!'

'You "feel" as if I did – but the reality is just that I don't. The day I overwhelm you, Mr Van—!' She let that pass, however; there was too much to say about it and there was something else much simpler. 'Girls understand now. It has got to be faced, as Tishy says.'

'Oh well,' Vanderbank laughed, 'we don't require Tishy to point that out to us. What are we all doing most of the time but trying to face it?'

'Doing? Aren't you doing rather something very different? You're just trying to dodge it. You're trying to make believe – not perhaps to yourselves but to *us* – that it isn't so.'

'But surely you don't want us to be any worse!'

She shook her head with brisk gravity. 'We don't care really what you are.'

His amusement now dropped to her straighter. 'Your "we" is awfully beautiful. It's charming to hear you speak for the whole lovely lot. Only you speak, you know, as if you were just the class apart that you yet complain of our – by our scruples – implying you to be.'

She considered this objection with her eyes on his face. 'Well then, we do care. Only—!'

'Only it's a big subject.'

'Oh yes – no doubt; it's a big subject.' She appeared to wish to meet him on everything reasonable. 'Even Mr Longdon admits that.'

Vanderbank wondered. 'You mean you talk over with him—'

'The subject of girls? Why, we scarcely discuss anything else.'

'Oh, no wonder then you're not bored. But you mean,'

Vanderbank asked, 'that he recognizes the inevitable change—?'

'He can't shut his eyes to the facts. He sees we're quite a different thing.'

'I dare say' – her friend was fully appreciative. 'Yet the old thing – what do *you* know of it?'

'I personally? Well, I've seen some change even in *my* short life. And aren't the old books full of us? Then Mr Longdon himself has told me.'

Vanderbank smoked and smoked. 'You've gone into it with him?'

'As far as a man and a woman can together.'

As he took her in at this with a turn of his eye he might have had in his ears the echo of all the times it had been dropped in Buckingham Crescent that Nanda was 'wonderful'. She *was* indeed. 'Oh, he's of course on certain sides shy.'

'Awfully – too beautifully. And then there's Aggie,' the girl pursued. 'I mean for the real old thing.'

'Yes, no doubt – if she *be* the real old thing. But what the deuce really *is* Aggie?'

'Well,' said Nanda with the frankest interest, 'she's a miracle. If one could be her exactly, absolutely, without the least little mite of change, one would probably do the best thing to close with it. Otherwise – except for anything *but* that – I'd rather brazen it out as myself.'

There fell between them on this a silence of some minutes, after which it would probably not have been possible for either to say if their eyes had met while it lasted. This was at any rate not the case as Vanderbank at last exclaimed: 'Your brass, my dear young lady, is pure gold!'

'Then it's of me, I think, that Harold ought to borrow.'

'You mean therefore that mine isn't?' Vanderbank inquired.

'Well, you really haven't any natural "cheek" – not like *some* of them. You're, in yourself, as uneasy, if anything's said and every one giggles or makes some face, as Mr Longdon, and if Lord Petherton hadn't once told me that a man hates almost as much to be called modest as a woman does, I would say that very often in London now you must pass some bad moments.'

The present might precisely have been one of them, we should doubtless have gathered, had we seen fully recorded in Vanderbank's face the degree to which this prompt response embarrassed or at least stupefied him. But he could always laugh. 'I like your "in London now"!'

'It's the tone and the current and the effect of all the others that push you along,' she went on as if she had not heard him. 'If such things are contagious, as every one says, you prove it perhaps as much as any one. But you don't begin' – she continued blandly enough to work it out for him: 'or you can't at least originally have begun. Any one would know that now – from the terrific effect I see I produce on you by talking this way. There it is – it's all out before one knows it, isn't it, and I can't help it any more than you can, can I?' So she appeared to put it to him, with something in her lucidity that would have been infinitely touching; a strange, grave, calm consciousness of their common doom and of what in especial in it would be worst for herself. He sprang up indeed after an instant as if he had been infinitely touched; he turned away, taking just near her a few steps to and fro, gazed about the place again, but this time without the air of particularly seeing it, and then came back to her as if from a greater distance. An observer at all initiated would, at the juncture, fairly have hung on his lips, and there was in fact on Vanderbank's part quite the look of the man – though it lasted but just while we seize it – in suspense about himself. The most initiated observer of all would have been poor Mr Longdon, who would now have been destined, however, to be also the most defeated and the sign of whose tension would have been a smothered 'Ah, if he doesn't do it *now*!' Well, Vanderbank didn't do it 'now', and the long, odd, irrelevant sigh that he gave out might have sufficed as the record of his recovery from a peril lasting just long enough to be measured. Had there been any measure of it meanwhile for Nanda? There was nothing at least to show either the presence or the relief of anxiety in the way in which, by a prompt transition, she left her last appeal to him simply to take care of itself. 'You haven't denied that Harold does borrow.'

Vanderbank gave a note as of cheer for this luckily firmer ground. 'My dear child, I never lent the silly boy five pounds in my life. In fact I like the way you talk of that. I don't know quite for what you take me, but the number of persons to whom I *have* lent five pounds—'

'Is so awfully small' – she took him up on it – 'as not to look so very well for you?' She held him an instant as with the fine intelligence of his meaning in this, and then, though not with sharpness, she broke out: 'Why are you trying to make out that you're nasty and stingy? Why do you misrepresent—'

'My natural generosity? I don't misrepresent anything, but I take, I think, rather markedly good care of money.' She had remained in her place and he was before her on the grass, his hands in his pockets and his manner perhaps a little awkward. 'The way you young things talk of it!'

'Harold talks of it – but I don't think *I* do. I'm not a bit expensive – ask mother, or even ask father. I do with awfully little – for clothes and things, and I could easily do with still less. Harold's a born consumer, as Mitchy says; he says also he's one of those people who will never really want.'

'Ah, for that, Mitchy himself will never let him.'

'Well then, with every one helping us all round aren't we a lovely family? I don't speak of it to tell tales, but when you mention hearing from Harold all sorts of things immediately come over me. We seem to be all living more or less on other people, all immensely "beholden". You can easily say of course that I'm the worst of all. The children and their people, at Bognor, are in borrowed quarters – mother got them lent her – as to which, no doubt, I'm perfectly aware that I ought to be there sharing them, taking care of my little brother and sister, instead of sitting here at Mr Longdon's expense to expose everything and criticize. Father and mother, in Scotland, are on a pro- gramme of places—! Well' – she pulled herself up – 'I'm not in *that* at any rate. Say you've lent Harold only five shillings,' she went on.

Vanderbank stood smiling. 'Well, say I have. I never lend any one whatever more.'

'It only adds to my conviction,' Nanda explained, 'that he writes to Mr Longdon.'

'But if Mr Longdon doesn't say so——?' Vanderbank objected.

'Oh, that proves nothing.' She got up as she spoke. 'Harold also works Granny.' He only laughed out at first for this, while she went on: 'You'll think I make myself out fearfully deep – I mean in the way of knowing everything without having to be told. That *is*, as you say, mamma's great accomplishment, so it must be hereditary. Besides, there seem to me only too many things one *is* told. Only Mr Longdon has in fact said nothing.'

She had looked about responsibly, as if not to leave in disorder the garden nook they had occupied, picking up a newspaper and changing the place of a cushion. 'I do think that with him you're remarkable,' Vanderbank observed – 'putting on one side all you seem to know and on the other all he holds his tongue about. What then *does* he say?' the young man asked after a slight pause and perhaps even with a slight irritation.

Nanda glanced round again – she was folding, rather carefully, her paper. Presently her glance met their friend, who, having come out of one of the long windows that opened to the lawn, had stopped there to watch them. 'He says just now that luncheon's ready.'

XXV

'I've made him,' Nanda said in the drawing-room to Mitchy, 'make Mr Van go with him.'

Mr Longdon, in the rain, which had come on since the morning, had betaken himself to church, and his other guest, with sufficiently marked good humour, had borne him company. The windows of the drawing-room looked at the wet garden, all vivid and rich in the summer shower, and Mitchy, after seeing Vanderbank turn up his trousers and fling back a last answer to the not quite sincere chaff

his submission had engendered, adopted freely and familiarly the prospect not only of a grateful, freshened lawn,
but of a good hour in the very pick, as he called it, of his
actual happy conditions. The favouring rain, the dear old
place, the charming serious house, the large inimitable
room, the absence of the others, the present vision of what
his young friend had given him to count on – the sense of
these delights was expressed in his fixed, generous glare.
He was at first too pleased even to sit down; he measured
the great space from end to end, admiring again everything
he had admired before and protesting afresh that no
modern ingenuity – not even his own, to which he did
justice – could create effects of such purity. The final touch
in the picture before them was just the composer's ignorance. Mr Longdon had not made his house, he had simply
lived it, and the 'taste' of the place – Mitchy in certain
connexions abominated the word – was nothing more than
the beauty of his life. Everything on every side had dropped
straight from heaven, with nowhere a bargaining thumb-
mark, a single sign of the shop. All this would have been a
wonderful theme for discourse in Buckingham Crescent –
so happy an exercise for the votaries of that temple of
analysis that he repeatedly spoke of their experience of it as
crying aloud for Mrs Brook. The questions it set in motion
for the perceptive mind were exactly those that, as he said,
most made them feel themselves. Vanderbank's plea for his
morning had been a pile of letters to work off, and
Mitchy – then coming down, as he announced from the
first, ready for anything – had gone to church with Mr
Longdon and Nanda in the finest spirit of curiosity. He
now – after the girl's remark – turned away from his view
of the rain, which he found different somehow from other
rain, as everything else was different, and replied that he
knew well enough what she could make Mr Longdon do,
but only wondered at Mr Longdon's secret for acting on
their friend. He was there before her with his hands in his
pockets and appreciation winking from every yellow spot
of his red neck-tie. 'Afternoon service of a wet Sunday in a
small country town is a large order. Does Van do everything the proprietor wants?'

'He may perhaps have had a suspicion of what *I* want,' Nanda explained. 'If I want particularly to talk to you—'

'He has got out of the way to give me a chance? Well then, he's as usual simply magnificent. How can I express the bliss of finding myself enclosed with you in this sweet old security, this really unimagined sanctity? Nothing is more charming than suddenly to come across something sharp and fresh after we've thought there was nothing more that could draw from us a groan. We've supposed we've had it all, have squeezed the last impression out of the last disappointment, penetrated to the last familiarity in the last surprise; then some fine day we find that we haven't done justice to life. There are little things that pop up and make us feel again. What *may* happen is after all incalculable. There's just a little chuck of the dice, and for three minutes we win. These, my dear young lady, are my three minutes. You wouldn't believe the amusement I get from them, and how can I possibly tell you? There's a faint, divine old fragrance here in the room – or doesn't it perhaps reach you? I sha'n't have lived without it, but I see now I had been afraid I should. You, on your side, won't have lived without some touch of greatness. This moment is great, and you've produced it. You were great when you felt all you *could* produce. Therefore,' Mitchy went on, pausing once more, as he walked, before a picture, 'I won't pull the whole thing down by the vulgarity of wishing that I too had a first-rate Cotman.'

'Have you given up some *very* big thing to come?' Nanda inquired.

'What in the world is very big, my child, but the beauty of this hour? I haven't the least idea *what*, when I got Mr Longdon's note, I gave up. Don't ask me for an account of anything; everything went – became imperceptible. I *will* say that for myself: I shed my badness, I do forget people, with a facility that makes me, for bits, for little patches, so far as they are concerned, cease to *be*; so that my life is spotted all over with momentary states in which I'm as the dead of whom nothing is said but good.' He had strolled toward her again while she smiled at him. 'I've died for this, Nanda.'

'The only difficulty I see,' she presently replied, 'is that you ought to marry a woman really clever and that I'm not quite sure what there may be of that in Aggie.'

'In Aggie?' her friend echoed very gently. 'Is *that* what you've sent for me for – to talk about Aggie?'

'Didn't it occur to you it might be?'

'That it couldn't possibly, you mean, be anything else?' He looked about for the place in which it would express the deepest surrender to the scene to sit, then sank down with a beautiful prompt submission. 'I've no idea of what occurred to me – nothing at least but the sense that I had occurred to *you*. The occurrence is clay in the hands of the potter. Do with me what you will.'

'You appreciate everything so wonderfully,' Nanda said, 'that it oughtn't to be hard for you to appreciate *her*. I do dream so that you may save her; and that's why I haven't waited.'

'The only thing that remains to me in life,' he answered, 'is a certain accessibility to the thought of what I may still do to figure a little in your eye; but that's precisely a thought you may assist to become clearer. You may for instance give me some pledge or sign that if I do figure – prance and caracole and sufficiently kick up the dust – your eye won't suffer itself to be distracted from me. I think there's no adventure I'm not ready to undertake for you; yet my passion – chastened, through all this, purified, austere – is still enough of this world not wholly to have renounced the fancy of some small reward.'

'How small?' the girl asked.

She spoke as if feeling that she must take from him, in common kindness, at least as much as she would make him take, and the serious, anxious patience such a consciousness gave to her tone was met by Mitchy with a charmed reasonableness that his habit of hyperbole did nothing to misrepresent. He glowed at her with the fullest recognition that there was something he was there to discuss with her, but with the assurance in every soft sound of him that no height to which she might lift the discussion would be too great for him to reach. His every cadence and every motion was an implication, as from one to the other, of the exquisite. Oh, he could sustain it! 'Well, I mean the establishment of something between us. I mean your arranging somehow that we shall be drawn more together – know together something nobody else knows. I should like so terrifically to have a secret with you.'

'Oh, if that's all you want you can be easily gratified. *Rien de plus facile*, as mamma says. I'm full of secrets – I think I'm really most secretive. I'll share almost any one of them with you – that is if it's a good one.'

Mitchy hesitated. 'You mean you'll choose it yourself? You won't let it be one of mine?'

Nanda wondered. 'But what's the difference?'

Her companion jumped up again and for a moment pervaded the place. 'When you say such things as that, you're of a beauty—! *May* it,' he asked as he stopped before her, 'be one of mine – a perfectly awful one?'

She showed her clearest interest. 'As I suppose the most awful secrets are the best – yes, certainly.'

'I'm hideously tempted.' But he hung fire; then dropping into his chair again: 'It would be too bad. I'm afraid I can't.'

'Then why won't *this* do, just as it is?'

'"This"?' He looked over the big bland room. 'Which?'

'Why, what you're here for?'

'My dear child, I'm here – most of all – to love you more than ever; and there's an absence of favouring mystery about *that*—'

She looked at him as if seeing what he meant and only asking to remedy it. 'There's a certain amount of mystery we can now *make* – that it strikes me in fact we *must* make. Dear Mitchy,' she continued almost with eagerness, 'I don't think we *can* really tell.'

He had fallen back in his chair, not looking at her now and with his hands, from his supported elbows, clasped to keep himself more quiet. 'Are you still talking about Aggie?'

'Why, I've scarcely begun!'

'Oh!' It was not irritation he appeared to express, but the slight strain of an effort to get into relation with the subject. Better to focus the image he closed his eyes awhile.

'You speak of something that may draw us together, and I simply reply that if you don't feel how near together we are in this I shouldn't imagine you ever would. You must have wonderful notions,' she presently went on, 'of the ideal state of union. I pack every one off for you – I banish everything that can interfere, and I don't in the least mind your knowing that I find the consequence delightful. *You* may talk, if you like, of what will have passed between us, but I shall never mention it to a soul; literally not to a living creature. What do you want more than that?' He opened his eyes in deference to the question, but replied only with a gaze as unassisted as if it had come through a hole in a curtain. 'You say you're ready for an adventure, and it's just an adventure that I propose. If I can make you feel for yourself as I feel *for* you the beauty of your chance to go in and save her—'

'Well, if you can?' – Mitchy at last broke in. 'I don't think, you know,' he said after a moment, 'you'll find it easy to make your two ends meet.'

She thought a little longer. 'One of the ends is yours, so that you'll act *with* me. If I wind you up so that you go—'

'You'll just happily sit and watch me spin? Thank you! *That* will be my reward?'

Nanda on this rose from her chair as with the impulse of protest. 'Sha'n't you care for my gratitude, my admiration?'

'Oh yes' – Mitchy seemed to muse. 'I shall care for *them*. But I don't quite see, you know, what you *owe* to Aggie. It isn't as if—!' But with this he faltered.

'As if she cared particularly for *me*? Ah, that has nothing to do with it; that's a thing without which surely it's but too possible to be exquisite. There are beautiful, quite beautiful people who don't care for me. The thing that's important to one is the thing one sees one's self, and it's quite enough if *I* see what can be made of that child. Marry her, Mitchy, and you'll see who she'll care for!'

Mitchy kept his position; he was for the moment – his image of shortly before reversed – the one who appeared to sit happily and watch. 'It's too awfully pleasant your asking me anything whatever!'

'Well then, as I say, beautifully, grandly save her.'

'As you say, yes' – he sympathetically inclined his head. 'But without making me feel exactly what you mean by it.'

'Keep her,' Nanda returned, 'from becoming like the Duchess.'

'But she isn't a bit like the Duchess in any of her elements. She's a totally different thing.'

It was only for an instant, however, that this objection seemed to count. 'That's exactly why she'll be so perfect for you. You'll get her away – take her out of her aunt's life.'

Mitchy met it all now in a sort of spellbound stillness. 'What do you know about her aunt's life?'

'Oh, I know everything!' She spoke with her first faint shade of impatience.

It produced for a little a hush between them, at the end of which her companion said with extraordinary gentleness and tenderness: 'Dear old Nanda!' Her own silence appeared consciously to continue, and the suggestion of it might have been that for intelligent ears there was nothing to add to the declaration she had just made and which Mitchy sat there taking in as with a new light. What he drew from it indeed he presently went on to show. 'You're too awfully interesting. Of course – you know a lot. How shouldn't you – and why?'

'"Why"? Oh, that's another affair! But you don't imagine what I know; I'm sure it's much more than you've a notion of. That's the kind of thing now one *is* – just except the little marvel of Aggie. What on earth,' the girl pursued, 'do you take us for?'

'Oh, it's all right!' breathed Mitchy, divinely pacific.

'I'm sure I don't know whether it is; I shouldn't wonder if it were in fact all wrong. But what at least is certainly right is for one not to pretend anything else. There I am for you at any rate. Now the beauty of Aggie is that she knows nothing – but absolutely, utterly: not the least little tittle of anything.'

It was barely visible that Mitchy hesitated, and he spoke quite gravely. 'Have you tried her?'

'Oh yes. And Tishy has.' His gravity had been less than

Nanda's. 'Nothing, nothing.' The memory of some scene or some passage might have come back to her with a charm. 'Ah, say what you will – it *is* the way we ought to be!'

Mitchy, after a minute of much intensity, had stopped watching her; changing his posture and with his elbows on his knees, he dropped for a while his face into his hands. Then he jerked himself to his feet. 'There's something I wish awfully I could say to you. But I can't.'

Nanda, after a slow head-shake, covered him with one of the dimmest of her smiles. 'You needn't say it. I know perfectly which it is.' She held him an instant, after which she went on: 'It's simply that you wish me fully to understand that *you're* one who, in perfect sincerity, doesn't mind one straw how awful—'

'Yes, how awful?' He had kindled, as she paused, with his new eagerness.

'Well, one's knowledge may be. It doesn't shock in you a single hereditary prejudice.'

'Oh, "hereditary"—!' Mitchy ecstatically murmured.

'You even rather like me the better for it; so that one of the reasons why you couldn't have told me – though not of course, I know, the only one – is that you would have been literally almost ashamed. Because, you know,' she went on, 'it *is* strange.'

'My lack of hereditary—?'

'Yes, discomfort in the presence of the fact I speak of. There's a kind of sense you don't possess.'

His appreciation again fairly goggled at her. 'Oh, you do know everything!'

'You're so good that nothing shocks you,' she lucidly persisted. 'There's a kind of delicacy you haven't got.'

He was more and more struck, 'I've only that – as it were – of the skin and the fingers?' he appealed.

'Oh, and that of the mind. And that of the soul. And some other kinds, certainly. But not *the* kind.'

'Yes' – he wondered – 'I suppose that's the only way one can name it.' It appeared to rise there before him. '*The* kind!'

'The kind that would make me painful to you. Or rather

not me perhaps,' she added as if to create between them the fullest possible light; 'but my situation, my exposure – all the results of them that I show. Doesn't one become a sort of a little drainpipe with everything flowing through?'

'Why don't you call it more gracefully,' Mitchy asked, freshly struck, 'a little aeolian harp set in the drawing-room window and vibrating in the breeze of conversation?'

'Oh, because the harp gives out a sound, and *we* – at least we try to – give out none.'

'What you take, you mean, you keep?'

'Well, it sticks to us. And that's what you don't mind!'

Their eyes met long on it. 'Yes – I see. I *don't* mind. I've the most extraordinary lacunae.'

'Oh, I don't know about others,' Nanda replied; 'I haven't noticed them. But you've that one, and it's enough.'

He continued to face her with his queer mixture of assent and speculation. 'Enough, my dear, for what? To have made me impossible for you because the only man you could, as they say, have "respected" would be a man who *would* have minded?' Then as under the cool, soft pressure of the question she looked at last away from him: 'The man with "*the* kind", as you call it, happens to be just the type you *can* love? But what's the use,' he persisted as she answered nothing, 'in loving a person with the prejudice – hereditary or other – to which you're precisely obnoxious? Do you positively *like* to love in vain?'

It was a question, the way she turned back to him seemed to say, that deserved a responsible answer. 'Yes.'

But she had moved off after speaking, and Mitchy's eyes followed her to different parts of the room as, with small pretexts of present atention to it, small touches for symmetry, she slowly measured it. 'What's extraordinary then is your idea of my finding any charm in Aggie's ignorance.'

She immediately put down an old snuff-box. 'Why, it's the one sort of thing you don't know. You can't imagine,' she said as she returned to him, 'the effect it will produce on you. You must get really near it and see it all come out to feel all its beauty. You'll like it, Mitchy' – and Nanda's gravity was wonderful – 'better than anything you *have* known.'

The clear sincerity of this, even had there been nothing else, imposed a consideration that Mitchy now flagrantly could give, and the deference of his suggestion of difficulty only grew more deep. 'I'm to do then, with this happy condition of hers, what you say *you've* done – to "try" it.' And then as her assent, so directly challenged, failed an instant: 'But won't my approach to it, however cautious, be just what will break it up and spoil it?'

Nanda thought. 'Why so – if mine wasn't?'

'Oh, you're not me.'

'But I'm just as bad.'

'Thank you, my dear!' Mitchy rang out.

'Without,' Nanda pursued, 'being as good.' She had on this, in a different key, her own sudden explosion. 'Don't you see, Mitchy dear – for the very heart of it all – how good I *believe* you?'

She had spoken as with a flare of impatience at some justice he failed to do her, and this brought him after a startled instant close enough to her to take up her hand. She let him have it, and, in mute, solemn reassurance he raised it to his lips, saying to her thus more things than he could say in any other way; which yet just after, when he had released it and a motionless pause had ensued, didn't prevent him from adding three words. 'Oh, Nanda, Nanda!'

The tone of them made her again extraordinarily gentle. 'Don't "try" anything then. Take everything for granted.'

He had turned away from her and walked mechanically, with his air of blind emotion, to the window, where for a minute he looked out. 'It has stopped raining,' he said at last; 'it's going to brighten.'

The place had three windows, and Nanda went to the next. 'Not quite yet – but I think it will.'

Mitchy soon faced back into the room, where after a brief hesitation he moved as quietly – almost as cautiously – as if on tiptoe to the seat occupied by his companion at the beginning of their talk. Here he sank down watching the girl, who stood awhile longer with her eyes on the garden. 'You want me, you say, to take her out of the Duchess's life; but where am I myself, if we come to that, but even more *in* the Duchess's life than Aggie is! I'm in it by my contacts, my associations, my indifferences – all my acceptances, knowledges, amusements. I'm in it by my cynicisms – those that circumstances somehow from the first, when I began for myself to look at life and the world, committed me to and steeped me in; I'm in it by a kind of desperation that I shouldn't have felt perhaps if you had got hold of me sooner with just this touch with which you've got hold of me today; and I'm in it more than all – you'll yourself admit – by the very fact that her aunt desires, as you know, much more even than you do, to bring the thing about. Then we *should* be – the Duchess and I – shoulder to shoulder!'

Nanda heard him motionless to the end, taking also another minute to turn over what he had said. 'What is it you like so in Lord Petherton?' she asked as she came to him.

'My dear child, if you could only tell me! It would be, wouldn't it? – it must have been – the subject of some fairytale, if fairy-tales were made now, or better still, of some Christmas pantomime: "The Gnome and the Giant".'

Nanda appeared to try – not with much success – to see it. 'Do you find Lord Petherton a Gnome?'

Mitchy at first, for all reward, only glared at her. 'Charming, Nanda – charming!'

'A man's giant enough for Lord Petherton,' she went on, 'when his fortune's gigantic. He preys upon you.'

His hands in his pockets and his legs much apart, Mitchy sat there as in a posture adapted to her simplicity. 'You're adorable. *You* don't. But it *is* rather horrid, isn't it?' he presently went on.

Her momentary silence would have been by itself enough of an answer. 'Nothing – of all you speak of,' she nevertheless returned, 'will matter then. She'll so simplify your life.' He remained just as he was, only with his eyes on her; and meanwhile she had turned again to her window, through which a faint sunstreak began to glimmer and play. At the sight of it she opened the casement to let in the warm freshness. 'The rain *has* stopped.'

'You say you want me to save her. But what you really

mean,' Mitchy resumed from the sofa, 'isn't at all exactly that.'

Nanda, without heeding the remark, took in the sunshine. 'It will be charming now in the garden.'

Her friend got up, found his wonderful crossbarred cap after a glance on a neighbouring chair, and with it came toward her. 'Your hope is that – as I'm good enough to be worth it – she'll save *me*.'

Nanda looked at him now. 'She will, Mitchy – she *will*!'

They stood a moment in the recovered brightness; after which he mechanically – as with the pressure of quite another consciousness – put on his cap. 'Well then, shall that hope between us be the thing—?'

'The thing?' – she just wondered.

'Why, that will have drawn us together – to hold us so, you know – this afternoon. I mean the secret we spoke of.'

She put out to him on this the hand he had taken a few minutes before, and he clasped it now only with the firmness it seemed to give and to ask for. 'Oh, it will do for that!' she said as they went out together.

XXVI

It had been understood that he was to take his leave on the morrow while Vanderbank was to stay another day. Mr Longdon had for the Sunday dinner invited three or four of his neighbours to 'meet' the two gentlemen from town, so that it was not till the company had departed, or in other words till near bedtime, that our four friends could again have become aware, as between themselves, of that directness of mutual relation which forms the subject of our picture. It had not, however, prevented Nanda's slipping upstairs as soon as the doctor and his wife had gone, and the manner indeed in which on the stroke of eleven Mr Longdon kept up his tradition of appropriating a particular candle was as positive an expression of it as any other. Nothing in him was more amiable than the terms maintained between the rigour of his personal habits and his free imagination of the habits of others. He deprecated as regards the former, it might have been seen, most signs of resemblance, and no one had ever dared to learn how he would have handled a show of imitation. 'The way to flatter him,' Mitchy threw off five minutes later, 'is not to make him think you're like him, but to let him see how different you perceive he can bear to think you. I mean of course without hating you.'

'But what interest have *you*,' Vanderbank asked, 'in the way to flatter him?'

'My dear fellow, more than you, I haven't been here all day without arriving at conclusions on the credit he has opened to you—!'

'Do you mean the amount he'll settle?'

'You have it in your power,' said Mitchy, 'to make it anything you like.'

'And is he then – so bloated?'

Mitchy was on his feet in the apartment in which their host had left them, and he had at first for this question but an expressive motion of the shoulders in respect to everything in the room. 'See, judge, guess, feel!'

But it was as if Vanderbank, before the fire, consciously controlled his attention. 'Oh, I don't care a hang!'

This passage took place in the library and as a consequence of their having confessed, as their friend faced them with his bedroom light, that a brief, discreet vigil and a box of cigarettes would fix better than anything else the fine impression of the day. Mitchy might at that moment, on the evidence of the eyes Mr Longdon turned to them and of which his innocent candle-flame betrayed the secret, have found matter for a measure of the almost extreme allowances he wanted them to want of him. They had only to see that the greater window was fast and to turn out the library lamp. It might really have amused them to stand a moment at the open door that, apart from this, was to testify to his conception of those who were not, in the smaller hours, as *he* was. He had in fact by his retreat – and but too sensibly – left them there with a deal of midnight company. If one of these presences was the mystery he had himself mixed, the manner of our young men showed a due expectation of the others. Mitchy, on hearing how little Vanderbank 'cared', only kept up a while longer that observant revolution in which he had spent much of his day, to which any fresh sense of any exhibition always promptly committed him and which, had it not been controlled by infinite tact, might have affected the nerves of those in whom enjoyment was less rotary. He was silent long enough to suggest his fearing that almost anything he might say would appear too allusive; then at last once more he took his risk. 'Awfully jolly old place!'

'It is indeed,' Van only said; but his posture in the large chair he had pushed towards the open window was of itself almost an opinion. The August night was hot and the air that came in charged and sweet. Vanderbank smoked with his face turned to the dusky garden and the dim stars; at the end of a few moments more of which he glanced round. 'Don't you think it rather stuffy with that big lamp? As those candles on the chimney are going we might put it out.'

'Like this?' The amiable Mitchy had straightway obliged his companion and he as promptly took in the effect of the diminished light on the character of the room, which he commended as if the depth of shadow produced were all this companion had sought. He might freshly have brought home to Vanderbank that a man sensitive to so many different things could never really be incommoded, though that personage presently indeed showed himself occupied with another thought.

'I think I ought to mention to you that I've told him how you and Mrs Brook now both know. I did so this afternoon on our way back from church – I hadn't done it before. He took me a walk round to show me more of the place, and that gave me my chance. But he doesn't mind,' Vanderbank continued. 'The only thing is that I've thought it may possibly make him speak to you, so that it's better you should know he knows. But he told me definitely Nanda doesn't.'

Mitchy took this in with an attention that spoke of his already recognizing how the less tempered darkness favoured talk. 'And is that all that passed between you?'

'Well, practically; except of course that I made him

understand, I think, how it happened that I haven't kept my own counsel.'

'Oh, but you *have* – didn't he at least feel? – or perhaps even have done better, when you've two such excellent persons to keep it *for* you? Can't he easily believe how we feel with you?'

Vanderbank appeared for a minute to leave this appeal unheeded; he continued to stare into the garden while he smoked and swung the long leg he had thrown over the arm of the chair. When he at last spoke, however, it was with some emphasis – perhaps even with some vulgarity. 'Oh rot!'

Mitchy hovered without an arrest. 'You mean he *can't* feel?'

'I mean it isn't true. I've no illusions about you. I know how you're both affected, though I of course perfectly trust you.'

Mitchy had a short silence. 'Trust us not to speak?'

'Not to speak to Nanda herself – though of course too if you spoke to others,' Vanderbank went on, 'they would immediately rush and tell her.'

'I've spoken to no one,' said Mitchy.

'I'm sure of it. And neither has Mrs Brook.'

'I'm glad you're sure of that also,' Mitchy returned, 'for it's only doing her justice.'

'Oh, I'm quite confident of it,' said Vanderbank.

'And without asking her?'

'Perfectly.'

'And you're equally sure, without asking, that *I* haven't betrayed you?' After which, while, as if to let the question lie there in its folly, Vanderbank said nothing, his friend pursued: 'I came, I must tell you, terribly near it today.'

'Why must you tell me? Your coming "near" doesn't concern me, and I take it you don't suppose I'm watching or sounding you. Mrs Brook will have come terribly near,' Vanderbank continued as if to make the matter free; 'but she won't have done it either. She will have been distinctly tempted—'

'But she won't have fallen?' Mitchy broke in. 'Exactly – there we are. *I* was distinctly tempted and I didn't fall. I think your certainty about Mrs Brook,' he added, 'shows you do know her. She's incapable of anything deliberately nasty.'

'Oh, of anything nasty in any way,' Vanderbank said musingly and kindly.

'Yes; one knows on the whole what she *won't* do.' After which for a period Mitchy roamed and reflected. 'But in spite of the assurance given you by Mr Longdon – or perhaps indeed just because of your having taken it – I think I ought to mention to you my belief that Nanda does know of his offer to you. I mean by having guessed it.'

'Oh!' said Vanderbank.

'There's in fact more still,' his companion pursued, 'that I feel I should like to mention to you.'

'Oh!' Vanderbank at first only repeated. But after a moment he said: 'My dear fellow, I'm much obliged.'

'The thing I speak of is something I should at any rate have said, and I should have looked out for some chance if we had not had this one.' Mitchy spoke as if his friend's last words were not of consequence, and he continued as Vanderbank got up and, moving rather aimlessly, came and stood with his back to the chimney. 'My only hesitation would have been caused by its entailing our going down into things in a way that, face to face – given the private nature of the things – I dare say most men don't particularly enjoy. But if you don't mind—'

'Oh, I don't mind. In fact, as I tell you, I recognize an obligation to you.' Vanderbank, with his shoulders against the high mantel, uttered this without a direct look; he smoked and smoked, then looked at the tip of his cigarette. 'You feel convinced she knows?' he inquired.

'Well, it's my impression.'

'Ah, any impression of yours – of that sort – is sure to be right. If you think I ought to have it from you I'm really grateful. Is that – a – what you wanted to say to me?' Vanderbank with a slight hesitation demanded.

Mitchy, watching him more than he watched Mitchy, shook a mildly decisive head. 'No.'

Vanderbank, his eyes on his smoke puffs, seemed to wonder. 'What you wanted is – something else?'

'Something else.'

'Oh!' said Vanderbank for the third time.

The ejaculation had been vague, but the movement that followed it was definite; the young man, turning away, found himself again near the chair he had quitted, and resumed possession of it as a sign of being at his friend's service. This friend, however, not only hung fire but finally went back to take a shot from a quarter they might have been supposed to have left. 'It strikes me as odd his imagining – awfully acute as he is – that she has *not* guessed. One wouldn't have thought he could live with her here in such an intimacy – seeing her every day and pretty much all day – and make such a mistake.'

Vanderbank, his great length all of a lounge again, turned it over. 'And yet I do thoroughly feel the mistake's not yours.'

Mitchy had a new serenity of affirmation. 'Oh, it's not mine.'

'Perhaps then' – it occurred to Vanderbank – 'he doesn't really believe it.'

'And only says so to make you feel more easy?'

'So that one may – in fairness to one's self – keep one's head, as it were, and decide quite on one's own grounds.'

'Then you *have* still to decide?'

Van took his time to answer. 'I've still to decide.' Mitchy became again on this, in the sociable dusk, a slow-circling, vaguely agitated element, and his friend continued: 'Is your idea very generously and handsomely to help that by letting me know—'

'That I do definitely renounce' – Mitchy took him up – 'any pretension and any hope? Well, I'm ready with a proof of it. I've passed my word that I'll apply elsewhere.'

Vanderbank turned more round to him. 'Apply to the Duchess for her niece?'

'It's practically settled.'

'But since when?'

Mitchy barely faltered. 'Since this afternoon.'

'Ah then, not with the Duchess herself.'

'With Nanda – whose plan from the first, you won't have forgotten, the thing has so charmingly been.'

Vanderbank could show that his not having in the least

forgotten was yet not a bar to his being now mystified. 'But, my dear man, what can Nanda "settle"?'

'My fate,' Mitchy said, pausing well before him.

Vanderbank sat now a minute with raised eyes, catching the indistinctness of his friend's strange expression. 'You're both beyond me!' he exclaimed at last. 'I don't see what you in particular gain.'

'I didn't either till she made it all out to me. One sees then, in such a matter, for one's self. And as everything's gain that isn't loss, there was nothing I *could* lose. It gets me,' Mitchy further explained, 'out of the way.'

'Out of the way of what?'

This, Mitchy frankly showed, was more difficult to say, but he in time brought it out. 'Well, of appearing to suggest to you that my existence, in a prolonged state of singleness, may ever represent for her any real alternative.'

'But alternative to what?'

'Why, to being *your* wife, damn you!' Mitchy, on these words turned away again, and his companion, in the presence of his renewed dim gyrations, sat for a minute dumb. Before Van had spoken indeed he was back again. 'Excuse my violence, but of course you really see.'

'I'm not pretending anything,' Vanderbank said – 'but a man *must* understand. What I catch hold of is that you offer me – in the fact that you're thus at any rate disposed of – a proof that I at any rate sha'n't, if I hesitate to "go in", have a pretext for saying to myself that I *may* deprive her—'

'Yes, precisely,' Mitchy now urbanely assented: 'of something, in the shape of a man with *my* amount of money, that she may live to regret and to languish for. My amount of money, don't you see,' he very simply added, 'is nothing to her.'

'And you want me to be sure that – so far as I may ever have had a scruple – she has had her chance and got rid of it.'

'Completely,' Mitchy smiled.

'Because' – Vanderbank, with the aid of his cigarette, thoughtfully pieced it out – 'that may possibly bring me to the point.'

'Possibly!' Mitchy laughed.

He had stood a moment longer, almost as if to see the possibility develop before his eyes, and had even started at the next sound of his friend's voice. What Vanderbank in fact brought out, however, only made him turn his back. 'Do you like so very much little Aggie?'

'Well,' said Mitchy, 'Nanda does. And I like Nanda.'

'You're too amazing,' Vanderbank mused. His musing had presently the effect of making him rise; reflection indeed possessed him after he was on his feet. 'I can't help its coming over me then that on such an extraordinary system you must also rather like *me*.'

'What will you have, my dear Van?' Mitchy frankly asked. 'It's the sort of thing you must be most used to. For at the present moment – look! – aren't we all at you at once?'

It was as if Vanderbank had managed to appear to wonder. ' "All"?'

'Nanda, Mrs Brook, Mr Longdon—'

'And you. I see.'

'Names of distinction. And all the others,' Mitchy pursued, 'that I don't count.'

'Oh, you're the best.'

'I?'

'You're the best,' Vanderbank simply repeated. 'It's at all events most extraordinary,' he declared. 'But I make you out on the whole better than I do Mr Longdon.'

'Ah, aren't we very much the same – simple lovers of life? That is, of that finer essence of it which appeals to the consciousness—'

'The consciousness?' – his companion took up his hesitation.

'Well, enlarged and improved.'

The words had made on Mitchy's lips an image by which his friend seemed for a moment to be held. 'One doesn't really know quite what to say or to do.'

'Oh, you must take it all quietly. You're of a special class; one of those who, as we said the other day – don't you remember? – are a source of the sacred terror. People made in such a way must take the consequences; just as people must take them,' Mitchy went on, 'who are made as *I* am. So cheer up!'

Mitchy, uttering this incitement, had moved to the empty chair by the window, in which he presently was sunk; and it might have been in emulation of his previous strolling and straying that Vanderbank himself now began to revolve. The meditation he next threw out, however, showed a certain resistance to Mitchy's advice. 'I'm glad at any rate I don't deprive her of a fortune.'

'You don't deprive her of mine of course,' Mitchy answered from the chair, 'but isn't her enjoyment of Mr Longdon's at least a good deal staked after all on your action?'

Vanderbank stopped short. 'It's his idea to settle it *all*?'

Mitchy gave out his glare. 'I thought you didn't "care a hang". I haven't been here so long,' he went on as his companion at first retorted nothing, 'without making up my mind for myself about his means. He *is* distinctly bloated.'

It sent Vanderbank off again. 'Oh well, she'll no more get all in the one event than she'll get nothing in the other. She'll only get a sort of a provision. But she'll get that whatever happens.'

'Oh, if you're sure—!' Mitchy simply commented.

'I'm not sure, confound it!' Then – for his voice had been irritated – Van spoke more quietly. 'Only I see her here – though on his wish of course – handling things quite as if they were her own and paying him a visit without apparently any calculated end. What's that on *his* part but a pledge?'

Oh, Mitchy could show off-hand that he knew what it was. 'It's a pledge, quite as much, to you. He shows you the whole thing. He likes you not a whit less than he likes her.'

'Oh thunder!' Van impatiently sighed.

'It's as "rum" as you please, but there it is,' said the inexorable Mitchy.

'Then does he think I'll do it for *this*?'

'For "this"?'

'For the place, the whole thing, as you call it, that he shows me.'

Mitchy had a short silence that might have represented a change of colour. 'It isn't good enough?' But he instantly took himself up. 'Of course he wants – as I do – to treat you with a tact!'

'Oh, it's all right,' Vanderbank immediately said. 'Your "tact" – yours and his – is marvellous, and Nanda's greatest of all.'

Mitchy's momentary renewal of stillness was addressed, he somehow managed not obscurely to convey, to the last clause of his friend's speech. 'If you're not sure,' he presently resumed, 'why can't you frankly ask him?'

Vanderbank again, as the phrase is, 'mooned' about a little. 'Because I don't know that it would do.'

'What do you mean by "do"?'

'Well, that it would be exactly – what do you call it? – "square". Or even quite delicate or decent. To take from him, in the way of an assurance so handsomely offered, so much and then to ask for more: I don't feel I can do it. Besides, I have my little conviction. To the question itself he might easily reply that it's none of my business.'

'I see,' Mitchy dropped. 'Such an inquiry might suggest to him moreover that you're hesitating more than you perhaps really are.'

'Oh, as to *that*,' said Vanderbank, 'I think he practically knows how much.'

'And how little?' He met this however with no more form than if it had been a poor joke, so that Mitchy also smoked for a moment in silence. 'It's your coming down here, you mean, for these three or four days, that will have fixed it?'

The question this time was one to which the speaker might have expected an answer, but Vanderbank's only immediate answer was to walk and walk. 'I want so awfully to be kind to her,' he at last said.

'I should think so!' Then, with irrelevance, Mitchy harked back. 'Shall *I* inquire?'

But Vanderbank, with another thought, had lost the thread. 'Inquire what?'

'Why, if she does get anything—!'

'If I'm not kind *enough*?' – Van had caught up again.

'Dear no; I'd rather you wouldn't speak unless first spoken to.'

'Well, *he* may speak – since he knows we know.'

'It isn't likely, for he can't make out why I told you.'

'You didn't tell *me*, you know,' said Mitchy. 'You told Mrs Brook.'

'Well, *she* told you, and her talking about it is the unpleasant idea. He can't get her down anyhow.'

'Poor Mrs Brook!' Mitchy meditated.

'Poor Mrs Brook!' his companion echoed.

'But I thought you said,' he went on, 'that he doesn't mind.'

'*Your* knowing? Well, I dare say he doesn't. But he doesn't want a lot of gossip and chatter.'

'Oh!' said Mitchy with meekness.

'I may absolutely take it from you then,' Vanderbank presently resumed, 'that Nanda has her idea?'

'Oh, she didn't tell me so. But it's none the less my belief.'

'Well,' Vanderbank at last threw off, 'I feel it for myself. If only because she knows everything,' he pursued without looking at Mitchy. 'She knows everything, everything.'

'Everything, everything.' Mitchy got up.

'She told me so herself yesterday,' said Van.

'And she told *me* so today.'

Vanderbank's hesitation might have shown he was struck with this. 'Well, I don't think it's information that either of us required. But of course she can't help it,' he added. 'Everything, literally everything, in London, in the world she lives in, is in the air she breathes – so that the longer *she's* in it the more she'll know.'

'The more she'll know, certainly,' Mitchy acknowledged. 'But she isn't in it, you see, down here.'

'No. Only she appears to have come down with such accumulations. And she won't be here for ever,' Vanderbank hastened to subjoin.

'Certainly not if you marry her.'

'But isn't that at the same time,' Vanderbank asked, 'just the difficulty?'

Mitchy looked vague. 'The difficulty?'

'Why, as a married woman she'll be steeped in it again.'

'Surely' – oh, Mitchy could be candid! 'But the difference will be that for a married woman it won't matter. It only matters for girls,' he plausibly continued – 'and then only for those on whom no one takes pity.'

'The trouble is,' said Vanderbank – but quite as if uttering only a general truth – 'that it's just a thing that may sometimes operate as a bar to pity. Isn't it for the non-marrying girls that it doesn't particularly matter? For the others it's such an odd preparation.'

'Oh! I don't mind it!' Mitchy declared.

Vanderbank visibly demurred. 'Ah, but your choice—'

'Is such a different sort of thing?' Mitchy, for the half-hour, in the ambiguous dusk, had never looked more droll. 'The young lady I named isn't my *choice*.'

'Well then, that's only a sign the more that you do these things more easily.'

'Oh, "easily"!' Mitchy murmured.

'We oughtn't, at any rate, to keep it up,' said Vanderbank, who had looked at his watch. 'Twelve twenty-five – good-night. Shall I blow out the candles?'

'Do, please. I'll close the window' – and Mitchy went to it. 'I'll follow you – good-night.' The candles after a minute, were out, and his friend had gone, but Mitchy, left in darkness, face to face with the vague, quiet garden, still stood there.

BOOK VIII

TISHY GRENDON

XXVII

THE footman, opening the door, mumbled his name without sincerity, and Vanderbank, passing in, found in fact – for he had caught the symptom – the chairs and tables, the lighted lamps and the flowers alone in possession. He looked at his watch, which exactly marked eight, then turned to speak again to the servant, who had however, without another sound and as if blushing for the house, already closed him in. There was nothing indeed but Mrs Grendon's want of promptness that failed of a welcome: her drawing-room, on the January night, showed its elegance through a suffusion of pink electricity which melted, at the end of the vista, into the faintly golden glow of a retreat still more sacred. Vanderbank walked after a moment into the second room, which also proved empty and which had its little globes of white fire – discreetly limited in number – coated with lemon-coloured silk. The walls, covered with delicate French mouldings, were so fair that they seemed vaguely silvered; the low French chimney had a French fire. There was a lemon-coloured stuff on the sofa and chairs, a wonderful polish on the floor that was largely exposed, and a copy of a French novel in blue paper on one of the spindle-legged tables. Vanderbank looked about him an instant as if generally struck, then gave himself to something that had particularly caught his eye. This was simply his own name written rather large on the cover of the French book and endowed, after he had taken the volume up, with the power to hold his attention the more closely the longer he looked at it. He uttered, for a private satisfaction, before letting the matter pass, a low confused sound; after which, flinging the book down with some emphasis in another place, he moved to the chimney-

piece, where his eyes for a little intently fixed the small
ashy wood fire. When he raised them again it was, on the
observation that the beautiful clock on the mantel was
wrong, to consult once more his watch and then give a
glance, in the chimney glass, at the state of his moustache,
of which he twisted for a moment with due care the ends.
While so engaged he became aware of something else and,
quickly facing about, recognized in the doorway of the
room the other figure the glass had just reflected.

'Oh *you*?' he said, with a quick hand-shake. 'Mrs
Grendon's down?' But he had already passed with Nanda,
on their greeting, back into the first room, which contained
only themselves, and she had mentioned that she believed
Tishy to have said 8.15, which meant of course anything
people liked.

'Oh then, there'll be nobody till nine. I didn't, I suppose,
sufficiently study my note; which didn't mention to me, by
the way,' Vanderbank added, 'that you were to be here.'

'Ah, but why *should* it?' the girl candidly exclaimed.
She spoke again, however, before he could reply. 'I dare
say that when she wrote to you she didn't know.'

'Know you would come up to meet me?' Vanderbank
laughed. 'Jolly at any rate, thanks to my mistake, to have
in this way a quiet moment with you. You came on ahead
of your mother?'

'Oh no – I'm staying here.'

'Oh!' said Vanderbank.

'Mr Longdon came up with me – I came here, Friday
last, straight.'

'You parted at the door?' he asked with marked gaiety.

She thought a moment – she was more serious. 'Yes –
but only for a day or two. He's coming tonight.'

'Good. How delightful!'

'He'll be glad to see you,' Nanda said, looking at the
flowers.

'Awfully kind of him when I've been such a brute.'

'How – a brute?'

'Well, I mean not writing – nor going back.'

'Oh, I see,' Nanda simply returned.

It was a simplicity that, clearly enough, made her friend

a little awkward. 'Has he – a – minded? But he can't have complained!' he quickly added.

'Oh, he never complains.'

'No, no – it isn't in him. But it's just that,' said Vanderbank, 'that makes one feel so base. I've been ferociously busy.'

'He knows that – he likes it,' Nanda returned. 'He delights in your work. And I've done what I can for him.'

'Ah,' said her companion, 'you've evidently brought him round. I mean to this lady.'

'To Tishy? Oh, of course I can't leave her – with nobody.'

'No' – Vanderbank became jocose again – 'that's a London necessity. You can't leave anybody with nobody – exposed to everybody.'

Mild as it was, however, Nanda missed the pleasantry. 'Mr Grendon's not here.'

'Ah, where is he?'

'Yachting – but she doesn't know.'

'Then she and you are just doing this together?'

'Well,' said Nanda, 'she's dreadfully frightened.'

'Oh, she mustn't allow herself,' he returned, 'to be too much carried away by it. But we're to have your mother?'

'Yes, and papa. It's really for Mitchy and Aggie,' the girl went on – 'before they go abroad.'

'Oh then, I see what you've come up for! Tishy and I are not in it. It's all for Mitchy.'

'If you mean there's nothing I wouldn't do for him, you're quite right. He has always been of a kindness to me—'

'That culminated in marrying your friend?' Vanderbank asked. 'It was charming, certainly, and I don't mean to diminish the merit of it. But Aggie herself, I gather, is of a charm now—!'

'Isn't she?' – Nanda was eager. 'Hasn't she come out?'

'With a bound – into the arena. But when a young person's out with Mitchy—!'

'Oh, you mustn't say anything against that. I've been out with him myself.'

'Ah, but my dear child—!' Van frankly argued.

It was not, however, a thing to notice. 'I knew it would be just so. It always is when they've been like that.'

'Do you mean as she apparently *was*? But doesn't it make one wonder a little *if* she was?'

'Oh, she was – I know she was. And we're also to have Harold,' Nanda continued – 'another of Mitchy's beneficiaries. It *would* be a banquet, wouldn't it? if we were to have them all.'

Vanderbank hesitated, and the look he fixed on the door might have suggested a certain open attention to the arrival of their hostess or the announcement of other guests. 'If you haven't got them all, you've got, in having me, I should suppose, about the biggest.'

'Ah, what has he done for you?' Nanda asked.

Again her friend hung fire. 'Do you remember something you said to me down there in August?'

She looked vague but quite unembarrassed. 'I remember but too well that I chattered.'

'You declared to me that you knew everything.'

'Oh yes – and I said so to Mitchy too.'

'Well, my dear child, you don't.'

'Because I don't know—?'

'Yes, what makes *me* the victim of his insatiable benevolence.'

'Ah, well, if you've no doubt of it yourself, that's all that's required. I'm quite *glad* to hear of something I don't know,' Nanda pursued. 'And we're glad to have Harold too,' she repeated.

'As a beneficiary? Then we *shall* fill up! Harold will give us a stamp.'

'Won't he? I hear of nothing but his success. Mother wrote me that people are frantic for him; and,' said the girl after an instant, 'do you know what Cousin Jane wrote me?'

'What *would* she now? I'm trying to think.'

Nanda relieved him of this effort. 'Why, that mother has transferred to him all the scruples that she felt – "even to excess" – in *my* time, about what we might pick up among you all that wouldn't be good for us.'

'That's a neat one for *me*!' Vanderbank declared. 'And I like your talk about your antediluvian "time".'

'Oh, it's all over.'

'What exactly is it,' Vanderbank presently demanded, 'that you describe in that manner?'

'Well, my little hour. And the danger of picking up.'

'There's none of it here?'

Nanda appeared frankly to judge. 'No – because, really, Tishy, don't you see? is natural. We just talk.'

Vanderbank showed his interest. 'Whereas at your mother's—?'

'Well, you were all afraid.'

Vanderbank laughed straight out. 'Do you mind my telling her that?'

'Oh, she knows it. I've heard her say herself you were.'

'Ah, *I* was,' he concurred. 'You know we've spoken of that before.'

'I'm speaking now of all of you,' said Nanda. 'But it was she who was most so, for she tried – I know she did, she told me so – to control you. And it was when you were most controlled—'

Van's amusement took it up. 'That we were most detrimental?'

'Yes, because of course what's so awfully unutterable is just what we most notice. Tishy knows that,' Nanda wonderfully observed.

As the reflection of her tone might have been caught by an observer in Vanderbank's face, it was in all probability caught by his interlocutress, who superficially, however, need have recognized there – what was all she showed – but the right manner of waiting for dinner. 'The better way then is to dash right in? That's what our friend here does?'

'Oh, you know what she does!' the girl replied as if with a sudden drop of interest in the question. She turned at the moment to the opening of the door.

It was Tishy who at last appeared, and her guest had his greeting ready. 'We're talking of the delicate matters as to which you think it's better to dash right in; but I'm bound to say your inviting a hungry man to dinner doesn't appear to be one of them.'

The sign of Tishy Grendon – as it had been often called in a society in which variety of reference had brought to high perfection, for usual safety, the sense of signs – was a retarded facial glimmer that, in respect to any subject, closed up the rear of the procession. It had been said of her indeed that when processions were at all rapid she was usually to be found, on a false impression of her whereabouts, mixed up with the next; so that now, for instance, by the time she had reached the point of saying to Vanderbank 'Are you *really* hungry?' Nanda had begun to appeal to him for some praise of their hostess's appearance. This was of course with soft looks, up and down, at her clothes. 'Isn't she too nice? Did you ever see anything so lovely?'

'I'm so faint with inanition,' Van replied to Mrs Grendon, 'that – like the traveller in the desert, isn't it? – I only make out, as an oasis or a mirage, a sweet green rustling blur. I don't trust you.'

'I don't trust *you*,' Nanda said on her friend's behalf. 'She isn't "green" – men are amazing: they don't know the dearest old blue that ever was seen.'

'*Is* it your "*old* blue"?' Vanderbank, monocular, very earnestly asked. 'I can imagine it was "dear", but I should have thought—'

'It was yellow' – Nanda helped him out – 'if I hadn't kindly told you.' Tishy's figure showed the confidence of objects consecrated by publicity; bodily speaking a beautiful human plant, it might have taken the last November gale to account for the completeness with which, in some quarters, she had shed her leaves. Her companions could only emphasize by the direction of their eyes the nature of the responsibility with which a spectator would have seen them saddled – a choice, as to consciousness, between the effect of her being and the effect of her not being dressed. 'Oh, I'm hideous – of course I know it,' said Tishy. 'I'm only just clean. Here's Nanda now, who's beautiful,' she vaguely continued, 'and Nanda—'

'Oh but, darling, Nanda's clean too!' the young lady in question interrupted; on which her fellow-guest could only laugh with her as in relief from the antithesis of which her presence of mind had averted the completion, little indeed, for the most part, as, in Mrs Grendon's talk that element of style was involved.

'There's nothing in such a matter,' Vanderbank observed as if it were the least he could decently say, 'like challenging inquiry; and here's Harold, precisely,' he went on in the next breath, 'as clear and crisp and undefiled as a fresh five-pound note.'

'A fresh one?' – Harold had passed in a flash from his hostess. 'A man who like me hasn't seen one for six months, could perfectly do, I assure you, with one that has lost its what-do-you-call-it.' He kissed Nanda with a friendly peck, then, more completely aware, had a straighter apprehension for Tishy. 'My dear child, *you* seem to have lost something, though I'll say for you that one doesn't miss it.'

Mrs Grendon looked from him to Nanda. 'Does he mean anything very nasty? I can only understand you when Nanda explains,' she returned to Harold. 'In fact there's scarcely anything I understand except when Nanda explains. It's too dreadful her being away so much now with strange people, whom I'm sure she can't begin to do for what she does for me; it makes me miss her all round. And the only thing I've come across that she *can't* explain,' Tishy launched straight at her friend, 'is what on earth she's doing there.'

'Why, she's working Mr Longdon, like a good true girl,' Harold said; 'like a good true daughter and even, though she doesn't love me nearly so much as I love *her*, I will say, like a good true sister. I'm bound to tell you, my dear Tishy,' he went on, 'that I think it awfully happy, with the trend of manners, for any really nice young thing to be a bit lost to sight. London, upon my honour, is quite too awful for girls, and any big house in the country is as much worse – with the promiscuities and opportunities and all that – as you know for yourselves. *I* know some places,' Harold declared, 'where, if I had any girls, I'd see 'em shot before I'd take 'em.'

'Oh, you know too much, my dear boy!' Vanderbank remarked with commiseration.

'Ah, my brave old Van,' the youth returned, 'don't speak

as if *you* had illusions. I know,' he pursued to the ladies, 'just where some of Van's must have perished, and some of the places I've in mind are just where he has left his tracks. A man must be wedded to sweet superstitions not nowadays to *have* to open his eyes. Nanda, love,' he benevolently concluded, 'stay where you are. So at least I sha'n't blush for you. That you've the good fortune to have reached your time of life with so little injury to your innocence makes you a case by yourself, of which we must recognize the claims. If Tishy can't stump you, that's nothing against you – Tishy comes of one of the few innocent English families that are left. Yes, you may all cry "Oho!" – but I defy you to name me, say, five, or at most seven, in which some awful thing or other hasn't happened. Of course ours is one, and Tishy's is one, and Van's is one, and Mr Longdon's is one, and that makes you, bang off, four. So there you are!' Harold gaily wound up.

'I see now why he's the rage!' Vanderbank observed to Nanda.

But Mrs Grendon expressed to their young friend a lingering wonder. 'Do you mean you go in for the adoption—?'

'Oh, Tishy!' Nanda mildly murmured.

Harold, however, had his own tact. 'The dear man's taking her quite over? Not altogether unreservedly. I'm with the governor: I think we ought to *get* something. "Oh yes, dear man, but what do you *give* us for her?" – that's what *I* should say to him. I mean, don't you know, that I don't think she's making quite the bargain she might. If he were to want *me* I don't say he mightn't have me, but I should have it on my conscience to make it in one way or another a good thing for my parents. You *are* nice, old woman' – he turned to his sister – 'and one can still feel, for the flower of your youth, something of the wonderful "reverence" that we were all brought up on. For God's sake therefore – all the more – don't really close with him till you've had another word or two with me. I'll be hanged' – he appealed to the company again – 'if he shall have her for nothing!'

'See rather,' Vanderbank said to Mrs Grendon, 'how

little it's like your really losing her that she should be able this evening fairly to bring the dear man to you. At this rate we don't lose her – we simply get him as well.'

'Ah, but is it quite the dear man's *company* we want?' – and Harold looked anxious and acute. 'If that's the best arrangement Nanda can make—!'

'If he hears us talking in this way, which strikes me as very horrible,' Nanda interposed very simply and gravely, 'I don't think we're likely to get anything.'

'Oh, Harold's talk,' Vanderbank protested, 'offers, I think, an extraordinary interest; only I'm bound to say it crushes me to the earth. I've to make at least, as I listen to him, a big effort to bear up. It doesn't seem long ago,' he pursued to his young friend, 'that I used to feel I was in it; but the way you bring home to me, dreadful youth, that I'm already *not*—!'

Harold looked earnest to understand. 'The hungry generations tread you down – is that it?'

Vanderbank gave a pleasant tragic head-shake. 'We speak a different language.'

'Ah, but I think I perfectly understand yours!'

'That's just my anguish – and your advantage. It's awfully curious,' Vanderbank went on to Nanda, 'but I feel as if I must figure to him, you know, very much as Mr Longdon figures to me. Mr Longdon doesn't somehow get into me. Yet I do, I think, into him. But we don't matter!'

'"We"?' – Nanda, with her eyes on him, echoed it.

'Mr Longdon and I. It can't be helped, I suppose,' he went on, for Tishy, with sociable sadness, 'but it *is* short innings.'

Mrs Grendon, who was clearly credulous, looked positively frightened. 'Ah but, my dear, thank you! I haven't begun to *live*.'

'Well, *I* have – that's just where it is,' said Harold. 'Thank you, all the more, old Van, for the tip.'

There was an announcement just now at the door, and Tishy turned to meet the Duchess, with Harold, almost as if he had been master of the house, figuring but a step behind her. 'Don't mind *her*,' Vanderbank immediately said to the companion with whom he was left, 'but tell me, while I still have hold of you, who wrote my name on the French novel that I noticed a few minutes since in the other room.'

Nanda at first only wondered. 'If it's there – didn't *you*?'

He just hesitated. 'If it were here you would see if it's my hand.'

Nanda faltered, and for somewhat longer. 'How should I see? What do I know of your hand?'

He looked at her hard. 'You *have* seen it.'

'Oh – so little!' she replied with a faint smile.

'Do you mean I've not written to you for so long? Surely I did in – when was it?'

'Yes, when? But why *should* you?' she asked in quite a different tone.

He was not prepared on this with the right statement, and what he did after a moment bring out had for the occasion, a little the sound of the wrong. 'The beauty of *you* is that you're too good: which, for me, is but another way of saying you're too clever. You make no demands. You let things go. You don't allow in particular for the human weakness that enjoys an occasional glimpse of the weakness of others.'

She had deeply attended to him. 'You mean perhaps one doesn't show enough what one wants?'

'I think that must be it. You're so fiendishly proud.'

She appeared again to wonder. 'Not too much so, at any rate, only to want from *you*—'

'Well, what?'

'Why, what's pleasant for yourself,' she simply said.

'Oh dear, that's poor bliss!' he declared. 'How does it come then,' he next said, 'that, with this barrenness of our intercourse, I know so well *your* hand?'

A series of announcements had meanwhile been made, with guests arriving to match them, and Nanda's eyes at this moment engaged themselves with Mr Longdon and her mother, who entered the room together. When she looked back to her companion she had had time to drop a consciousness of his question. 'If I'm proud, to you, I'm not good,' she said, 'and if I'm good – always to you – I'm not proud. I know at all events perfectly how immensely you're occupied, what a quantity of work you get through and how every minute, for you, counts. Don't make it a crime to me that I'm reasonable.'

'No, that would show, wouldn't it? that there isn't much else. But how it all comes back—!'

'Well, to what?' she asked.

'To the old story. You know how I'm occupied. You know how I work. You know how I manage my time.'

'Oh, I see,' said Nanda. 'It *is* my knowing, after all, everything.'

'Everything. The book I just mentioned is one that, months ago – I remember now – I lent to your mother.'

'Oh, a thing in a blue cover? I remember then too.' Nanda's face cleared up. 'I had forgotten it was lying about here, but I must have brought it – in fact, I remember I did – for Tishy. And I wrote your name on it so that we might know—'

'That I hadn't lent it to either of you? It didn't occur to you to write your own?' Vanderbank went on.

'Well, but if it isn't mine? It *isn't* mine, I'm sure.'

'Therefore, also, if it can't be Tishy's—'

'It's simple enough – it's mother's.'

' "Simple"?' Vanderbank laughed. 'I like you! And may I ask if you've read the remarkable work?'

'Oh yes.' Then she wonderfully said: 'For Tishy.'

'To see if it would do?'

'I've often done that,' the girl returned.

'And she takes your word?'

'Generally. I think I remember she did that time.'

'And read the confounded thing?'

'Oh no!' said Nanda.

He looked at her a moment longer. 'You're too particular!' he rather oddly sounded, turning away with it to meet Mr Longdon.

XXVIII

WHEN after dinner the company was restored to the upper rooms, the Duchess was on her feet as soon as the door opened for the entrance of the gentlemen. Then it might have been seen that she had a purpose, for as soon as the elements had again, with a due amount of the usual shuffling and mismatching, been mixed, her case proved the first to have been settled. She had got Mr Longdon beside her on a sofa that was just right for two. 'I've seized you without a scruple,' she frankly said, 'for there are things I want to say to you as well as very particularly to ask. More than anything else of course I want again to thank you.'

No collapse of Mr Longdon's was ever incompatible with his sitting well forward. ' "Again"?'

'Do you look so blank,' she demanded, 'because you've really forgotten the gratitude I expressed to you when you were so good as to bring Nanda up for Aggie's marriage? – or because you don't think it a matter I should trouble myself to return to? How can I help it,' she went on without waiting for his answer, 'if I see your hand in everything that has happened since the so interesting talk I had with you last summer at Mertle? There have been times when I've really thought of writing to you; I've even had a bold bad idea of proposing myself to you for a Sunday. Then the crisis, my momentary alarm, has struck me as blowing over, and I've felt I could wait for some luck like this, which would sooner or later come.' Her companion, however, appeared to leave the luck so on her hands that she could only snatch up, to cover its nudity, the next handsomest assumption. 'I see you cleverly guess that what I've been worried about is the effect on Mrs Brook of the loss of her dear Mitchy. If you've not at all events had your own impression of this effect, isn't that only because these last months you've seen so little of her? *I*'ve seen,' said the Duchess, 'enough and to spare.' She waited as if for her vision, on this, to be flashed back at her, but the only result of her speech was that her friend looked hard at somebody else. It was just this symptom indeed that perhaps sufficed her, for in a minute she was again afloat. 'Things have turned out so much as *I* desire them that I should really feel wicked not to have a humble heart. There's a quarter indeed,' she added with a noble unction, 'to which I don't fear to say for myself that no day and no night pass without my showing it. However, you English, I know, don't like one to speak of one's religion. I'm just as simply thankful for mine – I mean with as little sense of indecency or agony about it – as I am for my health or my carriage. My point is at any rate that I say in no cruel spirit of triumph, yet do none the less very distinctly say, that Mr Mitchett's disgusted patroness may be now to be feared.' These words had the sound of a climax, and she had brought them out as if, with her duty done, to leave them; but something that took place, for her eye, in the face Mr Longdon had half averted gave her after an instant what he might have called her second wind. 'Oh, I know you think she always *has* been. But you've exaggerated – as to that; and I don't say that even at present it's anything we sha'n't get the better of. Only we must keep our heads. We must remember that from her own point of view she has her grievance, and we must at least look as if we trusted her. That, you know, is what you've never quite done.'

Mr Longdon gave out a murmur of discomfort which produced in him a change of position, and the sequel to the change was that he presently accepted from his cushioned angle of the sofa the definite support it could offer. If his eyes moreover had not met his companion's they had been brought by the hand he repeatedly and somewhat distressfully passed over them closer to the question of which of the alien objects presented to his choice it would cost him least to profess to handle. What he had already paid, a spectator would easily have gathered from the long, suppressed wriggle that had ended in his falling back, was some sacrifice of his habit of not privately depreciating those to whom he was publicly civil. It was plain, however, that when he presently spoke his thought had taken a stretch. 'I'm sure I've fully intended to be everything that's proper. But I don't think Mr Vanderbank cares for her.'

It kindled in the Duchess an immediate light. '*Vous avez bien de l'esprit.* You put one at one's ease. I've been vaguely groping, while you're already there. It's really only for Nanda he cares.'

'Yes – really.'

The Duchess hesitated. 'And yet exactly how much?'

'I haven't asked him.'

She had another, but a briefer pause. 'Don't you think it about time you *should*?' Once more she waited, then seemed to feel that her opportunity wouldn't. 'We've worked a bit together, but you don't take me into your confidence. I dare say you don't believe I'm quite straight. Don't you really see how I *must* be?' She had a pleading note which made him at last fix her. 'Don't you see,' she went on with the advantage of it, 'that, having got all I want for myself, I haven't a motive in the world for spoiling the fun of another? I don't want in the least, I assure you, to spoil even Mrs Brook's; for how will she get a bit less out of him – I mean than she does now – if what you desire *should* take place? Honestly, my dear man, that's quite what I desire, and I only want, over and above, to help you. What I feel for Nanda, believe me, is pure pity. I won't say I'm frantically grateful to her, because in the long run – one way or another – she'll have found her account. It nevertheless worries me to see her, and all the more because of this very certitude, which you've so kindly just settled for me, that our young man hasn't really, with her mother—'

Whatever the certitude Mr Longdon had kindly settled, it was in another interest that he at this moment broke in. 'Is he *your* young man too?'

She was not too much amused to cast about her. 'Aren't such marked ornaments of life a little the property of all who admire and enjoy them?'

'You "enjoy" him?' Mr Longdon asked in the same straightforward way.

'Immensely.'

His silence for a little seemed the sign of a plan. 'What is it he hasn't done with Mrs Brook?'

'Well, the thing that *would* be the complication. He hasn't gone beyond a certain point. You may ask how one knows such matters, but I'm afraid I've not quite a receipt for it. A woman knows, but she can't tell. They haven't done, as it's called, anything wrong.'

Mr Longdon frowned. 'It would be extremely horrid if they had.'

'Ah but, for you and me who know life it isn't *that* that – if other things had made for it – would have prevented! As it happens, however, we've got off easily. She doesn't speak to him—!'

She had forms he could only take up. ' "Speak" to him—?'

'Why, as much as she would have liked to be able to believe.'

'Then where's the danger of which you appear to wish to warn me?'

'Just in her feeling in the case as most women would feel. You see she did what she could for her daughter. She did, I'm bound to say, as that sort of thing goes among you people, a good deal. She treasured up, she nursed along Mitchy, whom she would also, though of course not so much, have liked herself. Nanda with a word could have kept him on, becoming thereby for *your* plan so much the less accessible. That would have thoroughly obliged her mother, but your little English girls, in these altered times – oh, I know how you feel them! – don't stand on such trifles; and – even if you think it odd of me – I can't defend myself, though I've so directly profited, against a certain compassion also for Mrs Brook's upset. As a good-natured woman I feel in short for both of them; I deplore all round what's after all rather a sad relation. Only, as I tell you, Nanda's the one, I naturally say to myself, for me now most to think of: if I don't assume too much, that is, that you don't suffer by my freedom.'

Mr Longdon put by with a mere drop of his eyes the question of his suffering: there was so clearly for him an issue more relevant. 'What do you know of my "plan"?'

'Why, my dear man, haven't I told you that ever since Mertle I've made out your hand? What on earth for other people can your action look like but an adoption?'

'Of – a – *him*?'

'You're delightful. Of – a – *her*! If it does come to the same thing for you, so much the better. That at any rate is what we're all taking it for, and Mrs Brook herself *en tête*.

She sees – through your generosity – Nanda's life, more or less, at the worst, arranged for, and that's just what gives her a good conscience.'

If Mr Longdon breathed rather hard it seemed to show at least that he followed. 'What does she want of a good conscience?'

From under her high tiara an instant she almost looked down at him. 'Ah, you do hate her!'

He coloured, but held his ground. 'Don't you tell me yourself she's to be feared?'

'Yes, and watched. But – if possible – with amusement.'

'Amusement?' Mr Longdon faintly gasped.

'Look at her now,' his friend went on with an indication that was indeed easy to embrace. Separated from them by the width of the room, Mrs Brook was, though placed in profile, fully presented; the satisfaction with which she had lately sunk upon a light gilt chair marked itself as superficial and was moreover visibly not confirmed by the fact that Vanderbank's high-perched head, arrested before her in a general survey of opportunity, gave her eyes in conversation too prayerful a flight. Their companions were dispersed, some in the other room, and for the occupants of the Duchess's sofa they made, as a couple in communion, a picture, framed and detached, vaguely reduplicated in the high polish of the French floor. 'She *is* tremendously pretty.' The Duchess appeared to drop this as a plea for indulgence and to be impelled in fact by the interlocutor's silence to carry it further. 'I've never at all thought, you know, that Nanda touches her.'

Mr Longdon demurred. 'Do you mean for beauty?'

His friend, for his simplicity, discriminated. 'Ah, they've neither of them "beauty". That's not a word to make free with. But the mother has grace.'

'And the daughter hasn't?'

'Not a line. You answer me of course when I say *that*, with your adored Lady Julia, and will want to know what then becomes of the lucky resemblance. I quite grant you that Lady Julia must have had the thing we speak of. But that dear sweet blessed thing is very much the same lost secret as the dear sweet blessed *other* thing that went away with it – the decent leisure that, for the most part, we've also seen the last of. It's the thing at any rate that poor Nanda and all her kind have most effectually got rid of. Oh, if you'd trust me a little more you'd see that I'm quite at one with you on all the changes for the worse. I bear up, but I'm old enough to have known. All the same Mrs Brook has something – say what you like – when she bends that little brown head. *Dieu sait comme elle se coiffe*, but what she gets out of it! Only look.'

Mr Longdon conveyed in an indescribable manner that he had retired to a great distance; yet even from this position he must have launched a glance that arrived at a middle way. 'They both know you're watching them.'

'And don't they know *you* are? Poor Mr Van has a consciousness!'

'So should I if two terrible women—'

'Were admiring you both at once?' The Duchess folded the big feathered fan that had partly protected their range. 'Well *she*, poor dear, can't help it. She wants him herself.'

At the drop of the Duchess's fan he restored his nippers. 'And he doesn't – not a bit – want *her*!'

'There it is. She has put down her money, as it were, without a return. She has given Mitchy up and got nothing instead.'

There was delicacy, yet there was distinctness, in Mr Longdon's reserve. 'Do you call *me* nothing?'

The Duchess at this fairly swelled with her happy stare. 'Then it *is* an adoption?' She forbore to press, however; she only went on: 'It isn't a question, my dear man, of what *I* call it. *You* don't make love to her.'

'Dear me,' said Mr Longdon, 'what would she have had?'

'That could be more charming, you mean, than your famous "loyalty"? Oh, *caro mio*, she wants it straighter! But I shock you,' his companion quickly added.

The manner in which he firmly rose was scarce a denial; yet he stood for a moment in place. 'What after all can she do?'

'She can *keep* Mr Van.'

Mr Longdon wondered. 'Where?'

'I mean till it's too late. She can work on him.'

'But how?'

Covertly again the Duchess had followed the effect of her friend's perceived movement on Mrs Brook, who also got up. She gave a rap with her fan on his leg. 'Sit down – you'll see.'

XXIX

HE mechanically obeyed her, though it happened to lend him the air of taking Mrs Brook's approach for a signal to resume his seat. She came over to them, Vanderbank followed, and it was without again moving, with a vague upward gape, in fact, from his place, that Mr Longdon received as she stood before him a challenge of a sort to flash a point into what the Duchess had just said. 'Why do you hate me so?'

Vanderbank, who, beside Mrs Brook, looked at him with attention, might have suspected him of turning a trifle pale; though even Vanderbank, with reasons of his own for an observation of the sharpest, could scarce have read into the matter the particular dim vision that would have accounted for it – the flicker of fear of what Mrs Brook, whether as daughter or as mother, was at last so strangely and differently to show herself.

'I should warn you, sir,' the young man threw off, 'that we don't consider that – in Buckingham Crescent certainly – a fair question. It isn't playing the game – it's hitting below the belt. We hate and we love – the latter especially – but to tell each other why is to break that little tacit rule of finding out for ourselves which is the delight of our lives and the source of our triumphs. You can say, you know, if you like, but you're not obliged.'

Mr Longdon transferred to him something of the same colder apprehension, looking at him manifestly harder than ever before and finding in his eyes also no doubt a consciousness more charged. He presently got up, but, without answering Vanderbank, fixed again Mrs Brook, to whom he echoed without expression: 'Hate you?'

The next moment, while he remained in presence with Vanderbank, Mrs Brook was pointing out her meaning to him from the cushioned corner he had quitted. 'Why, when you come back to town, you come straight, as it were, here.'

'Ah, what's that,' the Duchess asked in his interest, 'but to follow Nanda as closely as possible, or at any rate to keep well with her?'

Mrs Brook however had no ear for this plea. 'And when I, coming here too and thinking only of my chance to "meet" you, do my very sweetest to catch your eye, you're entirely given up—'

'To trying of course,' the Duchess broke in afresh, 'to keep well with *me*!'

Mrs Brook now had a smile for her. 'Ah, that takes precautions then that *I* shall perhaps fail of if I too much interrupt your conversation.'

'Isn't she nice to me,' the Duchess asked of Mr Longdon, 'when I was in the very act of praising her to the skies?'

Their interlocutor's reply was not too rapid to anticipate Mrs Brook herself. 'My dear Jane, that only proves that he had reached some extravagance in the other sense that you had in mere decency to match. The truth is probably in the "mean" – isn't that what they call it? – between you. Don't *you* now take him away,' she went on to Vanderbank, who had glanced about for some better accommodation.

He immediately pushed forward the nearest chair, which happened to be by the Duchess's side of the sofa. 'Will you sit here, sir?'

'If you'll stay here to protect me.'

'That was really what I brought him over to you for,' Mrs Brook said while Mr Longdon took his place and Vanderbank looked out for another seat. 'But I didn't know,' she observed with her sweet, free curiosity, 'that he called you "sir".' She often made discoveries that were fairly childlike. 'He has done it twice.'

'Isn't that only your inevitable English surprise,' the Duchess demanded, 'at the civility quite the commonest in other societies? – so that one has to come here to find it regarded, in the way of ceremony, as the very end of the world!'

'Oh,' Mr Longdon remarked, 'it's a word I rather like myself even to employ to others.'

'I always ask here,' the Duchess continued to him, 'what word they've got instead. And do you know what they tell me?'

Mrs Brook wondered, then again, before he was ready, charmingly suggested, 'Our pretty manner?' Quickly too she appealed to Mr Longdon. 'Is *that* what you miss from me?'

He wondered however more than Mrs Brook. 'Your "pretty manner"?'

'Well, these grand old forms that the Duchess is such a mistress of.' Mrs Brook had with this one of her eagerest visions. 'Did mamma say "sir" to you? Ought *I*? Do you really get it, in private, out of Nanda? *She* has such depths of discretion,' she explained to the Duchess and to Vanderbank, who had come back with his chair, 'that it's just the kind of illustrative anecdote she never in the world gives me.'

Mr Longdon looked across at Van, placed now, after a moment's talk with Tishy in sight of them all, by Mrs Brook's arm of the sofa — 'You haven't protected — you've only exposed me.'

'Oh, there's no joy without danger—' Mrs Brook took it up with spirit. 'Perhaps one should even say there's no danger without joy.'

Vanderbank's eyes had followed Mrs Grendon after his brief passage with her, terminated by some need of her listless presence on the other side of the room. 'What do you say then, on that theory, to the extraordinary gloom of our hostess? Her safety, by such a rule, must be deep.'

The Duchess was this time the first to know what they said. 'The expression of Tishy's face comes precisely from our comparing it so unfavourably with that of her poor sister Carrie, who, though she isn't here tonight with the Cashmores — amazing enough even as coming *without* that! — has so often shown us that an *âme en peine*, constantly tottering, but, as Nanda guarantees us, usually recovering, may look after all as beatific as a Dutch doll.'

Mrs Brook's eyes had, on Tishy's passing away, taken the same course as Vanderbank's, whom she had visibly not neglected moreover while the pair stood there. 'I give you Carrie, as you know, and I throw Mr Cashmore in; but I'm lost in admiration tonight, as I always have been, at the way Tishy makes her ugliness serve. I should call it, if the word weren't so for ladies' maids, the most "elegant" thing I know.'

'My dear child,' the Duchess objected, 'what you describe as making her ugliness serve is what I should describe as concealing none of her beauty. There's nothing the matter surely with "elegant" as applied to Tishy save that as commonly used it refers rather to a charm that's artificial than to a state of pure nature. There should be for elegance a basis of clothing. Nanda rather stints her.'

Mrs Brook, perhaps more than usually thoughtful, just discriminated. 'There *is*, I think, one little place. I'll speak to her.'

'To Tishy?' Vanderbank asked.

'Oh, *that* would do no good. To Nanda. All the same,' she continued, 'it's an awfully superficial thing of you not to see that her dreariness – on which moreover I've set you right before – is a mere facial accident and doesn't correspond or, as they say, "rhyme" to anything within her that might make it a little interesting. What I like it for is just that it's so funny in itself. Her low spirits are nothing more than her features. Her gloom, as you call it, is merely her broken nose.'

'*Has* she a broken nose?' Mr Longdon demanded with an accent that for some reason touched in the others the spring of laughter.

'Has Nanda never mentioned it?' Mrs Brook inquired with this gaiety.

'That's the discretion you just spoke of,' said the Duchess. 'Only I should have expected from the cause you refer to rather the comic effect.'

'Mrs Grendon's broken nose, sir,' Vanderbank explained to Mr Longdon, 'is only the kinder way taken by these ladies to speak of Mrs Grendon's broken heart. You must know all about that.'

'Oh yes – *all*.' Mr Longdon spoke very simply, with the consequence this time, on the part of his companions, of a silence of some minutes, which he himself had at last to break. 'Mr Grendon doesn't like her.' The addition of these words apparently made the difference – as if they constituted a fresh link with the irresistible comedy of things. That he was unexpectedly diverting was, however, no check to Mr Longdon's delivering his full thought. 'Very horrid of two sisters to be both, in their marriages, so wretched.'

'Ah, but Tishy, I maintain,' Mrs Brook returned, '*isn't* wretched at all. If I were satisfied that she's really so I would never let Nanda come to her.'

'That's the most extraordinary doctrine, love,' the Duchess interposed. 'When you're satisfied a woman's "really" poor you never give her a crust?'

'Do you call Nanda a crust, Duchess?' Vanderbank amusedly asked.

'She's all at any rate, apparently, just now, that poor Tishy has to live on.'

'You're severe then,' the young man said, 'on our dinner of tonight.'

'Oh, Jane,' Mrs Brook declared, 'is never severe: she's only uncontrollably witty. It's only Tishy moreover who gives out that her husband doesn't like her. *He*, poor man, doesn't say anything of the sort.'

'Yes, but after all you know' – Vanderbank just put it to her – 'where the deuce, all the while, *is* he?'

'Heaven forbid,' the Duchess remarked, 'that we should too indiscreetly inquire.'

'There it is – exactly,' Mr Longdon subjoined.

He had once more his success of hilarity, though not indeed to the injury of the Duchess's next word. 'It's Nanda, you know, who speaks, and loud enough, for Harry Grendon's dislikes.'

'That's easy for her,' Mrs Brook declared, 'when she herself isn't one of them.'

'She isn't surely one of anybody's,' Mr Longdon gravely observed.

Mrs Brook gazed across at him. 'You *are* too dear! But I've none the less a crow to pick with you.'

Mr Longdon returned her look, but returned it somehow to Van. 'You frighten me, you know, out of my wits.'

'*I* do?' said Vanderbank.

Mr Longdon just hesitated. 'Yes.'

'It must be the sacred terror,' Mrs Brook suggested to Van, 'that Mitchy so often speaks of. *I'm* not trying with you,' she went on to Mr Longdon, 'for anything of that kind, but only for the short half-hour in private that I think you won't for the world grant me. Nothing will induce you to find yourself alone with me.'

'Why, what on earth,' Vanderbank asked, 'do you suspect him of supposing you want to do?'

'Oh, it isn't *that*,' Mrs Brook sadly said.

'It isn't what?' laughed the Duchess.

'That he fears I may want in any way to – what do you call it? – make up to him.' She spoke as if she only wished it had been. 'He has a deeper thought.'

'Well then, what in goodness is it?'

Mr Longdon had said nothing more, but Mrs Brook preferred none the less to treat the question as between themselves. She *was*, as the others said, wonderful. 'You can't help thinking me' – she spoke to him straight – 'rather tortuous.' The pause she thus momentarily produced was so intense as to give a sharpness that was almost vulgar to the little 'Oh!' by which it was presently broken and the source of which neither of her three companions could afterwards in the least have named. Neither would have endeavoured to fix an indecency of which each doubtless had been but too capable. 'It's only as a mother,' she added, 'that I want my chance.'

But the Duchess at this was again in the breach. 'Take it, for mercy's sake then, my dear, over Harold, who's an example to Nanda herself in the way that, behind the piano there, he's keeping it up with Lady Fanny.'

If this had been a herring that, in the interest of peace, the Duchess had wished to draw across the scent, it could scarce have been more effective. Mrs Brook, whose position had made just the difference that she lost the view of the other side of the piano, took a slight but immediate stretch. '*Is* Harold with Lady Fanny?'

'You ask it, my dear child,' said the Duchess, 'as if it were too grand to be believed. It's the note of eagerness,' she went on for Mr Longdon's benefit – 'it's almost the note of hope: one of those that *ces messieurs*, that we all in fact delight in and find so matchless. She desires for Harold the highest advantages.'

'Well then,' declared Vanderbank, who had achieved a glimpse, 'he's clearly having them. It brings home to one his success.'

'His success is true,' Mrs Brook insisted. 'How he does it I don't know.'

'Oh *don't* you?' trumpeted the Duchess.

'He's amazing,' Mrs Brook pursued. 'I watch – I hold my breath. But I'm bound to say also I rather admire. He somehow amuses them.'

'She's as pleased as Punch,' said the Duchess.

'Those great calm women – they like slighter creatures.'

'The great calm whales,' the Duchess laughed, 'swallow the little fishes.'

'Oh, my dear,' Mrs Brook returned, 'Harold can be tasted, if you like—'

'If *I* like?' the Duchess parenthetically jeered. 'Thank you, love!'

'But he can't, I think, be eaten. It all works out,' Mrs Brook expounded, 'to the highest end. If Lady Fanny's amused she'll be quiet.'

'Bless me,' cried the Duchess, 'of all the immoral speeches—! I put it to you, Longdon. Does she mean' – she appealed to their friend – 'that if she commits murder she won't commit anything else?'

'Oh, it won't be murder,' said Mrs Brook. 'I mean that if Harold, in one way and another, keeps her along, she won't get off.'

'Off where?' Mr Longdon inquired.

Vanderbank immediately informed him. 'To one of the smaller Italian towns. Don't you know?'

'Oh yes. Like – who is it? I forget.'

'Anna Karénine? You know about Anna?'

'Nanda,' said the Duchess, 'has told him. But I thought,'

she went on to Mrs Brook, 'that Lady Fanny, by this time, *must* have gone.'

'Petherton then,' Mrs Brook returned, 'doesn't keep you *au courant*?'

The Duchess blandly wondered. 'I seem to remember he had positively said so. And that she had come back.'

'Because this looks so like a fresh start? No. *We* know. You assume, besides,' Mrs Brook asked, 'that Mr Cashmore would have received her again?'

The Duchess fixed a little that gentleman and his actual companion. 'What will you have? He mightn't have noticed.'

'Oh, you're out of step, Duchess,' Vanderbank said. 'We used all to march abreast, but we're falling to pieces. It's all, saving your presence, Mitchy's marriage.'

'Ah,' Mrs Brook concurred, 'how thoroughly I feel that! Oh, I knew. The spell's broken; the harp has lost a string. We're not the same thing. *He's* not the same thing.'

'Frankly, my dear,' the Duchess answered. 'I don't think that you personally are either.'

'Oh, as for that – which is what matters least – we shall perhaps see.' With which Mrs Brook turned again to Mr Longdon. 'I haven't explained to you what I meant just now. We want Nanda.'

Mr Longdon stared. 'At home again?'

'In her little old nook. You must give her back.'

'Do you mean altogether?'

'Ah, that will be for you in a manner to arrange. But you've had her practically these five months, and, with no desire to be unreasonable, we yet have our natural feelings.'

This interchange, to which circumstances somehow gave a high effect of suddenness and strangeness, was listened to by the others in a quick silence that was like the sense of a blast of cold air, though with the difference between the spectators that Vanderbank attached his eyes hard to Mrs Brook and that the Duchess looked as straight at Mr Longdon, to whom clearly she wished to convey that if he had wondered a short time before how Mrs Brook would do it he must now be quite at his ease. He indulged in fact, after this lady's last words, in a pause that might have signified some of the fulness of a new light. He only said very quietly: 'I thought you liked it.'

At this his neighbour broke in. 'The care you take of the child? They *do*!' The Duchess as she spoke, became aware of the nearer presence of Edward Brookenham, who within a minute had come in from the other room; and the determination of her character leaped forth in her quick signal to him. 'Edward will tell you.' He was already before their semicircle. '*Do* you, dear,' she appealed, 'want Nanda back from Mr Longdon?'

Edward plainly could be trusted to feel in his quiet way that the oracle must be a match for the priestess. ' "Want" her, Jane? We wouldn't *take* her.' As if knowing quite what he was about he looked at his wife only after he had spoken.

XXX

His reply had complete success, to which there could scarce have afterwards been a positive denial that some sound of amusement even from Mr Longdon himself had in its degree contributed. Certain it was that Mrs Brook found, as she exclaimed that her husband was always so awfully civil, just the right note of resigned understanding; whereupon he for a minute presented to them blankly enough his fine dead face. ' "Civil" is just what I was afraid I wasn't. I mean, you know,' he continued to Mr Longdon, 'that you really mustn't look to us to let you off—'

'From a week or a day' – Mr Longdon took him up – 'of the time to which you consider I've pledged myself? My dear sir, please don't imagine it's for *me* the Duchess appeals.'

'It's from your wife, you delicious dull man,' that lady elucidated. 'If you wished to be stiff with our friend here you've really been so with *her*; which comes, no doubt, from the absence between you of proper preconcerted action. You spoke without your cue.'

'Oh!' said Edward Brookenham.

'That's it, Jane' – Mrs Brook continued to take it beautifully. 'We dressed today in a hurry and hadn't time for our usual rehearsal. Edward, when we dine out, generally brings three pocket-handkerchiefs and six jokes. I leave the management of the handkerchiefs to his own taste, but we mostly try together in advance to arrange a career for the other things. It's some charming light thing of my own that's supposed to give him the sign.'

'Only sometimes he confounds' – Vanderbank helped her out – 'your light and your heavy!' He had got up to make room for his host of so many occasions and, having forced him into the empty chair, now moved vaguely off to the quarter of the room occupied by Nanda and Mr Cashmore.

'That's very well,' the Duchess resumed, 'but it doesn't at all clear you, *cara mia*, of the misdemeanour of setting up as a felt domestic need something of which Edward proves deeply unconscious. He has put his finger on Nanda's true interest. He doesn't care a bit how it would *look* for you to want her.'

'Don't you mean rather, Jane, how it looks for us *not* to want her?' Mrs Brook inquired with a detachment now complete. 'Of course, dear old friend,' she continued to Mr Longdon, 'she quite puts me with my back to the wall when she helps you to see – what you otherwise mightn't guess – that Edward and I work it out between us to show off as tender parents and yet to get from you everything you'll give. I do the sentimental and he the practical; so that we, in one way and another, deck ourselves in the glory of our sacrifice without forfeiting the "keep" of our daughter. This must appeal to you as another useful illustration of what London manners have come to; unless indeed,' Mrs Brook prattled on, 'it only strikes you still more – and to a degree that blinds you to its other possible bearings – as the last proof that I'm too tortuous for you to know what I'd be at!'

Mr Longdon faced her, across his interval, with his original terror represented now only by such a lingering flush as might have formed a natural tribute to a brilliant scene. 'I haven't the glimmering of an idea of what you'd be at. But please understand,' he added, 'that I don't at all refuse you the private half-hour you referred to a while since.'

'Are you really willing to put the child up for the rest of the year?' Edward placidly demanded, speaking as if quite unaware that anything else had been said.

His wife fixed her eyes on him. 'The ingenuity of your companions, love, plays in the air like the lightning, but flashes round your head only, by good fortune, to leave it unscathed. Still, you have after all your own strange wit, and I'm not sure that any of ours ever compares with it. Only, confronted also with ours, how can poor Mr Longdon really choose which of the two he'll meet?'

Poor Mr Longdon now looked hard at Edward. 'Oh, Mr Brookenham's, I feel, any day. It's even with *you*, I confess,' he said to him, 'that I'd rather have that private half-hour.'

'Done!' Mrs Brook declared, 'I'll send him to you. But we *have*, you know, as Van says, gone to pieces,' she went on, twisting her pretty head and tossing it back over her shoulder to an auditor of whose approach to her from behind, though it was impossible she should have seen him, she had visibly within a minute become aware. 'It's your marriage, Mitchy, that has darkened our old, bright air, changed us more than we even yet know, and most grossly and horribly, my dear man, changed *you*. You steal up in a way that gives one the creeps, whereas in the good time that's gone you always burst in with music and song. Go round where I can see you: I mayn't love you now, but at least, I suppose, I may look at you. Direct your energies,' she pursued while Mitchy obeyed her, 'as much as possible, please, against our uncanny chill. Pile on the fire and close up the ranks; this *was* our best hour, you know – and all the more that Tishy, I see, is getting rid of her superfluities. Here comes back old Van,' she wound up, 'vanquished, I judge, in the attempt to divert Nanda from her prey. Won't Nanda sit with poor *us*?' she asked of Vanderbank, who now, meeting Mitchy in range of the others, remained standing with him and as at her commands.

'I didn't of course ask her,' the young man replied.

'Then what did you do?'

'I only took a little walk.'

Mrs Brook on this was woeful at Mitchy. 'See then what we've come to. When did we ever "walk" in *your* time save as a distinct part of the effect of our good things? Please return to Nanda,' she said to Vanderbank, 'and tell her I particularly wish her to come in for this delightful evening's end.'

'She's joining us of herself now,' said the Duchess, 'and so is Mr Cashmore, and so is Tishy – *voyez!* – who has kept on – bless her little bare back! – no one she oughtn't to keep. As nobody else will now arrive it would be quite cosy if she locked the door.'

'But what on earth, my dear Jane,' Mrs Brook plaintively wondered, 'are you proposing we should do?'

Mrs Brook, in her apprehension, had looked expressively at their friends, but the eye of the Duchess wandered no further than Harold and Lady Fanny. 'It would perhaps serve to keep that pair a little longer from escaping together.'

Mrs Brook took a pause no greater. 'But wouldn't it be, as regards another pair, locking the stable door after – what do you call it? Don't Petherton and Aggie appear already to have escaped together? Mitchy, man, where in the world's your wife?'

'I quite grant you,' said the Duchess gaily, 'that my niece is wherever Petherton is. This I'm sure of, for *there's* a friendship, if you please, that has not been interrupted. Petherton's not gone, is he?' she asked in her turn of Mitchy.

But again, before he could speak, it was taken up. 'Mitchy's silent, Mitchy's altered, Mitchy's queer!' Mrs Brook proclaimed, while the new recruits to the circle, Tishy and Nanda and Mr Cashmore, Lady Fanny and Harold too after a minute and on perceiving the movement of the others, ended by enlarging it, with mutual accommodation and aid, to a pleasant talkative ring in which the subject of their companion's ejaculation, on a low ottoman and glaring in his odd way in almost all directions at once, formed the conspicuous, attractive centre. Tishy was nearest

Mr Longdon, and Nanda, still flanked by Mr Cashmore, between that gentleman and his wife, who had Harold on her other side. Edward Brookenham was neighboured by his son and by Vanderbank, who might easily have felt himself, in spite of their separation and given, as it happened, their places in the group, rather publicly confronted with Mr Longdon. 'Is his wife in the other room?' Mrs Brook now put to Tishy.

Tishy, after a stare about, came back to consciousness to account for this guest. 'Oh yes – she's playing with him.'

'But with whom, dear?'

'Why, with Petherton. I thought you knew.'

'Knew they're playing—?' Mrs Brook was almost Socratic.

'She's regularly wound up,' her husband meanwhile, without resonance, observed to Vanderbank.

'Brilliant indeed!' Vanderbank replied.

'But she's rather naughty, you know,' Edward after a pause continued.

'Oh, villainous!' his interlocutor said with a short, smothered laugh that might have represented for a spectator a sudden start at such a flash of analysis from such a quarter.

When Vanderbank's attention at any rate was free again their hostess, assisted to the transition, was describing the play, as she had called it, of the absentees, 'She has hidden a book, and he's trying to find it.'

'Hide and seek? Why, isn't it innocent, Mitch!' Mrs Brook exclaimed.

Mitchy, speaking for the first time, faced her with extravagant gloom. 'Do you really think so?'

'That's *her* innocence!' the Duchess laughed.

'And don't you suppose he has found it *yet*?' Mrs Brook pursued earnestly to Tishy. 'Isn't it something we might *all* play at if—?' On which however, abruptly checking herself, she changed her note. 'Nanda, love, please go and invite them to join us.'

Mitchy, at this, on his ottoman, wheeled straight round to the girl, who looked at him before speaking. 'I'll go if Mitchy tells me.'

'But if he does fear,' said her mother, 'that there may be something in it—?'

Mitchy jerked back to Mrs Brook. 'Well, you see, I don't want to give way to my fear. Suppose there *should* be something! Let me not know.'

She met him tenderly. 'I see. You couldn't – so soon – bear it.'

'Ah but, *savez-vous*,' the Duchess interposed with some majesty, 'you're horrid!'

'Let them alone,' Mitchy continued. 'We don't want at all events a general romp.'

'Oh, I thought just that,' said Mrs Brook, 'was what the Duchess wished the door locked for! Perhaps moreover' – she returned to Tishy – 'he has not yet found the book.'

'He can't,' Tishy said with simplicity.

'But why in the world—?'

'You see she's sitting on it' – Tishy felt, it was plain, the responsibility of explanation. 'So that unless he pulls her off—'

'He can't compass his desperate end? Ah, I hope he won't pull her off!' Mrs Brook wonderfully murmured. It was said in a manner that stirred the circle, and unanimous laughter seemed already to have crowned her invocation, lately uttered, to the social spirit. 'But what in the world,' she pursued, 'is the book selected for such a position? I hope it's not a very big one.'

'Oh, aren't the books that are sat upon,' Mr Cashmore freely inquired, 'as a matter of course the bad ones?'

'Not a bit as a matter of course,' Harold as freely replied to him. 'They sit, all round, nowadays – I mean in the papers and places – on some awfully good stuff. Why, I myself read books that I couldn't – upon my honour I wouldn't risk it! – read out to you here.'

'What a pity,' his father dropped with the special shade of dryness that was all Edward's own, 'that you haven't got one of your favourites to try on us!'

Harold looked about as if it might have been after all a happy thought. 'Well, Nanda's the only girl.'

'And one's sister doesn't count,' said the Duchess.

'It's just because the thing's bad,' Tishy resumed for Mrs

Brook's more particular benefit, 'that Lord Petherton is trying to wrest it.'

Mrs Brook's pale interest deepened. 'Then it's a real hand-to-hand struggle?'

'He says she sha'n't read it – she says she will.'

'Ah, that's because – isn't it, Jane?' Mrs Brook appealed – 'he so long overlooked and advised her in those matters. Doesn't he feel by this time – so awfully clever as he is – the extraordinary way she has come out?'

' "By this time"?' Harold echoed. 'Dearest mummy, you're too sweet. It's only about ten weeks – isn't it, Mitch? You don't mind my saying that, I hope,' he solicitously added.

Mitchy had his back to him and, bending it a little, sat with head dropped and knees pressing his hands together. 'I don't mind any one's saying anything.'

'Lord, are you already past that?' Harold sociably laughed.

'He used to vibrate to everything. My dear man, what *is* the matter?' Mrs Brook demanded. 'Does it all move too fast for you?'

'Mercy on us, what *are* you talking about? That's what *I* want to know!' Mr Cashmore vivaciously declared.

'Well, she *has* gone at a pace – if Mitchy doesn't mind,' Harold interposed in the tone of tact and taste. 'But then don't they always – I mean when they're like Aggie and they once get loose – go at a pace? That's what *I* want to know. I don't suppose mother did, nor Tishy, nor the Duchess,' he communicated to the rest, 'but mother and Tishy and the Duchess, it strikes me, must either have been of the school that knew, don't you know? a deuce of a deal before, or of the type that takes it all more quietly after.'

'I think a woman can only speak for herself. *I* took it all quietly enough both before and after,' said Mrs Brook. Then she addressed to Mr Cashmore with a small formal nod one of her lovely wan smiles. 'What I'm talking about, *s'il vous plaît*, is marriage.'

'I wonder if you know,' the Duchess broke out on this, 'how silly you all sound! When did it ever, in any society that could call itself decently "good", *not* make a difference that an innocent young creature, a flower tended and guarded, should find from one day to the other her whole consciousness changed? People pull long faces and look wonderful looks and punch each other, in your English fashion, in the sides and say to each other in corners that my poor darling has "come out". *Je crois bien*, she has come out! I married her – I don't mind saying it now – exactly that she *should*, and I should be mightily ashamed of every one concerned if she hadn't. I didn't marry her, I give you to believe, that she should stay "in", and if any of you think to frighten Mitchy with it I imagine you'll do so as little as you frighten *me*. If it has taken her a very short time – as Harold so vividly puts it – to which of you did I ever pretend, I should like to know, that it would take her a very long one? I dare say there are girls it would have taken longer, just as there are certainly others who wouldn't have required so much as an hour. It surely isn't news to you that if some young persons among us all are very stupid and others very wise, *my* dear child was never either, but only perfectly bred and deliciously clever. Ah, *that* – rather! If she's so clever that you don't know what to do with her, it's scarcely *her* fault. But add to it that Mitchy's very kind, and you have the whole thing. What more do you want?'

Mrs Brook, who looked immensely struck, replied with the promptest sympathy, yet as if there might have been an alternative. 'I don't think' – and her eyes appealed to the others – 'that we want *any* more, do we? than the whole thing.'

'Gracious, I should hope not!' her husband remarked as privately as before to Vanderbank. 'Jane – for a mixed company – does go into it.'

Vanderbank, for a minute and with a special short arrest, took in the circle. 'Should you call us "mixed"? There's only *one* girl.'

Edward Brookenham glanced at his daughter. 'Yes, but I wish there were more.'

'*Do* you?' And Vanderbank's laugh at this odd view covered, for a little, the rest of the talk. But when he again began to follow no victory had yet been snatched.

It was Mrs Brook naturally who rattled the standard. 'When you say, dearest, that we don't know what to "do" with Aggie's cleverness, do you quite allow for the way we bow down before it and worship it? I don't quite see what else we – in here – can do with it, even though we *have* gathered that, just over there, Petherton is finding for it a different application. We can only each in our way do our best. Don't therefore succumb, Jane, to the delusive charm of a grievance. There would be nothing in it. You haven't got one. The beauty of the life that so many of us have so long led together' – and she showed that it was for Mr Longdon she more particularly brought this out – 'is precisely that nobody has ever had one. Nobody has dreamed of it – it would have been such a rough, false note, a note of violence out of all keeping. Did *you* ever hear of one, Van? Did you, my poor Mitchy? But you see for yourselves,' she wound up with a sigh and before either could answer, 'how inferior we've become when we have even in our defence to assert such things.'

Mitchy, who for a while past had sat gazing at the floor, now raised his good natural goggles and stretched his closed mouth to its widest. 'Oh, I think we're pretty good still!' he then replied.

Mrs Brook indeed appeared, after a pause and addressing herself again to Tishy, to give a reluctant illustration of it, coming back as from an excursion of the shortest to the question momentarily dropped. 'I'm bound to say, all the more you know, that I don't quite see what Aggie mayn't now read.' Suddenly, however, her look at their informant took on an anxiety. 'Is the book you speak of something *very* awful?'

Mrs Grendon, with so much these past minutes to have made her so, was at last visibly more present. 'That's what Lord Petherton says of it. From what he knows of the author.'

'So that he wants to keep her—?'

'Well, from trying it first. I think he wants to see if it's good for her.'

'That's one of the most charming cares, I think,' the Duchess said, 'that a gentleman may render to a young

woman to whom he desires to be useful. I won't say that
Petherton always knows how good a book may be, but I'd
trust him any day to say how bad.'

Mr Longdon, who had sat throughout silent and still,
quitted his seat at this and evidently in so doing gave
Mrs Brook as much occasion as she required. She also got
up, and her movement brought to her view at the door of
the further room something that drew from her a quick
exclamation. 'He can tell us now, then – for here they
come!' Lord Petherton, arriving with animation and
followed so swiftly by his young companion that she presented herself as pursuing him, shook triumphantly over his
head a small volume in blue paper. There was a general
movement at the sight of them, and by the time they had
rejoined their friends the company, pushing back seats and
causing a variety of mute expression smoothly to circulate,
was pretty well on its feet. 'See – he *has* pulled her off!'
said Mrs Brook.

Little Aggie, to whom plenty of pearls were singularly
becoming, met it as pleasant sympathy. 'Yes, and it was a
real pull. But of course,' she continued with the prettiest
humour and as if Mrs Brook would quite understand,
'from the moment one has a person's nails, and almost his
teeth, in one's flesh—!'

Mrs Brook's sympathy passed, however, with no great
ease from Aggie's pearls to her other charms; fixing the
former indeed so markedly that Harold had a quick word
about it for Lady Fanny. 'When poor mummy thinks, you
know, that Nanda might have had them—!'

Lady Fanny's attention, for that matter, had resisted
them as little. 'Well, I dare say that if I had wanted
I might!'

'Lord – *could* you have stood him?' the young man
returned. 'But I believe women can stand anything!' he
profoundly concluded. His mother meanwhile, recovering
herself, had begun to ejaculate on the prints on Aggie's
arms, and he was then diverted from the sense of what he
'personally' as he would have said, couldn't have stood, by
a glance at Lord Petherton's trophy, for which he made a
prompt grab. 'The bone of contention?' Lord Petherton

had let it go, and Harold remained arrested by the cover. 'Why, blest if it hasn't Van's name!'

'Van's?' – his mother was near enough to effect her own snatch, after which she swiftly faced the proprietor of the volume. 'Dear man, it's the last thing you lent me! But I don't think,' she added, turning to Tishy, 'that I ever passed such a production on to *you*.'

'It was just seeing Mr Van's hand,' Aggie conscientiously explained, 'that made me think one was free—!'

'But it isn't Mr Van's hand!' – Mrs Brook quite smiled at the error. She thrust the book straight at Mr Longdon. '*Is* that Mr Van's hand?'

Holding the disputed object, which he had put on his nippers to glance at, he presently, without speaking, looked over these aids straight at Nanda, who looked as straight back at him. 'It was I who wrote Mr Van's name.' The girl's eyes were on Mr Longdon, but her words as for the company. 'I brought the book here from Buckingham Crescent and left it by accident in the other room.'

'By accident, my dear,' her mother replied, 'I do quite hope. But what on earth did you bring it for? It's too hideous.'

Nanda seemed to wonder. 'Is it?' she murmured.

'Then you haven't read it?'

She just hesitated. 'One hardly knows now, I think, what is and what isn't.'

'She brought it only for *me* to read,' Tishy gravely interposed.

Mrs Brook looked strange. 'Nanda *recommended* it?'

'Oh no – the contrary.' Tishy, as if scared by so much publicity, floundered a little. 'She only told me—'

'The awful subject?' Mrs Brook wailed.

There was so deepening an echo of the drollery of this last passage that it was a minute before Vanderbank could be heard saying: 'The responsibility's wholly mine for setting the beastly thing in motion. Still,' he added good-humouredly and as if to minimize if not the cause at least the consequence, 'I think I agree with Nanda that it's no worse than anything else.'

Mrs Brook had recovered the volume from Mr Longdon's

relaxed hand and now, without another glance at it, held it behind her with an unusual air of firmness. 'Oh, how can you say that, my dear man, of anything so revolting?'

The discussion kept them for the instant well face to face. 'Then did *you* read it?'

She debated, then jerked the book into the nearest empty chair, where Mr Cashmore quickly pounced upon it. 'Wasn't it for that you brought it me?' she demanded. Yet before he could answer she again challenged her child. 'Have you read this work, Nanda?'

'Yes, mamma.'

'Oh, I say!' cried Mr Cashmore, hilarious and turning the leaves.

Mr Longdon had by this time ceremoniously approached Tishy. 'Good night.'

BOOK IX

VANDERBANK

XXXI

'I THINK then you had better wait,' Mrs Brook said, 'till I see if he has gone;' and on the arrival the next moment of the servants with the tea she was able to put her question. 'Is Mr Cashmore still with Miss Brookenham?'

'No ma'am,' the footman replied. 'I let Mr Cashmore out five minutes ago.'

Vanderbank showed for the next short time by his behaviour what he felt at not yet being free to take this up; moving pointlessly about the room while the servants arranged the tea-table and taking no trouble to make, for appearance, any other talk. Mrs Brook, on her side, took so little that the silence – which their temporary companions had all the effect of keeping up by conscious dawdling – became precisely one of those precious lights for the circle belowstairs which people fondly fancy they have not kindled when they have not spoken. But Vanderbank spoke again as soon as the door was closed. 'Does he run in and out that way without even speaking to *you*?'

Mrs Brook turned away from the fire that, late in May, was the only charm of the crude, cold afternoon. 'One would like to draw the curtains, wouldn't one? and gossip in the glow of the hearth.'

'Oh, "gossip"!' Vanderbank wearily said as he came to her pretty table.

In the act of serving him she checked herself. 'You wouldn't rather have it with *her*?'

He balanced a moment. 'Does she have a tea of her own?'

'Do you mean to say you don't know?' – Mrs Brook asked it with surprise. 'Such ignorance of what I do for her does tell, I think, the tale of how you've lately treated us.'

'In not coming for so long?'

'For more weeks, for more months than I can count. Scarcely since – when was it? – the end of January, that night of Tishy's dinner.'

'Yes, that awful night.'

'Awful, you call it?'

'Awful.'

'Well, the time without you,' Mrs Brook returned, 'has been so bad that I'm afraid I've lost the impression of anything before.' Then she offered the tea to his choice. '*Will* you have it upstairs?'

He received the cup. 'Yes, and here too.' After which he said nothing again till, first pouring in milk to cool it, he had drunk his tea down. 'That's not literally true, you know. I *have* been in.'

'Yes, but always with other people – you managed it somehow; the wrong ones. It hasn't counted.'

'Ah, in one way and another, I think everything counts. And you forget I've dined.'

'Oh – for once!'

'The once you asked me. So don't spoil the beauty of your own behaviour by mistimed reflections. You've been, as usual, superior.'

'Ah, but there has been no beauty in it. There has been nothing,' Mrs Brook went on, 'but bare, bleak recognition, the curse of my hideous intelligence. We've fallen to pieces, and at least I'm not such a fool as not to have felt it in time. From the moment one did feel it why should one insist on vain forms? If *you* felt it, and were so ready to drop them, my part was what it has always been – to accept the inevitable. We shall never grow together again. The smash was too great.'

Vanderbank for a little said nothing; then at last: 'You ought to know how great!'

Whatever had happened her lovely look here survived it. 'I?'

'The smash,' he replied, 'was indeed as complete, I think, as your intention. Each of the "pieces" testifies to your success. Five minutes did it.'

She appeared to wonder where he was going. 'But surely

not *my* minutes. Where have you discovered that I made Mitchy's marriage?'

'Mitchy's marriage has nothing to do with it.'

'I see.' She had the old interest at least still at their service. 'You think we might have survived that.' A new thought of it seemed to glimmer. 'I'm bound to say Mitchy's marriage promises elements.'

'You did it that night at Mrs Grendon's.' He spoke as if he had not heard her. 'It was a wonderful performance. You pulled us down – just closing with each of the great columns in its turn – as Samson pulled down the temple. I was at the time more or less bruised and buried, and I didn't in the agitation and confusion fully understand what had happened. But I understand now.'

'Are you very sure?' Mrs Brook earnestly asked.

'Well, I'm stupid compared with you, but you see I've taken my time. I've puzzled it out. I've lain awake on it: all the more that I've had to do it all myself – with the Mitchys in Italy and Greece. I've missed his aid.'

'You'll have it now,' Mrs Brook kindly said. 'They're coming back.'

'And when do they arrive?'

'Any day, I believe.'

'Has he written you?'

'No,' said Mrs Brook – 'there it is. That's just the way we've fallen to pieces. But you'll of course have heard something.'

'Never a word.'

'Ah then it's complete.'

Vanderbank thought a moment. 'Not quite, is it? – I mean it won't be altogether unless he hasn't written to Nanda.'

'Then *has* he?' – she was keen again.

'Oh, I'm assuming. Don't *you* know?'

'How *should* I?'

This too he turned over. 'Just as a consequence of your having, at Tishy's, so abruptly and wonderfully tackled the question that, a few days later as I afterwards gathered, was to be crowned with a measure of success not yet exhausted. Why, in other words – if it was to know so little about her and to get no nearer to her – did you secure Nanda's return?'

There was a clear reason, her face said, if she could only remember it. 'Why did I—?' Then as catching a light: 'Fancy your asking me – at this time of day!'

'Ah, you *have* noticed that I haven't asked before? However,' Van promptly added, 'I know well enough what you notice. Nanda hasn't mentioned to you whether or no she has heard?'

'Absolutely not. But you don't suppose, I take it, that it was to pry into her affairs that I called her in.'

Vanderbank on this lighted for the first time with a laugh. ' "Called her in"? How I like your expressions!'

'I do then, in spite of all,' she eagerly asked, 'remind you a little of the *bon temps*? Ah,' she sighed, 'I don't say anything good now. But of course I see Jane – though not so often either. It's from Jane I've heard of what she calls her "young things". It seems so odd to think of Mitchy as a young thing. He's as old as all time, and his wife, who the other day was about six, is now practically about forty. And I also saw Petherton,' Mrs Brook added, 'on his return.'

'His return from where?'

'Why, he was with them at Corfu, Malta, Cyprus – I don't know where; yachting, spending Mitchy's money, "larking", he called it – I don't know what. He was with them for weeks.'

'Till Jane, you mean, called him in?'

'I think it must have been that.'

'Well, that's better,' said Van, 'than if Mitchy had had to call him out.'

'Oh, Mitchy—!' Mrs Brook comprehensively sounded.

Her visitor quite assented. 'Isn't he amazing?'

'Unique.'

He had a short pause. 'But what's she up to?'

It was apparently for Mrs Brook a question of such a variety of application that she brought out experimentally: 'Jane?'

'Dear, no. I think we've fathomed "Jane", haven't we?'

'Well,' mused Mrs Brook, 'I'm by no means sure that *I* have. Just of late I've had a new sense!'

'Yes, of what now?' Van amusedly put it as she held the note.

'Oh, of depths below depths. But poor Jane – of course after all she's human. She's beside herself with one thing and another, but she can't in any consistency show it. She took her stand so on having with Petherton's aid formed Aggie for a *femme charmante*—'

'That it's too late to cry out that Petherton's aid can now be dispensed with? Do you mean then that he *is* such a brute that after all Mitchy has done for him—?' Vanderbank, at the rising image, pulled up in easy disgust.

'I think him quite capable of considering with a magnificent insolence of selfishness that what Mitchy has *most* done will have been to make Aggie accessible in a way that – for decency and delicacy of course, things on which Petherton highly prides himself – she could naturally *not* be as a girl. Her marriage has simplified it.'

Vanderbank took it all in. ' "Accessible" is good! Then – which was what I intended just now – Aggie has already become so?'

Mrs Brook, however, could as yet in fairness only wonder. 'That's just what I'm dying to see.'

Her companion smiled at it. ' "Even in our ashes live their wonted fires"! But what do you make, in such a box, of poor Mitchy himself? His marriage can scarcely to such an extent have simplified *him*.'

It was something, none the less, that Mrs Brook had to weigh. 'I don't know. I give it up. The thing was of a strangeness!'

Her friend also paused, and it was as if, for a little, they remained looking at each other over it and over what was unsaid between them. 'It *was* "rum"!' he at last merely dropped.

It was scarce for Mrs Brook, all the same – she seemed to feel after a moment – to surround the matter with an excess of silence. 'He did what a man does – especially in that business – when he doesn't do what he wants.'

'Did you mean what somebody else wanted?'

'Well, what he himself *didn't*. And if he's unhappy,' she went on, 'he'll know whom to pitch into.'

'Ah,' said Vanderbank, 'even if he is he won't be the man to what you might call "vent" it on her. He'll seek compensations elsewhere and won't mind any ridicule—'

'Whom are you speaking of as "her"?' Mrs Brook asked as on feeling that something in her face had made him stop. 'I wasn't referring,' she explained, 'to his wife.'

'Oh!' said Vanderbank.

'Aggie doesn't matter,' she went on.

'Oh!' he repeated. 'You meant the Duchess?' he then threw off.

'Don't be silly!' she rejoined. 'He *may* not become unhappy – God grant *not!*' she developed. 'But if he does he'll take it out of Nanda.'

Van appeared to challenge this, ' "Take it out" of her?'

'Well, want to know, as some American asked me the other day of somebody, what she's "going to do" about it.'

Vanderbank, who had remained on his feet, stood still at this for a longer time than at anything yet. 'But what *can* she "do"—?'

'That's again just what I'm curious to see.' Mrs Brook then spoke with a glance at the clock. 'But if you don't go up to her—'

'My notion of seeing her alone may be defeated by her coming down on learning that I'm here?' He had taken out his watch. 'I'll go in a moment. But, as a light on that danger, would *you*, in the circumstances, come down?'

Mrs Brook, however, for light could only look darkness. 'Oh, you don't love *me*.'

Vanderbank, still with his watch, stared then, as an alternative at the fire. 'You haven't yet told me, you know, if Mr Cashmore now comes *every* day.'

'My dear man, how can I say? You've just your occasion to find out.'

'From *her*, you mean?'

Mrs Brook hesitated. 'Unless you prefer the footman. Must I again remind you that, with her own sitting-room and one of the men, in addition to her maid, wholly at her orders, her independence is ideal?'

Vanderbank, who appeared to have been timing himself, put up his watch. 'I'm bound to say then that, with separations so established, I understand less than ever your unforgettable explosion.'

'Ah, you come back to that?' she wearily asked. 'And you find it, with all you've to think about, unforgettable?'

'Oh, but there was a wild light in your eye—!'

'Well,' Mrs Brook said, 'you see it now quite gone out.' She had spoken more sadly than sharply, but her impatience had the next moment a flicker. 'I called Nanda in because I wanted to.'

'Precisely; but what I don't make out, you see, is what you've since gained by it.'

'You mean she only hates me the more?'

Van's impatience, in the movement with which he turned from her, had a flare still sharper. 'You know I'm incapable of meaning anything of the sort.'

She waited a minute while his back was presented. 'I sometimes think in effect that you're incapable of anything straightforward.'

Vanderbank's movement had not been to the door, but he almost reached it after giving her, on this, a hard look. He then stopped short, however, to stare an instant still more fixedly into the hat he held in his hand; the consequence of which in turn was that he the next minute stood again before her chair. 'Don't you call it straightforward of me just not to have come for so long?'

She had again to take time to say. 'Is that an allusion to what – by the loss of your beautiful presence – I've failed to "gain"? I dare say at any rate' – she gave him no time to reply – 'that you feel you're quite as straightforward as I and that we're neither of us creatures of mere rash impulse. There was a time in fact, wasn't there? when we rather enjoyed each other's dim depths. If I wanted to fawn upon you,' she went on, 'I might say that, with such a comrade in obliquity to wind and double about with, I'd risk losing myself in the mine. But why retort or recriminate? Let us not, for God's sake, be vulgar – we haven't yet, bad as it is, come to *that*. I *can* be, no doubt – I some day *must* be: I feel it looming at me out of the awful future as an inevitable fate. But let it be for when I'm old and horrible; not an hour before. I do want to live a little even yet. So you ought to let me off easily – even as I let you.'

'Oh, I know,' said Vanderbank handsomely, 'that there are things you don't put to me! You show a tact!'

'There it is. And I like much better,' Mrs Brook went on, 'our speaking of it as delicacy than as duplicity. If you understand it's so much saved.'

'What I always understand more than anything else,' he returned, 'is the general truth that you're prodigious.'

It was perhaps a little as relapse from tension that she had nothing against that. 'As for instance when it *would* be so easy—'

'Yes, to take up what lies there, you yet so splendidly abstain.'

'You literally press upon me my opportunity? It's *you* who are splendid!' Mrs Brook rather strangely laughed.

'Don't you at least want to say,' he went on with a slight flush, 'what you *most* obviously and naturally might?'

Appealed to on the question of underlying desire, Mrs Brook went through the decent form of appearing to try to give it the benefit of any doubt. 'Don't I want, you mean, to find out before you go up what *you* want? Shall you be too disappointed,' she asked, 'if I say that, as I shall probably learn, as we used to be told as children, "all in good time", I can wait till the light comes out of itself?'

Vanderbank still lingered. 'You *are* deep!'

'You've only to be deeper.'

'That's easy to say. I'm afraid at any rate you won't think I am,' he pursued after a pause, 'if I ask you what in the world – since Harold does keep Lady Fanny so quiet – Cashmore still requires Nanda's direction for?'

'Ah, find out!' said Mrs Brook.

'Isn't Mrs Donner quite shelved?'

'Find out,' she repeated.

Vanderbank had reached the door and had his hand on the latch, but there was still something else. 'You scarce suppose, I imagine, that she has come to like him "for himself"?'

'Find out!' And Mrs Brook, who was now on her feet, turned away.

He watched her a moment more, then checked himself and left her.

XXXII

SHE remained alone for ten minutes, at the end of which her reflections – they would have been seen to be deep – were interrupted by the entrance of her husband. The interruption was indeed not so great as if the couple had not met, as they almost invariably met, in silence: she took at all events to begin with, no more account of his presence than to hand him a cup of tea accompanied with nothing but cream and sugar. Her having no word for him, how-ever, committed her no more to implying that he had come in only for his refreshment than it would have committed her to say: 'Here it is, Edward dear – just as you like it; so take it and sit down and be quiet.' No spectator worth his salt could have seen them more than a little together without feeling how everything that, under his eyes or not, she either did or omitted rested on a profound acquaintance with his ways. They formed, Edward's ways, a chapter by themselves, of which Mrs Brook was completely mistress and in respect to which the only drawback was that a part of her credit was by the nature of the case predestined to remain obscure. So many of them were so queer that no one but she *could* know them and know thereby into what crannies her reckoning had to penetrate. It was one of them for instance that if he was often most silent when most primed with matter, so when he had nothing to say he was always silent too – a peculiarity misleading, until mastered, for a lady who could have allowed in the latter case for almost any variety of remark. 'What do you think,' he said at last, 'of his turning up today?'

'Of old Van's?'

'Oh, has *he* turned up?'

'Half an hour ago, and asking almost in his first breath for Nanda. I sent him up to her and he's with her now.'

If Edward had his ways she had also some of her own; one of which, in talk with him, if talk it could be called, was never to produce anything until the need was marked. She had thus a card or two always in reserve, for it was her theory that she never knew what might happen. It nevertheless did occur that he sometimes went, as she would have called it, one better.

'He's not with her now. I've just been with her.'

'Then he didn't go up?' Mrs Brook was immensely interested. 'He left me, you know, to do so.'

'Know? – how should I know? I left her five minutes ago.'

'Then he went out without seeing her.' Mrs Brook took it in. 'He changed his mind out there on the stairs.'

'Well,' said Edward, 'it won't be the first mind that has been changed there. It's about the only thing a man can change.'

'Do you refer particularly to *my* stairs?' she asked with her whimsical woe. But meanwhile she had taken it in. 'Then whom were you speaking of?'

'Mr Longdon's coming to tea with her. She has had a note.'

'But when did he come to town?'

'Last night, I believe. The note, an hour or two ago, announced him – brought by hand and hoping she would be at home.'

Mrs Brook thought again. 'I'm glad she is. He's too sweet. By hand! – it must have been so he sent them to mamma. He wouldn't for the world wire.'

'Oh, Nanda has often wired to *him*,' her father returned.

'Then she ought to be ashamed of herself. But how,' said Mrs Brook, 'do you know?'

'Oh, I know when we're in a thing like this.'

'Yet you complain of her want of intimacy with you! It turns out that you're as thick as thieves.'

Edward looked at this charge as he looked at all old friends, without a sign – to call a sign – of recognition. 'I don't know of whose want of intimacy with me I've ever complained. There isn't much more of it, that I can see, that any of them could put on. What do you suppose I'd have them do? If I, on my side, don't get very far, I may have alluded to *that*.'

'Oh, but you do,' Mrs Brook declared. 'You think you don't, but you get very far indeed. You're always, as I said just now, bringing out something that you've got somewhere.'

'Yes, and seeing you flare up at it. What I bring out is only what they tell me.'

This limitation offered, however, for Mrs Brook no difficulty. 'Ah, but it seems to me that with the things people nowadays tell one—! What more do you want?'

'Well' – and Edward from his chair fixed the fire a while – 'the difference must be in what they tell *you*.'

'Things that are better?'

'Yes – worse. I dare say,' he went on, 'what I give them—'

'Isn't as bad as what I do? Oh, we must each do our best. But when I hear from you,' Mrs Brook pursued, 'that Nanda has ever permitted herself anything so dreadful as to wire to him, it comes over me afresh that *I* would have been the perfect one to deal with him if his detestation of me hadn't prevented.' She was by this time also – but on her feet – before the fire, into which like her husband she gazed. '*I* would never have wired. I would have gone in for little delicacies and odd things she has never thought of.'

'Oh, she doesn't go in for what you do,' Edward assented.

'She's as bleak as a chimney-top when the fire's out, and if it hadn't been after all for mamma—!' And she lost herself again in the reasons of things.

Her husband's silence seemed to mark for an instant a deference to her allusion, but there was a limit even to this combination. 'You make your mother, I think, keep it up pretty well. But if she *hadn't*, as you say, done so—?'

'Why, we shouldn't have been anywhere.'

'Well, where are we now? That's what *I* want to know.'

Following her own train, she had at first no heed for his inquiry. 'Without his hatred he would have liked me.' But she came back with a sigh to the actual. 'No matter. We must deal with what we've got.'

'What *have* we got?' Edward continued.

Again with no ear for his question his wife turned away, only however, after taking a few vague steps, to approach him with new decision. 'If Mr Longdon is due, will you do me a favour? Will you go back to Nanda – before he arrives – and let her know, though not of course as from *me*, that Van has been here half an hour, has had it put well before him that she's up there and at liberty, and has left the house without seeing her?'

Edward Brookenham made no motion. 'You don't like better to do it yourself?'

'If I liked better,' said Mrs Brook, 'I would have already done it. The way to make it not come from me is surely not for me to give it to her. Besides, I want to be here to receive him first.'

'Then can't she know it afterwards?'

'After Mr Longdon has gone? The whole point is that she should know it in time to let *him* know it.'

Edward still communed with the fire. 'And what's the point of *that*?' Her impatience, which visibly increased, carried her away again, and by the time she reached the window he had launched another question. 'Are you in such a hurry she should know that Van doesn't want her?'

'What do you call a hurry when I've waited nearly a year? Nanda may know or not as she likes – may know whenever: if she doesn't know pretty well by this time she's too stupid for it to matter. My only pressure's for Mr Longdon. She'll have it there for him when he arrives.'

'You mean she'll make haste to tell him?'

Mrs Brook, for a moment, raised her eyes to some upper immensity. 'She'll mention it.'

Her husband, on the other hand, with his legs out-stretched, looked straight at the toes of his boots. 'Are you very sure?' Then as he remained without an answer: 'Why should she if he hasn't told *her*—?'

'Of the way I so long ago let you know that he had put the matter to Van? It's not out between them in words, no doubt; but I fancy that, for things to pass, they've not to dot their i's quite so much, my dear, as we do. Without a syllable said to her, she's yet aware in every fibre of her little being of what has taken place.'

Edward gave a still longer space to taking this in. 'Poor little thing!'

'Does she strike you as so poor,' Mrs Brook asked, 'with so awfully much done for her?'

'Done by whom?'

It was as if she had not heard the question that she spoke again. 'She has got what every woman, young or old, wants.'

'Really?'

Edward's tone was of wonder, but she simply went on. 'She has got a man of her own.'

'Well, but if he's the wrong one?'

'Do you call Mr Longdon so very wrong? I wish,' she declared with a strange sigh, 'that *I* had had a Mr Longdon!'

'I wish very much you had. I wouldn't have taken it like Van.'

'Oh, it took Van,' Mrs Brook replied, 'to put *them* where they are.'

'But where *are* they? That's exactly it. In these three months, for instance,' Edward demanded, 'how has their connexion profited?'

Mrs Brook turned it over. 'Profited which?'

'Well, one cares most for one's child.'

'Then she has become for him what we've most hoped her to be – an object of compassion still more marked.'

'Is that what you've hoped her to be?'

Mrs Brook was obviously, for herself, so lucid that her renewed expression of impatience had plenty of point. 'How can you ask after seeing what I did——'

'That night at Mrs Grendon's? Well, it's the first time I *have* asked it.'

Mrs Brook had a silence more pregnant. 'It's for being with *us* that he pities her.'

Edward thought. 'With me too?'

'Not so much – but still you help.'

'I thought you thought I didn't – that night.'

'At Tishy's? Oh, you didn't matter,' said Mrs Brook. 'Everything, every one helps. Harold distinctly' – she seemed to figure it all out – 'and even the poor children,

I dare say, a little. Oh, but every one' – she warmed to the vision – 'it's perfect. Jane immensely, *par exemple*. Almost all the others who come to the house. Cashmore, Carrie, Tishy, Fanny – bless their hearts all! – each in their degree.'

Edward Brookenham, under the influence of this demonstration, had gradually risen from his seat, and as his wife approached that part of her process which might be expected to furnish the proof he placed himself before her with his back to the fire. 'And Mitchy, I suppose?'

But he was out. 'No. Mitchy's different.'

He wondered. 'Different?'

'Not a help. Quite a drawback.' Then as his face told how these *were* involutions, 'you needn't understand, but you can believe me,' she added. 'The one who does most is of course Van himself.' It was a statement by which his failure to apprehend was not diminished, and she completed her operation. 'By not liking her.'

Edward's gloom on this was not quite blankness, yet it was dense. 'Do you like his not liking her?'

'Dear no. No better than *he* does.'

'And he doesn't—?'

'Oh, he hates it.'

'Of course I haven't asked him,' Edward appeared to say more to himself than to his wife.

'And of course *I* haven't,' she returned – not at all in this case, plainly, for herself. 'But I know it. He'd like her if he could, but he can't. That,' Mrs Brook wound up, 'is what makes it sure.'

There was at last in Edward's gravity a positive pathos. 'Sure he won't propose?'

'Sure Mr Longdon won't now throw her over.'

'Of course if it *is* sure—'

'Well?'

'Why, it is. But of course if it isn't—'

'Well?'

'Why, she won't have anything. Anything but *us*,' he continued to reflect. 'Unless, you know, you're working it on a certainty—'

'That's just what I *am* working it on. I did nothing till I knew I was safe.'

'"Safe"?' he ambiguously echoed, while on this their eyes met longer.

'Safe. I knew he would stick.'

'But how did you know Van wouldn't?'

'No matter "how" — but better still. He hasn't stuck.' She said it very simply, but she turned away from him.

His eyes for a little followed her. 'We don't *know*, after all, the old chap's means.'

'I don't know what you mean by "we" don't. Nanda does.'

'But where's the support if she doesn't tell us?'

Mrs Brook, who had faced about, again turned from him. 'I hope you don't forget,' she remarked with superiority, 'that we don't ask her.'

'*You* don't?' Edward gloomed.

'Never. But I trust her.'

'Yes,' he mused afresh, 'one must trust one's child. Does Van?' he then inquired.

'Does he trust her?'

'Does he know anything of the general figure?'

She hesitated. 'Everything. It's high.'

'He has told you so?'

Mrs Brook, supremely impatient now, seemed to demur even to the question. 'We ask *him* even less.'

'Then how do we know?'

She was weary of explaining. 'Because that's just why he hates it.'

There was no end, however, apparently, to what Edward could take. 'But hates what?'

'Why, not liking her.'

Edward kept his back to the fire and his dead eyes on the cornice and the ceiling. 'I shouldn't think it would be so difficult.'

'Well, you see it isn't. Mr Longdon can manage it.'

'I don't see what the devil's the matter with her,' he coldly continued.

'Ah, that may not prevent—! It's fortunately the source at any rate of half Mr Longdon's interest.'

'But what the hell *is* it?' he drearily demanded.

She faltered a little, but she brought it out. 'It's *me*.'

'And what's the matter with "you"?'

She made, at this, a movement that drew his eyes to her own, and for a moment she dimly smiled at him. 'That's the nicest thing you ever said to me. But ever, *ever*, you know.'

'Is it?' She had her hand on his sleeve, and he looked almost awkward.

'Quite the very nicest. Consider that fact well and even if you only said it by accident don't be funny – as you know you sometimes *can* be – and take it back. It's all right. It's charming, isn't it? when our troubles bring us more together. Now go up to her.'

Edward kept a queer face, into which this succession of remarks introduced no light, but he finally moved and it was only when he had almost reached the door that he stopped again. 'Of course you know he has sent her no end of books.'

'Mr Longdon – of late? Oh yes, a deluge, so that her room looks like a bookseller's back shop: and all, in the loveliest bindings, the most standard English works. I not only know it, naturally, but I know – what you don't – why.'

'"Why?"?' Edward echoed. 'Why but that – unless he should send her money – it's about the only kindness he can show her at a distance?'

Mrs Brook hesitated; then with a little suppressed sigh: 'That's it!'

But it still held him. 'And perhaps he does send her money.'

'No. Not now.'

Edward lingered. 'Then is he taking it out—?'

'In books only?' It was wonderful – with its effect on him now visible – how she possessed her subject. 'Yes, that's his delicacy – for the present.'

'And you're not afraid for the future—?'

'Of his considering that the books will have worked it off? No. They're thrown in.'

Just perceptibly cheered, he reached the door, where, however, he had another pause. 'You don't think I had better see Van?'

She stared. 'What for?'

'Why, to ask what the devil he means.'

'If you should do anything so hideously vulgar,' she instantly replied, 'I would leave your house the next hour. Do you expect,' she asked, 'to be able to force your child down his throat?'

He was clearly not prepared with an account of his expectations, but he had a general memory that imposed itself. 'Then why in the world did he make up to us?'

'He didn't. We made up to *him*.'

'But why in the world—?'

'Well,' said Mrs Brook, really to finish, 'we were in love with him.'

'Oh!' Edward jerked. He had by this time opened the door, and the sound was partly the effect of the disclosure of a servant preceding a visitor. His greeting of the visitor before edging past and away was, however, of the briefest and might have implied that they had met but yesterday. 'How d'ye do, Mitchy? – At home? Oh, rather!'

XXXIII

VERY different was Mrs Brook's welcome of the restored wanderer, to whom, in a brief space, she addressed every expression of surprise and delight, though marking indeed at last, as a qualification of these things, her regret that he declined to partake of her tea or to allow her to make him what she called 'snug for a talk' in his customary corner of her sofa. He pleaded frankly agitation and embarrassment, reminded her even that he was awfully shy and that after separations, complications, whatever might at any time happen, he was conscious of the dust that had settled on intercourse and that he couldn't blow away in a single breath. She was only, according to her nature, to indulge him if, while he walked about and changed his place, he came to the surface but in patches and pieces. There was so much he wanted to know that – well, as they had arrived only the night before, she could judge. There was knowledge, it became clear, that Mrs Brook almost equally craved, so that it even looked at first as if, on either side, confidence might be choked by curiosity. This disaster was finally barred by the fact that the spirit of inquiry found for Mitchy material that was comparatively plastic. That was after all apparent enough when at the end of a few vain passes he brought out sociably: 'Well, has he done it?'

Still indeed there was something in Mrs Brook's face that seemed to reply 'Oh come – don't rush it, you know!' and something in the movement with which she turned away that described the state of their question as by no means so simple as that. On his refusal of tea she had rung for the removal of the table, and the bell was at this moment answered by the two men. Little ensued then, for some minutes, while the servants were present; she spoke only as the butler was about to close the door. 'If Mr Longdon presently comes show him into Mr Brookenham's room if Mr Brookenham isn't there. If he is, show him into the dining-room, and in either case, let me immediately know.'

The man waited, expressionless. 'And in case of his asking for Miss Brookenham—?'

'He won't!' she replied with a sharpness before which her interlocutor retired. 'He will!' she then added in quite another tone to Mitchy. 'That is, you know, he perfectly *may*. But oh the subtlety of servants!' she sighed.

Mitchy was now all there. 'Mr Longdon's in town then?'

'For the first time since you went away. He's to call this afternoon.'

'And you want to see him alone?'

Mrs Brook thought. 'I don't think I want to see him at all.'

'Then your keeping him below—?'

'Is so that he sha'n't burst in till I know. It's *you*, my dear, I want to see.'

Mitchy glared about. 'Well, don't take it ill if, in return for that, I say that I myself want to see every one. I could have done even just now with a little more of Edward.'

Mrs Brook, in her own manner, and with a slow head-shake, looked lovely. '*I* couldn't.' Then she puzzled it out with a pause: 'It even does come over me that if you don't mind—'

'What, my dear woman,' said Mitchy encouragingly, 'did I *ever* mind? I assure you,' he laughed, 'I haven't come back to begin!'

At this suddenly, dropping everything else, she laid her hand on him. 'Mitchy love, *are* you happy?'

So for a moment they stood confronted. 'Not perhaps as *you* would have tried to make me.'

'Well, you've still *got* me, you know.'

'Oh,' said Mitchy, 'I've got a great deal. How, if I really look at it, can a man of my peculiar nature – it *is*, you know, awfully peculiar – *not* be happy? Think, if one is driven to it for instance, of the breadth of my sympathies.'

Mrs Brook, as a result of thinking, appeared for a little to demur. 'Yes – but one mustn't be too much driven to it. It's by one's sympathies that one suffers. If you should do that I couldn't bear it.'

She clearly evoked for Mitchy a definite image. 'It *would* be funny, wouldn't it? But you wouldn't have to. I'd go off and do it alone somewhere – in a dark room, I think, or on a desert island; at any rate where nobody should see. Where's the harm moreover,' he went on, 'of any suffering that doesn't bore one, as I'm sure, however much its outer aspect might amuse some others, mine wouldn't bore me? What I should do in my desert island or my dark room, I feel, would be just to dance about with the thrill of it – which is exactly the exhibition of ludicrous gambols that I would fain have arranged to spare you. I assure you, dear Mrs Brook,' he wound up, 'that I'm not in the least bored now. Everything is so interesting.'

'You're beautiful!' she vaguely interposed.

But he pursued without heeding: 'Was it perhaps what you had in your head that *I* should see him—?'

She came back but slowly, however, to the moment. 'Mr Longdon? Well, yes. You know he can't bear *me*—'

'Yes, yes' – Mitchy was almost eager.

It had already sent her off again. 'You're too lovely. You *have* come back the same. It seemed to me,' she after an instant explained, 'that I wanted him to be seen—'

'Without inconvenience, as it were, either to himself or to you? Then,' said Mitchy, who visibly felt that he had taken her up successfully, 'it strikes me that I'm absolutely your man. It's delicious to come back to a use.'

But she was much more dim about it. 'Oh, what you've come back to!'

'It's just what I'm trying to get at. Van is still then where I left him?'

She was silent. 'Did you really believe he would move?'

Mitchy took a few turns, speaking almost with his back presented. 'Well, with all the reasons—!' After which, while she watched him, he was before her again with a question. 'Is it utterly off?'

'When was it ever really on?'

'Oh, I know your view, and that, I think,' said Mitchy, 'is the most extraordinary part of it. I can tell you it would have put *me* on.'

'My view?' Mrs Brook thought. 'Have you forgotten that I had for you too a view that didn't?'

'Ah, but we didn't differ, you and I. It wasn't a defiance and a prophecy. You wanted *me*.'

'I did indeed!' Mrs Brook said simply.

'And you didn't want him. For *her*, I mean. So you risked showing it.'

She looked surprised. '*Did* I?'

Again they were face to face. 'Your candour's divine!'

She wondered. 'Do you mean it was even then?'

Mitchy smiled at her till he was red. 'It's exquisite now.'

'Well,' she presently returned, 'I knew my Van!'

'*I* thought I knew "yours" too,' Mitchy said. Their eyes met a minute, and he added: 'But I didn't.' Then he exclaimed: 'How you've worked it!'

She looked barely conscious. ' "Worked it"?' After which, with a slightly sharper note: 'How do you know – while you've been amusing yourself in places that I'd give my head to see again, but never shall – what I've been doing?'

'Well I saw, you know, that night at Tishy's, just before we left England, your wonderful start. I got a look at your attitude, as it were, and your system.'

Her eyes were now far away, and she spoke after an

instant without moving them. 'And didn't I by the same token get a look at yours?'

'Mine?' Mitchy thought, but seemed to doubt. 'My dear child, I hadn't any then.'

'You mean that it has formed itself – your system – since?'

He shook his head with decision. 'I assure you I'm quite at sea. I've never had, and I have as little as ever now, anything but my general philosophy, which I won't attempt at present to go into and of which moreover I think you've had, first and last, your glimpses. What I made out in you that night was a perfect policy.'

Mrs Brook had another of her infantine stares. 'Every one that night seems to have made out something! All I can say is at any rate,' she went on, 'that in that case you were all far deeper than I was.'

'It was just a blind instinct, without a programme or a scheme? Perhaps then, since it has so perfectly succeeded, the name doesn't mater. I'm lost, as I tell you,' Mitchy declared, 'in admiration of its success.'

She looked, as before, so young, yet so grave. 'What do you call its success?'

'Let me ask you rather – mayn't I – what *you* call its failure.'

Mrs Brook, who had been standing for some minutes, seated herself at this as if to respond to his idea. But the next moment she had fallen back into thought. 'Have you often heard from him?'

'Never once.'

'And have you written?'

'Not a word either. I left it, you see,' Mitchy smiled, 'all to *you*.' After which he continued: 'Has he been with you much?'

She just hesitated. 'As little as possible. But, as it happens, he was here just now.'

Her visitor fairly flushed. 'And I've only missed him?'

Her pause again was of the briefest. 'You wouldn't if he *had* gone up.'

' "Gone up"?'

'To Nanda, who has now her own sitting-room, as you

know, for whom he immediately asked and for whose benefit, whatever you may think, I was, at the end of a quarter of an hour I assure you, perfectly ready to release him. He changed his mind, however, and went away without seeing her.'

Mitchy showed the deepest interest. 'And what made him change his mind?'

'Well, I'm thinking it out.'

He appeared to watch this labour. 'But with no light yet?'

'When it comes I'll tell you.'

He hung fire, once more, but an instant. 'You didn't yourself work the thing again?'

She rose at this in strange sincerity. 'I think, you know, you go very far.'

'Why, didn't we just now settle,' he promptly replied, 'that it's all instinctive and unconscious? If it was so that night at Tishy's—'

'Ah, *voyons, voyons*,' she broke in, 'what did I do even then?'

He laughed out at something in her tone. 'You'd like it again all pictured—?'

'I'm not afraid.'

'Why, you just simply – publicly – took her back.'

'And where was the monstrosity of that?'

'In the one little right place. In your removal of every doubt—'

'Well, of what?' He had appeared not quite to know how to put it.

But he saw at last. 'Why, of what we may still hope to do for her. Thanks to your care, there were specimens.' Then as she had the look of trying vainly to focus a few, 'I can't recover them one by one,' he pursued, 'but the whole thing was quite lurid enough to do us all credit.'

She met him after a little, but at such an odd point. 'Excuse me if I scarcely see how much of the credit was yours. For the first time since I've known you, you went in for decency.'

Mitchy's surprise showed as real. 'It struck you as decency—?'

Since he wished she thought it over. 'Oh, your be-haviour—'

'My behaviour was – my condition. Do you call *that* decent? No, you're quite out.' He spoke, in his good nature, with an approach to reproof. 'How can I ever—?'

But it had already brought her quite round, and to a firmer earth that she clearly preferred to tread. 'Are things really bad with you, Mitch?'

'Well, I'll tell you how they are. But not now.'

'Some other time? – on your honour?'

'You shall have them all. Don't be afraid.'

She dimly smiled. 'It will be like old times.'

He rather demurred. 'For you perhaps. But not for me.'

In spite of what he said it did hold her, and her hand again almost caressed him. 'But – till you do tell me – is it very, very dreadful?'

'That's just perhaps what I may have to get you to decide.'

'Then shall I help you?' she eagerly asked.

'I think it will be quite in your line.'

At the thought of her line – it sounded somehow so general – she released him a little with a sigh, yet still looking round as it were for possibilities. 'Jane, you know, is in a state.'

'Yes, Jane's in a state. That's a comfort!'

She continued in a manner to cling to him. 'But is it your only one?'

He was very kind and patient. 'Not perhaps quite.'

'*I'm* a little of one?'

'My dear child, as you see.'

Yes, she saw, but was still launched. 'And shall you have recourse—?'

'To what?' he asked as she appeared to falter.

'I don't mean to anything violent. But shall you tell Nanda?'

Mitchy wondered. 'Tell her—?'

'Well, everything. I think, you know,' Mrs Brook musingly observed, 'that it would really serve her right.'

Mitchy's silence, which lasted a minute, seemed to take

the idea, but not perhaps quite to know what to do with it. 'Ah, I'm afraid I shall never really serve her right!'

Just as he spoke the butler reappeared; at the sight of whom Mrs Brook immediately guessed. 'Mr Longdon?'

'In Mr Brookenham's room, ma'am. Mr Brookenham has gone out.'

'And where has he gone?'

'I think, ma'am, only for some evening papers.'

She had an intense look for Mitchy; then she said to the man: 'Ask him to wait three minutes – I'll ring;' turning again to her visitor as soon as they were alone. 'You don't know how I'm trusting you!'

'Trusting me?'

'Why, if he comes up to you.'

Mitchy thought. 'Hadn't I better go down?'

'No – you may have Edward back. If you see him you must see him here. If I don't myself, it's for a reason.'

Mitchy again just sounded her. 'His not, as you awhile ago hinted—?'

'Yes, caring for what I say.' She had a pause, but she brought it out. 'He doesn't believe a word—'

'Of what you tell him?' Mitchy was splendid. 'I see. And you want something said to him.'

'Yes, that he'll take from *you*. Only it's for you,' Mrs Brook went on, 'really and honestly, and as I trust you, to give it. But the comfort of you is that you'll do so if you promise.'

Mitchy was infinitely struck. 'But I haven't promised, eh? Of course I can't till I know what it is.'

'It's to put before him—'

'Oh, I see: the situation.'

'What has happened here today. Van's marked retreat, and how, with the time that has passed, it makes us at last know where we are. You of course for yourself,' Mrs Brook wound up, 'see that.'

'Where are we?' Mitchy took a turn and came back. 'But what then did Van come for? If you speak of a retreat, there must have been an advance.'

'Oh,' said Mrs Brook, 'he simply wanted not to look too brutal. After so much absence he *could* come.'

'Well, if he established that he wasn't brutal, where was the retreat?'

'In his not going up to Nanda. He came – frankly – to do that, but made up his mind on second thoughts that he couldn't risk even being civil to her.'

Mitchy had visibly warmed to his work. 'Well, and what made the difference?'

She wondered. 'What difference?'

'Why, of the effect, as you say, of his second thoughts. Thoughts of what?'

'Oh,' said Mrs Brook suddenly and as if it were quite simple – 'I know *that*! Suspicions.'

'And of whom?'

'Why, of *you*, you goose. Of your not having done—'

'Well, what?' he persisted as she paused.

'How shall I say it? The best thing for yourself. And of Nanda's feeling that. Don't you see?'

In the effort of seeing, or perhaps indeed in the full act of it, poor Mitchy glared as never before. 'Do you mean Van's *jealous* of me?'

Pressed as she was, there was something in his face that momentarily hushed her. 'There it is!' she achieved however at last.

'Of *me*?' Mitchy went on.

What was in his face so suddenly and strangely was the look of rising tears – at sight of which, as from a compunction as prompt, she showed a lovely flush. 'There it is, there it is,' she repeated. 'You ask me for a reason, and it's the only one I see. Of course if you don't care,' she added, 'he needn't come up. He can go straight to Nanda.'

Mitchy had turned away again as with the impulse of hiding the tears that had risen and that had not wholly disappeared even by the time he faced about. 'Did Nanda know he was to come?'

'Mr Longdon?'

'No, no. Was she expecting Van—?'

'My dear man,' Mrs Brook mildly wailed, 'when can she have *not* been?'

Mitchy looked hard for an instant at the floor. 'I mean does she know he has been and gone?'

Mrs Brook, from where she stood and through the window, looked rather at the sky. 'Her father will have told her.'

'Her father?' Mitchy frankly wondered. 'Is *he* in it?'

Mrs Brook at this had a longer pause. 'You assume, I suppose, Mitchy dear,' she then quavered, 'that I put him up—'

'Put Edward up?' he broke in.

'No – that of course. Put Van up to ideas—'

He caught it again. 'About *me* – what you call his suspicions?' He seemed to weigh the charge, but it ended, while he passed his hand hard over his eyes, in weariness and in the nearest approach to coldness he had ever shown Mrs Brook. 'It doesn't matter. It's every one's fate to be in one way or another the subject of ideas. Do then,' he continued, 'let Mr Longdon come up.'

She instantly rang the bell. 'Then I'll go to Nanda. But don't look frightened,' she added as she came back, 'as to what we may – Edward or I – do next. It's only to tell her that he'll be with her.'

'Good. I'll tell Tatton,' Mitchy replied.

Still, however, she lingered. 'Shall you ever care for me more?'

He had almost the air, as he waited for her to go, of the master of the house, for she had made herself before him, as he stood with his back to the fire, as humble as a relegated visitor. 'Oh, just as much. Where's the difference? Aren't our ties in fact rather multiplied?'

'That's the way *I* want to feel it. And from the moment you recognize with me—'

'Yes?'

'Well, that he never, you know, really *would*—'

He took her mercifully up. 'There's no harm done?' Mitchy thought of it.

It made her still hover. 'Nanda will be rich. Toward that you *can* help, and it's really, I may now tell you, what it came into my head you should see our friend here *for*.'

He maintained his waiting attitude. 'Thanks, thanks.'

'You're our guardian angel!' she exclaimed.

At this he laughed out. 'Wait till you see what Mr Longdon does!'

hostess doesn't appear, I mustn't forget myself. I too came
back but yesterday and I've an engagement – for which
I'm already late – with Miss Brookenham, who has been so
good as to ask me to tea.'

The divided mind, the express civility, the decent 'Miss
Brookenham', the escape from their hostess – these were all
things Mitchy could quickly take in, and they gave him in
a moment his light for not missing his occasion. 'I see,
I see – I shall make you keep Nanda waiting. But there's
something I shall ask you to take from me as quite a
sufficient basis for that: which is simply that after all, you
know – for I think you do know, don't you? – I'm nearly as
much attached to her as you are.'

Mr Longdon had looked suddenly apprehensive and even
a trifle embarrassed, but he spoke with due presence of
mind. 'Of course I understand that perfectly. If you hadn't
liked her so much—'

'Well?' said Mitchy as he checked himself.

'I would never, last year, have gone to stay with you.'

'Thank you!' Mitchy laughed.

'Though I like you also – and extremely,' Mr Longdon
gravely pursued, 'for yourself.'

Mitchy made a sign of acknowledgement. 'You like me
better for *her* than you do for anybody else *but* myself.'

'You put it, I think, correctly. Of course I've not seen so
much of Nanda – if between my age and hers, that is, any
real contact is possible – without knowing that she now
regards you as one of the very best of her friends, treating
you, I almost fancy, with a degree of confidence—'

Mitchy gave a laugh of interruption. 'That she doesn't
show even to you?'

Mr Longdon's poised glasses faced him. 'Even! I don't
mind,' the old man went on, 'as the opportunity has come
up, telling you frankly – and as from my time of life to
your own – all the comfort I take in the sense that in any
case of need or trouble she might look to you for whatever
advice or support the affair might demand.'

'She has told you she feels I'd be there?' Mitchy after an
instant asked.

'I'm not sure,' his friend replied, 'that I ought quite to

mention anything she has "told" me. I speak of what I've made out for myself.'

'Then I thank you more than I can say for your penetration. Her mother, I should let you know,' Mitchy continued, 'is with her just now.'

Mr Longdon took off his glasses with a jerk. 'Has anything happened to her?'

'To account for the fact I refer to?' Mitchy said in amusement at his start. 'She's not ill, that I know of, thank goodness, and she has not broken her leg. But something, none the less, has happened to her – that I think I may say. To tell you all in a word, it's the reason, such as it is, of my being here to meet you. Mrs Brook asked me to wait. She'll see you herself some other time.'

Mr Longdon wondered. 'And Nanda too?'

'Oh, that must be between yourselves. Only, while I keep you here—'

'She understands my delay?'

Mitchy thought. 'Mrs Brook must have explained.' Then as his companion took this in silence, 'But you don't like it?' he inquired.

'It only comes to me that Mrs Brook's explanations—!'

'Are often so odd? Oh yes; but Nanda, you know, allows for that oddity. And Mrs Brook, by the same token,' Mitchy developed, 'knows herself – no one better – what may frequently be thought of it. That's precisely the reason of her desire that you should have on this occasion explanations from a source that she's so good as to pronounce, for the immediate purpose, superior. As for Nanda,' he wound up, 'to be aware that we're here together won't strike her as so bad a sign.'

'No,' Mr Longdon attentively assented; 'she'll hardly fear we're plotting her ruin. But what has happened to her?' he more sharply demanded.

'Well,' said Mitchy, 'it's you, I think, who will have to give it a name. I know you know what I've known.'

Mr Longdon, with his nippers again placed, hesitated. 'Yes, I know.'

'And you've accepted it.'

'How could I help it? To reckon with such cleverness—'

'Was beyond you? Ah, it wasn't my cleverness,' Mitchy said. 'There's a greater than mine. There's a greater even than Van's. That's the whole point,' he went on while his friend looked at him hard. 'You don't even like it just a little?'

Mr Longdon wondered. 'The existence of such an element—?'

'No; the existence simply of my knowledge of your idea.'

'I suppose I'm bound to keep in mind in fairness the existence of my own knowledge of yours.'

But Mitchy gave that the go-by. 'Oh, I've so many "ideas"! I'm always getting hold of some new one and for the most part trying it – generally to let it go as a failure. Yes, I had one six months ago. I tried that. I'm trying it still.'

'Then I hope,' said Mr Longdon, with a gaiety slightly strained, 'that, contrary to your usual rule, it's a success.'

It was a gaiety, for that matter, that Mitchy's could match. 'It does promise well! But I've another idea even now, and it's just what I'm again trying.'

'On me?' Mr Longdon still somewhat extravagantly smiled.

Mitchy thought. 'Well, on two or three persons, of whom you *are* the first for me to tackle. But what I must begin with is having from you that you recognize she trusts us.'

'Nanda?'

Mitchy's idea after an instant had visibly gone further. 'Both of them – the two women up there at present so strangely together. Mrs Brook must too, immensely. But for that you won't care.'

Mr Longdon had relapsed into an anxiety more natural than his expression of a moment before. 'It's about time! But if Nanda didn't trust us,' he went on, 'her case would indeed be a sorry one. She has nobody else to trust.'

'Yes.' Mitchy's concurrence was grave. 'Only you and me.'

'Only you and me.'

The eyes of the two men met over it in a pause terminated at last by Mitchy's saying: 'We must make it all up to her.'

'Is that your idea?'

'Ah,' said Mitchy gently, 'don't laugh at it.'

His friend's grey gloom again covered him. 'But what *can*—?' Then as Mitchy showed a face that seemed to wince with a silent 'What *could*?' the old man completed his objection. 'Think of the magnitude of the loss.'

'Oh, I don't for a moment suggest,' Mitchy hastened to reply, 'that it isn't immense.'

'She does care for him, you know,' said Mr Longdon.

Mitchy at this gave a long wide glare. ' "Know—"?' he ever so delicately murmured.

His irony had quite touched. 'But of course you know! You know everything – Nanda and you.'

There was a tone in it that moved a spring, and Mitchy laughed out. 'I like your putting me with her! But we're all together. With Nanda,' he next added, 'it *is* deep.'

His companion took it from him. 'Deep.'

'And yet somehow it isn't abject.'

The old man wondered. ' "Abject"?'

'I mean it isn't pitiful. In its way,' Mitchy developed, 'it's happy.'

This too, though rather ruefully, Mr Longdon could take from him. 'Yes – in its way.'

'Any passion so great, so complete,' Mitchy went on, 'is – satisfied or unsatisfied – a life.' Mr Longdon looked so interested that his fellow-visitor, evidently touched by what was now an appeal and a dependence, grew still more bland, or at least more assured, for affirmation. 'She's not *too* sorry for herself.'

'Ah, she's so proud!'

'Yes, but that's a help.'

'Oh – not for *us*!'

It arrested Mitchy, but his ingenuity could only rebound. 'In *one* way: that of reducing us to feel that the desire to "make up" to her is – well, mainly for *our* relief. If she "trusts" us, as I said just now, it isn't for *that* she does so.' As his friend appeared to wait then to hear, it was presently with positive joy that he showed he could meet the last difficulty. 'What she trusts us to do' – oh, Mitchy had worked it out! – 'is to let *him* off.'

'Let him off?' It still left Mr Longdon dim.

'Easily. That's all.'

'But what would letting him off hard be? It seems to me he's – on any terms – already beyond us. He *is* off.'

Mr Longdon had given it a sound that suddenly made Mitchy appear to collapse under a sharper sense of the matter. 'He *is* off,' he moodily echoed.

His companion, again a little bewildered, watched him; then with impatience: 'Do, please, tell me what has happened.'

He quickly pulled himself round. 'Well, he was, after a long absence, here a while since as if expressly to see her. But after spending half an hour he went away without it.'

Mr Longdon's watch continued. 'He spent the half-hour with her mother instead?'

'Oh "instead" – it was hardly that. He at all events dropped his idea.'

'And what had it been, his idea?'

'You speak as if he had as many as I!' Mitchy replied. 'In a manner indeed he has,' he continued as if for himself. 'But they're of a different kind,' he said to Mr Longdon.

'What had it been, his idea?' the old man, however, simply repeated.

Mitchy's confession at this seemed to explain his previous evasion. 'We shall never know.'

Mr Longdon hesitated, 'He won't tell *you*?'

'Me?' Mitchy had a pause. 'Less than any one.'

Many things they had not spoken had already passed between them, and something evidently, to the sense of each, passed during the moment that followed this. 'While you were abroad,' Mr Longdon presently asked, 'did you hear from him?'

'Never. And I wrote nothing.'

'Like me,' said Mr Longdon. 'I've neither written nor heard.'

'Ah, but with you it will be different.' Mr Longdon, as if with the outbreak of an agitation hitherto controlled, had turned abruptly away and, with the usual swing of his glass, begun almost wildly to wander. 'You *will* hear.'

'I shall be curious.'

'Oh, but what Nanda wants, you know, is that you shouldn't be too much so.'

Mr Longdon thoughtfully rambled. 'Too much—?'

'To let him off, as we were saying, easily.'

The elder man for a while said nothing more, but he at last came back. 'She'd like me actually to give him something?'

'I dare say!'

'Money?'

Mitchy smiled. 'A handsome present.' They were face to face again with more mute interchange. 'She doesn't want *him* to have lost—!' Mr Longdon, however, on this once more broke off while Mitchy's eyes followed him. 'Doesn't it give a sort of measure of what she may feel—?'

He had paused, working it out again with the effect of his friend's returning afresh to be fed with his light. 'Doesn't what give it?'

'Why, the fact that we still like him.'

Mr Longdon stared. 'Do *you* still like him?'

'If I didn't how should I mind—?' But on the utterance of it Mitchy fairly pulled up.

His companion, after another look, laid a mild hand on his shoulder. 'What is it you mind?'

'From *him*? Oh, nothing!' He could trust himself again 'There are people like that – great cases of privilege.'

'He *is* one!' Mr Longdon mused.

'There it is. They go through life, somehow, guaranteed. They can't help pleasing.'

'Ah,' Mr Longdon murmured, 'if it hadn't been for that—!'

'They hold, they keep every one,' Mitchy went on. 'It's the sacred terror.'

The companions for a little seemed to stand together in this element; after which the elder turned once more away and appeared to continue to walk in it. 'Poor Nanda!' then, in a far-off sigh, came across from him to Mitchy. Mitchy on this turned vaguely around to the fire, into which he remained gazing till he heard again Mr Longdon's voice. 'I knew it of course after all. It was what I came up for. That night, before you went abroad, at Mrs Grendon's—'

'Yes?' – Mitchy was with him again.

'Well, made me see the future. It was then already too late.'

Mitchy assented with emphasis. 'Too late. She was spoiled for him.'

If Mr Longdon had to take it he took it at least quietly, only saying after a time: 'And her mother *isn't*?'

'Oh yes. Quite.'

'And does Mrs Brook know it?'

'Yes, but doesn't mind. She resembles you and me. She "still likes" him.'

'But what good will that do her?'

Mitchy sketched a shrug. 'What good does it do *us*?'

Mr Longdon thought. 'We can at least respect ourselves.'

'*Can* we?' Mitchy smiled.

'And *he* can respect us,' his friend, as if not hearing him, went on.

Mitchy seemed almost to demur. 'He must think we're "rum".'

'Well, Mrs Brook's worse than "rum". He can't respect *her*.'

'Oh, that will be perhaps,' Mitchy laughed, 'what she'll get just most out of!' It was the first time, however, of Mr Longdon's showing that even after a minute he had not understood him; so that as quickly as possible he passed to another point. 'If you do anything may I be in it?'

'But what can I do? If it's over it's over.'

'For *him*, yes. But not for her or for you or for me.'

'Oh, I'm not for long!' the old man wearily said, turning the next moment to the door, at which one of the footmen had appeared.

'Mrs Brookenham's compliments, please sir,' this messenger articulated, 'and Miss Brookenham is now alone.'

'Thanks – I'll come up.'

The servant withdrew, and the eyes of the two visitors again met for a minute, after which Mitchy looked about for his hat. 'Good-bye. I'll go.'

Mr Longdon watched him while, having found his hat, he looked about for his stick. 'You want to be in *everything*?'

Mitchy, without answering, smoothed his hat down; then he replied: 'You say you're not for long, but you won't abandon her.'

'Oh, I mean I sha'n't last for ever.'

'Well, since you so expressed it yourself, that's what I mean too. I assure you *I* sha'n't desert her. And if I can help you—'

'Help me?' Mr Longdon interrupted, looking at him hard.

It made him a little awkward. 'Help you to help her, you know—!'

'You're very wonderful,' Mr Longdon presently returned. 'A year and a half ago you wanted to help me to help Mr Vanderbank.'

'Well,' said Mitchy, 'you can't quite say I haven't.'

'But your ideas of help are of a splendour!'

'Oh, I've told you about my ideas.' Mitchy was almost apologetic.

Mr Longdon hesitated. 'I suppose I'm not indiscreet then in recognizing your marriage as one of them. And that, with a responsibility so great already assumed, you appear fairly eager for another—!'

'Makes me out a kind of monster of benevolence?' Mitchy looked at it with a flushed face. 'The two responsibilities are very much one and the same. My marriage has brought me, as it were, only nearer to Nanda. My wife and she, don't you see? are particular friends.'

Mr Longdon, on his side, turned a trifle pale; he looked rather hard at the floor. 'I see – I see.' Then he raised his eyes. 'But – to an old fellow like me – it's all so strange.'

'It *is* strange.' Mitchy spoke very kindly. 'But it's all right.'

Mr Longdon gave a head-shake that was both sad and sharp. 'It's all wrong. But *you're* all right!' he added in a different tone as he walked hastily away.

BOOK X

NANDA

XXXV

NANDA BROOKENHAM, for a fortnight after Mr Longdon's return, had found much to think of; but the bustle of business became, visibly for us, particularly great with her on a certain Friday afternoon in June. She was in unusual possession of that chamber of comfort in which so much of her life had lately been passed, the redecorated and rededicated room, upstairs, in which she had enjoyed a due measure both of solitude and society. Passing the objects about her in review she gave especial attention to her rather marked wealth of books; changed repeatedly for five minutes the position of various volumes, transferred to tables those that were on shelves and rearranged shelves with an eye to the effect of backs. She was flagrantly engaged throughout indeed in the study of effect, which moreover, had the law of an extreme freshness not inveterately prevailed there, might have been observed to be traceable in the very detail of her own appearance. 'Company' in short was in the air and expectation in the picture. The flowers on the little tables bloomed with a consciousness sharply taken up by the glitter of knick-knacks and reproduced in turn in the light exuberance of cushions on sofas and the measured drop of blinds in windows. The friends in the photographs in particular were highly prepared, with small intense faces each, that happened in every case to be turned to the door. The pair of eyes most dilated perhaps was that of old Van, present under a polished glass and in a frame of gilt-edged morocco that spoke out, across the room, of Piccadilly and Christmas, and visibly widening his gaze at the opening of the door, the announcement of a name by a footman and the entrance of a gentleman remarkably like him save as the resemblance was on the gentleman's part flattered. Vanderbank had not been in the room ten seconds before he showed that he had arrived to be kind. Kindness therefore becomes for us, by a quick turn of the glass that reflects the whole scene, the high pitch of the concert – a kindness that almost immediately filled the place, to the exclusion of everything else, with a familiar, friendly voice, a brightness of good looks and good intentions, a constant though perhaps sometimes misapplied laugh, a super-abundance almost of interest, inattention and movement.

The first thing the young man said was that he was tremendously glad she had written. 'I think it was most particularly nice of you.' And this thought precisely seemed as he spoke a flower of the general bloom – as if the niceness he had brought in was so great that it straightway converted everything to its image. 'The only thing that upset me a little,' he went on, 'was your saying that before writing it you had so hesitated and waited. I hope very much, you know, that you'll never do anything of that kind again. If you've ever the slightest desire to see me – for no matter what reason; if there's ever the smallest thing of any sort I can do for you, I promise you I sha'n't easily forgive you if you stand on ceremony. It seems to me that when people have known each other as long as you and I there's one comfort at least they may treat themselves to. I mean of course,' Van developed, 'that of being easy and frank and natural. There are such a lot of relations in which one isn't, in which it doesn't pay, in which "ease" in fact would be the greatest of troubles and "nature" the greatest of falsities. However,' he continued while he suddenly got up to change the place in which he had put his hat, 'I don't really know why I'm preaching at such a rate, for I've a perfect consciousness of not myself requiring it. One does half the time preach more or less for one's self, eh? I'm not mistaken at all events, I think, about the right thing with *you*. And a hint's enough for you, I'm sure, on the right thing with me.' He had been looking all round while he talked and had twice shifted his seat; so that it was quite in consonance with his general admiring notice that the next impression he broke out with should have achieved some air of relevance. 'What extraordinarily lovely flowers you have and how charming you've made everything! You're always doing something – women are always changing the position of their furniture. If you happen to come in in the dark – no matter how well you know the place – you sit down on a hat or a puppy-dog. But of course you'll say one doesn't come in in the dark, or at least if one does deserves what one gets. Only you know the way some women keep their rooms. I'm bound to say *you* don't, do you? – you don't go in for flower-pots in the windows and half-a-dozen blinds. Why *should* you? You *have* got a lot to show!' He rose with this for the third time, as the better to command the scene. 'What I mean is that sofa – which, by the way, is awfully good: you do, my dear Nanda, go it! It certainly was *here* the last time, wasn't it? and this thing was there. The last time – I mean the last time I was up here – was fearfully long ago: when, by the way, *was* it? But you see I *have* been and that I remember it. And you've a lot more things now. You're laying up treasure. Really the increase of luxury—! What an awfully jolly lot of books – have you read them all? Where did you learn so much about bindings?'

He continued to talk; he took things up and put them down; Nanda sat in her place, where her stillness, fixed and colourless, contrasted with his rather flushed freedom, and appeared only to wait, half in surprise, half in surrender, for the flow of his suggestiveness to run its course, so that, having herself provoked the occasion, she might do a little more to meet it. It was by no means, however, that his presence in any degree ceased to prevail; for there were minutes during which her face, the only thing in her that moved, turning with his turns and following his glances, actually had a look inconsistent with anything but sub-mission to almost any accident. It might have expressed a desire for his talk to last and last, an acceptance of any treatment of the hour or any version, or want of version, of her act that would best suit his ease, even in fact a resigned prevision of the occurrence of something that would leave her, quenched and blank, with the appearance of having made him come simply that she might look at him. She might indeed have been aware of an inability to look at him

little enough to make it flagrant that she had appealed to
him for something quite different. Keeping the situation
meanwhile thus in his hands he recognized over the chimney
a new alteration. 'There used to be a big print – wasn't
there? a thing of the fifties – we had lots of them at home;
some place or other "in the olden time". And now there's
that lovely French glass. So you see.' He spoke as if she had
in some way gainsaid him, whereas he had not left her time
even to answer a question. But he broke out anew on the
beauty of her flowers. 'You have awfully good ones – where
do you get them? Flowers and pictures and – what are the
other things people have when they're happy and superior?
– books and birds. You ought to have a bird or two, though
I dare say you think that by the noise I make I'm as good
myself as a dozen. Isn't there some girl in some story – it
isn't Scott; what is it? – who had domestic difficulties and a
cage in her window and whom one associates with chick-
weed and virtue? It isn't Esmeralda – Esmeralda had a
poodle, hadn't she? – or have I got my heroines mixed?
You're up here yourself like a heroine; you're perched in
your tower or what do you call it? – your bower. You quite
hang over the place, you know – the great wicked city, the
wonderful London sky and the monuments looming
through: or am I again only muddling up my Zola? You
must have the sunsets – haven't you? No – what am I talking about? Of course you look north. Well, they strike me
as about the only thing you haven't. At the same time it's
not only because I envy you that I feel humiliated. I ought
to have sent you some flowers.' He smote himself with
horror, throwing back his head with a sudden thought.
'Why in goodness when I got your note didn't I for once in
my life do something really graceful? I simply liked it and
answered it. Here I am. But I've brought nothing. I haven't
even brought a box of sweets. I'm not a man of the world.'

'Most of the flowers here,' Nanda at last said, 'come
from Mr Longdon. Don't you remember his garden?'

Vanderbank, in quick response, called it up. 'Dear yes –
wasn't it charming? And that morning you and I spent
there' – he was so careful to be easy about it – 'talking
under the trees.'

'You had gone out to be quiet and read—'

'And you came out to look after me. Well, I remember,' Van went on, 'that we had some good talk.'

The talk, Nanda's face implied, had become dim to her; but there were other things. 'You know he's a great gardener — I mean really one of the greatest. His garden is like a dinner in a house where the person — the person of the house — thoroughly knows and cares.'

'I see. And he sends you dishes from the table.'

'Often — every week. That is, now that he's in town his gardener does it.'

'Charming of them both!' Vanderbank exclaimed. 'But his gardener — that extraordinarily tall fellow with the long red beard — was almost as nice as himself. I had talks with *him* too, and I remember every word he said. I remember he told me you asked questions that showed "a deal of study". But I thought I had never seen all round such a charming lot of people — I mean as those down there that our friend has got about him. It's an awfully good note for a man, pleasant servants, I always think, don't you? Mr Longdon's — and quite without their saying anything; just from the sort of type and manner they had — struck me as a kind of chorus of praise. The same with Mitchy's at Mertle, I remember,' Van rambled on. 'Mitchy's the sort of chap who might have awful ones, but I recollect telling him that one quite felt as if it were with *them* one had come to stay. Good note, good note,' he cheerfully repeated. 'I'm bound to say, you know,' he continued in this key, 'that you've a jolly sense for getting in with people who make you comfortable. Then, by the way, he's still in town?'

Nanda hesitated. 'Do you mean Mr Mitchy?'

'Oh, *he* is, I know — I met them two nights ago; and by the way again — don't let me forget — I want to speak to you about his wife. But I've not seen, do you know? Mr Longdon — which is really too awful. Twice, thrice I think, have I at moments like this one snatched myself from pressure; but there's no finding the old demon at any earthly hour. When do *you* go — or does he only come here? Of course I see you've got the place arranged for him. When I asked at his hotel at what hour he ever *was* in, blest if the fellow didn't say "Very often, sir, about ten!" And when I said "Ten P.M.?" he quite laughed at my innocence over a person of such habits. What *are* his habits then now, and what are you putting him up to? Seriously,' Vanderbank pursued, 'I *am* awfully sorry, and I wonder if, the first time you've a chance, you'd kindly tell him you've heard me say so and that I mean yet to run him to earth. The same really with the Mitchys. I didn't, somehow, the other night, in such a lot of people, get at them. But I sat opposite to Aggie all through dinner, and that puts me in mind. I should like volumes from you about Aggie, please. It's too revolting of me not to go to see her. But every one knows I'm busy. We're up to our necks!'

'I can't tell you,' said Nanda, 'how kind I think it of you to have found, with all you have to do, a moment for *this*. But please, without delay, let me tell you—'

Practically, however, he would let her tell him nothing; his almost aggressive friendly optimism clung so to references of short range. 'Don't mention it, please. It's too charming of you to squeeze me in. To see *you* moreover does me good. Quite distinct good. And your writing me touched me – oh, but really. There were all sorts of old things in it.' Then he broke out once more on her books, one of which for some minutes past he had held in his hand. 'I see you go in for sets – and, my dear child, upon my word, I see, *big* sets. What's this? – "Vol. 23: The British Poets." Vol. 23 is delightful – do tell me about Vol. 23. Are you doing much in the British Poets? But when the deuce, you wonderful being, do you find time to read? *I* don't find any – it's too hideous. One relapses in London into illiteracy and barbarism. I have to keep up a false glitter to hide in conversation my rapidly increasing ignorance: I should be so ashamed after all to see other people *not* shocked by it. But teach me, teach me!' he gaily went on.

'The British Poets,' Nanda immediately answered, 'were given me by Mr Longdon, who has given me all the good books except a few – those in that top row – that have been given me at different times by Mr Mitchy. Mr Mitchy has sent me flowers too, as well as Mr Longdon. And they're

both – since we've spoken of my seeing them – coming by
appointment this afternoon; not together, but Mr Mitchy
at 5.30 and Mr Longdon at 6.30.'

She had spoken as with conscious promptitude, making
up for what she had not yet succeeded in saying by a quick,
complete statement of her case. She was evidently also
going on with more, but her actual visitor with a laugh had
already taken her up. 'You *are* making a day of it and you
run us like railway trains!' He looked at his watch. 'Have
I then time?'

'It seems to me I should say "Have *I*?" But it's not half-
past four,' Nanda went on, 'and though I've something
very particular of course to say to you it won't take long.
They don't bring tea till five, and you must surely stay till
that. I had already written to you when they each, for the
same reason, proposed this afternoon. They go out of town
tomorrow for Sunday.'

'Oh, I see – and they have to see you first. What an
influence you exert, you know, on people's behaviour!'

She continued as literal as her friend was facetious:
'Well, it just happened so, and it didn't matter, since, on
my asking you, don't you know? to choose your time, you
had taken, as suiting you best, this comparatively early
hour.'

'Oh perfectly.' But he again had his watch out. 'I've a
job, perversely – that was my reason – on the other side of
the world; which, by the way, I'm afraid, won't permit me
to wait for tea. My tea doesn't matter.' The watch went
back to his pocket. 'I'm sorry to say I must be off before
five. It has been delightful at all events to see you again.'

He was on his feet as he spoke, and though he had been
half the time on his feet his last words gave the effect of his
moving almost immediately to the door. It appeared to
come out with them rather clearer than before that he was
embarrassed enough really to need help, and it was
doubtless the measure she after an instant took of this that
enabled Nanda, with a quietness all her own, to draw to
herself a little more of the situation. The quietness was
plainly determined for her by a quick vision of its being the
best assistance she could show. Had he an inward terror

that explained his superficial nervousness, the incoherence of a loquacity designed, it would seem, to check in each direction her advance? He only fed it in that case by allowing his precautionary benevolence to put him in so much deeper. Where indeed could he have supposed that she wanted to come out, and what that she could ever do for him would really be so beautiful as this present chance to smooth his confusion and add as much as possible to that refined satisfaction with himself which would proceed from his having dealt with a difficult hour in a gallant and delicate way? To force upon him an awkwardness was like forcing a disfigurement or a hurt, so that at the end of a minute, during which the expression of her face became a kind of uplifted view of her opportunity, she arrived at the appearance of having changed places with him and of their being together precisely in order that he – not she – should be let down easily.

XXXVI

'But surely you're not going already?' she asked. 'Why in the world then do you suppose I appealed to you?'

'Bless me, no; I've lots of time.' He dropped, laughing for very eagerness, straight into another chair. 'You're too awfully interesting. Is it really an "appeal"?' Putting the question indeed, he could scarce even yet allow her a chance to answer it. 'It's only that you make me a little nervous with your account of all the people who are going to tumble in. And there's one thing more,' he quickly went on: 'I just want to make the point in case we should be interrupted. The whole fun is in seeing you this way alone.'

'Is *that* the point?' Nanda, as he took breath, gravely asked.

'That's a part of it – I feel it, I assure you, to be charming. But what I meant – if you'd only give me time, you know, to put in a word – is what for that matter I've already told you: that it almost spoils my pleasure for you to keep reminding me that a bit of luck like this – luck for *me*: I see you coming! – is after all for you but a question of business. Hang business! Good – don't stab me with that paper-knife. I listen. What *is* the great affair?' Then as it looked for an instant as if the words she had prepared had just, in the supreme pinch of her need, fallen apart, he once more tried his advantage. 'Oh, if there's any difficulty about it, let it go – we'll take it for granted. There's one thing at any rate – do let me say this – that I *should* like you to keep before me: I want before I go, to make you light up for me the question of little Aggie. Oh, there are other questions too as to which I regard you as a perfect fountain of curious knowledge! However, we'll take them one by one – the next some other time. You always seem to me to hold the strings of such a lot of queer little dramas. Have something on the shelf for me when we meet again. *The* thing just now is the outlook for Mitchy's affair. One cares enough for old Mitch to fancy one may feel safer for a lead or two. In fact I want regularly to turn you on.'

'Ah, but the thing I happen to have taken it into my head to say to you,' Nanda now placidly enough replied, 'hasn't the least bit to do, I assure you, either with Aggie or with "old Mitch". If you don't want to hear it – want some way of getting off – please believe *they* won't help you a bit.' It was quite in fact that she felt herself at last to have found the right tone. Nothing less than a conviction of this could have made her after an instant add: 'What in the world, Mr Van, are you afraid of?'

Well, that it *was* the right tone a single little minute was sufficient to prove – a minute, I must yet haste to say, big enough in spite of its smallness to contain the longest look ever, on any occasion, exchanged between these friends. It was one of those looks – not so frequent, it must be admitted, as the muse of history, dealing at best in short cuts, is often by the conditions of her trade reduced to representing them – which after they have come and gone are felt not only to have changed relations but absolutely to have cleared the air. It certainly helped Vanderbank to find his answer. 'I'm only afraid, I think, of your conscience.'

He had been indeed for the space more helped than she. 'My conscience?'

'Think it over – quite at your leisure – and some day

you'll understand. There's no hurry,' he continued – 'no hurry. And when you do understand, it needn't make your existence a burden to you to fancy you must tell me.' Oh he was so kind – kinder than ever now. 'The thing is, you see, that *I* haven't a conscience. I only want my fun.'

They had on this a second look, also decidedly comfortable, though discounted, as the phrase is, by the other, which had really in its way exhausted the possibilities of looks. 'Oh, I want *my* fun too,' said Nanda, 'and little as it may strike you in some ways as looking like it, just this, I beg you to believe, is the real thing. What's at the bottom of it,' she went on, 'is a talk I had not long ago with mother.'

'Oh yes,' Van returned with brightly blushing interest. 'The fun,' he laughed, 'that's to be got out of "mother"!'

'Oh, I'm not thinking so much of that. I'm thinking of any that she herself may be still in a position to pick up. Mine now, don't you see? is in making out how I can manage for this. Of course it's rather difficult,' the girl pursued, 'for me to tell you exactly what I mean.'

'Oh, but it isn't a bit difficult for me to understand you!' Vanderbank spoke in his geniality as if this were in fact the veriest trifle. 'You've got your mother on your mind. That's very much what I mean by your conscience.'

Nanda had a fresh hesitation, but evidently unaccompanied at present by any pain. 'Don't you still *like* mamma?' she at any rate quite successfully brought out. 'I must tell you,' she quickly subjoined, 'that though I've mentioned my talk with her as having finally led to my writing to you, it isn't in the least that she then suggested my putting you the question. I put it,' she explained, 'quite off my own bat.'

The explanation, as an effect immediately produced, manifestly for Vanderbank – and also on the spot – improved it. He sat back in his chair with a pleased – a distinctly exhilarated – sense of the combination. 'You're an adorable family!'

'Well then, if mother's adorable why give her up? That I don't mind admitting she did, the day I speak of, let me see that she feels you've done; but without suggesting

either — not a scrap, please believe — that I should make
you any sort of scene about it. Of course in the first place
she knows perfectly that anything like a scene would be no
use. You couldn't make out even if you wanted,' Nanda
went on, 'that *this* is one. She won't hear us — will she? —
smashing the furniture. I didn't think for a while that I
could do anything at all, and I worried myself with that
idea half to death. Then suddenly it came to me that I
could do just what I'm doing now. You said a while ago
that we must never be — you and I — anything but frank
and natural. That's what I said to myself also — why not?
Here I am for you therefore as natural as a cold in your
head. I just ask you — I even press you. It's because, as she
said, you've practically ceased coming. Of course I know
everything changes. It's the law — what is it? — "the great
law" of something or other. All sorts of things happen —
things come to an end. She has more or less — by his
marriage — lost Mitchy. I don't want her to lose everything.
Do stick to her. What I really wanted to say to you — to
bring it straight out — is that I don't believe you thoroughly
know how awfully she likes you. I hope my saying such a
thing doesn't affect you as "immodest". One never knows —
but I don't much care if it does. I suppose it *would* be
immodest if I were to say that I verily believe she's in love
with you. Not, for that matter, that father would mind —
he wouldn't mind, as he says, a twopenny rap. So' — she
extraordinarily kept it up — 'you're welcome to any good
the information may have for you: though that, I dare say,
does sound hideous. No matter — if I produce any effect on
you. That's the only thing I want. When I think of her
downstairs there so often nowadays practically alone I feel
as if I could scarcely bear it. She's so fearfully young.'

This time at least her speech, while she went from point
to point, completely hushed him, though after a full
glimpse of the direction it was taking he ceased to meet her
eyes and only sat staring hard at the pattern of the rug.
Even when at last he spoke it was without looking up.
'You're indeed, as she herself used to say, the modern
daughter! It takes that type to wish to make a career for
her parents.'

'Oh,' said Nanda very simply, 'it isn't a "career" exactly, is it – keeping hold of an old friend; but it may console a little, mayn't it, for the absence of one? At all events I didn't want not to have spoken before it's too late. Of course I don't know what's the matter between you, or if anything's really the matter at all. I don't care, at any rate, *what* is – it can't be anything very bad. Make it up, make it up – forget it. I don't pretend that's a career for *you* any more than for her; but there it is. I know how I sound – most patronizing and pushing; but nothing venture nothing have. You *can't* know how much you are to her. You're more to her, I verily believe, than any one *ever* was. I hate to have the appearance of plotting anything about her behind her back; so I'll say it once for all. She said once, in speaking of it to a person who repeated it to me, that you had done more for her than any one, because it was you who had really brought her out. It *was* – you did. I saw it at the time myself. I was very small, but I *could* see it. You'll say I must have been a most uncanny little wretch, and I dare say I was and am keeping now the pleasant promise. That doesn't prevent one's feeling that when a person has brought a person out—'

'A person should take the consequences,' Vanderbank broke in, 'and see a person through?' He could meet her now perfectly and proceeded admirably to do it. 'There's an immense deal in that, I admit – I admit. I'm bound to say I don't know quite what I did – one does these things, no doubt, with a fine unconsciousness: I should have thought indeed it was the other way round. But I assure you I accept all consequences and all responsibilities. If you don't know what's the matter between us I'm sure *I* don't either. It can't be much – we'll look into it. I don't mean you and I – *you* mustn't be any more worried; but she and her so unwittingly faithless one. I *haven't* been so often, I know' – Van pleasantly kept his course. 'But there's a tide in the affairs of men – and of women too, and of girls and of every one. You know what I mean – you know it for yourself. The great thing is that – bless both your hearts! – one doesn't, one simply *can't* if one would, give your mother up. It's absurd to talk about it. Nobody ever did such a thing in his life. There she is, like the moon or the Marble Arch. I don't say, mind you,' he candidly explained, 'that every one *likes* her equally: that's another affair. But no one who ever *has* liked her can afford ever again for any long period to do without her. There are too many stupid people – there's too much dull company. That, in London, is to be had by the ton; your mother's intelligence, on the other hand, will always have its price. One can talk with her for a change. She's fine, fine, fine. So, my dear child, be quiet. She's a fixed star.'

'Oh, I know she is,' Nanda said. 'It's *you*—'

'Who may be only the flashing meteor?' He sat and smiled at her. 'I promise you then that your words have stayed me in my course. You've made me stand as still as Joshua made the sun.' With which he got straight up. '"Young", you say she is?' he, as if to make up for it, all the more sociably continued. 'It's not like anything else. She's youth. She's *my* youth – she *was* mine. And if you ever have a chance,' he wound up, 'do put in for me that, if she wants *really* to know, she's booked for my old age. She's clever enough, you know' – and Vanderbank, laughing, went over for his hat – 'to understand what you tell her.'

Nanda took this in with due attention; she was also now on her feet. 'And then she's so lovely.'

'Awfully pretty!'

'I don't say it, as they say, you know,' the girl continued, '*because* she's mother, but I often think when we're out that wherever she is—'

'There's no one that, all round, really touches her?' Vanderbank took it up with zeal. 'Oh, so every one thinks, and in fact one's appreciation of the charming things that, in that way, are so intensely her own, can scarcely breathe on them all lightly enough. And then, hang it, she has perceptions – which are not things that run about the streets. She has surprises.' He almost broke down for vividness. 'She has little ways.'

'Well, I'm glad you do like her,' Nanda gravely replied.

At this again he fairly faced her, his momentary silence making it still more direct. 'I like, you know, about as well as I ever liked anything, this wonderful idea of yours of putting in a plea for her solitude and her youth. Don't think I do it injustice if I say – which is saying much – that it's quite as charming as it's amusing. And now good-bye.'

He had put out his hand, but Nanda hesitated. 'You won't wait for tea?'

'My dear child, I can't.' He seemed to feel, however, that something more must be said. 'We shall meet again. But it's getting on, isn't it, toward the general scatter?'

'Yes, and I hope that this year,' she answered, 'you'll have a good holiday.'

'Oh, we shall meet before that. I shall do what I can, but upon my word I feel, you know,' he laughed, 'that such a tuning-up as *you've* given me will last me a long time. It's like the high Alps.' Then with his hand out again he added: 'Have you any plans yourself?'

So many, it might have seemed, that she had to take no time to think. 'I dare say I shall be away a good deal.'

He candidly wondered. 'With Mr Longdon?'

'Yes – with him most.'

He had another pause. 'Really for a long time?'

'A long, long one, I hope.'

'Your mother's willing again?'

'Oh perfectly. And you see that's why.'

'Why?' She had said nothing more, and he failed to understand.

'Why you mustn't too much leave her alone. *Don't!*' Nanda brought out.

'I won't. But,' he presently added, 'there are one or two things.'

'Well, what are they?'

He produced in some seriousness the first. 'Won't she after all see the Mitchys?'

'Not so much either. That of course is now very different.'

Vanderbank hesitated. 'But not for *you*, I gather – is it? Don't you expect to see them?'

'Oh yes – I hope they'll come down.'

He moved away a little – not straight to the door. 'To Beccles? Funny place for them, a little though, isn't it?'

He had put the question as if for amusement, but Nanda

took it literally. 'Ah, not when they're invited so very very charmingly. Not when he wants them so.'

'Mr Longdon? Then that keeps up?'

'"That"?' – she was at a loss.

'I mean his intimacy – with Mitchy.'

'So far as it *is* an intimacy.'

'But didn't you, by the way' – and he looked again at his watch – 'tell me they're just about to turn up together?'

'Oh, not so very particularly together.'

'Mitchy first alone?' Vanderbank asked.

She had a smile that was dim, that was slightly strange. 'Unless you'll stay for company.'

'Thanks – impossible. And then Mr Longdon alone?'

'Unless Mitchy stays.'

He had another pause. 'You haven't after all told me about the efflorescence of his wife.'

'How can I if you don't give me time?'

'I see – of course not.' He seemed to feel for an instant the return of his curiosity. 'Yet it won't do, will it? to have her out before *him*? No, I must go.' He came back to her, and at present she gave him a hand. 'But if you do see Mr Longdon alone will you do me a service? I mean indeed not simply today, but with all other good chances?'

She waited. '*Any* service. But which first?'

'Well,' he returned in a moment, 'let us call it a bargain. I look after your mother—'

'And I—?' She had had to wait again.

'Look after my good name. I mean for common decency to *him*. He has been of a kindness to me that, when I think of my failure to return it, makes me blush from head to foot. I've odiously neglected him – by a complication of accidents. There are things I ought to have done that I haven't. There's one in particular – but it doesn't matter. And I haven't even explained about *that*. I've been a brute and I didn't mean it and I couldn't help it. But there it is. Say a good word for me. Make out somehow or other that I'm *not* a brute. In short,' the young man said, quite flushed once more with the intensity of his thought, 'let us have it that you may quite trust *me* if you'll let me a little – just for my character as a gentleman – trust *you*.'

'Ah, you may trust me,' Nanda replied with her hand-shake.

'Good-bye then!' he called from the door.

'Good-bye,' she said after he had closed it.

XXXVII

IT was half-past five when Mitchy turned up; and her relapse had in the meantime known no arrest but the arrival of tea, which, however, she had left unnoticed. He expressed on entering the fear that he had failed of exactitude, to which she replied by the assurance that he was on the contrary remarkably near it and by the mention of all the aid to patience she had drawn from the pleasure of half an hour with Mr Van – an allusion that of course immediately provoked on Mitchy's part the liveliest interest. 'He *has* risked it at last then? How tremendously exciting! And your mother?' he went on; after which, as she said nothing: 'Did *she* see him, I mean, and is he perhaps with her now?'

'No; she won't have come in – unless you asked.'

'I didn't ask. I asked only for you.'

Nanda thought an instant. 'But you will still sometimes come to see her, won't you? I mean you won't ever give her up?'

Mitchy, at this, laughed out. 'My dear child, you're an adorable family!'

She took it placidly enough. 'That's what Mr Van said. He said I'm trying to make a career for her.'

'Did he?' Her visitor, though without prejudice to his amusement, appeared struck. 'You must have got in with him rather deep.'

She again considered. 'Well, I think I did rather. He was awfully beautiful and kind.'

'Oh,' Mitchy concurred, 'trust him always for that!'

'He wrote me on my note,' Nanda pursued, 'a tremendously good answer.'

Mitchy was struck afresh. 'Your note? What note?'

'To ask him to come. I wrote at the beginning of the week.'

'Oh – I see,' Mitchy observed as if this were rather different. 'He couldn't then of course have done less than come.'

Yet his companion again thought. 'I don't know.'

'Oh come – I say: you do know,' Mitchy laughed. 'I should like to see him – or you either!' There would have been for a continuous spectator of these episodes an odd resemblance between the manner and all the movements that had followed his entrance and those that had accompanied the installation of his predecessor. He laid his hat, as Vanderbank had done, in three places in succession and appeared to have very much the same various views about the security of his stick and the retention in his hand of his gloves. He postponed the final selection of a seat and he looked at the objects about him while he spoke of other matters. Quite in the same fashion indeed at last these objects impressed him. 'How charmingly you've made your room and what a lot of nice things you've got!'

'That's just what Mr Van said too. He seemed immensely struck.'

But Mitchy hereupon once more had a drop to extravagance. 'Can I do nothing then but repeat him? I came, you know, to be original.'

'It would be original for *you*,' Nanda promptly returned, 'to be at all like him. But you *won't*,' she went back, 'not sometimes come for mother only? You'll have plenty of chances.'

This he took up with more gravity. 'What do you mean by chances? That you're going away? That *will* add to the attraction!' he exclaimed as she kept silence.

'I shall have to wait,' she answered at last, 'to tell you definitely what I'm to do. It's all in the air – yet I think I shall know today. I'm to see Mr Longdon.'

Mitchy wondered. 'Today?'

'He's coming at half-past six.'

'And then you'll know?'

'Well – *he* will.'

'Mr Longdon?'

'I meant Mr Longdon,' she said after a moment.

Mitchy had his watch out. 'Then shall I interfere?'

'There are quantities of time. You must have your tea. You see at any rate,' the girl continued, 'what I mean by your chances.'

She had made him his tea, which he had taken. 'You do squeeze us in!'

'Well, it's an accident your coming together – except of course that you're *not* together. I simply took the time that you each independently proposed. But it would have been all right even if you *had* met. That is, I mean,' she explained, 'even if you and Mr Longdon do. Mr Van, I confess, I did want alone.'

Mitchy had been glaring at her over his tea. 'You're more and more remarkable!'

'Well then, if I improve so give me your promise.'

Mitchy, as he partook of refreshment, kept up his thoughtful gaze. 'I shall presently want some more, please. But do you mind my asking if Van knew——'

'That Mr Longdon's to come? Oh yes, I told him, and he left with me a message for him.'

'A message? How awfully interesting!'

Nanda thought. 'It *will* be awfully – to Mr Longdon.'

'Some more *now*, please,' said Mitchy while she took his cup. 'And to Mr Longdon only, eh? Is that a way of saying that it's none of *my* business?'

The fact of her attending – and with a happy show of particular care – to his immediate material want added somehow, as she replied, to her effect of sincerity. 'Ah, Mr Mitchy, the business of mine that has not by this time ever so naturally become a business of yours – well, I can't think of any just now, and I wouldn't, you know, if I could!'

'I can promise you then that there's none of mine,' Mitchy declared, 'that hasn't made by the same token quite the same shift. Keep it well before you, please, that if ever a young woman had a grave lookout——!'

'What do you mean,' she interrupted, 'by a grave lookout?'

'Well, the certainty of finding herself saddled for all time to come with the affairs of a gentleman whom she can never get rid of on the specious plea that he's only her husband or her lover or her father or her son or her brother or her uncle or her cousin. There, as none of these characters, he just stands.'

'Yes,' Nanda kindly mused, 'he's simply her Mitchy.'

'Precisely. And a Mitchy, you see, is – what do you call it? – simply indissoluble. He's moreover inordinately inquisitive. He goes to the length of wondering whether Van also learned that you were expecting *me*.'

'Oh yes – I told him everything.'

Mitchy smiled. 'Everything?'

'I told him – I told him,' she replied with impatience.

Mitchy hesitated. 'And did he then leave me also a message?'

'No, nothing. What I'm to do for him with Mr Longdon,' she immediately explained, 'is to make practically a kind of apology.'

'Ah, and for me' – Mitchy quickly took it up – 'there can be no question of anything of that kind. I see. He has done me no wrong.'

Nanda, with her eyes now on the window, turned it over. 'I don't much think he would know even if I had.'

'I see, I see. And we wouldn't tell him.'

She turned with some abruptness from the outer view. 'We wouldn't tell him. But he was beautiful all round,' she went on. 'No one could have been nicer about having for so long, for instance, come so little to the house. As if he hadn't only too many other things to do! He didn't even make them out nearly the good reasons he might. But fancy, with his important duties – all the great affairs on his hands – our making vulgar little rows about being "neglected"! He actually made so little of what he might easily plead – speaking so, I mean, as if he were all in the wrong – that one had almost positively to *show* him his excuses. As if' – she really kept it up – 'he hasn't plenty!'

'It's only people like me,' Mitchy threw out, 'who have none?'

'Yes – people like you. People of no use, of no occupation and no importance. Like you, you know,' she pursued, 'there are so many.' Then it was with no transition of tone that she added: 'If you're bad Mitchy, I won't tell you anything.'

'And if I'm good what will you tell me? What I want

really most to *know* is why he should be, as you said just now, "apologetic" to Mr Longdon. What's the wrong he allows he has done *him*?'

'Oh, he has "neglected" him – if that's any comfort to us – quite as much.'

'Hasn't looked him up and that sort of thing?'

'Yes – and he mentioned some other matter.'

Mitchy wondered. 'Mentioned it?'

'In which,' said Nanda, 'he hasn't pleased him.'

Mitchy, after an instant, risked it. 'But what other matter?'

'Oh, he says that when I speak to him Mr Longdon will know.'

Mitchy gravely took this in. 'And shall you speak to him?'

'For Mr Van?' How, she seemed to ask, could he doubt it? 'Why, the very first thing.'

'And then will Mr Longdon tell you?'

'What Mr Van means?' Nanda thought. 'Well – I hope not.'

Mitchy followed it up. 'You "hope"—?'

'Why, if it's anything that could possibly make any one like him any less. I mean I sha'n't in that case in the least want to hear it.'

Mitchy looked as if he could understand that and yet could also imagine something of a conflict. 'But if Mr Longdon insists—?'

'On making me know? I sha'n't let him insist. Would *you*?' she put to him.

'Oh, I'm not in question!'

'Yes, you are!' she quite rang out.

'Ah—!' Mitchy laughed. After which he added: 'Well then, I might overbear you.'

'No, you mightn't,' she as positively declared again, 'and you wouldn't at any rate desire to.'

This he finally showed he could take from her – showed it in the silence in which for a minute their eyes met; then showed it perhaps even more in his deep exclamation: 'You're complete!'

For such a proposition as well she had the same detached

sense. 'I don't think I am in anything but the wish to keep *you* so.'

'Well – keep me, keep me! It strikes me that I'm not at all now on a footing, you know, of keeping myself. I quite give you notice in fact,' Mitchy went on, 'that I'm going to come to you henceforth for everything. But you're too wonderful,' he wound up as she at first said nothing to this. 'I don't even frighten you.'

'Yes – fortunately for you.'

'Ah, but I distinctly warn you that I mean to do my very best for it!'

Nanda viewed it all with as near an approach to gaiety as she often achieved. 'Well, if you should ever succeed it would be a dark day for you.'

'You bristle with your own guns,' he pursued, 'but the ingenuity of a lifetime shall be devoted to taking you on some quarter on which you're not prepared.'

'And what quarter, pray, will that be?'

'Ah, I'm not such a fool as to begin by giving you a cue!' Mitchy, on this, turned off with an ambiguous but unmistakably natural sigh; he looked at photographs, he took up a book or two as Vanderbank had done, and for a couple of minutes there was silence between them. 'What does stretch before me,' he resumed after an interval during which clearly, in spite of his movements, he had looked at nothing – 'what does stretch before me is the happy prospect of my feeling that I have found in you a friend with whom, so utterly and unreservedly, I can always go to the bottom of things. This luxury, you see now, of our freedom to look facts in the face is one of which, I promise you, I mean fully to avail myself.' He stopped before her again, and again she was silent. 'It's so awfully jolly, isn't it? that there's not at last a single thing that we can't take our ease about. I mean that we can't intelligibly name and comfortably challenge. We've worked through the long tunnel of artificial reserves and superstitious mysteries, and I at least shall have only to feel that in showing every confidence and dotting every "i" I follow the example you so admirably set. You go down to the roots? Good. It's all I ask!'

He had dropped into a chair as he talked, and so long as

she remained in her own they were confronted; but she presently got up and, the next moment, while he kept his place, was busy restoring order to the objects that both her visitors had disarranged. 'If you weren't delightful you'd be dreadful!'

'There we are! I could easily, in other words, frighten you if I would.'

She took no notice of the remark, only, after a few more scattered touches, producing an observation of her own. 'He's going, all the same, Mr Van, to be charming to mother. We've settled that.'

'Ah, then he *can* make time—?'

She hesitated. 'For as much as *that* – yes. For as much, I mean, as may sufficiently show her that he has not given her up. So don't you recognize how much more time *you* can make?'

'Ah – see precisely – there we are again!' Mitchy promptly ejaculated.

Yet he had gone, it seemed, further than she followed. 'But where?'

'Why, as I say, at the roots and in the depths of things.'

'Oh!' she dropped to an indifference that was but part of her general patience for all his irony.

'It's needless to go into the question of not giving your mother up. One simply *doesn't* give her up. One can't. There she is.'

'That's exactly what *he* says. There she is.'

'Ah, but I don't want to say nothing but what "he" says!' Mitchy laughed. 'He can't at all events have mentioned to you any such link as the one that in my case is now almost the most sensible. *I've* got a wife, you know.'

'Oh, Mitchy!' the girl protestingly though vaguely murmured.

'And my wife – did you know it?' Mitchy went on, 'is positively getting thick with your mother. Of course it isn't new to you that she's wonderful for wives. Now that our marriage is an accomplished fact she takes the greatest interest in it – or bids fair to, if her attention can only be thoroughly secured – and more particularly in what I believe is generally called our peculiar situation: for it appears, you know, that we're in the most conspicuous manner possible *in* a peculiar situation. Aggie is therefore already, and is likely to be still more, in what's universally recognized as your mother's regular line. Your mother will attract her, study her, finally "understand" her. In fact, she'll "help", as she has "helped" so many before and will "help" so many still to come. With Aggie thus as a satellite and a frequenter – in a degree in which she never yet *has* been,' he continued, 'what will the whole thing be but a practical multiplication of our points of contact? You may remind me of Mrs Brook's contention that if she did in her time keep something of a saloon the saloon is now, in consequence of events, but a collection of fortuitous atoms; but that, my dear Nanda, will become none the less to your clearer sense but a pious echo of her momentary modesty or – call it at the worst – her momentary despair. The generations will come and go, and the *personnel*, as the newspapers say, of the saloon will shift and change, but the institution itself, as resting on a deep human need, has a long course yet to run and a good work yet to do. *We* sha'n't last, but your mother will, and as Aggie is happily very young she's therefore provided for, in the time to come, on a scale sufficiently considerable to leave us just now at peace. Meanwhile, as you're almost as good for husbands as Mrs Brook is for wives, why aren't we, as a couple, we Mitchys, quite ideally arranged for, and why mayn't I speak to you of my future as sufficiently guaranteed? The only appreciable shadow I make out comes, for me, from the question of what may today be between you and Mr Longdon. Do I understand,' Mitchy asked, 'that he's presently to arrive for an answer to something he has put to you?'

Nanda looked at him a while with a sort of solemnity of tenderness, and her voice, when she at last spoke, trembled with a feeling that clearly had grown in her as she listened to the string of whimsicalities, bitter and sweet, that he had just unrolled. 'You're wild,' she said simply – 'you're wild.'

He wonderfully glared. 'Am I then already frightening you?' He shook his head rather sadly. 'I'm not in the least trying yet. There's something,' he added after an instant, 'that I do want too awfully to ask you.'

'Well, then—!' If she had not eagerness she had at least charity.

'Oh, but you see I reflect that though you show all the courage to go to the roots and depths with *me*, I'm not – I never have been – fully conscious of the nerve for doing as much with you. It's a question,' Mitchy explained, 'of how much – of a particular matter – you know.'

She continued ever so kindly to face him. 'Hasn't it come out all round now that I know everything?'

Her reply, in this form, took a minute or two to operate, but when it began to do so it fairly diffused a light. Mitchy's face turned of a colour that might have been produced by her holding close to it some lantern wonderfully glazed. 'You know, you know!' he then rang out.

'Of course I know.'

'You know, you know!' Mitchy repeated.

'Everything,' she imperturbably went on, 'but what you're talking about.'

He was silent a little, with his eyes on her. 'May I kiss your hand?'

'No,' she answered: 'that's what I call wild.'

He had risen with his inquiry and after her reply he remained a moment on the spot. 'See – I've frightened you. It proves as easy as that. But I only wanted to show you and to be sure for myself. Now that I've the mental certitude I shall never wish otherwise to use it.' He turned away to begin again one of his absorbed revolutions. 'Mr Longdon has asked you this time for a grand public adhesion, and what he turns up for now is to receive your ultimatum? A final, irrevocable flight with him is the line he advises, and he'll be ready for it on the spot with the post-chaise and the pistols?'

The image appeared really to have for Nanda a certain vividness, and she looked at it a space without a hint of a smile. 'We sha'n't need any pistols, whatever may be decided about the post-chaise; and any flight we may undertake together will need no cover of secrecy or night. Mother, as I've told you—'

'Won't fling herself across your reckless path? I remember,' said Mitchy – 'you alluded to her magnificent resignation. But father?' he oddly inquired.

Nanda thought for this a moment longer. 'Well, Mr Longdon has – off in the country – a good deal of shooting.'

'So that Edward can sometimes come down with his old gun? Good then too – if it isn't, as he takes you by the way, to shoot *you*. You've got it all shipshape and arranged, in other words, and have only, if the fancy does move you, to clear out. You clear out – you make all sorts of room. It *is* interesting,' Mitchy exclaimed, 'arriving thus with you at the depths! I look all round and see every one squared and every one but one or two suited. Why then reflection and delay?'

'You don't, dear Mr Mitchy,' Nanda took her time to return, 'know nearly as much as you think.'

'But isn't my question absolutely a confession of ignorance and a renunciation of thought? I put myself from this moment forth with you,' Mitchy declared, 'on the footing of knowing nothing whatever and of receiving literally from your hands all information and all life. Let my continued attitude of inquiry, my dear Nanda, show it. Any hesitation you may yet feel, you imply, proceeds from a sense of duties in London not to be lightly renounced? Oh,' he thoughtfully said, 'I do at least know you *have* them.'

She watched him with the same mildness while he vaguely circled about. 'You're wild, you're wild,' she insisted. 'But it doesn't in the least matter. I sha'n't abandon you.'

He stopped short. 'Ah, that's what I wanted from you in so many clear-cut golden words – though I won't in the least of course pretend that I've felt I literally need it. I don't literally need the big turquoise in my neck-tie; which incidently means, by the way, that if you should admire it you're quite welcome to it. Such words – that's my point – are like jewels: the pride, you see, of one's heart. They're mere vanity, but they help along. You've got of course always poor Tishy,' he continued.

'Will you leave it all to *me*?' Nanda said as if she had not heard him.

'And then you've got poor Carrie,' he went on, 'though *her* of course you rather divide with your mother.'

'Will you leave it all to *me*?' the girl repeated.

'To say nothing of poor Cashmore,' he pursued, 'whom you take *all*, I believe, yourself?'

'Will you leave it all to me?' she once more repeated.

This time he pulled up, suddenly and expressively wondering. 'Are you going to do anything about it at present? – I mean with our friend?'

She appeared to have a scruple of saying, but at last she produced it. 'Yes – he doesn't mind now.'

Mitchy again laughed out. 'You *are*, as a family—!' But he had already checked himself. 'Mr Longdon will at any rate, you imply, be somehow interested—'

'In *my* interests? Of course – since he has gone so far. You expressed surprise at my wanting to wait and think; but how can I not wait and not think when so much depends on the question – now so definite – of how much further he *will* go?'

'I see,' said Mitchy, profoundly impressed. 'And how much does that depend on?'

She had to reflect. 'On how much further I, for my part, *must*.'

Mitchy's grasp was already complete. 'And he's coming then to learn from you how far this is?'

'Yes – very much.'

Mitchy looked about for his hat. 'So that of course I see my time's about up as you'll want to be quite alone together.'

Nanda glanced at the clock. 'Oh, you've a margin yet.'

'But don't you want an interval for your thinking—?'

'Now that I've seen you?' Nanda was already very obviously thoughtful.

'I mean if you've an important decision to take.'

'Well,' she returned, 'seeing you *has* helped me.'

'Ah, but at the same time worried you. Therefore—' And he picked up his umbrella.

Her eyes rested on its curious handle. 'If you cling to your idea that I'm frightened you'll be disappointed. It will never be given you to reassure me.'

'You mean by that that I am primarily so solid—'

'Yes, that till I see you yourself afraid—'

'Well?'

'Well, I won't admit that anything isn't exactly what I was prepared for.'

Mitchy looked with interest into his hat. 'Then what is it I'm to "leave" to you?' After which, as she turned away from him with a suppressed sound and said, while he watched her, nothing else, 'It's no doubt natural for you to talk,' he went on, 'but I do make you nervous. Good-bye – good-bye.'

She had stayed him however by a fresh movement as he reached the door. 'Aggie's only trying to find out—'

'Yes – what?' he asked, waiting.

'Why, what sort of person she is. How can she ever have known? It was carefully, elaborately hidden from her – kept so obscure that she could make out nothing. She isn't now like *me*.'

He wonderingly attended. 'Like you?'

'Why, I get the benefit of the fact that there was never a time when I didn't know *something* or other and that I became more and more aware, as I grew older, of a hundred little chinks of daylight.'

Mitchy stared. 'You're stupendous, my dear!' he murmured.

Ah, but she kept it up. '*I* had my idea about Aggie.'

'Oh, don't I know you had? And how you were positive about the sort of person—'

'That she didn't even suspect herself,' Nanda broke in, 'to be? I'm equally positive now. It's quite what I believed, only there's ever so much more of it. More *has* come – and more will yet. You see, when there has been nothing before, it all has to come with a rush. So that, if even I am surprised, of course *she* is.'

'And of course *I* am!' Mitchy's interest, though even now not wholly unqualified with amusement, had visibly deepened. 'You admit then,' he continued, 'that you *are* surprised?'

Nanda just hesitated. 'At the mere scale of it. I think it's splendid. The only person whose astonishment I don't quite understand,' she added, 'is Cousin Jane.'

'Oh, Cousin Jane's astonishment serves her right!'

'If she held so,' Nanda pursued, 'that marriage should do everything—'

'She shouldn't be in such a funk at finding what it *is* doing? Oh no, she's the last one!' Mitchy declared. 'I vow I enjoy her scare.'

'But it's very bad, you know,' said Nanda.

'Oh, too awful!'

'Well, of course,' the girl appeared assentingly to muse, 'she couldn't after all have dreamed—!' But she took herself up. 'The great thing is to be helpful.'

'And in what way—?' Mitchy asked with his wonderful air of inviting competitive suggestions.

'Toward Aggie's finding herself. Do you think,' she immediately continued, 'that Lord Petherton really is?'

Mitchy frankly considered. 'Helpful? Oh, he does his best, I gather. Yes,' he presently added – 'Petherton's all right.'

'It's you yourself, naturally,' his companion threw off, 'who can help most.'

'Certainly, and I'm doing my best too. So that with such good assistance' – he seemed at last to have taken it all from her – 'what is it, I again ask, that, as you request, I'm to leave to you?'

Nanda required, while he still waited, some time to reply. 'To keep my promise.'

'Your promise?'

'Not to abandon you.'

'Ah,' cried Mitchy, 'that's better!'

'Then good-bye!' she said.

'Good-bye.' But he came a few steps forward. 'I *mayn't* kiss your hand?'

'Never.'

'Never?'

'Never.'

'Oh!' he oddly sounded as he quickly went out.

XXXVIII

THE interval he had represented as likely to be useful to
her was in fact, however, not a little abbreviated by a
punctuality of arrival on Mr Longdon's part so extreme as
to lead the first thing to a word almost of apology. 'You
can't say,' her new visitor immediately began, 'that I
haven't left you alone, these many days, as much as I
promised on coming up to you that afternoon when after
my return to town I found Mr Mitchett instead of your
mother awaiting me in the drawing-room.'

'Yes,' said Nanda, 'you've really done quite as I asked
you.'

'Well,' he returned, 'I felt half an hour ago that, near as
I was to relief, I could keep it up no longer; so that though
I knew it would bring me much too soon I started at six
sharp for our trysting-place.'

'And I've no tea, after all, to reward you!' It was but
now clearly that she noticed it. 'They must have removed
the things without my heeding.'

Her old friend looked at her with some intensity. 'Were
you in the room?'

'Yes – but I didn't see the man come in.'

'What then were you doing?'

Nanda thought; her smile was as usual the faintest
discernible outward sign. 'Thinking of *you.*'

'So tremendously hard?'

'Well, of other things too and of other persons. Of everything really that in our last talk I told you, you know, it
seemed to me best I should have out with myself before
meeting you for what I suppose you've now in mind.'

Mr Longdon had kept his eyes on her, but at this he
turned away; not, however, as an alternative, embracing
her material situation with the embarrassed optimism of
Vanderbank or the mitigated gloom of Mitchy. 'Ah' – he
took her up with some dryness – 'you've been having things
out with yourself?' But he went on before she answered: 'I
don't want any tea, thank you. I found myself, after five,
in such a fidget that I went three times in the course of the

hour to my club, where I have the impression that I each time had it. I dare say it wasn't there, though, that I did have it,' he after an instant pursued, 'for I've somehow a confused image of a shop in Oxford Street – or was it rather in Regent? – into which I gloomily wandered to beguile the moments with a liquid that if I strike you as upset I beg you to set it all down to. Do you know in fact what I've been doing for the last ten minutes? Roaming hither and thither in your beautiful Crescent till I could venture to come in.'

'Then did you see Mitchy go out? But no, you wouldn't' – Nanda corrected herself. 'He has been gone longer than that.'

Her visitor had dropped upon a sofa, where, propped by the back, he sat rather upright, his glasses on his nose, his hands in his pockets and his elbows much turned out. 'Mitchy left you more than ten minutes ago, and yet your state on his departure remains such that there could be a bustle of servants in the room without your being aware? Kindly give me some light then on the condition into which he has plunged you.'

She hovered before him with her obscure smile. 'You see it for yourself.'

He shook his head with decision. 'I don't see anything for myself, and I beg you to understand that it's not what I've come here today to do. Anything I may yet see which I don't already see will be only, I warn you, so far as you shall make it very clear. There – you've work cut out. And is it with Mr Mitchett, may I ask, that you've been, as you mention, cutting it?'

Nanda looked about her as if weighing many things; after which her eyes came back to him. 'Do you mind if I don't sit down?'

'I don't mind if you stand on your head – at the pass we've come to.'

'I shall not try your patience,' the girl good-humouredly replied, 'so far as that. I only want you not to be worried if I walk about a little.'

Mr Longdon, without a movement, kept his posture. 'Oh, I can't oblige you there. I *shall* be worried. I've come on purpose to be worried, and the more I surrender myself to the rack the more, I seem to feel, we shall have threshed our business out. So you may dance, if you like, on the absolutely passive thing you've made of me.'

'Well, what I *have* had from Mitchy,' she cheerfully responded, 'is practically a lesson in dancing; by which I perhaps mean rather a lesson in sitting, myself, as I want you to do while *I* talk, as still as a mouse. They take,' she declared, 'while *they* talk, an amount of exercise!'

'They?' Mr Longdon wondered. 'Was his wife with him?'

'Dear no – he and Mr Van.'

'Was Mr Van with him?'

'Oh no – before, alone. All over the place.'

Mr Longdon had a pause so rich in inquiry that when he at last spoke his question was itself like an answer. 'Mr Van has been to see you?'

'Yes. I wrote and asked him.'

'Oh!' said Mr Longdon.

'But don't get up.' She raised her hand. 'Don't!'

'Why should I?' He had never budged.

'He was most kind; stayed half an hour and, when I told him you were coming, left a good message for you.'

Mr Longdon appeared to wait for this tribute, which was not immediately produced. 'What do you call a "good" message?'

'I'm to make it all right with you.'

'To make what?'

'Why, that he has not, for so long, been to see you or written to you. That he has seemed to neglect you.'

Nanda's visitor looked so far about as to take the neighbourhood in general into the confidence of his surprise. 'To neglect *me*?'

'Well, others too, I believe – with whom we're not concerned. He has been so taken up. But you above all.'

Mr Longdon showed on this a coldness that somehow spoke for itself as the greatest with which he had ever in his life met an act of reparation and that was infinitely confirmed by his sustained immobility. 'But of what have I complained?'

'Oh, I don't think he fancies you've complained.'

'And how could he have come to see me,' he continued,

'when for so many months past I've been so little in town?'

He was not more ready with objections, however, than his companion had by this time become with answers. 'He must have been thinking of the time of your present stay. He said he hadn't seen you.'

'He has quite sufficiently tried – he has left cards,' Mr Longdon returned. 'What more does he want?'

Nanda looked at him with her long, grave straightness, which had often a play of light beyond any smile. 'Oh you know, he does want more.'

'Then it was open to him—'

'So he so strongly feels' – she quickly took him up – 'that you must have felt. And therefore it is that I speak for him.'

'Don't!' said Mr Longdon.

'But I promised him I would.'

'Don't!' the old man repeated.

She had kept for the time all her fine clearness turned to him; but she might on this have been taken as giving him up with a movement of obedience and a strange soft sigh. The smothered sound might even have represented to a listener at all initiated a consenting retreat before an effort greater than her reckoning – a retreat that was in so far the snap of a sharp tension. The next minute, none the less, she evidently found a fresh provocation in the sight of the pale and positively excessive rigour she had imposed, so that, though her friend was only accommodating himself to her wish, she had a sudden impulse of criticism. 'You're proud about it – too proud!'

'Well, what if I am?' He looked at her with a complexity of communication that no words could have meddled with. 'Pride's all right when it helps one to bear things.'

'Ah,' said Nanda, 'but that's only when one wants to take least from them. When one wants to take the most—'

'Well?' – he spoke, as she faltered, with a certain small hardness of interest.

She faltered, however, indeed. 'Oh, I don't know how to say it.' She fairly coloured with the attempt. 'One must let the sense of all that I speak of – well, all come. One must rather like it. I don't know – but I suppose one must rather grovel.'

Mr Longdon, though with visible reluctance, turned it over. 'That's very fine – but you're a woman.'

'Yes – that must make a difference. But being a woman in such a case has then,' Nanda went on, 'its advantages.'

On this point perhaps her friend might presently have been taken as relaxing. 'It strikes me that, even at that, the advantages are mainly for others. I'm glad, God knows, that you're not also a young man.'

'Then we're suited all round.'

She had spoken with a promptitude that appeared again to act on him slightly as an irritant, for he met it – with more delay – by a long, derisive murmur. 'Oh, *my* pride—!' But this she in no manner took up; so that he was left for a little to his thoughts. 'That's what you were plotting when you told me the other day that you wanted time?'

'Ah, I wasn't plotting – though I was, I confess, trying to work things out. That particular idea of simply asking Mr Van by letter to present himself – that particular flight of fancy hadn't in fact then at all occurred to me.'

'It never occurred, I'm bound to say, to *me*,' said Mr Longdon. 'I've never thought of writing to him.'

'Very good. But you haven't the reasons. I wanted to attack him.'

'Not about me, I hope to God!' Mr Longdon, distinctly a little paler, rejoined.

'Don't be afraid. I think I had an instinct of how you would have taken *that*. It was about mother.'

'Oh!' said her visitor.

'He has been worse to her than to you,' she continued. 'But he'll make it all right.'

Mr Longdon's attention retained its grimness. 'If he has such a remedy for the more then, what has he for the less?'

Nanda, however, was but for an instant checked. 'Oh, it's I who make it up to *you*. To mother, you see, there's no one otherwise to make it up.'

This at first unmistakably sounded to him too complicated for acceptance. But his face changed as light dawned. 'That puts it then that you *will* come?'

'I'll come if you'll take me as I am – which is, more than I've ever done before, what I must previously explain to you. But what *he* means by what you call his remedy is my making you feel better about himself.'

The old man gazed at her. '"Your" doing it is too beautiful! And he could really come to you for the purpose of asking you?'

'Oh no,' said the girl briskly, 'he came simply for the purpose of doing what he *had* to do. After my letter how could he not come? Then he met most kindly what I said to him for mother and what he quite understood to be all my business with him; so that his appeal to me to plead with you for – well, for his credit – was only thrown in because he had so good a chance.'

This speech brought Mr Longdon abruptly to his feet, but before she could warn him again of the patience she continued to need he had already, as if what she evoked for him left him too stupefied, dropped back into submission. 'The man stood there for you to render him a service? – for you to help and praise him?'

'Ah, but it wasn't to go out of my way, don't you see? He knew you were presently to be here.' Her anxiety that he should understand gave her a rare, strained smile. 'I mustn't make – as a request from him – too much of it, and I've not a doubt that, rather than you should think any ill of him for wishing me to say a word, he would gladly be left with whatever bad appearance he may actually happen to have.' She pulled up on these words as if with a quick sense of their really, by their mere sound, putting her in deeper; and could only give her friend one of the looks that expressed: 'If I could trust you not to assent even more than I want, I should say "You know what I mean!"' She allowed him at all events – or tried to allow him – no time for uttered irony before going on: 'He was everything you could have wished; quite as beautiful about *you*—'

'As about you?' – Mr Longdon took her up.

She demurred. 'As about mother.' With which she turned away as if it handsomely settled the question.

But it only left him, as she went to the window, sitting there sombre. 'I like, you know,' he brought out as his eyes followed her, 'your saying you're not proud! Thank God you *are*, my dear. Yes – it's better for us.'

At this, after a moment in her place, she turned round to him. 'I'm glad I'm anything – whatever you may call it and though I can't call it the same – that's good for *you*.'

He said nothing more for a little, as if by such a speech something in him were simplified and softened. 'It would be good for me – by which I mean it would be easier for me – if you didn't quite so immensely care for him.'

'Oh!' came from Nanda with an accent of attenuation at once so precipitate and so vague that it only made her attitude at first rather awkward. 'Oh!' she immediately repeated, but with an increase of the same effect. After which, conscious, she made as if to save herself a quick addition. 'Dear Mr Longdon, isn't it rather yourself most—?'

'It would be easier for me,' he went on heedless, 'if you didn't, my poor child, so wonderfully love him.'

'Ah, but I don't – please believe me when I assure you I *don't*!' she broke out. It burst from her, flaring up, in a queer quaver that ended in something queerer still – in her abrupt collapse, on the spot, into the nearest chair, where she choked with a torrent of tears. Her buried face could only after a moment give way to the flood, and she sobbed in a passion as sharp and brief as the flurry of a wild thing for an instant uncaged; her old friend meantime keeping his place in the silence broken by her sound and distantly – across the room – closing his eyes to his helplessness and her shame. Thus they sat together while their trouble both conjoined and divided them. She recovered herself, however, with an effort worthy of her fall and was on her feet again as she stammeringly spoke and angrily brushed at her eyes. 'What difference in the world does it make – what difference ever?' Then, clearly, even with the words, her checked tears suffered her to see that it made the difference that he too had been crying; so that 'I don't know why you mind!' she, on this, with extravagance, wailed.

'You don't know what I would have done for him. You don't know, you don't know!' he repeated – while she looked as if she naturally couldn't – as with a renewal of his dream of beneficence and of the soreness of his personal wound.

'Well, but *he* does you justice – he knows. So it shows, so it shows—!'

But in this direction too, unable to say what it showed, she had again broken down and again could only hold herself and let her companion sit there. 'Ah, Nanda, Nanda!' he deeply murmured; and the depth of the pity was, vainly and blindly, as the depth of a reproach.

'It's I – it's I, therefore,' she said as if she must then so look at it with him, 'it's I who am the horrible impossible and who have covered everything else with my own impossibility. For some different person you *could* have done what you speak of, and for some different person you can do it still.'

He stared at her with his barren sorrow. 'A person different from him?'

'A person different from *me*.'

'And what interest have I in any such person?'

'But your interest in me – you see well enough where *that* lands us.'

Mr Longdon now got to his feet and somewhat stiffly remained; after which, for all answer, 'You say you *will* come then?' he asked. Then as – seemingly with her last thought – she kept silent: 'You understand clearly, I take it, that this time it's never again to leave me – or to *be* left.'

'I understand,' she presently replied. 'Never again. That,' she continued, 'is why I asked you for these days.'

'Well then, since you've taken them—'

'Ah, but have *you*?' said Nanda. They were close to each other now, and with a tenderness of warning that was helped by their almost equal stature she laid her hand upon his shoulder. 'What I did more than anything else write to him for,' she had now regained her clearness enough to explain, 'was that – with whatever idea you had – you should see for yourself how he could come and go.'

'And what good was that to do me? *Hadn't* I seen for myself?'

'Well – you've seen once more. Here he was. I didn't care what he thought. Here I brought him. And his reasons remain.'

She kept her eyes on her companion's face, but his own now and afterwards seemed to wander far. 'What do I care for his reasons so long as they're not mine?'

She thought an instant, still holding him gently and as if for successful argument. 'But perhaps you don't altogether understand them.'

'And why the devil, altogether, *should* I?'

'Ah, because you distinctly want to,' said Nanda ever so kindly. 'You've admitted as much when we've talked—'

'Oh, but when *have* we talked?' he sharply interrupted.

This time he had challenged her so straight that it was her own look that strayed. 'When?'

'When.'

She hesitated. 'When *haven't* we?'

'Well, *you* may have: if that's what you call talking – never saying a word. But I haven't. I've only to do, at any rate, in the way of reasons, with my own.'

'And yours too then remain? Because, you know,' the girl pursued, 'I *am* like that.'

'Like what?'

'Like what he thinks.' Then so gravely that it was almost a supplication, 'Don't tell me,' she added, 'that you don't *know* what he thinks. You do know.'

Their eyes, on that strange ground, could meet at last, and the effect of it was presently for Mr Longdon. 'I do know.'

'Well?'

'Well!' He raised his hands and took her face, which he drew so close to his own that, as she gently let him, he could kiss her with solemnity on the forehead. 'Come!' he then very firmly said – quite indeed as if it were a question of their moving on the spot.

It literally made her smile, which, with a certain compunction, she immediately corrected by doing for him in the pressure of her lips to his cheek what he had just done for herself. 'Today?' she more seriously asked.

He looked at his watch. 'Tomorrow.'

She paused, but clearly for assent. 'That's what I mean by your taking me as I am. It *is*, you know, for a girl – extraordinary.'

'Oh, I know what it is!' he exclaimed with an odd fatigue in his tenderness.

But she continued, with the shadow of her scruple, to explain. 'We're many of us, we're most of us – as you long ago saw and showed you felt – extraordinary now. We can't help it. It isn't really our fault. There's so much else that's extraordinary that if we're in it all so much *we* must naturally be.' It was all obviously clearer to her than it had ever been, and her sense of it found renewed expression; so that she might have been, as she wound up, a very much older person than her friend. 'Everything's different from what it used to be.'

'Yes, everything,' he returned with an air of final indoctrination. 'That's what he ought to have recognized.'

'As *you* have?' Nanda was once more – and completely now – enthroned in high justice. 'Oh, he's more old-fashioned than you.'

'Much more,' said Mr Longdon with a queer face.

'He tried,' the girl went on – 'he did his best. But he couldn't. And he's so right – for himself.'

Her visitor, before meeting this, gathered in his hat and stick, which for a minute occupied his attention. 'He ought to have married—'

'Little Aggie? Yes,' said Nanda.

They had gained the door, where Mr Longdon again met her eyes. 'And then Mitchy—'

But she checked him with a quick gesture. 'No – not even then!'

So again before he went they were for a minute confronted. 'Are you anxious about Mitchy?'

She faltered, but at last brought it out. 'Yes. Do you see? There I am.'

'I see. There we are. Well,' said Mr Longdon – 'tomorrow.'

NOTES

(The references are to page and line numbers)

xxx. 20. *my scant but quite ponderable germ*: Recorded in James's notebook for 4 March 1895:

> The idea of the little London girl who grows up to 'sit with' the free-talking modern young mother – reaches 17, 18, etc. – comes out – and, not marrying, has to 'be there' – and, though the conversation is supposed to be expurgated for her, inevitably hears, overhears, guesses, follows, takes in, becomes acquainted with, horrors. A real little subject in this, I think – a real little situation for a short tale – if circumstance and setting is really given it. A young man who likes her – wants to take her out of it – feeling how she's exposed, etc. Attitude of the mother, the father, etc. The young man hesitates, because he thinks she already knows too much; but all the while he hesitates she knows, she learns, more and more. He finds out somehow how much she *does* know; and, terrified at it, drops her: all her ignorance, to his sense, is gone. His attitude to her mother – whom he has liked, visited, talked freely with, taken pleasure in. But when it comes to taking *her* daughter – ! She has appealed to him to do it – begged him to take her away. 'Oh, if some one would only marry her. I know – I have a bad conscience about her.' She may be an ugly one – who has also a passion for the world – for life – likes to be there – to hear, to know. There may be the contrasted clever, *avisée* foreign or foreignized friend or sister, who has married her daughter, very virtuously and very badly, unhappily, just to get her out of the atmosphere of her own talk and entourage – and takes *my* little lady to task for her inferior system and inferior virtue. Something in this really, I think – especially if one makes it take in something of the question of the non-marrying of girls, the desperation of mothers, the whole alteration of manners – in the sense of the *osé* – and tone, while our theory of the participation, the *presence* of the young, remains unaffected by it. Then the type of the little girl who is conscious and aware. 'I am modern – I'm supposed to know – I'm not a *jeune fille*,' etc. (*Notebooks*, p. 192)

xxxii. 7. *terribly at the mercy of his mind*: In his criticism James constantly stresses the inevitable role played by the perceiving imagination. In 'The Art of Fiction' (1884), he defines the novel as 'a personal, a direct impression of life' (*Partial Portraits*, p. 384). The observation is relativist in its implications but the influence of Arnoldian evaluative criticism persists in James's further comment that 'the deepest quality of a work of art will always be the quality of the mind of the producer. In proportion as that intelligence is fine will the novel, the picture, the statue partake of the substance of beauty and truth' (ibid. 406). And this criterion of moral judgment is still operating twenty years later in the Preface to *The Portrait of a Lady*:

> The question comes back ... to the kind and the degree of the artist's prime sensibility, which is the soil out of which his subject springs. The quality and capacity of that soil, its ability to 'grow' with due freshness and straightness any vision of life, represents, strongly or weakly, the projected morality. (*The Art of the Novel*, p. 45)

xxxii. 14. *to frame in the square, the circle, the charming oval*: James echoes his famous description from the Preface to *Roderick Hudson* of the artist's challenging difficulty of combining verisimilitude with formal rigour:

> Really, universally, relations stop nowhere, and the exquisite problem of the artist is eternally but to draw, by a geometry of his own, the circle within which they shall happily *appear* to do so. (*The Art of the Novel*, p. 5)

xxxvi. 20. '*Gyp*': The pen-name of Countess Sibylle Gabrielle Marie-Antoinette de Martel de Janville whose novels, for example *Ginette's Happiness* (*Le Bonheur de Ginette*) and *Bijou*, were popular in translation during the 1890s. As James suggests, they are written largely in dialogue – of an empty and functional kind – and deal with sexual intrigue in French society. Adultery is accepted (with some scruples – Gyp's heroines are reluctant to enter relationships with married men for fear of hurting their wives), and the novels are explicit on exactly those kinds of factual detail about which *The Awkward Age* is silent. The comparison suggests the irony in James citing Gyp as an apparently serious model.

xxxvii. 39. *M. Henri Lavedan*: Lavedan (1859–1940) was a popular dramatist and author of comedies of manners. James probably knew *Le Prince d'Aurec* (1894), one of his most successful works.

xxxviii. 38. '*complete disrespect*': *The Awkward Age* was published in book form on 25 April 1899, the first and only issue consisting of 2,000 copies. A popular novel could expect to sell around 50,000. The reviews were guarded, but slightly less negative than James implies. The novel received at least one perceptive notice, in the *Academy* (see Introduction, p. xxi), but the common complaint was that it was over-worked. A review in the *Dial* is typical: 'displaying workmanship of the highest cherry-stone order, and yet we are inexpressibly wearied by it, because it has so little to do with anything that makes life really worth having'. These and other reviews are reprinted in *Henry James: The Critical Heritage* (see 'Further reading').

xxxix. 19. *artistic rage*: James's phrase recalls the ancient notion of the artist as divinely inspired, classically described in Plato's *Phaedrus* and *Ion* and echoed in, for example, Coleridge's *Kubla Khan* ('Weave a circle round him thrice,/And close your eyes with holy dread'). James, characteristically, stresses not the inspirational but the technical aspects of the 'artistic rage' and goes on to describe the process of creation in a typical architectural image. (Cf. note to 112. 40.)

xlii. 10. *'Don't attempt to crush us with Dumas and Ibsen'*: Alexandre Dumas *fils* and Henrik Ibsen were the dramatists James most admired and whom he looked to as models during his period of writing for the theatre in the early 1890s. Dumas *fils* (1824–95), natural son of the novelist, is perhaps best known as the author of *La Dame aux Camélias* (1848), but he was also one of the most successful dramatists of the Second Empire and his plays about Parisian manners often have a strong didactic element. When he died James, a lifelong admirer of the Théâtre Français, wrote a commemorative essay, reprinted in *Notes on Novelists*, in which he regretfully observed British indifference to Dumas and described his 'extraordinarily firm grasp of his hard refractory art': 'The theatre of his time, wherever it has been serious, has on the ground of general method lived on him; wherever it has not done so it has not lived at all' (*Notes on Novelists*, pp. 293, 303). He also linked Dumas's name with that of Ibsen (1828–1906), as his rather different heir in serious drama: 'The energy that went forth blooming as Dumas has come back grizzled as Ibsen, and would under the latter form, I am sure, very freely acknowledge its debt' (ibid. 303). By 1895, when James wrote the essay on Dumas, and certainly by the time he wrote the Preface, the controversy over Ibsen's plays had largely subsided into acceptance, but during the late 1880s and early 1890s they were fiercely attacked as immoral. James is distinguished as an early admirer. He wrote reviews of *Hedda Gabler* and *The Master-Builder* in 1891 and 1893 (reprinted in *Essays in London and Elsewhere*) in which he described the attacks on Ibsen as 'one of those cries of outraged purity which have so often and so pathetically resounded through the Anglo-Saxon world', and in which he registered his fascination with Ibsen's ability to make his drama out of 'that supposedly undramatic thing, the picture not of an action but of a condition', a comment with obvious relevance to James's own method (*Essays in London*, pp. 244, 252). The 'disdainers of the contemporary drama' (xli. 25) whom James satirizes here objected to its seriousness, preferring the titillation of light French comedies to Ibsen's 'immorality'. They are typified by W. L. Courtney, a respected critic and academic, who in 1896 in the *Athenaeum* advised young dramatists: 'There must be a little psychological analysis but not too much; a little girding at social conventions, but social conventions must ultimately prevail; there must not be too much logic, but there must be romance and sentiment' (quoted by Michael Egan in *Ibsen: The Critical Heritage* (London and Boston, 1972), pp. 13–14).

xliii. 29. *the logic of but one way*: The technical challenge which drew James to the drama in the early 1890s. In a letter to William James of 6 February 1891 he wrote: 'I feel at last as if I had found my *real* form, which I am capable of carrying far, and for which the pale little art of fiction, as I have practised it, has been, for me, but a limited and restricted substitute.' By December 1893 he was writing of returning to 'more elevated and more independent courses. The whole odiousness of the thing lies in the connection between the drama and the theatre' (*Letters*, ed. Edel, III, 329, 452). Final disillusionment came with the failure of *Guy Domville* at the beginning of 1895 and James returned to fiction to apply the lessons learnt from the more compressed form.

xlv. 9. *the grave distinction between substance and form*: The interaction of subject and form has long been a critical commonplace, but in 1908 James's insight was radically new, particularly applied to prose fiction.

3. 1. *He might almost have been a priest*: Vanderbank's vision of Mr Longdon starts a train of suggestive imagery. Later Mr Longdon is to be the 'doorkeeper' of Nanda's 'temple of peace' (148. 27); Nanda is the sacrificial lamb (159. 14); and there is repeatedly talk of salvation – Vanderbank's potential for it (22.20), Mitchy and Aggie's mutual salvation (236. 16, 244. 8), and of course, unspoken, Mr Longdon's of Nanda.

3. 23. *the product of Beccles*: James asked the photographer Alvin Langdon Coburn to supply photographs as frontispieces for the New York Edition of his novels. The photograph in *The Awkward Age*, entitled 'Mr Longdon's', is of James's own home, Lamb House in Rye, Sussex. James moved to Lamb House in the autumn of 1898 and finished writing *The Awkward Age* there. His quiet autobiographical joke throws interesting light on the novel's pastoral symbolism: the positive associations of Mr Longdon's house and garden at Beccles reflect James's love for his own country home.

3. 38. *The General Audit*: Like Edward Brookenham who is in 'Rivers and Lakes' (5. 23), Vanderbank is high in the Civil Service. The very carefully depicted edges of society include people who have to earn their living – in Edward's case, the younger son of minor landed gentry, the need for a job reflects the increasing financial difficulties of his class. Entry to the Civil Service by competitive examination had been established over

forty years before, but some appointments were still outside the examination system and Edward is able to secure a position through patronage.

10. 34. *'have you got her?'*: The unattractively proprietorial implications of Vanderbank's room of 'many, too many photographs' (4. 39) are brought out in Mr Longdon's colloquial 'got'.

13. 24. *a visible scruple for the sweeping concession*: Mr Longdon mistrusts Vanderbank's hyperbole – an example for him of language falsifying its referent.

17. 4. *obvious, knock-down beauty*: Vanderbank refers to the success of 'Professional Beauties', most famous of whom was the Prince of Wales's mistress Lily Langtry, 'the Jersey Lily'.

18. 14. End of first serial episode.

25. 13. *Louis Seize*: Louis Quinze in the serial edition. The lines of Louis Seize are generally much squarer. Mrs Brookenham reflects the contemporary taste for French furniture.

26. 9. *the label of a circulating library*: By the 1890s the power of the circulating libraries (the most famous of which was Mudie's) over publishing practices was declining, though they still bought 10,000 of a successful novel's average of 50,000 copies. Earlier in the century they were largely responsible for maintaining the expensive three-volume format in which novels were published and this, together with a concern for respectability which amounted to censorship, earned them the criticism of writers. George Moore's pamphlet *Literature at Nurse or Circulating Morals* (1885) was instrumental in their decline. Here the image is of respectability, in contrast with the French novels read by the Brook circle.

29. 15. *'It wasn't an invitation ... ?'*: Mrs Brookenham stretches acceptable etiquette in the interests of finding cheap accommodation for Harold.

31. 10. End of second serial episode.

32. 18. *'She's not an American and she's not on the stage'*: The Duchess refers disparagingly to the ease with which actors and Americans were able to enter London society. 'Le succès de l'Américain' was commented on by 'Brada' (*Notebooks*, p. 195).

33. 31. *She was a person of no small presence*: The novel comes closest to authoritative authorial commentary, though still without 'going behind', in physical descriptions like this of the Duchess, or of Lord Petherton (pp. 51–2), near-caricatures in which James's satire is reminiscent of Dickens.

48. 17. *unlike the augurs behind the altar*: A reference to Cicero, *De Divinatione* ii. 51: 'The old saying of Cato is very neat: he said he was surprised that one diviner could see another without laughing'. The saying actually refers to low-class professional diviners (*haruspices*) who used the entrails of animals, but

it is often quoted as applying to augurs, who were upper-class and divined from the flight of birds.

50. 8. *She saw it steadily and saw it whole*: An echo of Arnold's description of Sophocles in his sonnet 'To a Friend': 'Who saw life steadily and saw it whole'.

51. 28. End of third serial episode.

53. 18. *those two French books*: French novels were still popularly identified with indecency. In 1888 the publisher Henry Vizetelly had been prosecuted and imprisoned for selling Zola's novels in translation. James always strongly disapproved of this English moral squeamishness.

54. 32. *'The most abominable –'*: No doubt a collection of erotica, common beneath the surface of Victorian propriety.

55. 21. *'the most dreadful sums'*: The question of Harold's borrowing runs like a leitmotif throughout the novel. His un-ashamed mercenariness contrasts clearly with Nanda's integrity, establishing the brother as a bad example (in contrast with the 'New Woman' novels which stressed brothers' freedom as a model for their sisters), but there is also the recurrent question of whether he actually *does* borrow large sums and the uncertainty is typical of the novel's consistent refusal to solve questions of fact – such as the exact nature of Vanderbank's relationship with Mrs Brooken-ham.

63. 3. *a gathered garden lily*: James's obvious use of typological symbols – later the Duchess describes Tishy Grendon as ' "though not perhaps herself quite the rose, she is decidedly, in these days, too near it" ' (69. 14) – reinforces the image of Nanda as poised awkwardly between the chaste and the sensual female alternatives.

70. 21. *'English periodical public washings of dirty linen'*: Divorce cases with any public interest were reported in detail in the press. Some of the most famous were the Dilke case of 1885 (in which James knew many of those involved), Lady Colin Campbell's case of 1886, and in 1889 the revelation of Parnell's relationship with Kitty O'Shea (James attended the 'thrilling, throbbing Parnell trial' (*Letters*, ed. Edel, III, 253)).

78. 24. End of fourth serial episode.

82. 7, 31. *'I'm a hater' . . . 'I'm Mr Longdon'*: Mr Longdon registers his ideological difference from Mrs Brookenham's set: for their uncommitted 'observation' he substitutes moral action, and his belief in certain identity is represented in his name which remains unsusceptible to change.

86. 27. *An observer disposed to interpret*: An interesting gloss on James's 'observer' can be found in his essay of 1888 on Guy de Maupassant. James takes issue with Maupassant's contention

that ' "psychology should be hidden in a book, as it is hidden in reality under the facts of existence" ':

> all depends upon the observer, the nature of one's observation, and one's curiosity. For some people motives, reasons, relations, explanations, are a part of the very surface of the drama, with the footlights beating full upon them. For me an act, an incident, an attitude, may be a sharp, detached, isolated thing, of which I give you a full account in saying that in such and such a way it came off. For you it may be hung about with implications, with relations, and conditions as necessary to help you to recognise it as the clothes of your friends are to help you to know them in the street. (*Partial Portraits*, pp. 256–7)

The Awkward Age's tentative interpretations endorse neither kind of response.

97. 14, 15. *Sir Thomas Lawrence . . . Gainsborough*: Vanderbank and Mr Longdon's comparisons of Nanda with the fashionable portraits of Lawrence (1769–1830) and Gainsborough (1727–1788) identify her with an ever-receding past – yet another illustration of their commitment to an outmoded ideal of womanhood.

97. 31. *Mrs Radcliffe*: Ann Radcliffe (1764–1823) was the author of popular Gothic novels, the most famous of which are *The Mysteries of Udolpho* (1794) and *The Italian* (1797).

103. 39. End of fifth serial episode.

108. 30. '*Do you mean she's so "fast"?*': James makes fine distinctions between the idioms of the various characters. Mr Cashmore's slang, mischievously echoed in the narrator's cliché 'keep the ball rolling', is cruder than that permitted in Mrs Brookenham's inner circle and suggests a comparative lack of sensitivity.

112. 40. *It was as if a fabric had crumbled*: Architectural images for assumptions and narratives which are largely the precarious product of characters' imaginations are common in late James. Cf. *The Sacred Fount* (1901) when the narrator feels his elaborate theory about the other characters threatened: ' "you're costing me a perfect palace of thought!" ' (chap. XIV). The imagery suggests the precariousness of all narrative and carries an echo of Prospero's famous speech in *The Tempest* (IV 1. 148–58).

117. 37. '*She's the delight of our life*': Carrie's indecisiveness about eloping with the facetiously named Captain Dent-Douglas, in offering a subject for endless speculation, is much more interesting to Mrs Brookenham than a conventional scandal – another reflection of the novel's own reticence about facts.

132. 28. '*have latch-key*': One of the hallmarks of the modern daughter.

133. 17. End of sixth serial episode.

137. 26. '*May* I?': Women smoking was still far from generally accepted. According to Alison Adburgham's *Punch History of Manners and Modes* (see 'Further reading'), a woman first smoked in public in 1896.

145. 4. *the fifties and the sixties*: 'The forties and the fifties' in the serial edition – which would put Mr Longdon's age at over seventy.

145. 22. '*the violation of their homes*': Mr Longdon's old-fashioned surprise at the modern habit of letting country houses is another reminder of the financial difficulties which contributed to breaking down the inviolability of society.

154. 39. End of seventh serial episode.

175. 16. *the young man's honesty*: As so often in the novel, silence suggests honesty or feeling.

176. 22. '*I've been seeing, feeling, thinking.*': In spite of his earlier denial of being an 'observer' (p. 82), Mr Longdon is learning some of the ways of Buckingham Crescent – but in order to act with his oddly blatant offer of money. In his ability to learn and in identifying himself as 'a man of imagination', he is a precursor of Strether in *The Ambassadors* (1903). By the end of the novel (322. 1), he can speak of ' "what I've made out for myself" '.

177. 17. *none but to rise from his place*: The movements in this scene are very carefully plotted. Authorial 'stage directions' make is very like watching a play.

185. 8. End of eighth serial episode – and with this crucial scene between Vanderbank and Mr Longdon just over half-way through the novel, the 'plot' is set in motion.

187. 21. '*like Anna Karénine*': In Tolstoy's novel (1875–7), Anna elopes to Italy with her lover Vronsky.

188. 29. '*that – what do you call it? – investigating Society*': Mrs Brookenham means the Society for Psychical Research, founded in 1882. James himself was never a member, but two of his friends, F. W. H. Myers and Edmund Gurney, were founder members and William James was a corresponding member and later vice-president and president. James always read the Society's Proceedings with interest and some of the cases probably contributed to the governess's story in *The Turn of the Screw*.

188. 33. *Baireuth*: The town in Bavaria where Wagner's Festival Theatre opened in 1876. Home of the annual Wagner Festival.

198. 9. '*You won't do it*': It is impossible to say whether Mrs Brookenham's 'knowledge' of Vanderbank is descriptive or prescriptive.

206. 29. '*Now that is cheap paradox!*': Mitchy's 'cheap paradox' recalls the style of dialogue in Oscar Wilde's plays and is perhaps

a bit of quiet revenge on Wilde whose plays were so much more successful than James's own. But it also of course expresses Mitchy's painful situation which Vanderbank's joke avoids.

210. 40. End of ninth serial episode.

212. 4. ' *"Our antagonist is our helper"* ': From Edmund Burke's *Reflections on the Revolution in France* (1790): 'He that wrestles with us strengthens our nerves, and sharpens our skill. Our antagonist is our helper. This amicable conflict with difficulty obliges us to an intimate acquaintance with our object, and compels us to consider it in all its relations. It will not suffer us to be superficial.'

223. 1. *three acres*: Rather larger than the garden at Lamb House, but walled like James's garden (and Eden).

244. 8. *'she'll save* me': In a letter of late 1899 to Henrietta Reubell, James explained:

> Mitchy marries Aggie by a calculation – in consequence of a state of mind – delicate and deep, but that I meant to show on his part as highly conceivable. It's absolute to him that N. will never have him – and she *appeals* to him for another girl, whom she sees him as 'saving' (from things – realities she sees). If he does it (and she shows how she values him by wanting it) it is still a way of getting and keeping near her – of making for *her*, to him, a tie of happiness – they can't (*especially if the marriage goes ill*) *not* be – given the girl that Nanda is – more, rather than less, together. And the *finale* of the picture *justifies* him: it leaves Nanda, precisely, with his case on her hands. Far-fetched? Well, I daresay: but so are diamonds and pearls and the beautiful Reubell turquoises! (*Letters*, ed. Lubbock, I, 342)

244. 20. End of tenth serial episode.

256. 17. *delicate French mouldings*: Tishy's rooms, with their fashionable French fittings, are the most up to date in the novel.

262. 16. *'Does he mean anything very nasty?'*: The characters' various 'languages' are brought together at Tishy's party. Like Aggie, Tishy speaks a completely different language from that spoken at Buckingham Crescent. Her simple discourse (' "We just talk" ', 260. 9) ironically qualifies her as an image of corruption.

270. 6. *'She doesn't speak to him – !'*: An interesting use of 'speak', suggesting both 'influence' and, possibly, 'sexually attract'.

273. 6. End of eleventh serial episode.

297. 25. ' *"Even in our ashes live their wonted fires"* ': From Gray's *Elegy Written in a Country Churchyard*, st. 23:

> On some fond breast the parting soul relies
> Some pious drops the closing eye requires;
> Ev'n from the tomb the voice of nature cries,
> Ev'n in our ashes live their wonted fires.

301. 4. End of twelfth serial episode.

328. 34. *'But* you're *all right!'*: Mr Longdon's echo of Mitchy's consolatory cliché restores it to meaning.

329. *Book X: Nanda*: The novel's books have moved, significantly, from 'Lady Julia' to 'Nanda' via 'Mrs Brook' and in this last book a new scene is set – Nanda's own room where, like her mother, she entertains and directs her guests. Its collection of photographs recalls Vanderbank's room in Book I.

332. 15. *'Isn't there some girl in some story'*: The various heroines Vanderbank mixes up here have been interestingly identified by Jean Frantz Blackall (see 'Further reading'). Esmeralda in Victor Hugo's *Notre-Dame de Paris* did have a bird-cage in her window, as did Molly, the heroine of *The Two Prisoners*, a popular novel by Thomas Nelson Page. The heroine who owns a poodle could be James's own Christina Light in *Roderick Hudson* and the Zola heroine Vanderbank seems vaguely to recall could be Camille Duvard in *Paris*. As Blackall suggests, Vanderbank's confusion suggests an ambivalent view of Nanda: his various heroines range from the innocent to the manipulative.

336. 17. End of thirteenth serial episode. In the serial edition the paragraph continues: 'Some such quick passage of things is at any rate no more than a fair translation of the expression just mentioned' – an unnecessarily clumsy intrusion by the uncertain narrator.

363. 21. *a torrent of tears*: Briefly, and for the only time in the novel (Mitchy's 'rising' tears, 317. 25, remain under control), passion breaks the surface of words – only to be quickly suppressed again.